Also by
EMILY SKRUTSKIE

Hullmetal Girls
The Abyss Surrounds Us
The Edge of the Abyss

BONDS OF BRASS

BONDS OF BRASS

BOOK ONE OF THE BLOODRIGHT TRILOGY

EMILY SKRUTSKIE

DEL REY

NEW YORK

Copyright © 2020 by Emily Skrutskie

Published in the United States by Del Rey,
an imprint of Random House, a division of
Penguin Random House LLC, New York.

DEL REY and the HOUSE colophon are registered trademarks of
Penguin Random House LLC.

ISBN 978-0-593-12889-3
Ebook ISBN 978-0-593-12890-9

Printed in the United States of America on acid-free paper

randomhousebooks.com

2 4 6 8 9 7 5 3 1

First Edition

Book Design by Edwin Vazquez

To the 2010 *A-Team* movie,
without which this book
would be a whole lot smarter.

And to Ivy,
because I wrote the whole damn thing
with her sitting on my feet.

BONDS OF BRASS

CHAPTER I

MY STOMACH DROPS when I see it. Not in horror—something closer to exasperation sculpts the feeling of my mess-hall-slop breakfast bottoming out. The hangar outside the equipment room rumbles with activity. Engines firing, boots on concrete, the crackle of announcements over the intercoms. I give the cacophony only dry silence in return, because Gal Veres has forgotten his helmet.

Again.

"One of these days, you're not going to have me to cover for you," I mutter under my breath as I cross the room and scoop it off the shelf. "One of these days, the officers are going to come down *hard* on your ass, and I won't do a thing to stop it—I swear on the gods of all systems."

But not today, and probably not tomorrow, either, and I'm already out the door with Gal's helmet under one arm and my own under the other.

The hangar swallows me whole, folding me into the Umber Imperial Academy's mad scramble. On a busy morning like this, at least three different flight drills are running simultaneously. The cavernous vault of the ceiling rattles at unsteady intervals as a line of ships passes overhead. People scamper back and forth—cadets, officers, mechanics—all of them moving with frantic purpose along the designated pathways painted between the spacecrafts.

This hangar plays host to every conceivable sort of ship, from narrow, sleek fighters to massive carriers that can skip between star systems at superluminal speeds. Every hull is marked with the obsidian and brass of the Umber Empire, shimmering in the low light. There's not a junker in sight—all of these ships are less than five years old, their metal fresh from the mined-out asteroid belts of the former Archon Territories. I'm forced to stop as a Razor taxis toward the hangar doors, a hungry promise in the thrum of its engines. My heart lifts as the vibrations rattle down my spine. *Soon,* the pump of my blood swears. Soon I'll be in the air. Soon I'll be nothing but the raw impulse it takes to pilot a fighter.

Just as I'm about to take off at a run, a hand comes down on my shoulder, yanking me to the side. "What the rut—" I choke, but already they're dragging me into the shadow of a skipship's wing. I twist out of the grip and find myself staring down the suspiciously perfect teeth of Tatsun Seely. Three of his friends hover behind him, blocking us from the main path.

"Ettian Nassun," Seely says, all charm and no sincerity. In the two and a half years we've been at the academy together, I think I've had about three conversations with the guy. Now he's smiling up at me like we share some secret, and I'm not keen on finding out what it is.

"We're gonna be late," I tell him. Not that it matters to Seely—his whole crowd treats exercises with willful disdain bordering on open resentment. Which I understand. Really, I do. Seely's an orphan of the former Archon Empire, like me. One of millions of kids whose lives were upended when Umber took our homeworlds seven years ago. Like me, his frame is stick-thin from half a life on Archon portions, barely rounded out from seven years of Umber abundance, though I'm a little taller and my skin is several shades darker. Like me, he was shuffled into the Umber military establishment once they opened this academy on the planet Rana, mere miles away from the former Archon Imperial Seat.

Unlike me, he's got a massive chip on his shoulder about it.

Which brings me back to his teeth and my suspicions. Because Seely's chompers are not your everyday set. They speak to years of good dental work—the *finest* dental work, stuff that must have started long before the Umber Empire's victory. You see teeth like his on governors, high-ranking officials, and probably even on imperials themselves.

And, presumably, on their heirs. At ten years old, Seely would have been far too young to be revealed to the rough-and-tumble world of galactic politics when the Archon Empire fell. If he was someone's next in line—maybe one of the planetary governors in an interior system—he would have been tucked safely in the shadows, raised in secret for a role his blood destined him to play. And when Iva emp-Umber won her war and claimed her spoils, she stole his bloodright out from under him.

It's a bit of a reach to explain why he half-asses everything, and it requires some logistical leaps to justify how he made it to the academy after the empire collapsed. But it's probably the most interesting thing about Tatsun Seely, so I entertain the notion.

"Ettian, hey—" Seely snaps his fingers in front of my eyes, and I fix him with a glare.

"Seely," I say coolly, "get to the tarmac."

I try to shrug his arm off my shoulders, but he clamps down tighter, pulling our heads close together. "Yeah, I'm not taking orders from you," Seely mutters, his voice dropping low and serious. His face contorts as he tries to maintain an amicable smile. "Doesn't matter what fancy call sign the higher-ups give you—you're one of us. And we need to talk about the company you keep." His eyes track an officer as she bustles past, but in the shadow of the skipship, we're off her radar.

"Really?" I snap. Now I get what this is about. I've caught the scornful looks Seely and his crew throw my way more than once. They know I was born right here on Rana. I come from the nearby city of Trost, the capital and heart of the former Archon Empire. Theoretically, I should be more pissed than any of them about the

Umber conquest, but instead I've thrown myself headlong into the new establishment. We've been at the academy together for two and a half years—I'm surprised it's taken them this long to confront me about it.

Archon is dead. It's gone. I can't carry it with me. The only productive thing I *can* do is latch on to the opportunities that rise out of the postwar reconstruction. That's what's kept me alive for the past seven years.

Seely's pride doesn't allow for that sort of thinking. It's a miracle he's survived this long. His lips curl up over those uncanny teeth. "Face it, *Gold One,* you've rolled right over for Umber. But we can help you fix that. There's a chance to regain a little dignity. A little honor."

His fingers start to fidget on my shoulder. To the untrained eye, it looks like a simple nervous tic, but every child born on Archon soil knows better. He's tapping a rhythm against my bones, one of the ancient beats that sculpted the old empire's culture. Some are soft and comforting, a resting pulse. Others scream of triumph in fast, emphatic strokes.

Seely's beat is urgent. Rising. A call to arms.

It freezes my blood. Seely feels me lock up against him. He leans close, his breath in my ear. "Remember the knights?" he whispers. "Remember how it felt to see one flying over a city? A single human in a powersuit that could tear the wing off a fighter craft? We're gonna be heroes like them."

And just like that, I'm unstuck. I duck out of Seely's grip, clutching the helmets uncomfortably against my hips. Sure, I remember the suited knights. The heroes of the Archon Empire, keeping the peace and fighting for justice across the systems.

They were the first thing Iva emp-Umber set her sights on when she decided to take our homeworlds and their abundance of metal-rich asteroid belts for her own. Thirty coordinated strikes destroyed every knight, their staffs, their headquarters. Not even a single powersuit remained in the aftermath. Knightfall, they called it. A declaration of war, painted in the blood of every single person we were dumb enough to call our heroes.

"I like my head where it is," I tell Seely sharply. Guilt prickles through me as his expression drops to a stony glare. Usually the choice to fall in line with Umber rests comfortably on my shoulders— and in my well-fed gut—but when a fellow war orphan is scowling at me like I'm dirt, it's hard not to feel it. "Look, for your sake, whatever it is you think you're going to do . . . Don't."

"Told you he wouldn't bite," one of Seely's companions says with a sniff. She glances over her shoulder. "He's a waste of time."

"Agreed," I tell her, plastering a false, cheery smile over my face as I back toward the marked walkways.

"See you in the black, Gold One," Seely calls. "And for *your* sake, stay out of my way."

I scoff as I dodge back into the flow of traffic out of the hangar. Seely's all talk—anyone who thinks they can do anything for the old empire at this point is all talk. If the Umber victory wasn't secure when they won the war and executed the Archon imperials seven years ago, it was rock-solid by the time they opened the academy's doors. Now Archon-born children grow up with good Umber foundations that keep the drums from pounding rhythms into their hearts. Reliable supply lines run from the richness of the Umber interior to all-but-barren Archon soil, and hungry new governors— often second children with no bloodright claim in their home territories—have stepped in to bring order to the newly acquired worlds. The region's finally stabilized after the war cracked it open, and gods of all systems help anyone who thinks it's a good idea to disturb that peace.

I break from the hangar's shadow and into the bright winter sun. A curl of wind from the east brings with it the dusty scent of prairie grass, and some of it settles the frayed ends of my nerves. Between getting Gal his forgotten helmet and my run-in with the other Archon brats, there's a good chance *I'm* going to be the one on the receiving end of an imperial-level dressing-down from the officers.

I lengthen my strides as I hustle down the tarmac, making for the row of Vipers lined up in their staging zones like knives in a drawer. My focus locks onto the third ship in the row—and as a result, I nearly run headlong into a young officer on her way back to the hangar. It takes me an extra second to recognize Jana as I try to keep from tripping over my boots.

"Ettian, hey!" she says, her smile bright as she resettles the shoulders of her crisp black uniform. Her eyes drop to the second helmet I'm carrying. "Again, huh?"

Jana's one of an entire cohort of upperclassmen Gal charmed into adopting him the second he arrived at the academy. Even though she graduated to the officer ranks two years ago, she still checks in from time to time, and it's not uncommon for her to come knocking at our door for a conversation that usually devolves into mindless gossip about ten minutes in.

I return her grin, backpedaling to keep my momentum going. "Again!" I tell her. I wish I had time to stop and chat, but there's fire under my heels. Knowing Jana, she'll probably swing by our room later tonight anyway.

She tips an informal salute at me, and I turn around and break into a jog. As I run past, some of the other cadets call out greetings that I try my best to acknowledge with quick jerks of my head. A few of them are already perched in their cockpits, doing their preflight checks. It spurs me faster.

By the time I make it to the Gold Twenty-Eight Viper, I'm clawing for breath, both helmets dragging me down like twenty-pound weights. But when Gal Veres turns around and sees me, it's easy to forget all that. His smile glows, the breath he lets out fogging in the chilled air. He's unfairly handsome, his skin a warm golden brown, his hair perpetually perfectly tousled, and his frame sturdily built from a lifetime in Umber abundance. *How dare you,* part of me groans. I need to be in my Viper already, comfortably settled in my gel-seat so I can forget how a single look from Gal sometimes feels like it might take my legs out from underneath me.

Before he has a chance to get a word in, I pitch his helmet at him. He catches it with a slight *oomph*.

"You owe me one," I tell him. It's not true, strictly speaking—I've been carrying his ass in classes since day one, but he's carried me through our time at the academy in ways I can never fully repay.

But it's Gal, so of course he plays along. He leans casually against the ladder to his cockpit, settling the helmet over his unruly undercut. "Thanks for covering for me—knew you'd have my back. I would have commed you to make sure, but . . ."

And then his smile goes wicked, and he slips my earpiece out of his pocket.

Hollow exasperation hits me like a gut punch for the second time today. "You've got to be kidding me," I groan.

Gal doesn't toss it—he makes me come and pluck the device daintily out of his palm, his hooded eyes sparkling with delight. "Noticed you forgot to make your way to the comm station, figured you'd gotten distracted by something, you know the rest. And we're supposed to trust you to lead us today?"

"Better me than you."

"Rut off. I could be an *amazing* leader."

"Your test scores say otherwise. And last week you couldn't even get one other person in the cantina to try streaking the officer quarters with you."

"No one was drunk enough. But it's gonna happen someday. We'll make academy history—first to make it to the head's door and back."

I knock my shoulder into his, laughing softly as I slip my earpiece in. Behind Gal, I catch a glimpse of Hanji, another cadet in our year, as she moseys toward her station in the control tower. She gives me a wave, then makes a suggestive gesture involving both of her hands and a wicked tilt of her eyebrow. I grapple with the urge to pull a face at her, keeping my stare pinned on Gal instead.

Hanji and Ollins, another member of her merry band of miscreants, made a bet where Gal and I are concerned. If Gal finds out the terms of that bet, I might as well float my Viper into the path of an oncoming dreadnought.

"What?" Gal asks, and I realize I've stared a moment too long.

"Huh? Oh, just . . . I saw Jana on my way over," I blurt. *Smooth, Ettian.*

"Yeah, she came by to say hi."

I glance around at the tarmac, the line of Vipers, the distance from here to the hangar. *"Came by?"*

"Jealous? I can ask if she's got friends who are into, y'know, all of this," he says, gesturing from my head to my toes.

"Who isn't?" I shoot back, setting my helmet over my head.

Gal snorts. "Got me there," he says, and something skitters sideways in my stomach. Before the comment has a chance to settle, he claps me on the shoulder. "C'mon, Ettian. Big day. Let's get these ruttin' birds in the sky."

I cuff him back, grinning, then lift a finger to my earpiece and flick my comms on. "This is Gold One. All units report in."

As I jog to my own Viper at the opposite end of the staging zone, my ears fill with the noise of thirty rowdy cadets sounding off. At my back, Viper engines whine through their preflight checks, rattling my bones. I clamber into my own cockpit, dropping into my gel-seat as I will myself to focus. It's just noise. No rhythm beneath it. No thoughts of the past. Only the wide-open future, the black above, and the sureness of the ship beneath my hands as I taxi onto the runway.

When the tower signals, I throw everything I have into the Viper's thrusters. I rocket for the fringes of Rana's atmosphere with the formation at my rear, begging for my heart to calm down.

But the frantic *thump-thump-thump* in my chest is a little too close to drums for my liking.

CHAPTER 2

THE HUMAN MIND isn't built to process hurtling through a vacuum at skin-peeling speeds in a cockpit just big enough for a single pilot and all of his fear. The Viper around me is sleek and athletic, and the engines at my back roar as I urge a little extra speed out of them. The vast dark of space envelops me, the stars washed out by the daytime glow of Rana five hundred miles beneath us. I should be pissing myself.

And yet.

My mind goes a little inhuman in the cockpit of a Viper. My awareness pushes its limits, my body forgotten in favor of the ship around me. My eyes unfocus. My heartbeat steadies. Any residual anxieties vaporize in the void, yielding to the immediacy of flying, and instinct takes over the way my hands twist and pull the craft's controls. The readouts spit information about the vector my ship is sailing on, but I don't need it.

All I need is the *feeling*. That's what keeps me in formation as we sweep through the black. The distance between each ship is measured, but instinct is what holds us there.

"This is Gold One. Execute first maneuver," I announce to the comm.

I fire the attitude thrusters, pulling my nose up. My Viper's engine drives a frantic tattoo into my spine. The burn is silent outside the craft, deadened by the vacuum, but inside my radio goes live. Thirty Vipers fill with the howls and whistles of cadets being jammed down into their gel-seats by the vicious inertia.

The glowing curve of Rana eases into view and then slides back out as we complete our arc and level off. At the edge of my vision, I catch the shine of Viper noses as the rest of the formation follows my lead. "Gold Twenty-Eight, get that vector straightened out," I grumble as one of them lists off-track.

"Sorry, Ettian."

My teeth set on edge, but I can't help the smile that tugs the corners of my lips. I've given up on trying to get Gal to use call signs during exercises, and so has most of the senior staff—though they certainly won't cut me any slack for letting him get away with it. His Viper jerks in my periphery, settling shakily back into formation.

"No apologies, Gold Twenty-Eight. Get it right." It's hard to say with a straight face, and I can picture the way Gal's smirking in his own cockpit. "Rest of you, this is Gold One. Execute second maneuver."

I close my eyes and spin up my gyros with a twist of the controls. I could flip my Viper with a preset, but where's the fun in that? Pure instinct sends my craft end over end—540 degrees, for show—and pure instinct fires the engines at the right moment, the attitude thrusters locking the Viper straight along the inverse of its former vector as the main burn kicks, driving me into my seat with the force of a missile strike.

That pure instinct is why I'm Gold One.

"Ruttin' showoff," Gal mutters over the comm, and bursts of laughter snap through from the other pilots.

"Jealous bastard," I shoot back, and Gal chuckles.

"Keep it professional, Ettian," he warns.

"Cut the chatter, Gold Twenty-Eight," I reply, but he knows I'd rather he didn't. Even though this is technically *my* drill and I should be keeping things serious, these flight exercises are a formality. Rana's Imperial Academy is a playground, a regimen of basic training that puts us in the shoes of pilots before we graduate for the leadership tracks. In true combat, none of us would be flying Vipers. We're destined for the command centers of a dreadnought, overseeing troops that will deploy from the cityships.

I wish it were otherwise. I prefer the Viper. In this cockpit, everything's under my control. It's simple and pure. I'm responsible for myself and myself alone.

Not today though. As leader of this exercise, I'm expected to keep all thirty cadets on my wing under control. Even with the Viper demanding my attention, a part of me pulses with constant awareness that the senior staff will be watching every move I make. They can excuse some friendly chatter, but if anything serious goes sideways, it's my hide on the line. I know for certain some of the officers aren't thrilled about an Archon whelp holding steady at the top of our class, and they're just waiting for an excuse to rip my command away.

"This is Gold One. Execute—"

"Wraith Squadron, detach," a familiar voice announces, cold and clear. A single fighter peels off the back of our formation.

Wraith? My gaze drops to the Viper's instruments. "Seely—Gold Eight, what the hell are you doing?" I snap. "This is Gold One, and I do *not* authorize whatever—"

A shriek of static cuts through the radio, and in my periphery, nineteen more Viper hulls fall away. Something goes fuzzy in my brain as I watch my control dissolve. My formation flies on, cut by two-thirds, holes torn in its former perfection. This can't be happening. *Why* is this happening? Sure, Seely hates me, but how in any system's hell did he convince nineteen of our classmates to ruin my drill? There's no way the bitter little rutter has that much clout.

My heart rate doubles, my mind reeling as I try to inventory which fighters have fallen back. At my left, I spot the glint of sunlight off a Viper's nose—Gal's Viper. He's still with me.

"This is Wraith One. Form up on me," Seely announces.

"Seely, what the hell is going on?" I shout, wrestling with my controls. Another spin of the gyros flips my Viper around, pointing me at the stray flock as I continue to sail backward in what's left of my formation.

They're shifting into an arrowhead. An attack pattern. My mouth goes dry. This isn't disobedience. This isn't just to stick it to me. This is something more. Something worse.

"Gods," Gal whispers over the comm. "Not now. Not . . . Ett—"

Seely's voice overpowers the line, full of authority I never suspected him of possessing. "Wraith One, authorizing weapons free."

Every lesson I've ever had about leadership under pressure crystalizes in my mind. "Gold One, evasive action *immediately*," I scream at what's left of my fighters. The Vipers split like they've been cleaved by a knife.

All except for Gal, who bolts across the black with no regard for pattern, for order, for any sort of direction that might save his ass.

Something in his brain has gone animal. Not the pack-animal mentality you sometimes slip into when you're flying in formation. No, Gal's just doing everything in his power to run.

"Heavens and hells," I swear, twist out of formation, and take off after him. The comms go live with confusion, the other pilots uncertain whether they're supposed to follow me.

Above the chatter, Seely's voice comes through loud and clear: "This is Wraith One. Shoot to kill."

I throw everything I have into the engines as the vacuum around me comes alive with the flash of boltfire. Gal swerves erratically, and my heart leaps into my throat as one of the bolts skims his Viper's wing. I hazard another glance at my instrumentation. Watch as the twenty defectors point their arrowhead directly at Gal's retreating tail. Not at the remaining nine Vipers holding formation as they flee across the black.

Just Gal.

"What the rut do you think you're doing?" I seethe through my teeth. I watch Gal on the instruments, my face heating with fury as another burst to the engines drives me deeper into my seat. This isn't the Gal I know—the Gal I've known for years, the one who pranks the senior staff, who struggles to keep even the most stalwart ships flying steady, who doesn't fear anything the way he should. Something's terribly wrong.

My calm evaporates into the vacuum.

I flip a switch on my radio controls, activating every distress beacon on my dashboard. "Base, this is Gold One. Twenty of my squad have . . . They're not following orders, and they've turned on one of my pilots. They're shooting to kill. Requesting—"

I hesitate. I shouldn't hesitate—the whole point of the academy is training me to *act* when the situation is dire. I twitch my controls to dodge another round of boltfire that streaks across my Viper's nose.

"Requesting ground support and awaiting further instructions," I conclude. The Viper rattles around me as my engines max out their burn. I flip the radio back over to the exercise channel, where Seely's still spinning orders to his mutiny. A note of indignation lances through my panic. It's bad enough Seely's trying to kill Gal, but with the single line available between our ships, everyone has to listen to him do it.

"Gold One, the rest of you go to ground," I shout over Seely's noise.

"Wraith One, split it. Let's cut him."

The drumming starts as a single beat, a single hand slapping a dashboard, the noise big enough to fill a single cockpit. One hand, then ten, then twenty as the defectors' formation cracks in half. Variations slip into the rhythm, and my vision goes fuzzy as I watch the nine cadets still under my command bolt for Rana's gravity.

I know this beat too. It's been seven years since I heard it last, but the rhythm of an Archon war cadence is etched into my heart. It's the rallying cry of our fallen empire, and for a terrifying moment, I forget every word I told Seely this morning.

The defectors cast their net wide, herding Gal, playing off the way fear is driving him. But fear's not driving me—not in the same way. As Gal swerves again, burning off his speed, I nose up along his wing.

"Gal," I say, and his vector steadies. Even over the rumble of the drumming, he hears me.

"Ettian, I'm so sorry—"

"No apologies." I try not to flinch as another scattering of bolts slices past us. Gal's Viper jerks, and I'm forced to swerve, tipping my gyros enough to dodge him. Even in all this confusion, my reflexes are as sharp as they were in the years after the empire fell. That time taught me a lot of things, but above all else, it taught me to improvise.

"Hold steady. I'm going to try something," I grunt.

"Easier said."

"I know." I twist my gyros, flipping my craft belly-up, and punch the attitude thrusters. My Viper slots neatly underneath his.

Gal's voice is on the edge of panicked laughter. "Don't you dare hump my ship."

"Thank me later." I yank my landing gear's release and jam the button that spins up my electromagnets. These things are meant to hold a Viper to the skin of a dreadnought, but they work just as well on the metal of another light craft. My ship snaps against his with a dull thud, and Gal yelps.

"You're going to get us both killed," he mutters, but he's already cutting his engine and stilling his gyros.

If he can't fly his way out of this, I'm going to do it for him.

With a heavy burst from my thrusters, I pull us into an arc, taking stock of the defector formation closing in on us. Two lines of ships spread out in a V, meaning to herd and crosscut us with their fire. Already they're adjusting course to follow where we lead. The drumming fades—the pilots need both hands now.

My vision goes dark at the edges as I tighten our vector. Vipers were designed to move around the pilot, keeping inertial forces on the body as minor as possible. Flying in curved lines is bad for biology, doubly so when the ship's center of mass is no longer focused on your head.

"Gal, you with me?" I choke, leveling us off. "You gotta talk, elsewise I'm going to think you blacked out."

"Or one of these bastards got me."

"That too." I glance up through my windshield, trying to pinpoint the academy on Rana's vast surface. I don't know if they're responding to my distress call. It'll take time for missiles to claw their way out of the planet's gravity. I don't know if I can keep us clear of the boltfire for that long. "Gal," I warn as another violent twist of the gyros steals my sight.

"Remember that time we got leave and went to Ikar?"

I grin. "Not particularly."

"You got so hammered, you started singing the Umber Anthem at the top of your lungs in an open market. In a former Archon territory," Gal chokes out as we level off onto a new vector.

"I remember the bruises. I won the fight, right?"

"If you call being left facedown in a garbage can 'winning,' I'll eject now."

My flying's working. With twenty of them and one of us, it's child's play to tease their formation into chaos—especially with our chatter covering up the orders Seely's screaming into the comm. "At least I actually fight my battles," I snap. It's harsh, given our current situation, but Gal knows what's in my head better than anyone, and he gives me exactly what I expect.

"And I talk my way out of them like a rational human being."

"Couldn't talk your way out of this?"

"That's what I have you for."

I appreciate the confidence, but I don't know how long I can keep this up. Feinting around boltfire and messing with their formations is only going to keep us alive for so long. Getting to safety is another matter entirely. Vipers can't trip past superluminal speeds, and our fastest isn't going to be enough to outrun them with this many on our tail. I don't see any way out.

And then I realize our escape has been looming over us the entire time. My eyes shift up to Rana—to my big, glorious, green homeworld. Nine specks of flame mark where the remainder of the squad is hitting the atmosphere, and those nine little flares set off one big one in my head.

Seely sees what I'm about to do the second before I do it. "Wraith One, close the net," he shrieks, and the formation shifts around us as I twist our Vipers through the mess. No time for feinting, no time for dodging the bolts—my vector is direct, and speed is my only concern. We plunge for the planet, my engine whining as I urge it past its limits. The metal of the Viper's hull creaks around me.

"Ettian, you *maniac*," Gal mutters.

"Keep talking," I tell him. Not because I need to make sure he's conscious—our acceleration isn't heavy enough for that to be a concern—but because I need his voice to keep me steady.

"What about?"

"You can start by explaining why there are twenty Vipers on our ass." At the edge of my wing, I catch the first wisps of the planet's outer atmosphere starting to drag at us. I kill the engines. No need for acceleration when Rana's mass is beginning to yank us in.

"I—I *can't* explain."

A vicious edge slips into my voice as the last of my patience dissolves. "No, that's a lie. Why the rut is this happening?"

On the instrumentation, I see the defectors locking onto our tail, some of them already oriented for reentry.

"Ettian—"

"Tell me, Gal, or so help me I'll keep you latched and burn us both."

As is, we're cutting it close. The Viper's heat shields are on the underbelly. If we hit the hard part of the atmosphere with our ships strapped together, we both go down in flames.

There's a sharp inhale on Gal's end of the line. A decision being made in the span of a breath. "I never wanted you to find out—not like this," Gal says.

We've got seconds. "Spit it out!" I yell.

"I'm the Umber heir."

I jam the button, releasing the electromagnets, and fire my attitude thrusters to break away from Gal's underbelly. He can't have said what I think he said. I have to put my ship right. I won't let my brain get stuck on what Gal's confessed and what it means. Another twist of my controls reorients my Viper, my heat shield braced to hit the atmosphere the second it hits back.

I didn't hear it right—that must be it. I glance out the windshield to my left, where Gal's wrestling his own ship into reentry position. Through the plastics separating us, I spot the tense line of his jaw. His eyes are shaded by his helmet and goggles, but somehow I know they're closed. I know Gal. I know him inside and out.

Or I thought I did.

Heat flares around me, my flight suit's coolant struggling to combat it as we plunge into the atmosphere. I extend every drag fin on my ship, gritting my teeth as the deceleration yanks at the flesh on my face, pressing me so deep into my seat's gel that I feel the bracing board beneath it.

Gal is the Umber heir. The thought consumes me more than any worry I might have about the reentry, about the twenty Vipers plunging after us, about what might await us back at the academy base.

The Umber Empire has stood for thousands of years. It was seeded from the first settlements made on stable worlds as wandering generation ships roved down the galactic arm, founded on planets that took to crops with so little effort that the people who made a home there managed to twist it into some sort of divine right. Mankind delved deeper into the galaxy, discovering the metal-rich Archon worlds and the fringe planets of Corinth, but none took root and expanded so boldly and decisively as Umber. Nowadays, the empire spans at least a hundred systems. Their imperial bloodline has conquest in its veins, and Empress Iva and Emperor Yltrast are its pinnacle. Seven years ago, they shredded the Archon Empire and took it for their own. They're the most fearsome force the galaxy has ever seen.

And Gal—

No, it's impossible. There has to be some kind of mistake. It's another of Gal's jokes, like the time he pretended to be the youngest general ever promoted to impress a girl in a bar. A laugh builds in the back of my throat. He had me going there for a moment. Thinking he was the son of—

The cold shock of truth catches up to me. None of Gal's jokes have put twenty Vipers on our rear. None of Gal's jokes have left him turning tail and running like the gates of every hell have opened.

And he's never left me out of one.

"Rut me sideways, you're not kidding," I groan.

Suddenly my suspicions about Seely's teeth seem downright petty. I'd always figured there would be shadow heirs installed at the academy. The Archon territories are notorious hotbeds of opportunity for up-and-coming bloodlines. Governors on every tier of power—continental, planetary, and even system—would jump at the chance to place their kids in the heart of the former empire to train them for command. But this is another thing entirely. Gal's a rutting *prince*. The Umber heir is destined by blood to *own* these systems someday. And twenty of our classmates, including Seely, still hear the Archon drums in their hearts. No wonder they're raining boltfire on his rear.

"Someone must have found out," Gal chokes over the rumble of reentry. "Sleepers didn't stop them."

Of course he has sleeper agents. Of course he wouldn't be here without protection in a seven-year-old territory. And whoever organized this hit knew it—they waited until he was isolated. Surrounded him with more enemies than he could evade on his own. If it hadn't been for me—

The ground's coming up too fast. My hands are numb against my Viper's controls. I steal another glance out the windshield, through the flames wrapped around our hulls. Gal's focus is on his instruments, but his mind must be miles away. I try to picture him beneath his helmet and visor, try to see his parents in him. Iva's dark, hooded eyes. Yltrast's golden skin. The proud brow distinct to the Umber line. No, I just see Gal as I've always seen him. Gal, who's always been a bad liar and a good friend—except something in my darker spaces is urging me to say it's the other way around.

And from those dark spaces, an intrusive thought hits hard and heavy. *Fall back,* it demands. *This is the heir to the bloodline that* rained hell on your homeworld. *That stole your life out from underneath you, broke you, and remade you in its image. You belong with Seely. You can redeem yourself.*

The fire dies around us as we slow into the atmosphere's cradle. My fingers tighten on the controls. Thirty seconds, tops, until the Vipers on our tail start chugging boltfire into our asses again.

Fall back.

It's where you belong.

Fall back.

Redemption.

I let out a long breath.

And a missile shrieks past my cockpit. Two seconds later, a thunderclap booms at our rear. On my dash, the command channel goes live. "Base to Gold One, watch for shrapnel," Hanji's voice announces, flat with raw horror. It's the most serious I've ever heard her. "Runway Three's been cleared for your approach."

Fourteen of the defector Vipers are gone. Reduced to nothing but shredded, heated metal that spatters across our backs like rain. A hollow, terrible feeling rips through me. They were assassins. Classmates. Archon kids like me.

Obliterated.

The clatter of debris on my hull shocks me back into reality. This is what happens to everyone who goes up against the Umber Empire. To suited knights and generals and even the imperials themselves. You don't become a hero.

You just get killed.

The six remaining Vipers scatter, pursued by a volley of heatseekers that scream up from beneath us. We don't have time to see what happens to them. The ground's rolling up fast, and the spires of the academy's buildings are rising to meet us. I punch my thrusters and adjust my drag flaps, and Gal falls in at my wing. Our approach cuts wide across the plains and finally—*finally*—there's the tarmac of Runway Three.

I extend my Viper's landing gear. Pull my nose up. Yards. Feet.

Inches. The Viper hits the pavement hard, and I feel something snap. Hear the shriek of rending metal. Know without seeing that I've ripped my wheels off.

"Base to Gold One, you're dragging fire," Hanji chirps helpfully in my ear.

My flight suit's coolant isn't enough—the cockpit's cooking as my Viper skins its belly on the tarmac. Sweat trickles down the back of my neck. My fingers fumble on the controls, scrabbling for the release.

There. Grab. Pull. The cockpit pops open, my seat ejects, and I catapult into the mercifully cool air. A whoop escapes my lips as I watch my flaming ship skitter away beneath me, outstripped by Gal's Viper. He streaks down the runway unhindered, leaving me in the dust and ashes. My parachutes deploy, yanking me out of my fall. I try to twist, to direct my descent, but I have no control—I'm at the mercy of the cold winds blowing in off the prairie.

By the time I touch down, Gal's already out of his Viper. I land fifty yards away from him and immediately start tearing at my restraints. Farther down the tarmac, people are swarming Gal. First a doctor, for whom everyone clears the way, then a security team flanked by high-level academy officials.

I stagger to my feet. My legs shake beneath me. I have to get to Gal, have to *talk,* have to wrap my head around what's happening. Hanji chatters in my ear, but I rip my helmet off and tear out my earpiece before I can register what she's saying.

I stumble down the tarmac. A fire crew screams past me, bound for the wreckage of my Viper. As the siren fades, I start to make sense of the hubbub surrounding Gal. They're talking about putting him in isolation. Summoning the governor Berr sys-Tosa from his winter estate on Imre, an inner world of the system. Arranging for transport to the Imperial Seat in the distant Umber interior.

Gal stands in the middle of the storm, his uncertain gaze flicking from face to face. His eyes find mine, and he lunges toward me. One of the security officers clamps a hand down on his shoulder. "Your Majesty," she says urgently.

I try to push through the people, but someone grabs me. "Gal," I wheeze, still trying to recover from the shock of the ejection and landing. None of this makes sense. I need him to *make this make sense.*

"Ettian, something's—" Gal breaks off abruptly. "I . . . I'm so sorry."

I'm so used to brushing those words off. So used to forgiving him instantly. But now, for once, as the security officers bundle my best friend away to whatever fate awaits him, I stand in the hollow silence left over and let him mean it.

CHAPTER 3

THE INSTRUCTOR'S ON her third iteration of my name by the time I realize she's calling on me. "Cadet Nassun," she declares. "We'd appreciate your input, if you'd be kind enough to join us."

I blink. Thirteen pairs of eyes blink back at me. I'm used to dozing off in this particular leadership seminar, but our numbers have decreased dramatically this morning, leaving it remarkably easy to catch me zoning out. Four of us were among the twenty shredded in the sky by academy missiles, and the usual occupant of the empty seat to my left is sitting gods-know-where, waiting for someone to cart him home to his parents.

At least, I think that's what's happening with Gal. No one's seen him since the security officers pulled him off the tarmac, no one's told me anything, and if I think too long about either of those facts, I end up wanting to break something.

Plenty of rumors are flying back and forth. By now, the whole academy knows the Umber heir is within our walls. The base is on lockdown, and all communications have been blocked. The thinly veiled threats in the academy head's morning announcement made the consequences of letting the heir's identity slip past the base's fences unquestionable. And everyone knows the traitorous connection among the other empty seats in our classrooms. Every single cadet born on Archon soil walks with caution today.

My empty stomach keens, but I can't fathom eating. Not when Tatsun Seely and nineteen other Archon-born kids were reduced to ashes yesterday. Not when he tried to co-opt me into my best friend's murder less than an hour beforehand. Not when that traitorous voice crept into my head seconds before the missile strike.

I can't shake that hopeful spark in Seely's eyes when he put his arm around my shoulders. I wonder if I was the last person he ever touched.

I didn't sleep much last night.

"Nassun," the instructor repeats, and I straighten in my chair. "We were discussing the failure of the joint effort by the Corinthian Empire and the Archon general Maxo Iral in their gambit for the Utar System. Specifically, the personal decisions made by Iral which led to—"

My mouth goes dry, a tickle of nausea climbing my throat. "The Utar campaign failed due to a fundamental lack of resources," I mutter. "The joint forces expected to be able to mine the system's moons for fuel, but they didn't establish the supply lines necessary to sustain that operation. With superior reserves, the Umber forces easily overwhelmed them."

Too late I realize it's the kind of answer Gal would have given— one that completely undermines the point of the question. This is a leadership seminar, and we're supposed to be deconstructing the faults and failures of Maxo Iral, not unpacking the mechanics of intersystem warfare. The subtle point I'm *supposed* to be making, the one the instructor wants to hear, is how Archon leadership was inherently unfit, making Umber intervention not just necessary but downright humane in comparison. But I'm not keen on thinking about the ways the general failed.

After Knightfall, he was the next hero the Archon people hung their hopes on—myself included. We realized that we couldn't rely on one person in a powersuit to come swooping in and save us. We needed people like Iral, people who could command hearts and minds, who could convince you to be your own goddamn hero.

Five years after they slaughtered the suited knights, the Umber imperials hung Maxo Iral on an electrified crucifix.

So much for heroes.

The instructor raises a brow. "Do try to be *present* the next time you show up for class," she says, and moves her imperious gaze to the next cadet.

I scowl. None of this makes any goddamn sense. Gal is a prince, we nearly got *killed* yesterday, twenty kids died, and somehow I'm back in class. Somehow the academy is carrying on like the galaxy hasn't suddenly reversed its spin. No time to catch my breath. Not even time to catch some decent sleep.

I let my eyes slide shut.

We were fifteen when we met. Both of us wide-eyed, clutching duffels, dressed in the simple grays of first-year cadets. His nose was too big for his face in the same way my ears were. We'd been assigned to the same bunk after the ceremony that marked our induction into the Umber Imperial Academy. I didn't know what I was getting into when he shook my hand and introduced himself as Gal Veres. I smiled and told him my name was Ettian Nassun and he could have the top bunk if he wanted. Maybe I should have noticed the imperialism in his blood when he took it immediately.

At first, we were only friends in the way proximity demanded. Neither of us knew anyone else—me because I'd been spat out by the postwar reconstruction and him because he'd been shipped in from a distant world in the Umber interior, far removed from the lower schools where many of our classmates met.

In those early days, we'd eat together in the mess, wrapped in the bubble of the other cadets' noise. I got the sense he was afraid of me then—I assumed because something about me screamed that I'd lived through the worst of the war, and no kid from the interior wanted to touch that. But after a week of quiet chewing, Gal started asking questions. Easy ones first—diplomatic, polite, the kind you ask when you're getting to know anyone. Favorite food, favorite color, where I was born, what kind of movies I liked best. Then the harder ones—ones about the three years I spent being shuttled between foster homes before my acceptance to the academy.

He started asking questions about further back, too, but quickly stopped when he realized I wouldn't—*couldn't*—talk about anything that happened to me before I was twelve. The war and the two years that followed were a bleeding wound waiting to scar, and thinking about anything before that time shut me down. I was always afraid he'd guess what filled in those missing parts of my history, but apparently Gal was just as afraid I'd guess the missing parts of his. Looking back now, I'm certain he asked all of those questions to keep me from realizing he wasn't answering any of mine.

But it didn't matter. For the first time since the war ended, I felt known. I wasn't part of the landscape, another faceless orphan shuffled into military service meant to replace the parents who fell with our homeworlds. I was *someone*. I had a story, and Gal was interested in hearing it.

And Gal was . . . Well, even then I could tell he was something glorious. He was magnetic, charming, and chaotic. His pranks were legendary, his clout with the upperclassmen uncanny, and it wasn't long before he had most of our fellow cadets vying for a spot at our table.

But more than that, he had heart. Some friends pull you out of the trash when they find you facedown in it. Gal was the kind who lay down next to you until you were ready to get up on your own. He'd always throw himself right into the mess alongside me, and I didn't fully grasp how important that was until the first time someone took a swing at me for my Archon origins and Gal swung back.

After he'd been released from a two-hour dressing-down and scheduled for three rotations of janitorial detention, he'd grinned at me, his black eye nearly swollen shut, and mouthed, *"Worth it."*

I did my best to keep a straight face, but something went supernova in my mind the moment those words left his mouth. *He doesn't know what I am, what I've been through,* part of me insisted. *Worthy,* the rest screamed so loudly that for once the other part barely seemed to matter. I weigh that moment against what I'm feeling now, and my gut boils with confusion, betrayal, guilt, and disgrace.

When I was ten, the Umber Empire stripped away everything I had and everything I was. When I was fifteen, the academy gave it back. *Gal* gave it back. I was proud to turn my nose up at Seely's willful disobedience, proud to wear a uniform decorated with brass and obsidian, proud to take part in the machine that was putting the worlds back together stronger than before, bringing the wealth of the Umber Empire to the Archon people who so desperately needed it. Proud to have reassembled myself into something more than the twelve-year-old nobody who crawled out of the rubble of Trost.

And now I remember who destroyed those streets in the first place. What bloodline saw Archon as its rightful conquest, burned the empire to ash, stripped our worlds of their value, and rebuilt what was left into its image, from the cities themselves to the children funneled through its shining new academies. I remember Gal's real name isn't Veres. His bloodright demands that he be addressed with the breadth of his holdings attached by the imperial honorific, a tradition that dates back to the foundations of every empire. No higher bloodright exists that could overwrite it through marriage, and he has no other true name to adopt. For as long as he lives, no matter whether he takes his throne or not, his name is Gal emp-Umber.

And Gal emp-Umber stands to inherit the empire that crushed us.

That crushed *me.*

Stashed away in the bottom of my drawer, there's a little velvet bag I've never been able to let go of. Inside is the last memento I have left of my parents. And now that I know who Gal is, an ember has ignited inside me, reminding me why I've kept it all these years.

"Cadet Nassun," a sharp voice snaps.

I come back to myself all at once, my chin jerking up toward the sound as I break eye contact with my own reflection. The academy head stares down at me over his large nose, at once imperious and strangely nonthreatening. It's always been difficult for me to take this reedy man's rank seriously, and today his nervous energy is making it exceptionally hard. The head has never liked me—never liked the fact that an Archon kid plucked off the streets has risen to the top of a year chock-full of well-fed, well-educated Umber kids. If there was talk of slapping a brass medal on my chest for the valor I showed yesterday, there's no doubt he shut it down.

The fluorescents overhead wash the interrogation room in a sickly, pale light. Ten people are packed in here, all higher-ups in the academy's administration. I've already told them every detail of the attack I can recall. They've looked over my history ten times, trying to figure out if I carry any loyalty to the former empire. Outside this room, there's a long line of Archon-born students waiting for their turn to be scrutinized.

The academy head clears his throat and taps the datapad in front of me. "We need your print to verify—"

"Where's Gal?" My tone veers on petulant, but I don't particularly care. My actions yesterday have granted me a certain sort of immunity in the eyes of the administration. They even know that Seely approached me beforehand, but after what I did to save Gal's life, there's no way they can spin that into an accusation.

The head's lips curl. "The prince is safe. That's all the information your clearance allows."

I don't trust his tone. I don't trust his intentions. I've never trusted much, but I thought I'd been getting better in the past two years. In the time since I met Gal.

Now I'm back where I started, the world upside down and nothing certain beyond the truths I know inside myself.

I glance down at the datapad. Not at the open circle on its screen, waiting for my print as a signature at the foot of the repetitive statement I've given, but at the clock in the upper right-hand corner. It's been nearly a full day since they took Gal away. My head spins with calculations—the distance from the Imperial Seat to here, the amount of time it would take a ship to reach Rana from the inner worlds of the Tosa System, the probability of Gal doing something rash or stupid in the time between now and then.

"Cadet Nassun," the academy head warns again.

I press my fingers to the screen.

"Ettian. Hey. EttianEttianEttian." A hand comes down hard on my back, startling me so badly that I snap upright and jolt the entire table. The noise barely registers in the clamor of the mess, which feels ten times more crowded than usual with all of the gossip rumbling through it. I glance up to find Hanji throwing herself and an overstuffed tray of cafeteria slop down beside me. Before I can get a word in, Rin slides up on my other side, Ollins straddles the bench across from me, and Rhodes shoves Ollins forward to make enough room for himself.

This is how it all breaks down. Ollins Cordello is the kind of guy who keeps a secret stash of fireworks tucked where most cadets hide far more unmentionable things. If you ask where Ollins got the fireworks, the answer would most likely be Rin Atsana—behind her sweet face and her diminutive stature lurks a mind that will build anything it's set to, no matter the danger. If you ask who taught Rin how to build fireworks, the answer would probably be Rhodes Tsampa, who spends most of his time in the library—a place no one had pegged as the most dangerous building on the academy's campus until he started getting ideas from it.

And if you were to ask who told Ollins it would be a great idea to set off said fireworks in the officer showers, the likely answer would be Hanji Iwam, who's now peering at me so intently that I have half a mind to yank her glasses off her face.

"You knew," Hanji says.

"There's no way he couldn't have known," Ollins butts in, speaking around a hefty mouthful of bread. "You must have been briefed when they bunked you together."

Rin rolls her eyes. "You think they'd put the Umber heir in with a random? Ettian's one of his personal guard, ain't that right?"

"If he were one of his personal guard, he'd be at the prince's side. Not munching garbage in the mess with us," Rhodes counters. I'd hardly call the rich, nutrient-packed meal served in generous spoonfuls garbage, but Umber kids have a different perspective on these things. I point a silent finger at him, and a hush falls over the table.

"So you didn't know," Ollins says. The noise comes back all at once, and I pick at my food as the gossip washes over me.

"Ruttin' hell."

"Did *anyone* know?"

"I kind of suspected."

"You did *not* suspect—who'd suspect that *Gold Twenty-Eight* was heir to the whole ruttin' empire? You've seen his grades. You've read those goofy little pacifist essays he wastes the instructors' time with. How could you even imagine *that guy* was Iva emp-Umber's son?"

"Thought he was a system governor's kid at minimum."

"I heard Sia Ramon is really Sia con-Tet. The jackass declared his identity, proclaimed he no longer felt safe at the academy, and the second the embargo lifts, he's hopping on a shuttle straight home to mother's knee."

"No one's going to try killing a continental governor's kid— what does that get you?"

"Well, now they're saying there might be a full-on Archon separatist ring here. Heard they had every native kid lined up for interrogations this morning."

I duck my head, stuff a large helping of stew in my mouth, and pray that none of them are thinking about where *I* came from. They're my friends, sure, but I've already sat through way too much grilling today.

"Archon's been dead for seven years—it's probably one of the other governors, trying to make a play for the crown. If Gal's the only heir they've got, Iva and Yltrast don't have time to pop out another one."

"They could freeze and use a surrogate."

"And wait for that one to grow?"

"Hold on, what if it's Corinth?"

As the four of them continue to gossip, more and more people pack around our table, all of them leaning close to catch the freshest takes. No one's sure of anything. Everyone's spinning their wheels, coming up with increasingly ludicrous theories, or making noise for the sake of making noise. By the time one of them remembers I'm there, Ollins is trying to convince the table that Gal offered him governorship of a border system in exchange for keeping his secret all this time.

Rin taps me on the shoulder. "Heard you saved his ass. Good going, Ettian."

"The missiles took out the Vipers. I just kept him from getting hit."

"Don't downplay it, dude," Hanji chuckles from my other side. "I was in the tower when it went down—you strapped your ship to his like a maniac and flew him through the soup."

"Someone had to do it."

Ollins joins in. "You pancaked your Viper on Runway Three."

"Yeah, landing gear was damaged from the maneuver."

"You sure you're not related to any of those suited idiots?" Hanji says, taking a swig of her drink. "Pretty sure ten years ago, that shit would have had the Archon imperials busting down your door."

My food sours on my tongue. "Every seven-year-old's dream," I try to joke, choking down the fact that it *was* my dream, at seven years old, to strap on a powersuit and go be a knight.

Hanji shrugs. "All I'm saying is we're lucky to have you. You're a ruttin' *hero,* Ettian. They'll probably give you a medal. A recommendation. You'll have a dreadnought of your own straight out of the academy."

I nearly choke on a laugh at the thought, thinking of the academy head's vendetta against me, but my humor twists into nausea before I can draw another breath. Would they fly me to Lucia and present me before the Imperial Seat? For a moment I'm consumed by the bloodcurdling image of Iva emp-Umber settling a brass-and-obsidian medallion around my neck before the masses with Gal looking on, his brow crowned in the metal and stone of his future empire, and betrayal in my gut from all sides.

"No need to look so put out." Ollins sniffs. "Honestly, Ettian, you look like someone's pissed in your boots."

"Does he ever not?"

I join the laughter that rolls down the table. Better to put on a smiling face for my classmates. It's what we all need right now. Beneath the glee and the joking and the wild theories, everyone's shell-shocked. Out of nowhere, a guy we've trained alongside for two and a half years turned out to be an imperial. Twenty of our classmates turned from comrades and friends to assassins and corpses. The entire base has been grounded, locked down, fenced in—even with miles of open prairie within the academy's bounds, it's impossible not to feel trapped. Every eye in the mess is suspicious. Everyone's wondering who's next.

"End of day, drinks are on me," Rin says, clapping me on the shoulder. "For the hero of the empire."

"I'll hold you to that," I tell her, and take another bite.

But come sundown, I don't head to the cantina. Instead, I go straight back to the room that Gal and I share—*shared,* I have to remind myself as I kick the door open. The narrow space feels smaller without Gal in it. His bunk rests above mine, the sheets still a jumbled mess the way he left them yesterday morning. Between classes, drills, and the three debriefings that left me with more questions than they answered, I'm ready to collapse.

My fingers fumble for the lock. We never used to lock it, but there's a deep-set fear in my bones that even a bolt isn't enough to put aside. At least twenty people wanted Gal dead yesterday. I saved him. Someone could be gunning for me now. I haven't felt this kind of fear in the halls of the academy since my first days here.

I grind my knuckles against my forehead, scowling. I'm thinking like the kid I was three years ago. *Feeling* like him too. I'm supposed to be better than that now. I'm supposed to be more. But maybe the only thing that really changed was having Gal at my side.

And now he's gone.

The datapad in my bag chirps. Probably Rin, wondering why I haven't joined them down in the cantina. As I reach into my bag to fish it out, I bump Gal's desk and wake the screen of his workstation. He's logged in, like he always leaves it. He's too goddamn trusting. The tactics essay he was working on two nights ago is still open. I should give it a read-through and turn it in for hi—*no, nope, not relevant anymore.*

But even so, I find myself skimming Gal's words. He's always been the class anarchist, trying to thread loopholes in the teachers' carefully laid lesson plans. This one is no exception. The solution to the scenario we were given is textbook. You swallow your pride, tuck your humanity in a nice little box, and raze your way through the system, burning anything you leave behind so nothing remains for your enemy to cobble together. Anyone who knows their history knows it's exactly what the Umber imperials did to the Nusi System in the War of Expansion.

Gal, as usual, has tried to dismantle it. He's ignoring civilian centers entirely in favor of running his fleet headlong at the enemy's, refusing to throw up the blockades and sieges necessary to cut off the supply lines. His quarrel is with the opposing fleet alone, and he's doing everything in his power to keep the common people—the *enemy's* people—out of the fight.

I mean, it's nice of him, but it's not actually going to work. And if you asked me to pick the next ruler of the galaxy out of my academy class, it definitely wouldn't be the dipshit trying to jam ethics into the middle of Umber warfare.

I dig my datapad out of my bag and flop backward onto the bottom bunk. But when I see the message waiting, every molecule of exhaustion evaporates from my body at once.

It's not from Rin.

Ettian,

I don't know if you're going to get this or if you're going to respond—I don't even know if it'll make it to you without getting caught in some firewall, but I have to try. The system governor will arrive by morning, and the guards are supposed to keep me safe until then. But these aren't my guards. Something's wrong. There are sleepers who were supposed to take over my protection the moment something happened.

But none of them were on the tarmac yesterday, and I haven't seen any of them since then. The only person I've been allowed to talk to is the academy head, and he's not telling me something. I don't think I'm safe here. I need to get out before the governor arrives, and you're the only one I trust. They're keeping me in the head's private quarters.

Please, try.

–Gal

A disbelieving snort escapes me before anything else. The only one he trusts? He shouldn't trust *anyone* at this point—not after twenty of us turned on him out of nowhere. But I did go right after him yesterday, and that speaks to something I can't dispute.

I stare out the slit of our window as the cool gray of dusk settles over the prairie. The word "sleepers" lances through me like a needle. How could Gal have been monitored at the academy without anyone discovering his identity? How could he be protected so thoroughly that Seely's mutineers had to make their attempt during a flight drill? I've spent two and a half years sleeping beneath Gal. I thought I was clever for noticing Seely's teeth. So how could I have missed—

The realization hits me like a static shock. I scramble out of bed and barrel out the door, breezing past a pair of grayed-out first years who flatten themselves against the wall as I rocket by.

If Gal hasn't seen the sleepers—

If they aren't protecting him—

If no one's protecting *them*—

I leap up the stairs three at a time until I've reached the top level of the dorms, where the young officers sleep. This hall's much more quiet and orderly than the cadet bunks below, but there's an eerie layer to the silence that settles over me as I stagger out of the stairwell and up to Jana's door.

With Gal's magnetic personality, it made sense that he befriended even the upperclassmen. No one questioned it. No one could blame them for continuing to check in on him, even after they'd graduated. I think of all the times they stopped by our room, all the times I caught him waving to one of them across the mess, the way they were such a constant, comfortable presence in our lives.

Always keeping an eye on him. Just the way they were supposed to.

"Jana?" I call out, rapping twice on the door. The quiet around me is stifling. I feel like I'm the only one breathing on this floor. *Calm down, Ettian,* I scold myself. *You saw her yesterday.* But I saw Gal yesterday, and now I might never see him again. I saw Seely yesterday and now he's nothing but scattered pieces across several miles of Rana's surface.

I try the door. Unlocked. Jana never leaves her room unlocked—hasn't since she found herself on the receiving end of one of Gal's pranks when she was still a cadet.

Gods of all systems, so that's how he was able to get away with—

The first things I notice are the scuffmarks. Long streaks of peeled rubber tell the story of boots dragged across the floor unwillingly. The bed's a little untidy, but for Jana that speaks volumes.

I step into the room, turn, and find the most telling marks of all. The wall by the door is pocked with the impact scars from three blaster bolts.

Someone removed Jana from this room. Whoever it was, she fought them tooth and nail to stop it. Whoever it was, they were confident enough that they didn't feel a need to mask what happened here. Whoever it was must run this place.

I slip back out the door, closing it carefully behind me, and duck into the stairwell. Leaning against the wall, I drop into the dark behind my eyelids.

Yesterday, I acted on instinct. Today it's a choice—a choice I've spent so long burying that I'd fooled myself into thinking I'd escaped it entirely. But Archon's not as dead as I once thought, and the apathy that's cloaked me ever since the empire fell is starting to constrict. Now I have to decide what's more important: the empire that built me up with promises of heroics and then abandoned me, or the boy who had to be dragged away from my side, who's fought for me like no one has.

The boy who talks his way out of fights like a rational human being.

The boy whose stupid, pacifistic essays I've been proofreading and turning in for years.

My breath catches in my throat.

Now I see the long game—the one he's been secretly playing the whole time. Gal's spent his entire academy career training himself not to emulate his parents' violence but to rip its teeth out.

My choice is as clear as the void. I gotta get him off this planet. I gotta get his ass on the throne.

But first things first, I *really* need that drink.

CHAPTER 4

THREE HOURS LATER, I've managed to waste five shots of polish over my shoulder and gained an entourage nearly thirty people strong. The cantina is packed to bursting, and true to her word, Rin's buying—not just for me, but for every cadet in the bar. Gods of all systems bless her parents' deep pockets. As far as I know, they're the heads of a mining corporation that struck exclusive rights to one of the newly acquired Archon belts, although Gal has gone and made it difficult to take even *that* at face value.

"TO THE HERO OF THE EMPIRE," Ollins roars from the top of a table, and the crowd roars back at him, hoisting their drinks in the air. The legal imperial age is eighteen, but the academy cantina has always made an exception for upperclassmen—otherwise it'd be full of sad officers and no money.

A few of those officers glower at the rest of us from a table in the back corner. My eyes are on them as I fake another sip. *That's right. Dumb, drunk cadets. No reason to sound any alarms.*

I wish there weren't so much on my mind. I want to soak this in. If it were any other night, Gal would be by my side, matching me drink for drink and lamenting that we're less than a year away from graduating to the officer ranks. Some of us will stick around for command training at the academy, harvesting the opportunities present in the new territories, but many will be assigned closer to the interior, where the appointments are more prestigious and the competition is a thousand times more cutthroat.

For now, the air is sweaty and electric, my drink is cold enough to numb my hand, and the noise and crush of people is overwhelming. Some aggressive, melodic Umber rock anthem blasts from the speakers—the type of music no one but the older officers and Hanji enjoys unironically. Two boys are making out in the corner, anonymous in the blur of bodies stuffing the cantina, and a pang of cheerstained jealousy twinges in my chest.

I want to be wrapped in this night forever. We have only so many of them left to go.

"I can't believe we have class tomorrow," Rin groans, clinging to my waist with one arm as she tries to steady herself. "I'm going to vomit on the drill field."

"I'll be right there with you," Hanji cackles from her other side. "What about you, Ettian? You feeling strong?"

"Oh, I'm feeling strong." I slide my arm around Rin's shoulders, and she tucks her head against my ribs.

"How strong are you feeling?"

Hanji doesn't realize what she's handed me. I grin, trying my best to look like I've just had the idea. "Feeling like I could streak the officers' quarters."

There are some words that have a little magic in them. Some words you have to be careful tossing around because they dig into people's consciousness in such visceral ways. Some words you know are dangerous, especially on a dangerous day like today.

I've said some of those words.

A hush falls over the people packed around me, and Ollins wobbles on his table. "You're ruttin' kidding me," he says. "You would actually—"

"Wouldn't you?"

"Hell yeah, I would! Bet I'd get farther than you too. Bet I could go all the way up to the head's door and back." Murmurs and laughter rise from the cadets around us.

I tip my glass at him. "Let's do it. Let's *all* do it."

For a moment, Ollins stares at me. Then he hoists his glass high and screams, "HELL YEAH." The crowd roars along with him, and the officers in the back slump lower in their seats, clutching their drinks tighter.

I down my polish in three quick gulps. Partly because with all eyes on me, there's no avoiding it. Mostly because I'm going to need all the courage I can get.

We gain people as we go. The thirty in the cantina are drunk enough to accept the notion immediately, but as we make our way to the barracks, they start recruiting from whoever's passing by. We're a chaotic, shrieking herd of animals, whooping and hollering as we stumble through the halls, and we've swollen to a number I can't accurately count.

Somehow I have to dislodge myself from them, but that means dislodging Rin from me first. She's still got her arm snaked around my waist, and it feels like I'm the only thing keeping her upright. Every time I try to slip her grip, she only holds on tighter. She stopped saying words that made sense around the time we stood up from the bar.

Desperate times call for desperate measures. I grab the hem of my shirt, and predictably enough, she lets go immediately, shrieking in delight.

"Damn, Nassun's going for it!" Hanji hollers behind me as I pull my shirt off and throw it aside. And like that, the chain reaction's off. Not to be outdone, Ollins is already staggering out of his pants. Rin yanks her tank over her head, and as the tidal wave of haphazardly disrobing cadets rounds a corner, it's too easy to slip away.

I didn't anticipate losing my shirt, but with the rate the drunken crowd is moving, there's no time to go back for it. I duck out through a side door, cursing as the chill of the night hits me. Overhead, the sky is clear, the distant lights of roving transports tracing lines between the stars. With nothing but open plains surrounding the academy, the vast dark of the universe seems monstrous.

No time to admire it. I haul ass along the barracks to the rows of poorly maintained hedges that decorate part of the green. My head's buzzing from the polish, and it takes me several extra seconds to figure out which one has my bag in it.

The whoops and yells inside the dorms are growing louder. Lights flicker on in the officers' quarters. There's a distant, muffled crash.

I sling the bag over my shoulder and take off running again, fixing my eyes on the uppermost floor of the officer barracks. The top brass sleeps up there, and I'm fairly certain the windows at the far end correspond to the head's rooms. There's a faint glow inside. Gods of all systems, I hope I'm right. Otherwise this is going to get awkward fast.

It takes my polish-blunted fingers way more time than I anticipated to get the ascension harness on properly. Four attempts to clip my blaster to my belt. Three tries to shoot the grappling line in the right place. But my head clears right away when my feet leave the ground. I steal up the side of the barracks, pressed flat against the stone, trying my best to keep away from the windows. As I climb, the chaos inside climbs with me. Ollins has the luck of a devil when it comes to betting, but he had better make good on this one—if this is going to work, my mob of streakers has to make it to the sixth floor.

But they aren't meeting any resistance, and who can blame the officers for not trying? It's hard to keep a smile off my face, imagining the scene inside. I wish I could be in there with them, naked, drunk, and manic. Instead I'm outside, dangling from a rope, freezing my ass off, and waiting for the moment their chaos hits the corridor inside the window I've chosen for my entrance.

Now I have time, so I hang my head back and admire the stars. The lights of the academy compound drown out all but the brightest. A few of our system's planets are visible tonight. I pick out the inner world of Imre and imagine the furious vector the system governor must be burning to get here from his winter estate. The trip will take him two days minimum with the intrasystem limits on travel speed, but every second of delay brings us closer to the moment he steps in with blood-granted authority that no one but an imperial can question. And something tells me that once Berr sys-Tosa arrives, he won't be yielding to the command of an unripened Umber. Gal has to get out of here before that happens.

Even with the distant movements of satellites, stations, and ships above, everything feels far too still for the way my heart is racing.

Unintelligible shouting from inside snaps me back into reality. I recognize Ollins's voice, and a grin splits my face even as a shudder of anticipation runs down my spine. I pull my blaster off my belt, brace against the stone, and fire a quick line of pulses along the base of the window. It splinters, then shatters, the glass falling away in a glimmering shower.

I whisper a prayer of thanks to all gods listening that the academy head chose comfort over security when he locked Gal away. With a kick off the wall, I swing into the window frame, using my boots to knock away the last of the glass.

The suite inside is plush. Far nicer than anything I've seen in my time at the academy. Fancy carpets, velvet drapery, soft orbs of warm light scattered around. And in the middle of it all, looking scared to pieces but still somehow smiling, is Gal emp-Umber.

"Ettian," he says, crossing his arms. "Why aren't you wearing a shirt?"

CHAPTER 5

I SCOWL, BUT I can't commit to it. Seeing him safe is too much of a relief. If I weren't worried about the broken glass, I'd sag against the window frame.

No time for that. Already the ruckus is moving past us in the corridor outside the suite. "We need to move," I say, glancing around the room in case there are more guards than the ones I knew would be posted in the hall outside his door. When my gaze lands on Gal again, I frown. "What the hell are you wearing?"

Gal shrugs. The fact of the matter is he's wearing a brightly colored robe, loose silk pants, and no shoes.

"You're joking. You asked for a rescue, and you're dressed for bed?"

"You're not wearing a shirt."

"Go put shoes on."

"I don't have shoes."

"You don't have shoes?"

"They gave me these stupid slipper things—took away my boots and my flight suit." He spreads his arms. Apparently the robe has ridiculous billowy sleeves.

"There's broken glass everywhere."

"That's on you." A sudden *thump* at the door followed by the sounds of fleeing feet sends Gal whirling around. "The hell was that?"

Ollins, I think, glowing with pride, but it's only going to distract Gal. "We don't have time for this," I say instead.

"Agreed." Gal crosses the room in two quick strides, his robe flapping as he sweeps up to the window. Some of the glass fell inward, and his eyes drop to the shards sticking out of the carpet.

I lean out into the room, the grappling line at my waist keeping me from toppling into the minefield below, and stretch out my arms. "C'mere," I mutter. The chaos is fading outside. Soon someone's going to check on their pet princeling.

Gal wraps his arms around my neck, pulling me into a tight hug.

I freeze. "I'm not hugging you, moron—I'm trying to pick you up."

"Oh."

"Let's go. Time's wasting." Before Gal can get another word in, I slip his grip and duck, hoisting him up on my shoulder. He's way heavier than I expected, even without boots and a flight suit weighing him down. My knees buckle, and I let out an involuntary grunt.

"Ruttin' hell, we're high up," Gal mutters as he gets his first good look at the drop awaiting us. I lean back, and he stiffens, his hands finding purchase on my ascension harness as his knees clench around my rib cage. My arm tightens around his waist, and my fingers fumble on the winch controls.

Deeper in the room, I hear the click of a doorknob turning.

I don't need to be told twice. I jump clear of the sill, punching the winch release, and Gal bites down on a scream as the ground comes flying up to meet us. I land hard, the extra weight nearly knocking me to my knees in the shattered glass that surrounds us. We sway forward, and I plant my forearm against the barracks to brace us.

One breath.

Two breaths.

The thunder of Gal's heart slams against my shoulder.

Drums in my ears.

Not again. I won't let that little voice that tried to convince me to fall back with Seely into my head, no matter how loud it shouts. Before any of my doubts have time to sink in, someone up above shouts, "He's gone!"

"Time to run," Gal whispers urgently.

I unsnap the grappling line from my harness and leave it, staggering three steps clear of the glass before I dare to let Gal down. He leans against me as he gets his legs underneath him, and I glance up at the window again. There's a shadow up there—no doubt one of the guards sticking their head out. We're cloaked in the darkness down here, tucked against the wall, but it's only a matter of time before they spot us.

But just when I'm certain we're hosed, a side door slams open and five naked cadets go shrieking into the night.

Gal stares after them, his mouth hanging open as I drag him into the barracks. "What did you *do*?"

"What I had to."

"At the door, up there, that was—"

"Someone making academy history. Ollins, I think."

He beams and pats me on the back. "I don't deserve you."

I flash a taut smile that's probably invisible in the darkness. "Let's move. We can make it to the room in—"

"The room, seriously? We don't have *time*—"

"Clothes, Gal. Supplies. *Shoes*."

He glances down at his bare feet and his flimsy robe. Then at my bare chest. His eyebrows lift. "Fair point," he says. "We make it fast. They'd expect us to bolt for a ship right away anyway."

"Now you're getting it. We gear up, lay low, wait for the chaos to die down, and *then* . . ." I trail off, waiting for him to fill in the rest. What his plan is, whom he needs to contact, where he needs to go to be safe again.

But Gal only turns tail and starts running.

We make it back to the room unspotted, but I'm not celebrating our luck yet. I lock the door behind us, and by the time I turn around, Gal's already stripped down and started rooting in his drawers. "Now what?" he asks, pulling out a primly folded pair of pants.

"You're asking *me*?" I sputter.

He turns, surprised by the harshness of my tone.

"Look at yourself. If it weren't for the way everyone's losing their goddamn minds, I wouldn't even believe you're a prince. You have no plan, no backups, no . . . *sense*."

"I . . ." Gal stares at the pants in his hand, plucking absently at a bit of lint. "I have you," he mumbles. "I was supposed to have more. There was a whole system to protect me, and it fell apart the moment I actually needed it. But *you* were there. I don't know what's happening right now. I don't know where's safe, or what I'm supposed to do, or even who to trust. But I have you. Right?"

My heart stutters. Gal's been shaken. Yesterday he had twenty people gunning for him, and gods know how many more enemies lurk in these halls. The sleepers meant to protect him have disappeared. I almost tell him what I found in Jana's room, but I know it's only going to worsen his focus, and I need him sharp. There's nothing we can do for her when we've barely got a plan for ourselves.

Something larger is in motion, sinister mechanics turning with Gal at the center. He's spent the past two and a half years training as a soldier and a leader, and in the span of a day he's been torn away from everything he was working toward, stuffed into a fancy robe and slippers, and placed under guard to wait until he's called on.

Gal's had his life stolen from him. He's just hoping there's a way to put it back together.

I close my eyes, pinching the bridge of my nose. "Put your damn pants on. We'll figure this out."

He follows orders, but I know him well enough to know I haven't put his mind at ease. If the way his eyes fix pointedly on the floor is any indication, Gal's thoughts are eating him alive. "Ettian," he says as he grabs a T-shirt and yanks it over his head. "I can jack a shuttle by myself and get out of here."

"Can you, though?"

"Ettian." He nods to my bed, to the two bags packed there. Only one of them is for him.

The walls of this room feel too close. Gal's eyes too intent. I take a deep breath, pulling on a tank as I try to prolong the inevitable. But he already knows exactly what I'm going to say.

"You can't leave the academy," Gal says. "You've worked so hard—you're the top pilot in our class. They're going to give you a dreadnought command someday."

I roll my eyes. "That's nothing. You're going to be an *emperor.* And look—I know you better than anyone. I know the kind of ruler you're going to be, the difference you're going to make. Getting you on that throne is a thousand times more important than anything I could ever accomplish at this stupid school."

I drop onto my bunk, pulling the bag I've packed into my lap to avoid looking at whatever that declaration has done to Gal's face. I can never double-check my gear enough, even though there's only one thing worth taking from this room. My fingers sink to the bottom of the bag, brushing velvet.

"Ettian." Suddenly Gal's right in front of me, those deep brown eyes staring with every ounce of their intensity, his knees inches from mine.

"Don't," I groan, stifling a laugh. I don't know when this was decided. Was it when I realized what Gal's rule would mean for the galaxy? When I locked my Viper to his? When I shook his hand on that first day in this room?

I'm going with him. I'm not letting him do this alone. And I'm not letting him leave me behind.

He needs someone at his side now more than ever. Someone who has his back without question. Someone with the street sense to keep him from stumbling into all the traps ahead. Someone who can fly him where he needs to go. And somehow—whether by fate, coincidence, or the hands of the gods themselves—I'm the best guy for the job. Maybe the only one.

I pull on my jacket, still not looking at him. Outside, the halls are quiet, but it won't be long until the streakers and their ruckus get herded back into the dorms. "We need to get moving." I sling his bag at him, and he catches it, tucking it under his arm.

His breath hitches, hesitant.

Gal sets a hand on my shoulder, his fingers curving lightly along the ridge of my bones. I can't look at him. We've been in this room together for so long. These narrow walls are the closest I've felt to home since the war. He knows how much it means for me to leave them behind. As Gal's thumb runs a gentle line up my neck, my thoughts stray. There were notions I had before my roommate turned out to be a prince. Notions we never got a chance to explore—not the way we might have wanted to.

Now I'm not sure what's left for us. I meet his eyes at last, and we both jolt like we've been hit by a stunner round. It's too much—all of it. Gal takes a step back.

"A ship," I whisper.

"Time to go," he agrees.

It dawns on me somewhere between the barracks and the main hangar that I'm not mentally "all here." Between the sleep deprivation, the stress, and the polish I couldn't avoid drinking, I'm deteriorating fast.

Gal's sharp, at least, driven by the tension of being out in the open for the first time since the assassination attempt. He keeps us clear of the frazzled patrols that sweep through the academy compound, chasing down our inebriated friends. More than once, we're forced to duck into the shadows as yet another naked cadet gets marched past us.

"Gods, how many of them were there?" Gal says, impressed and slightly miffed. We're crammed against a stack of cargo by the main hangar, but he's craning his neck around it to watch the scene unfolding on a distant drill field, where six people are doing their best to herd a determined streaker back toward the barracks. I think it might be Hanji.

"Focus, Gal," I remind him, though if it's Hanji, I don't blame him for staring. I glance back and forth, but no other patrols seem to be in the area. The distant lights are all focused on the roads, gates, and fences—the obvious exits from the academy compound.

But we're not heading out by land. Not if I can help it. I grab Gal by the collar, and together we make a run for the hangar's side door. Locked, as expected. Stealth has gotten us this far, but it won't get us through a bolt. I pull the blaster from my belt and hand it to Gal. "Want to do the honors?"

"Thought you'd never ask." Gal pummels three quick shots into the door, one at each of the hinges. Smoke whispers out of the holes, and I throw my shoulder against the door, smashing clear through.

Alarms wail, and lights snap on across the hangar floor, obliterating my vision. There's a slight pressure at my waist as Gal slips my blaster back into its holster. I blink away the spots in my eyes, following the guidance of Gal's hand on my back as we take off at a run.

When I see what we're running for, I balk.

"A Beamer? Seriously, Gal?"

Gal glances between me and the ship. "Problem?"

Even with the panic coursing through me, begging me to take the ship and get out of here before the alarms bring trouble down hard on our asses, I can think of a *host* of problems. Beamers are cheerfully wide and squat things, meant to do little more than travel in straight lines. They're built outlandishly heavy, a design made possible only by Archon metal flowing into Umber-held shipyards, so they're perfect for kids new to flying and families who need a friendly, reliable transport. They're the minivan of starships. They are *not* what I want to be flying when I make my escape from the academy.

"We don't have time to be picky," Gal urges. The shriek of the alarm sirens nearly drowns out his words.

"I'm not being picky, I'm being practical. Look, this way—" Across the hangar sits a row of sleek skipships, the kind of thing an imperial should be flying. Those ships are so athletic, armed, and

armored that you could safely fly an emperor through an active battlefield in one without getting a single scratch on it. One of them has
a hatch wide open, practically begging for us to take it. We just have
to cross the open hangar floor.

I grab Gal's shirt, trying to tug him along, but he plants his feet.
It's surprisingly effective, given that he's nearly fifty pounds lighter
than I am. "There isn't time, Ettian."

"It's right there."

But Gal's eyes aren't on the ship. I turn, following the line of his
gaze, and my stomach drops. A patrol has answered the sirens' howl.
Seven soldiers sprint across the hangar, each of them carrying a rifle.
They square up twenty yards away from us and lift their guns.

Gal steps in front of me.

Something transforms in him. He lifts his chin, his shoulders
squaring. The mask he's worn for two and a half years falls away.
He's no longer hiding behind terrible grades, a foul mouth, or his
horrible posture. Now I see it. Iva's blood. Yltrast's too. The brow
meant to wear a crown of obsidian and brass. The confidence that
could bring entire systems to their knees. This isn't Gal Veres, the
easygoing cadet, a good shot and a terrible pilot. Here he stands,
Gal emp-Umber. The Umber heir.

Stepping without hesitation between me and seven gun barrels.

"Lower your weapons," he says.

I've heard this voice before. Smooth, cultured, and difficult to
disobey. It's the voice that makes him a nightmare around the
drunken, the weak-willed, and basically anyone with ears. I always
wondered where it came from and why he didn't use it all the time.
But this voice is a weapon, and you don't point it lightly. And as to
where it came from . . .

Well, it's not exactly a mystery anymore.

The patrol hesitates. With a jolt, I realize Rhodes is among
them—I forgot he was on duty tonight. His gun dips a hair lower
than his fellows'.

"I'm sure your orders are to bring me in unharmed," Gal says.
"And most likely to eliminate anyone who's with me."

Rhodes nods helplessly before his superiors can stop him.

"But, as I'm sure you've noticed, I'm not being forced. Not being coerced. No one's bundling me off in the night. I am simply . . . leaving."

Someone turns off the alarm. The hangar plunges into a deathly quiet, filled only with an empty ringing and the panting breaths of nine people who don't want to be there. I press down the urge to reach out for Gal. What happens next is entirely up to him.

"Lower your guns," he urges. "Let us leave."

I hold my breath as all seven barrels dip lower. Gal's magic voice is doing its best work.

But then the woman at the center of the squad cocks her head to the side and snaps her rifle back up. Whatever's coming into her earpiece is changing her mind, and her motion leads the rest of the patrol. "Sorry, Umber. Head's orders," she says.

Gal's jaw goes taut, but he keeps his head high. "Who are you going to listen to? The academy head, or the blood that rules you?"

"The academy head is the academy head. But you're not an emperor yet."

Gal might be a great negotiator, but here's where he fails. When all it takes to twist a situation are your words, you're never good at telling when you're beaten. This is the part where I come in.

I lunge forward and grab Gal's collar, yanking him back and turning as the first stunner rounds let fly. He spins into my grip, slapping down a button on my chest, and the deflector armor under my jacket goes live as a bolt skips off my back. The kinetics of it knock me forward, but Gal's there to catch me. His gaze flicks to the skipships, but I'm already pulling us both into a sprint for the nearest Beamer.

Another bolt drives into me, knocking me to my knees. Gal hesitates, but I wave him on. "Pop the hatch," I shout. He ducks under the Beamer's wing, and I roll, yanking my blaster off my belt. The patrol's taken cover to reload, and as I stagger to my feet, I spot Rhodes with his head too high, fumbling with an ammunition pack. I raise my gun.

I've shot at classmates a thousand times, dropped a hundred of them with stunner rounds, but somehow it's different when it's real. Am I shooting at him as an Umber soldier in defense of an imperial? As a deserter in defiance of the Umber Empire? As an Archon—

I hesitate, and the hesitation throws everything off. My fingers stutter on the trigger. The shot goes wide, and Rhodes ducks lower beneath his cover. Before I have a chance to regret it, a bolt slams into my chest, knocking me flat on my back. My head cracks against concrete, and the armor on my chest beeps a warning that slices through my disorientation. The charge it carries can only deflect so much kinetic energy, and the hits I've taken have drained it almost completely.

"Ettian!"

Hands find my shoulders. The floor drags against my back. I try my best to pull my legs under me, but Gal's not letting that happen. He yanks me up the Beamer's ramp and into the cargo hold before I can yell at him for abandoning the ship's safety. The door hisses shut with a dull thud behind us. "Get it running," I choke.

Gal doesn't need to be told twice. He takes off for the ship's cockpit. I push myself upright, groaning as my head throbs, and rip my bag off my back. With the ship's walls around us, we're safe for the time being, but we need to get off the ground before the patrol finds a way to cut through the hull. I snap off the armor, slumping in relief as its electric rattle leaves my teeth. I'd rather Gal wore it, but we both knew I'd be the one they wouldn't hesitate to shoot.

The ship lurches, lights snapping on as Gal fires up the engines. I stand, steadying myself with a hand on the wall. We're off the ground and listing to one side already. Typical Gal. Why couldn't the "bad pilot" thing be part of his act too?

I get three steps up the ladder out of the hold before a massive *boom* knocks the ship sideways, throwing me off the rungs. I tuck and roll, my skin shrieking against the metal of the floor. "Gal?" I shout, scrambling to my feet the second I'm able.

"Yeah?"

"What—heavens and hells, what's—" I can't even get the words out. I think this is my brain careening past its breaking point. It's been deprived, drugged, and tossed around too much for one night, and now my rationality is running on fumes. I scramble up the ladder and tear down the hall into the Beamer's cockpit.

The first thing I notice is that it's dark. The second is that we're outside. The ship's lifters thrum cheerfully as we rocket low over the prairie. I flop into the copilot's seat, struggling to wrap my aching head around what I'm seeing.

"Gal?"

"Yeah?"

"We're outside."

"Yeah."

"We were in the hangar. The hangar doors were down."

"I blew through them."

"You—" I sit upright, fighting against the ship's acceleration as we lift higher and higher. "You did *what*?"

"Used the Beamer's guns to take out the doors. Punched a big enough hole in them that we could fly right through."

I slump back down. "I had clearance codes. You didn't have to— *shit, Gal!*" I lunge across the cockpit and yank the controls, throwing the Beamer into a vicious swerve to avoid clipping the massive communications tower that's suddenly loomed out of the darkness.

Gal's wide eyes turn up to meet mine.

I slap him lightly. "Face front, dumbass. Eyes on the sky if you're gonna drive. Gods of all systems, that was the academy's main relay. If you'd taken it down, you'd have knocked out the military comms keystone for this entire system."

Gal lets out an anxious scoff. "Hey, worst-case scenario, they sue my parents for the damages."

We both crack at the same time. The laugh comes from my stomach, blasting out of me so violently that I almost choke. The ship's vector wobbles as Gal bends over the controls, wheezing. He's trying his best to bite down on his hysteria, but when I'm laughing, he can never stop. I lean back in the copilot's chair, letting out a wild howl as we blast toward the stars above.

Then an alert flashes on the dash. Gal glances down at the warning, rubbing the tears from his eyes as he tries to make it out. "Rut me sideways," he says.

"Now what?"

"They've launched missiles."

CHAPTER 6

OUR EYES MEET. "Switch," we whisper simultaneously.

I didn't strap in, but Gal did. As I rocket out of my chair and scramble to the other side of the cockpit, he struggles with the restraints, his sweaty fingers slipping over the belts. The ship lists dangerously, and I lean over him to grab the controls before we start to plunge. The panel beneath me shows the inbound missiles. Thirty seconds until we're bits.

As Gal keeps floundering, I crank the engines up as hot as they'll go, practically daring the heat seekers to hump us. The Beamer handles like a bar of soap, a far cry from the Vipers I'm used to.

"Gal," I warn.

"I'm trying, I just—"

I know what I need to do. I twist over the seat, trying my best to keep the controls steady as I climb into Gal's lap. The cockpit clearly wasn't meant for this—I barely have room to maneuver, but at least I can reach everything I need to.

"Ruttin' unreal," Gal chokes from beneath me.

"One, you brought this on yourself. Two, I'm really, really sorry about this," I snap, then yank the controls and point our nose to the sky.

Acceleration crushes us as we climb. Gal whimpers, and it occurs to me that I'm probably not going to like the consequences of collapsing an Umber prince's rib cage. My eyes are on the instruments as the missiles close. I have to time this right. Two inbound heat seekers fly in parallel, dissolving the distance between us far too fast for my liking.

"Gal?"

I get a grunt. Can't blame him.

"Hold on."

He takes a second to catch my meaning. When his arms lock around my chest, I twist the Beamer's controls, throwing us into a tight spin. This ship can barely handle these kinds of forces—the whole thing creaks and groans. It's a struggle to keep my eyes open and focused. With no belts to hold me in, Gal's the only thing keeping me from flying across the cockpit. Even in the tumult, the warmth of his chest pressed against my back isn't lost on me.

Focus. I need to focus. Just for a minute more.

The spin has thrown the heat seekers into a spiral that twists wide. Wide enough? We're about to find out. Because here's the problem with heat seekers: they get a little confused when you go cold.

I cut the engines with a flip of a switch. Our acceleration drains away. The Beamer goes terrifyingly quiet. Nothing but our breaths, our heartbeats, and the rush of air around us. Nothing but the incoming shriek of the missiles.

We reach apogee. We drop. Gal's grip around me goes tighter. The instrumentation whistles a warning. I squeeze my eyes shut.

Nothing I do can save us now.

The missiles scream past us, recalculating, converging. A fraction of a second later, there's a bloom of light beyond my eyelids and an explosion that shakes us like a world shattering.

My eardrums ring, but distantly I hear Gal's scream. The engines are still dead, and the ship is just shy of tumbling out of control. We've gone weightless, but Gal clings to me, keeping me anchored to the pilot's seat. My hands find the controls again, my fingers shaking as I flip the engines back on. Feel the ship warm beneath me. Feel Gal press his forehead into my shoulder.

I open my eyes, jamming down the attitude thrusters to tear us out of our spin. The stars outside steady, and I twist the Beamer until we're pointed at the vast dark of the open prairie below. The ship moves grudgingly, and I groan. These things weren't designed to maneuver like a Viper, and I'm getting nowhere trying to fly it like one. My fingers itch for drag fins that aren't there, and dimly it dawns on me that I might have humped our chances of walking away from this.

Gods of all systems, I'd better not have. If Gal and I die together and it's my fault, the afterlife is not going to be a pleasant place. And there's no way in any system's hell I'm dying in a goddamn Beamer.

I let the engines spin up, then turn them loose. The Beamer creaks in protest, but slowly we pull out of our plummet. My shoulders go slack as we streak across the night, climbing once more for the stars.

I don't release the tension completely until we're pushing toward the outer limits of Rana's atmosphere. Finally, as the planet's gravity starts to loosen its hold on us, I flip on the autopilot and rise, shrugging out of Gal's grip. In the micrograv, a little push takes me to the ceiling of the cockpit, but Rana's still there to bring me drifting back down.

Back down to meet Gal's bugged-out eyes.

"I told you . . ." I wheeze, "I had clearance codes. So we wouldn't trigger the academy's *ruttin' automated defense systems* by taking off with an unauthorized ship and nearly flying it right into the main relay."

Gal squirms guiltily underneath me, glancing sideways as if his excuse is somewhere in the copilot's headrest. "Whoops?" he offers.

"Out of my chair."

Gal obliges, scrambling out of his restraints and sinking into the other seat. He instinctively reaches for the harness, then thinks better of it. I slide into the pilot's chair in his wake.

"That was . . . I don't know how you do it, honestly."

"If you had paid attention *once* in Dr. Ridan's sim class—"

"Don't even start."

"Just . . . Just let me do the flying from now on, okay?"

"She's all yours," Gal says shakily, patting the dashboard. The whisper of rushing air fades around us. We're past the realm of Rana's breath. I flip another switch and wince as the grav generators spin up with a tug that feels like a hook snagging my bones. Gal groans as he's pulled even deeper into his seat. "I didn't think . . . I didn't know . . ."

"Hey, it's okay. We're clear. We're off Rana. We fly for a day, get to a superluminal zone, and then we're going to be on a direct vector to the Imperial Seat."

The words hit like a hand on the back of my neck, and an instant, unshakable fear roots in me. Maybe Gal thinks of the Imperial Seat as his natural home, of the Umber core's abundance as his birthright. Maybe he looks at Iva and Yltrast and loves them unconditionally, even if they stuffed him under a rug for the first seventeen years of his life.

I think of it and see my homeworld in ruins.

Rana's sun-facing horizon glows beneath us, the night side of the planet dotted with the lights of cities. But my eyes find something else in the darkness—the subtle shadow of a massive crater north of Trost's glimmer.

We call it the Warning Shot. Seven years ago, the Archon imperials were on their last legs, unwilling to yield even as the war reached the core of their shattering empire. Trost was under bombardment so thorough it was like the enemy had raked fiery talons across the city. And when the first Umber dreadnought broke through the defenses around Rana, it set its sights north of the Archon Imperial Seat and let off a single burst from its main gun, along with a message broadcast throughout the system. The Archon imperials were to surrender, or the next shot would wipe Trost from the planet's surface.

Less than an hour later, the war was over, and the Archon imperials were on their way to the Umber interior in chains.

I look at that big, stupid hole in the ground, and I feel it inside me. A history so thoroughly annihilated that the only thing remaining is a huge empty scar. The Warning Shot is a reminder of how easily Umber takes, how blessed we've been that they didn't take more. Rana used to be proud. A shining capital planet with a shining capital city, the heart of an empire comfortably bordered by Umber along one axis and Corinth along another. Spare in arable land but wealthy in metal, with some of the most advanced technologies the galaxy has ever seen. A place where it was common to see a human-shaped powersuit rocket over a city as a knight rushed off to save the day. A place where anyone with the drive to defend the empire and the prowess to wear one of those suits could *be* a knight, whether or not you had bloodright to your name. Now it's just another battered jewel on the belt of Umber's conquests.

And it still hurts to see.

I forsook the Archon Empire long ago. It felt like the only choice that would let me *live,* free from the guilt and horror and the way my stomach felt like it might empty every time someone mocked the empire's platinum and emerald. It took years to build the walls I needed. I thought they were strong enough to hold.

But when you find out your best friend is blood of the blood that rained hell on Rana, it has a way of ripping open the wounds you thought had scarred.

An alert flashes on the dash, and I bolt upright, ice threading my veins. If the academy's scrambled ships to bring us back, this Beamer is in for the flight of its life. It takes me a moment to make sense of what the instrumentation is telling me. Gal leans over it too, looking puzzled.

And then it clicks. I sink back in my seat, staring out the cockpit windows. As a pilot, I thought I understood fear. Escaping the academy, the missiles, and the planet tonight, I thought I'd run through the purest forms of that emotion. But the fear I feel now dwarfs anything I've felt before. That was fear of pain, of capture, of death. This is fear on a new scale.

This is fear of annihilation.

Two of them are visible. The other eight appear only on our

readouts, somewhere off on the light side of Rana. They ring the planet, their noses pointed away from her pull, their engines firing in steady pulses with enough force to put a cigarette burn on a moon.

Dreadnoughts.

"Heavens and hells," I whisper. The planet's under blockade.

Gal leans forward over the controls, pinging satellites for information about the ships surrounding us. There's so much *hope* on his face. A twinge of nausea rattles through me at the thought that someone could see one of these monstrous war machines and feel anything but a deep, rooted terror. There's enough firepower ringing the planet to wipe out all life on its surface, and Gal thinks his parents must have sent it as a reckoning.

But not for long. His face falls as he finds what he was looking for. "Not Umber imperial," he says. That's obvious enough. If there were imperial dreadnoughts in orbit, the academy would already be blasted off the map for allowing an automated defense system to fire on us. "Looks like these all belong to . . . No, that can't be right."

"What?"

"The computer says they're under the command of Governor Berr sys-Tosa. Not by proxy. By *presence*."

Impossible. The system governor's vector from Imre would take him two full days to complete under the mandated travel speeds that keep intrasystem traffic safe. He could be court-martialed for burning that hard within Tosa System's radius, especially if he went superluminal. But apparently that doesn't matter. Because unless the computers are lying, Governor Berr is aboard one of these dreadnoughts. He's come for the Umber heir, and he's brought his entire arsenal to keep Gal from slipping through his grip. And with the governor aboard, the chain of command is unquestionable, with no room for Gal emp-Umber's golden voice to wrest control away.

There's no way we're clearing the system, let alone the planet's orbit. No wonder no pursuit has locked onto our tail in the time since we fled the academy. They already knew we'd never make it past these ships.

"They're hailing us," Gal murmurs. His finger hovers over the button to accept the call. He looks to me as if I have any say in the matter, and it grounds me in my convictions—his decency makes him a different creature entirely from his parents. He *has* to take the throne.

I give Gal a slow nod. Better to let the negotiator have a crack at saving our skins. There's nothing I can do with the planet caged by ten dreadnoughts, especially not flying a Beamer.

Gal presses down, and Berr sys-Tosa's face fills the screen. The system governor is aging, his pale skin lined and veined. But beneath his papery complexion, there's vigor. Hunger. His eyes aren't focused on the camera, but rather something off to the side. Most likely our ship's return signal. Most likely the face of the Umber heir, revealed to him after two years of hiding underneath his nose.

"Gal emp-Umber," he says. It's the first time I've heard Gal's true title aloud, with his territory attached to his name instead of a family. I hate that it came from this man's mouth. A whole host of opportunistic vultures swept in to claim positions of power when Archon fell, but none did it faster than Berr sys-Tosa. Tosa was formerly the younger brother of an Umber system governor, his blood-right not strong enough to overthrow his sister for the post. Instead he fell to commanding her war fleet, leading it in the campaign against Archon at the empress's behest—but all the while he was scheming for something greater. Before the surrender, he'd already assembled an entire government underneath himself that he installed in the former Archon core the second the imperials handed it over. His forward thinking earned him the favor of the empress and served as a template that allowed Umber to rapidly take root in its newly acquired territories. He's ruthless, relentless, shameless, and now the sound of Gal's name on his tongue echoes in my head. I try not to let my disgust show.

Gal doesn't. He flinches like he's been struck, and his own greeting gets caught in his throat. "Berr . . . Governor Berr sys-Tosa. Well met," he manages.

The governor laughs. "I've never known an imperial with a sense of humor."

"And I've never known a system governor to survive what you're attempting," Gal shoots back, sitting straighter in his chair.

Berr sys-Tosa's lips go thin. "You float, my prince. You have no leverage. No tether. No ships at your command, no power at your disposal, no troops to follow your orders."

Not true. Gal has a single soldier on his side, and gods of all systems, I hope I'm enough.

"The only cards you hold are your blood and your name," Tosa continues. "And those are not enough to stop a dreadnought."

"You would risk the wrath of Iva emp-Umber? Of Yltrast emp-Umber? Of the full force of the Imperial Fleet, of the hundreds of dreadnoughts at their command?"

The way they're talking is making my head hurt. Imperial-speak. *Umber* imperial–speak. You wouldn't hear this kind of talk from any Archon leader, but the Umber Empire is rank with the notion that the value of a ruler boils down to how much power they can wield. It often ends with the little people diving out of the way as larger powers try to prove their point. It's the kind of posturing that gets worlds destroyed. I try not to look sick, and give thanks for the way my darker complexion masks the blood draining from my face.

The governor gives us a grim smile. "Your parents don't know you've been revealed yet, Majesty. The academy hasn't released the information, and I've given the head instructions to keep your little secret under wraps until you turn yourself over."

Gal shifts uncomfortably in his chair. "You expect me to come willingly? Why trust you not to pull—"

The governor cuts him off with a bold laugh. "Child, there is no *trust.* Not in this empire. There is only blood-proven power. Bow to mine, and you may stand a chance of inheriting yours. When you come of age, of course—which you could do in the comfort of my court. I can even offer my heirs at your disposal, should you wish to factor my blood's power into your ascension."

A flicker of disgust shows on Gal's face. "Are you . . . threatening me into taking refuge with you? Even if the empress doesn't find out,

how do you imagine that plays out for you when I begin my succession?"

"A lot can change in six months."

Gal scoffs. He's trying to project the cool confidence, the negotiator exterior. It isn't working, and I hope I'm the only one who can
tell how much this situation unnerves him. "Governor, you've yet to
make a concrete proposal of how you intend to use all this *power* of
yours. What'll it be? Boltfire if we dare to move? Will you be sending
an emissary to fetch us, or are we meant to come to you? Which ship
are we bound for?"

I slide my hands forward, the controls slipping under my fingertips. Better to have the engines ready to go.

Gal's response has thrown the governor. Seems he hasn't decided
what he wants to do with us. He glances back over his shoulder, no
doubt to the officers he commands. "I'm a man with a generous
heart, Gal emp-Umber. I'll give you a chance to handle this with
dignity and nobility. Prove I don't have to fetch you like the child you
are. I await you aboard the *Fulcrum*. Your . . . *ship* . . . should be able
to identify it."

Gal gives me a nod. "Adjust our vector." He points on the console.

Not to the dreadnought our readouts identify as the *Fulcrum*,
but to an empty space slightly above it.

His other hand taps quietly on his side of the controls. I map my
gaze to the equivalent on my instrumentation. My stomach drops. I
shake my head.

"Do it, Nassun," Gal demands through his teeth. "We're out-
matched against the governor. This is our only course."

Berr sys-Tosa beams. "I'm glad you see reason. You'll make a fine
leader someday."

I spur the thrusters, setting the Beamer on a vector bound directly for the *Fulcrum*. I can feel the weight of Gal's anxious stare on
my neck as I lean forward over the controls and urge the Beamer up
to speed.

"I look forward to meeting you in person, Gal emp-Umber," Berr sys-Tosa says, giving us a sickening smile.

I nudge the Beamer's vector—barely enough to be noticeable, but enough to start a gentle list toward the empty space Gal pointed to.

Gal meets the governor's eyes, flashing a taut smile. "Likewise." He closes the line, and the two of us let out a long, needed sigh.

Acceleration sinks us back in our seats as we close on the *Fulcrum*. From far away, the cityship was barely more than a point of light. The closer we get, the more we comprehend its scale. Dreadnoughts are assembled in the metal-rich asteroid belts of solar systems, free from the gravity of a planet. Free to be built like steel-wrapped gods. From tip to tail, the *Fulcrum* is twenty miles long, every inch of it carved for domination.

No purer emblem for the Umber war machine exists. The Umber interior is littered with mined-out belts, depleted both by the power-hungry system governors battling for influence within the empire and by the imperials struggling to keep them in line over the past thousand years. When Umber's need for more dreadnoughts eclipsed the resources in their territory, they set their sights on their Archon neighbors, who had never fathomed a need for ships this big and brutal. The empress told her soldiers that the Archon imperials had mismanaged their sparse resources and were allowing their citizens to starve. Propaganda packaged the war as a humanitarian effort to save these territories from their leadership. But anyone with half a brain knows in the end, it was all about that metal.

I have no doubt that every single one of the ships in this blockade is less than seven years old.

I don't like what we're about to do. I don't like that I'm about to do it in a Beamer. I don't like any of this. But when it comes down to it, this is our best option—as long as they don't catch on in time.

Another hail pops up as we approach. Gal answers again. "*Fulcrum*, this is the Umber heir."

"Apologies, Your Majesty." It's not the system governor this time—instead, a nervous-looking communications officer appears onscreen. "Our telemetry shows you drifting nearly a mile off-course. Adjust accordingly."

Gal flashes that irresistibly charming apologetic smile he keeps tucked away in his arsenal. "Sorry, it's the Beamer being an asshole. Never can get these things to handle properly, am I right?"

We're seconds away from getting busted, and he knows it. He slides his hand onto the empty spot on his side of the dash. Taps once, twice, three times, each more insistent than the last. *Do it,* he's saying. *Do it now, before we lose this window. Do it, or I'll jump across the cockpit and do it for you.*

I've committed crimes in dozens of degrees tonight. Unleashed a mob of naked, drunken cadets on the officer quarters. Broken a window. Kidnapped a prince. Stolen a military ship. Compared to all of that, speeding should rank as a minor sin.

I check our vector, whisper a prayer, and jam down the superluminal booster.

My body tenses, anticipating a sudden snap of acceleration that doesn't come. It's an instinct I can't fight—something in my brain knows how fast we're about to go and braces for it. But going superluminal defies the natural order of physics. There's no lurch forward, no vicious, uncompromising acceleration. There's only a sudden stillness as the thrusters go quiet, the drives fire up with a whine, and the black goes gray outside our cockpit windows.

"How long until they lock on?" Gal asks, staring intently at the instrumentation.

"We've got a thirty-second head start. Enough time to get on course." Now that they've been given due cause, the dreadnoughts are immune to intrasystem speed limits—they'll be on our tail as soon as the system governor gets his wits about him. Already I'm tugging at the controls to get us on our escape vector. The Beamer can move like a devil on a linear path, wondrously enough, but it's another kind of nightmare to get it oriented.

"Ettian."

"What?"

"We should be headed for the interior. Why are we—"

"We'd never make it all the way to the Imperial Seat with ten dreadnoughts on our tail. We can't outrun them—we have to scrape them off somehow. So we go where they can't follow."

Gal pales. I almost apologize. He had no idea he was signing up for this when he got on this ship. Neither did I. But there's only one course we can set that has a chance of peeling these cityships off our ass. We have to cross a border they'd never dare follow us over. We have to leave the Umber Empire entirely.

So I've set us on a course for Corinth.

CHAPTER 7

OUR THIRTY-SECOND HEAD start translates into an entire day of superluminal with the dreadnoughts safely at our rear. It's enough to take us from the heart of the former Archon Empire to its border-worlds, and by the time we reach the fringes of the neutral zone that separates our empire from Corinth, the dreadnoughts have fallen off our tail. They know our gambit, and they're forced to let us pull it.

To catch us, they'll have to decelerate—and the instant they do, they'll be detectable by Corinthian instrumentation. To do so in Corinthian space would be interpreted as an act of war on behalf of the Umber Empire. For a rogue system governor trying to steal the Umber Crown's heir without the empress and emperor noticing, sparking a border skirmish would be downright disastrous. Berr sys-Tosa has no choice but to let us go.

But that doesn't mean Gal has to be happy about it.

It's been nearly a full day of silence. He left the cockpit and shut himself in the Beamer's crew bunk, emerging only to grab a ration pack, heat it in the kitchenette, and then retreat once more. I stay at the controls, even though they barely need my attention now that our vector is fixed and we're wrapped in the cocoon of grayed-out superluminal. All I have to do is sit back and let the Beamer do what it does best: fly in a straight line.

In the meantime, I try to sleep. Free from the cycle dictated by Rana's rotation, the Beamer has switched its timekeeping over to the galactic standard, slipping an extra hour into the way its lights shift from day to night. Nothing about our situation lets me stay unconscious for more than an hour at a time, but I'm able to doze enough while slumped in the pilot's chair that by the time Gal reenters the cockpit and flops down in the copilot's seat, I feel nearly rested.

My head still throbs from where it hit the hangar floor, my mouth is sour, and I don't even want to think about the way I smell. The environmental lights that stripe the cockpit are phasing out of dusk, melting from a pearly gray into darkness.

"We need to talk," Gal says, rubbing his hands over his eyes.

"Understatement," I mutter. Then I straighten and extend my hand to him. "Hi, my name's Ettian Nassun. Nice to meet you."

Gal plays along, taking it and giving it a firm shake. "Gal emp-Umber, future ruler of the galaxy at your service," he replies with a grimace.

"It's a pleasure, Your Highness. Or is it 'Your Majesty'? I can never keep the two straight."

"Rut off," he says and chuckles.

"What's your favorite color?"

"Still green, even though I don't look good in it. And my favorite food's still that meringue we found in the night market on Soata."

"And I still say desserts are bullshit favorite foods," I reply, but I can feel the tension loosening in my chest all the same. He may be the blood of Yltrast and Iva, the blood meant to rule the Umber Empire, but he's still the Gal I know, the Gal I'd follow to the edge of the universe. Which is good, because I just burned down my life for this idiot.

I just . . .

A day's worth of processing catches up to me like a ship at superluminal. "Gal, what the *hell*?" I blurt, and his head whips up.

"Are you . . . mad at me?" he asks.

"Yeah, I am!" I reply, sounding just as startled about it as he is. "All this time—"

"I couldn't have told you—"

"All this time—"

"No one was supposed to know until after we graduated—"

"This. Entire. Time."

"What should I have done? Violated seventeen years of tightly held protocol that protected the future of the *empire* just so you didn't feel left out?"

I seethe through my teeth. "I'm not mad at you for not telling me who you are. I'm . . ." It takes a moment for the words to come. "I'm mad you let me get so close. I mean, I can't blame myself for getting close to you—I didn't know. But you knew. You knew exactly who you are and *what* you are, you knew where I came from, and you knew what the truth about you might do to me, and you let all this happen anyway."

Gal scowls. "What was I supposed to do? Be a shitty roommate? A shitty friend? Hold everyone at arm's length during the only time of my life when I don't have to act like an imperial?"

"If you had any consideration for the rest of us, then *yes*." My voice is rising steadily. I let it. We're alone in the Beamer, nothing but vacuum around us—who cares how loud I get? Maybe if I yell loud enough, it'll make it through Gal's thick, imperial skull. "It's like . . . you don't exist on the same plane as the rest of us. You were never meant to. And you let us think . . ."

"Ettian," he whispers.

"I destroyed my whole life here for you, Gal. Everything I've built since the war, since your parents . . ." Horror swells in me as my eyes start to go damp. "Even knowing what you are, I knew I had to get you out of there at any cost. That's what you've done to me. You knowingly let me get to the point where I would be willing to give up everything I worked for to save your ass. So yeah, I'm pissed, and I don't think you can fault me for it."

"I didn't make you do anything," Gal replies with a surprising amount of venom in his voice. He still won't look at me. "You chose.

You knew you were choosing. You keep choosing over and over. Don't you dare blame me—"

"Don't *you* dare act like you're free of guilt."

"Ettian!" he shouts, throwing his hands up. "What else was I supposed to do? Who else could I go to?"

"Anyone else. There was a whole academy full of cadets back there—*Umber-born* cadets. You were friendly with Ollins. With Rhodes. With a whole bunch of other people who easily could have done what I did."

"'Can' and 'will' are very different words," Gal says, his voice softening. "Ollins is good for a laugh or a wager, but Ollins didn't strap his Viper to mine when twenty Archon sympathizers turned on me out of nowhere."

I squeeze my eyes shut as the sour taste in my mouth gets keener. "Those drums . . ."

Gal lets out a soft sigh, barely audible over the hum of the Beamer's instrumentation. "I don't understand how any of this could happen. The academy head told me there was an entire resistance ring grown under their noses. All twenty of those kids who turned on me yesterday were from former Archon territories, and they were coordinated by an officer who'd pinpointed my identity through an affair with one of my sleepers. They . . . The head brought me to that officer, and they got her to confess everything. They made her do it in front of me . . . And then—" Gal's voice chokes off, but I know the look in his eyes.

"They fried her," I say, so he doesn't have to. They electrocuted the traitor, and Gal had to watch.

Now isn't the best time to bring up the historical precedent. I know he's shaken. I know the wound is fresh. But I also know that Gal has seen executions before. Ones with far more spectacle and far more celebration involved. He would have been ten years old, same as me, on the day the Archon imperials fell.

They broadcasted it across the Umber Empire, across the freshly acquired Archon territories—hells, I'm sure even Corinth got the video. Everyone saw the triumph parade. Saw the brass-and-obsidian chariot moving through the Imperial Seat. Iva and Yltrast stood on top, cloaked in shining robes and crowned in their empire's metal and stone.

And dragged along behind it—

The cameras weren't close enough to capture the fear in their eyes. Marc and Henrietta, emperor and empress, former wearers of the Archon crown, stripped of their names and the worlds encompassed by them. The power of their blood yielded to Umber's might. Instead of platinum, they were wrapped in brass chains. Instead of emerald, their necks were bound in an obsidian yoke. Trussed up in the metal and stone of their enemy. Their feet bare, bloodied from being dragged so far.

The imperials marched them up the steps of the citadel. Iva held the chains. Yltrast bore the ax. The cameras followed, greedy.

It was barbaric, but it was necessary. To let the fallen empire see the forfeit of its ruling blood. To see that blood spilled down the steps of the Umber capital.

They kept the skulls, after.

"Ettian?"

I unclench my fists, slumping back in the pilot's seat and burying my face in my hands. "Sorry," I croak, trying not to shake as the horror of the memory dissipates.

"No apologies," he says. But he sounds worried. Maybe he's remembering that Rana was my homeworld. That I lived at the heart of the Archon Empire before his parents tore it out. That there are years in my history that are still too painful to touch, all because of his bloodline's conquest. "Are you okay? How are you holding up?" His voice is soft—too soft for the thoughts running wild in my head.

I shrug halfheartedly. *It's dead. It's gone. I can't carry it with me.* "Still flying," I tell him, trying to convince myself it's true.

But the notion of an Archon insurgency continues to rattle me. The idea that there are people out there devoted to raising the empire from the ashes used to seem so impossible. And some of them were organized enough to make a serious attempt on the Umber heir's life. Nothing's come close to a victory for the Archon Empire since General Maxo Iral waged his fringe wars in the wake of the Umber conquest. Though he fell in the end, while he fought, there was hope that our defeat wasn't final. That hope's been buried for so long.

I haven't had time to process it. The drums are thundering in my ears, in my heart, in the hollows of my chest.

"I know this is . . . complicated for you," Gal says cautiously. "I know you suffered under my parents' campaign." I throw a sharp glance his way, and he holds up his hands, just like every other time he's pried too closely at the gaping, Warning Shot–sized hole in my past. "You didn't sign up for any of this, you're not one of my sleepers—"

"Jana," I say, no time between the formation of the thought and her name leaving my lips.

Gal flinches.

"I went to her room after I got your message. I saw . . . She put up a fight. I should have tried to find out what they did with her and the other sleepers. They could have helped—"

He gives his head the slightest shake, closing his eyes. "When she came by that morning before the drill, it was to warn me. The sleepers didn't think it'd be safe to fly, but I thought it'd be too suspicious if I backed out at the last second. I should have listened to her—if I'd just listened to her, none of this would have happened. And now . . ." Gal scrubs the heel of his hand over one eye, inhaling sharply. "Their job was to protect me. It would have gone against every oath they swore to risk my safety for their sakes."

I cling tight to the way those words tear out of his throat—reluctantly, like it's ripping him in half to admit the necessity of leaving Jana behind. This is the Gal I've always known. The Gal who could never make his parents' choices. The Gal who could change the galaxy for the better if he takes his mother's throne.

For a little while, we stare out into the gray. Superluminal travel is disturbingly peaceful. It doesn't feel like we're snapping across systems faster than the speed of light. The ship is quiet but for the whine of the electronics and the distant hum of the drives. It's like being on a raft, the lights turned out, the lake still, nothing but fog on all sides.

I'm starting to appreciate the Beamer more. Maybe it's because it's holding me hostage and I have no other options, but any ship that can put good distance between myself and a dreadnought deserves a little respect. I glance over at Gal, curled up in the copilot's seat. He's dressed in an oversized jacket, his feet bare, and everything about it makes him look far too young to be dealing with any of this.

"When did you leave Lucia?" I ask.

Gal sighs. "Originally they had planned to start shadowing me at ten, but then General Iral wouldn't go down. It wasn't safe for me to be out among the people, even in secret, while he was out there. When we fried him two years later, I was finally allowed to attend a pre-military school on Naberrie. Then they graduated me to the academy when I was fifteen."

It matches the story he told in those early days at the academy—though of course, he'd told me he grew up on Naberrie, another fertile Umber core world, instead of Lucia, the Imperial Seat itself, and that his parents were an old military family. He's even visited Naberrie on personal leave a few times. "And before that?"

"Before that, I barely saw the light of day. I grew up deep inside the citadel. Everything I needed was brought to me. Everyone who interacted with me was vetted and, I assume, threatened. Nurses, tutors, even the chefs who knew there was an extra mouth within the citadel walls to feed. I made some friends on Naberrie, but keeping me in one place for too long was dangerous. And supposedly keeping me in the interior would have made me too complacent, so when I graduated the pre-mil school, they packed me off to Rana and had me start all over."

He wears it all so heavily. I used to think Gal always looked more tired than he should. Now I understand the weight he's been carrying all his life. He's been denied friends, denied normalcy, denied stability and safety. The practice of shadowing heirs—a common one, a *necessary* one across all levels of galactic government—

demands that sacrifice for the sake of his future rule. His own family can't publicly acknowledge him until he turns eighteen, when he can legally begin the succession process. Until then, he's a pressure point for greedy system governors to exploit.

"It's gonna be worth it though, right?" I ask. From the way Gal stiffens, I don't think I've managed to strike the casual tone I was aiming for.

"It's gotta be," he says softly, staring at his knees again. "It's the whole reason I'm alive. But more than that, it's a chance no one else in the galaxy has. I spent my entire academy career trying to figure out how I could do it my way—how I could *get away* with doing it my way. No more wars, no more expansion, no more conquest. Just negotiation and levelheadedness."

"You? Levelheaded?"

"Rut off," he says with a smirk. "Being part of the Umber royal line means I'm part of something greater than myself. Don't be so surprised I've thought about my life's focal point once or twice." Gal lets out a long, heavy sigh. "Look, when I turn eighteen, they'll walk me out in front of the public and put a crown on my head. Succession spans a seven-year period before my parents step down and I assume my full bloodright, but even when I'm sharing the throne, I think I could still manage some good. And once the crown's mine alone . . . If I could make that work then yeah, it'll be worth it."

If there were any anger left in me from my outburst, those words wash it away. I have a million other questions that should fill the next spaces in this conversation, but I feel like I'm wringing him out, like every new answer is draining him more than the one before. Gal needs rest. He's got a big future ahead, one I'm going to fight like hell to make sure he sees.

So the next thing I blurt is, "I'm thinking of naming the Beamer."

Gal laughs. "You can't."

"C'mon, it's served us well. It deserves something in return."

He shakes his head. "It's clearly a stolen military ship. We're going to have to dump it the second we make berth in Corinth."

"So?"

"You name it, you're going to start getting attached to it. I thought you hated it. Seem to recall some feet-dragging at a critical moment."

I roll my eyes, patting the dash affectionately. "Don't listen to him, baby. He's jealous."

"Ruttin' hell," Gal groans, an exasperated twinkle in his eye.

"Fine."

"Fine?"

"*Ruttin' Hell*. That's what we're calling her. After your decidedly unprincely tongue."

"Fine, but you're the one who's feeding her and taking her for walks." Gal chuckles. His laughter deflates as he stares out into the eerie superluminal gray, but a soft smile is quick to replace it. "You know, I'm actually looking forward to this. Is that weird to say?"

I shake my head. I know exactly what he's trying to get at. For the first time in his life, he's completely abandoning his responsibility, and the freedom from that weight is like being able to breathe for the first time. We're on a mad dash to a system completely outside the sphere of his power, an entirely different empire, and even though the risk of being discovered remains, the end of this journey feels full of possibility. It's just the two of us. No titles. No blood-rights. Nothing but what we carry.

In the span of a day, Gal's lost the anonymity that kept him safe. He *liked* being Gal Veres. He wanted the six months between now and his eighteenth birthday, the time the revelation stole from him. Maybe he can get a little of that time back in Corinth.

And maybe there's a part of me that wants those months too. My gaze slides guiltily over Gal, over the whole of him, over everything I'm just getting to know and everything I might never have.

Gal catches me looking. "Ettian?" he says.

"Yeah?"

"You smell like ass. Go shower."

The *Ruttin' Hell* is surprisingly well stocked. I always assumed the academy kept these things around to give new cadets something harmless to cut their teeth on, but this ship's outfitted like it's meant for officer transport. It even has towels.

The shower's not luxurious, but it does the trick. I scrub for ages, trying to get rid of every particle of dried sweat that clings to my skin. When I emerge at last, feeling raw, my fingers have shriveled like prunes. I grimace at my reflection in the plate-sized mirror bolted to the wall. My eyes are bloodshot, my chin grown-in with wiry stubble. I run one hand over my close-cropped hair, then root around in the cabinets until I find a shaving kit.

Bit by bit, I carve away the last remains of yesterday's stress, yesterday's fear, yesterday's sheer, manic focus on staying alive. Bit by bit, I pull myself back together until my reflection could be the same one I saw every morning in the dorm bathroom mirrors.

I try to smile, but it doesn't quite reach my eyes. I look haunted— which I suppose is fair enough. The past three days have been dragging back from the grave the part of me I tried my best to kill. I can't deny that I still thrill over mentions of suited knights and valiant deeds in the name of the Archon Empire. The promise of heroics turned Seely from a war orphan to a would-be murderer to ashes. And now here I am, clocking in heroic act after heroic act—all for the sake of the Umber Crown and everything it represents.

I'm starting to tear down the middle, and I'm scared shitless of what it could do to me.

When I finally step into the crew cabin, Gal's sitting in my bunk. Well, to be fair, we never explicitly said whose bunk was whose, but he's taken the top bunk in every dorm room we've ever slept in. He has the decency to look guilty when he sees me at the door. His hands fall away from the datapad in his lap.

"What are you writing?" I ask, moving for the drawers built into the wall. Gal's already taken the liberty of unpacking both our bags, emptying our clothes into the drawers and folding them neatly. He does this every damn time we go somewhere new—says it helps settle his nerves.

"Right now?" Gal sighs. "A list of people who've tried to kill me and why."

"Am I on it?"

Gal bares his teeth. "I suppose I should count the drop from the window."

"And the flying—don't forget the flying." I towel away the last of the shower's dampness and pull on fresh clothes.

When I turn around, Gal's got his lips pursed. "The system governor's the biggest threat at the moment."

"Not the potential Archon uprising?"

He waves a hand. "They have no power—only people. And probably not many, at that." Those words sting and relieve in equal measure, but I try not to let the former show. "Berr sys-Tosa has dreadnoughts at his command. To make it to the interior, we'll have to go through Tosa System again, and if he triangulates our vector, there's no way we clear it without getting scooped up."

His fingertips twitch over the datapad's screen, pulling up a galactic map. The star systems glitter as he scales them, and even from a distance, I recognize the layout of the Umber interior. The origin of the map, where the three major axes defining its space intersect, points squarely at Acua, the shining star at the heart of the empire's capital system. Lucia orbits it, marked by a brassy sigil that signifies the home of the Imperial Seat.

Gal drops a marker on his homeworld and pulls back, collapsing the system until he's considering the vast dark between the stars. He zooms out farther to find the shining mark of Tosa nestled at the center of the other former Archon systems down the galactic arm. Then farther still, until he finds us, hauling ass in the opposite direction, toward the distant reaches of Corinth. His expression goes taut.

I clear my throat. "So we ditch the Beamer in Corinth . . ."

Gal nods. "We need a different ship. Maybe we can cut some sort of deal for this one—but the sale of a stolen military vehicle is going to raise some red flags, so we have to be prepared to book it right away. Tosa's going to be watching for it. We need . . . I dunno, a *plan*. Something more concrete than switching ships and going back the way we came." He looks up, noticing the way I've frozen against the drawers. Wordlessly, he pats the blanket next to him.

"You've got two days to worry yourself into something more concrete," I mutter, collapsing on the bed. At least he's thinking about plans now and not leaving them up to me. I thought I'd gotten enough rest dozing in the pilot's seat, but the mattress beneath me is telling me I was so, so wrong. I close my eyes, my brain already racing toward unconsciousness. Distantly, I feel Gal roll back and hear the clatter of him tossing the datapad aside.

"Ettian?" he asks, before I can go completely.

"Mhm?"

"I should have said it already, but . . . thank you."

Those two words and the reverent way he whispers them are the last things I grasp before the emptiness of sleep takes over.

CHAPTER 8

THE NEXT TWO days pass far too slowly.

On every other interstellar voyage I've made, I was part of a larger crew—usually a pack of cadets on a training mission or a retreat or a brief period of leave. No matter the destination, the journey was never dull.

But aboard the *Ruttin' Hell,* our options are limited. There's always sleeping—I'm grateful for that. At the academy, we rose with the sun and our assignments kept us up late into the night. Over the two days of travel, I'm catching up on two and a half years of sleep, making full use of the galactic standard's extra hour. When we're not sleeping, we spend most of our time planning our approach to Delos, a borderworld on the Corinthian fringe, and plotting how we'll make berth in a foreign empire without incurring suspicion.

When we're not doing that, we're bored. I try my best to avoid thinking of some ways we could relieve our boredom, ways that take advantage of the fact that for now we're two nobodies, the only life forms for a million miles, wrapped in the silence of the void. No leering fellow cadets, no warnings about fraternization, no fear of destroying our friendship and continuing to share a room in the aftermath.

Keep it together, I think over and over. I try my damnedest to distract myself, but entertainment on the ship is limited to the saccharine pop library Gal's downloaded onto his datapad and a few stuffy war novels I checked out on mine—all recommended to me by officers and all barely more than jingoistic Umber propaganda written by ex-soldiers. It's not enough to keep my mind away from where it can't help straying. There are far greater things at stake than my own heart, and letting it into the mess of what's happening is asking for trouble.

But Gal keeps sleeping in my bed.

Neither of us acknowledge the second bunk above our heads. We barely acknowledge each other, apart from quick apologies if, gods forbid, one of us bumps into the other. We sleep back-to-back, still and tense, and act like nothing's happening.

Confront him, half of me insists. *Because when all of this is over, he's either dead or a prince, and he'll have nothing to do with you then.* But it's hard to let go of a fear you've nurtured for so long.

And I don't even know how long I've been afraid of this. There was no moment of sudden clarity. No clouds parting, no sunbeam shining down at the right moment. No single gaze that pierced me through the chest. It was more like a pot set on a low heat, coming to boil. A gradual acknowledgment that yes, this could be an option.

Except, well, soon it won't be. Soon Gal will be buried in the Umber citadel, back in the sunless isolation where he spent the first twelve years of his life. Six months from now, if all goes well, he'll be revealed to the public as the Umber heir. His hand will likely be pawned off in a political marriage to a system governor's child—sooner rather than later, before the infighting among the system governors with eligible heirs comes to bloodshed. And I'll be . . . No, I can't even think that far into the future. Can't focus on anything but getting Gal to safety.

I remember being this kind of creature back in the days after the Archon Empire fell. Reduced to survival instinct and nothing more, living one day to the next with my only goal to keep on living. It wasn't until the academy that I started reaching for something greater.

Now I might be overreaching.

We approach Delos from the morning side, slipping into the atmosphere over the soft seam that separates night and day. The sun blazes at our backs, the light chasing us across the continents. I set a course for a stretch of wilderness several hours away from the planetary capital city of Isla. The *Ruttin' Hell* rattles like a washing machine as reentry fires flare around us, and this time we both strap in good and tight.

A combination of prayer and talent gets us decelerated without losing a wing, and I bring us in low over the trees. From a distance, we've been listening to the planet's chatter. We've watched how ships approach Delos without a fuss and land without any threat of getting shot down. The military presence here is minor, a hallmark of a long-settled empire. Still, I fly low. Better to be cautious.

The Beamer needs no runway, just a few insistent bursts from the rotary thrusters to slow it. I drop us in a clearing carpeted by sand and bracken, in sight of a river that winds all the way to the capital. The *Ruttin' Hell* hits the ground with a heavy thud. Gal gives me a pointed look, and I'm quick to point out it's far more graceful than the last landing I made.

My first instinct was to head straight to Isla, but fortunately I'm not the only one making the plans anymore. As Gal rightly noted, there are Umber markings on our hull, stripes of deep black and tainted gold that call attention to our ship's point of origin.

Luckily for us, there are also toolboxes in the cargo hold.

The second I'm sure the ship has settled with no risk of tipping over, I slam down the button that releases the rear ramp, my other hand spinning up the ship's fans. Warm air rushes over me, carrying with it the crisp scent of distant pines. It's summer in this hemisphere of Delos, and after months of bitter, dry winter on Rana, everything about it is glorious.

Gal's already unstrapped himself, stumbling on unsteady legs as he tears through the ship. I stagger after him, unbalanced by the readjustment to planetary gravity. He jumps the ladder into the cargo hold, tucking into a roll that carries him down the ramp and into the sand. With a wicked grin, he tips his head back and howls his triumph, throwing two fists in the air like he's conquered this planet.

I roll my eyes, sliding down the ladder after him. Rather than rush for Delos's dirt, I cross to the equipment lockers and pull a pair of scrapers from the toolbox. When I descend the ramp, I do it slowly, savoring each step until my boots sink into the sand of an empire I've never known.

We couldn't have picked a prettier spot. The distant ribbon of the river slices across the horizon, catching the light of the rising sun so vividly that it seems like it's glowing. Mist curls through the forest that hems the clearing, and everything is *green*. Not the dusky, patched green of a prairie spring at the academy. This part of Delos is downright verdant.

It's the perfect place to catch your breath, and that's exactly what I do as I sink into the sand next to Gal. In through the nose. Out through the mouth. As if I could drink in the entire world this way.

"You're infatuated," Gal says, and I stiffen before I realize he means *with the planet*.

I toss him one of the scrapers. "Time to put some calluses on those princely fingers."

The paint that marks the *Ruttin' Hell* as Umber property is tougher than it looks. Worse, it's hard to get at, even with the ladders we find tucked in the cargo hold's equipment lockers. Both of us can't work at the same time—someone has to hold the ladder steady while someone else works until his arms get too sore to carry on.

I take a certain amount of pleasure in peeling off the black and brass bit by bit. Flakes of paint fall away, leaving nothing but pure hullmetal untempered by the heat of reentry. There's no hiding that we've removed markings from the ship. We'd need an acid wash to restore it to its factory state. But there's something deeply satisfying about taking something Umber has layered itself over and making it clean again.

When it's my turn to hold the ladder, I don't look up.

We break at midday when the sun gets unbearable, retreating into the Beamer's cargo hold, sealing ourselves inside, and cycling the coolant until our sweat-stained shirts feel like they're about to freeze to our skin. Over a ration-pack meal, we reevaluate. We'd thought it would only take the morning to get the *Ruttin' Hell* scrubbed, and we'd be in Isla before sundown. Clearly that isn't happening.

"We finish the job today, sleep, and hit Isla first thing tomorrow," Gal declares, taking a swig of water as I cut the air and reopen the cargo ramp. The delay's eating at him. His nervous energy has been building with no ceiling ever since we set foot on this planet. Every extra day we spend on foreign soil is a risk. We can't linger on Delos.

Even if I sort of wish we could.

I've never spent an extended amount of time in the wilderness. I'm used to cities, to the constancy and solidity of buildings and pavement and people all around. That or the quiet of the void, with only the hum of a ship to fill the air. A different kind of hum pervades this space. It's like the planet is an engine, its heart beating with the distant motion of the river and the dull roar of the winds that cuts above the tree line. Here, I can almost forget everything that matters, every force driving us, every piece of history nipping at our heels.

There's time to kill before the afternoon heat breaks, so we trek across the sandy clearing to the banks of the river. The water looks clean, cool, and inviting. Naturally my shirt's over my head and my boots are off before Gal can get a single note of worrying in. The water's only three feet deep, but I immerse myself anyway, dropping to my knees and then rolling onto my back as its chill sinks through me. When I glance back at the shore, Gal's still looking indecisive.

"Problem, *Your Majesty*?" I smirk.

"Ruttin' hell," he sighs, and my stare snaps guiltily away as he yanks his shirt off.

I close my eyes and let my head drop back, a muffled gurgle filling my ears. Distantly I hear the sloshing of Gal's footsteps as he wades into the river. Then a crash as he trips over a rock and goes down hard.

I sit upright in time to catch the sight of a disgruntled Umber prince sputtering and gasping as he flounders for his footing. "It's *cold*," he says, his voice so indignant that it's almost a shriek. "How the rut did you . . . flop in like that?"

I shrug. "You adjust fast."

"You have a death wish, Ettian Nassun."

"A little river's not going to kill you, Gal."

He glances around, shrugging. "The plants look healthy enough. Probably no weird chemicals in this water." Gal wanders over to my side and sinks gingerly into the water, as if it's finally deigned to meet his standards. "Okay, fine, this is nice," he concedes, stretching out his legs.

I give him about three seconds to enjoy it, then splash him.

"Ettian!" he chokes, shielding his face before another wave hits him. I scuttle back as he swings his arm around and lets a volley of water fly. I try to duck behind my elbow, but Gal grabs my arm and twists, cackling as he manages to get another handful of water in my face. My attempt to retaliate is blocked by him grabbing my other wrist, and I lose my balance to complete the indignity of it all, collapsing back into the shallows.

And of course, because he has an uncanny knack for putting me in the worst possible situation, Gal comes down on top of me. One of his elbows digs hard into my stomach, and his weight crushes my chest, driving the breath out of my lungs. I inhale water as my head goes under, then come up choking to find Gal bent over me. He's breathless, his mop of unruly hair dripping into his eyes, down his nose, onto my collarbone.

I try to clear my throat, but it comes out as a weak noise, halfway to a whimper. I don't know what to do with the way he looks at me. With the way he's got one arm braced in the water over my shoulder. With his other hand hovering over my chest.

There's a dangerous instinct that kicks in sometimes when you're flying. The adrenaline pushes you into doing the most reckless thing you can think of the second the option appears. Recognizing that instinct is hard.

Stopping it is harder.

My hand curves up over his waist, running along the line between his skin and his soaking pants as I push myself up. Push closer. His eyes go half-closed, his gaze dropping to my lips. Ten inches. Two.

His hand presses against my chest, stopping me short. I jolt backward as the haze around my brain clears in a horrible instant. "Gal—"

"I—"

"I'm so sorry."

He rockets to his feet and steps over me, rubbing his hands over his face. Without a backward glance, he wades out of the shallows and up onto the riverbank. I watch him tramp back toward the ship with his boots in one hand and shirt in the other, contemplating the option of slipping under the surface of the river, never to be heard from again.

My mind sputters with excuses—*I was playing, it wasn't serious, I didn't mean*—but all of them fizzle out. Gal knows me too well to believe any lie I spin. He knows exactly what that was, and now I know exactly how all of my questions get answered. Now we're stuck with knowing.

Any illusions I had about lingering in the wild drain from my head. Better to hit Isla as quickly as possible, before I have a chance to rut this up even more.

When I return to the *Ruttin' Hell,* Gal's already up on a precariously balanced ladder, scraping furiously at the paint. His datapad sticks out of his waistband, blasting a chipper pop tune that drowns out the grating noise of metal against metal. He's changed into dry clothes, but his hair is still damp, and if he notices my approach, he's choosing to ignore it.

I duck into the Beamer to change and reemerge to discover that he's cleared nearly two feet of paint. Deep down, I know it's better to let him wear himself out rather than say something, but I need to make sure he doesn't hurt himself in the process. So I take up my position at the base of the ladder, bracing against it as I stare down into the sand and ferns that surround our landing site. Scorched patches mark where the Beamer's rotary thrusters fired to stabilize our landing, wreathed by the curled and blackened stems of the plants I destroyed when I dropped the ship here.

I close my eyes.

I knew it would go like this. I don't know why I thought it would turn out any differently. I've watched Gal and romance from afar, and they're not a good pair. He'll flirt and flit, but he dances around anything serious, leaving a trail of frustrated people in his wake. In retrospect, his reasons are clear. He knows the responsibility on his shoulders. For his future empire's sake, he's learned to guard his heart.

I wish I could have done the same. I got caught up in the river, in the moment of escape, in the way this place made me forget everything we carry with us. There's no taking back what I tried. We're trapped in the aftermath.

But maybe it's better this way. There's absolutely no future for anything between us—not when he's going to be the ruler of the galaxy and I'll only ever be an orphan who crawled out of the ruins of Trost. We'd never stand as equals, and I can't believe I let myself think otherwise.

He was smart to reject me. Right to reject me. If he knew anything about what I've survived—and I've made damn sure he doesn't—he wouldn't want anything to do with me. There's nothing about me that deserves the love of an Umber prince, especially not the love of one who might actually do some *good* in this rutted-up universe.

Gal can't afford the distraction, and neither can I. I need to get my head on straight and start thinking like the loyal soldier he needs. Gal doesn't need a lover. He needs a pilot. The best thing I can do for him isn't kissing him—it's bringing him home.

I keep my post at the base of the ladder, waiting for Gal to offer a switch, but he only comes down, kicks it a few feet over, and then climbs right back up. The afternoon drags on into evening, the paint chips keep falling, and by the time the sun's disappeared into the tree line, he's cleared the last of his family's colors from the ship. As he descends the ladder for the last time, I retreat to the cargo bay ramp and lean against the edge of the hull there, stuffing my hands in my pockets and trying to ignore the rattle of Gal's footsteps.

The setting sun paints the sky above us a hazy, soft purple. Unfamiliar stars peek out between the sparse clouds, and the distant lights of air traffic trace vectors toward Isla in the north. I tip my head back, knocking my skull against the *Ruttin' Hell*. The dusk is lovely, and the freedom of the wilderness is intoxicating, but it's all an illusion. Our lives are no less in danger, and we can't afford to get swept away.

The thought barely has time to settle before Gal's fingers wrap around the back of my neck, pulling me down. I let out a startled yelp, nearly losing my footing in the sand as I catch his shoulders, stopping his lips inches from mine. A look of confusion flickers across his face, his hands slipping hesitantly down over my collarbones. I shy back from his touch, pressing against the sun-warmed hull behind me.

"But you . . ." he says. "But I . . ."

"We *can't*," I croak, even though a part of me is violently raging to throw all that thinking and resolving I did aside. "*You* . . . I thought . . . In the river . . ."

"Yeah, well, you were covered in river water then," Gal snaps, taking a few steps back and running a hand through his sweat-fluffed hair. "And I needed time to think it over—it was a lot to process, and it all happened so fast. What happened between then and now?"

I have absolutely no idea what to do with my hands, but they're starting to shake. "*I* thought it over. I realized it's stupid—it's so stupid—"

"It's not," he murmurs, lunging suddenly forward, but he pulls up short when he sees the way I tense. His wide brown eyes bore deep into mine, and there's something about the half-light that makes them a thousand times more intense. "Ettian, I have so little time left to make my own choices. I want to do everything I can to make the most of it."

I suppress a shiver, forcing myself to hold his gaze. My hands curl into fists at my sides. "And when your time is up, you want to leave me like this?"

"I won't leave you," he swears with a fierce shake of his head.

I wish I could believe that. I don't tell him how badly I wish for it—I'm afraid if the words leave my mouth, I'll somehow fool myself into thinking we *could* make this work. "You will," I mutter. "You have to. You should."

"I'm the Umber heir," Gal protests. "I can make a place for you. There's always going to be a place for you at my side."

"As what, your consort?"

"Don't be crass."

"Your chauffeur?"

"Ettian."

"Your pressure point?"

And that gets him. His eyes dart guiltily away as the blow registers, his lips twisting in a scowl. He knows the games imperials play. Gal's whole life has been spent in hiding to keep him from being used by power-hungry system governors. He's already dragged me into enough of his mess, but if it got out that the Umber heir had given his heart to some kid from the former Archon Empire, I'd be the target of every single knife the governors might want to bury in his back. Swinging for a prince might have serious consequences, but nobody gives a shit about Ettian Nassun.

Nobody except Gal, who's looking at me again in a way I can't stand. "It might be my last chance to have something real," he whispers, and I feel like my heart's being pulled out of my throat.

We have to kill this thing before it's too late.

I shake my head, dropping my gaze to the poor scorched plants withering in the sand. "It can't work," I mutter, hating every breath of the truth that slips between my teeth. "It's better like this."

There's a long pause, filled only by the soft chatter of the distant river and the hum of insects awakening in the twilight. Gal looks around helplessly, hugging his arms to his chest and hunching in a way that makes him look even smaller. "But you're still . . . with me, right?" he finally asks.

Part of me wants to fire the snappy retort trying to force itself from my lungs, but I bite down on it. "Yeah, of course. Always."

"Well, not *always*," Gal points out.

"Fine—until we reach the Seat. Until then, I've *always* got your back."

He flashes a weary smile, and I hate that it's enough. "I . . . scraped most of the paint off a ship, and my arms are about to fall off."

"You know, I *would* have taken a turn, but . . ."

He rolls his eyes, starting up the *Ruttin' Hell*'s ramp at an unsteady gait. "We have to get moving bright and early tomorrow. Dawn at the latest."

I nod but don't follow. As he disappears into the dark of the ship, I tip my head back, staring up at the unfamiliar stars of this system. Even though I feel a yawning, terrible ache in my chest, there's a thread of giddiness trying to sew it shut that brings a soft smile out of the corners of my lips. I wasn't making it up. There was something there. Something mutual. Something that has to end, but it was *real*.

When I finally make my way to bed, I find Gal's taken the top bunk.

CHAPTER 9

WE LEAVE BEFORE sunrise, and by the time the summer heat's begun to shimmer on our wings, the *Ruttin' Hell* is on its approach to Isla. The planetary capital sprawls out ahead of us, and a ping of misplaced jealousy rattles through me as I think of Trost. Isla has never been the site of any war of conquest, and this city grows tall in a way my home was never allowed to. Traffic hails and insistent drones shunt us into a regulated lane once we move over the suburbs, and my teeth grate as our speed slows and slows.

Gal's propped up on his elbows, peering at the skyline rolling beneath us. Ships in the lower lanes cut across our view, and briefly I wonder if it's strange or liberating for him, seeing people he won't rule one day. He doesn't have to think about anyone here as his future subject, and I can't ignore the bitter taste of that reminder.

"Eyes on the sky, Ettian," Gal warns, and only then do I realize I've been staring at him.

I turn my gaze to the buildings below, biting down on a scowl.

"I mean, you can enjoy the view, but your eyes are making promises you don't intend to keep."

My lips twitch. He's been like this all morning—constantly re-

minding me that for two mismatched seconds yesterday, the door was wide open. I thought watching Gal flirt with other people at the academy was bad enough, but I underestimated how much it sucks to be in his sights and know I can't do anything about it.

I mean, I *could*, but—

I focus harder on the city. Isla's built with precision, relying on subtleties of shape and carving to distinguish skyscrapers nearly identical in build. Its character is brutalist and square, everything arranged along a clean-cut grid. Most of the downtown buildings are capped with granite carvings and ironwork in homage to the Corinthian Empire's metal and stone. Corinth coalesced from the settlements made by the people who ventured the farthest along the galactic arm back in the generation-ship days, and their choice of crude metal and rough stone represents their pride in hacking it on the fringes. The sight of such deep, established patriotism is unsettling after seven years in a conquered territory.

Gal's knuckles go pale when I drop us into the next lane below, the Beamer doing its damnedest to let gravity take us even lower. The closer we get to the ground, the more stressed he gets. "It's a city of two million," I remind him. "No one's going to know who you are."

"Unless Berr sys-Tosa got desperate. He could have broadcasted my name and face to every Corinthian borderworld a signal could reach."

"If he did that, he's probably already been hauled to the interior and beheaded on the citadel steps. Trying to ransom you for power is one kind of stupidity—revealing you to a foreign empire is another kind entirely."

Gal nods.

"He could have sent bounty hunters though."

He groans.

"Again, city of two million. We keep a low profile, and there's nothing to worry about."

Gal sticks his lower lip out as our lane dives into the forest of skyscrapers. He folds his arms across his chest, leaning back in his chair and sticking a careless foot up on the dash. I studiously ignore how good he looks doing it. "Why do I get the feeling that's easier said than done?"

If you want to have a good time in a city, you visit its shiny bits. The places they polish up specifically to welcome outsiders. The places they show in pictures. But if you want to *know* a city, you visit its underbelly.

Isla's overcity is shining, stalwart, blocky, and organized.

And the undercity . . .

Well, the best word would be "skewed." The difference starts with the architecture itself. The clean-cut edges of the skyscrapers melt into slanted storefronts. The iron here is rusted, unprotected by the chemical treatment that keeps the upper parts of Isla looking freshly forged, and any granite is barefaced and unpolished.

The people dress to match. Gal and I look rough enough to blend in without suspicion in our drab civilian garb. I trail in his wake as he weaves through the pedestrians, staring down at his datapad and tapping furiously. He listed the Beamer the second we connected to the city's network, and received a solid offer before we'd even landed on a lot.

"Up ahead, to the right," Gal says with a jerk of his head, eyes still fixed on the screen. "Should be marked by a green sash," he adds, holding up the pad so I can see the photo. Leaning a little closer than necessary too.

The light's different today, draping the storefront in indistinct shadows, but it's the same place for sure. The green sash he mentioned winds around a pole out front, faded by age and torn by wind. Gal pockets his datapad, a hungry grin breaking over his face. "The offer's not much, but . . ."

"You can talk it up, I know." I step up and haul open the door, holding out a hand to block him from charging in as I scope out the place.

The shop's interior is dark, the surfaces dusted, the chairs stacked on tables. Suspicion prickles inside me, and I turn to check the door for a broken bolt.

When I turn back, a flint strikes in the shadows. "You must be the sellers," a voice says as a cigar glows to life. Her accent is strange—Corinthian, but not entirely—and she speaks with a slow, easy cadence. "Beamer, model N-67. Military outfit, manufactured in the Otosan Belt of the Archon territories."

"It's not mil—"

"You stupid little shits expect me to believe that?" The shadows take form, a woman stepping out of them with a wildcat's grace. She's short and built with lean muscle, somewhere in her thirties, her dark, uneven hair hanging in her face. The cigar dangles dangerously from her lips. "God of Cret, you're children. Where the rut did you get a Beamer?"

"That's not important." Gal steps around me, drawing himself up to his full height as if he's trying to lord the inch he has on her. "What's important is your offer's too low. We don't go under 9K."

She lets out another short laugh around a mouthful of smoke. "Seven K's my offer, and you won't get another."

"You underestimate our persistence."

"No, kiddo. You underestimate how much fear I can instill in the hearts of others. I buy your ship for 7K, or you never sell it. And judging by the eagerness that brought you to my door, I don't think you're in a position to turn me down."

"Nine K," Gal replies coolly. "If you want it so bad. Which I suspect you do, given the speed of your offer."

The woman doesn't reply. She reaches up and plucks the cigar from her lips, letting out another smoky breath as she twirls it between fingers made of metal. My gaze drops to the point where flesh meets cybernetics halfway down her forearm. Assistive tech like this is rare in the Umber Empire, where metal is prioritized for more brutal uses. This woman's business must be thriving for her to afford a piece like this. She catches me staring and bares her yellowed teeth. "You should have seen the other guy." Taking her cigar up in her other hand, she sticks out the metal one to shake. "Adela Esperza."

"Ettian," I say, stepping around Gal to take it first. "This is Gal." Gal's lips go taut, and too late I remember that we probably shouldn't be using the names Berr sys-Tosa will be looking for.

"Pleasure," Adela says with a grin, her grip going tight around mine. Her fingers are warm and full of sharp edges. "Now, if you really want to negotiate, how about you take me to the ship?"

Adela Esperza looks at the Beamer like she wants to eat it. Gal and I stand to the side of the vacant lot, leaning back against a chain-link fence as we watch her circle the *Ruttin' Hell,* running her hands over every part of the ship she can reach. More than once, she traces her mechanical fingers over the lines left by our hasty paint removal, smirking like she knows exactly what we've done and what it means.

"I don't like this," I murmur.

"Agreed," Gal says.

"We're in over our heads."

"Yep."

"I think she *likes* the ship."

"Eh."

I have to agree with that assessment. Though Adela's smiling through her inspection of the Beamer's hull, it isn't necessarily a good smile. It's a butcher's smile, and it promises things I'm finding remarkably difficult to stomach. My mind spins with visions of chop shops, sparks flying as circular saws shriek. I didn't mean to get so attached to this ship—didn't even think it was possible. But the *Ruttin' Hell* has been shelter and safety since we flung ourselves out into the unknown. It may handle like a brick taped to a cat, but it outran a dreadnought, and when we sell it, we'll be striking out into a foreign territory with nothing but what we carry on our backs.

Adela ducks around the wing, finally throwing a glance our way. "Interior?" she asks, rapping her knuckles against the rear.

Gal pushes off the fence and crosses the lot to open the cargo ramp for her. I don't want to watch her greedy eyes take in the space that's been our refuge, but I also wouldn't dare leave the Umber heir alone with her. I follow Gal across the lot, wincing when the hazy layer of cloud shifts and sunlight beams down on the back of my neck. The afternoon heat is nowhere near as oppressive as yesterday, but any bit of sun changes that fast.

By the time I duck into the Beamer's cool, dark interior, Adela's already scrambling up the cargo-bay ladder, making a beeline for the cockpit. She ignores the crew bunks, the head, and the kitchenette—she only has eyes for the ship's controls. I glance into our room as I pass it, the lump in my throat growing at the sight of two slept-in beds.

"Console outfit looks standard," Adela calls from the cockpit. She's planted herself in the pilot's chair already, and something in me bristles territorially. "Nothing's obviously missing. Few enhancements here and there, but that's what you'd expect when a ship's . . . Well, you know."

Neither of us confirm what she's fishing for, but neither of us has to. The ship's stolen military property from another empire. If we let her use that fact to negotiate, we'll get slaughtered.

"Let's see how she flies. Hold on, kiddos."

Gal dives for the copilot's chair, and I wrap my hands around the headrest as Adela spins up the engines with a casual flick of her wrist. The rotary thrusters roar, bumping the ship a few feet off the ground, and we wheel in the air, the vacant lot shrinking beneath us. "We never agreed to a test drive," Gal mutters, but Adela only cackles in reply.

I grip the headrest tighter, my legs braced for the worst. We gain altitude at a miserable rate, complaints echoing from all sides as the *Ruttin' Hell* puts up its best fight against its pilot. Adela flies like a drunkard at first glance, but there's a method to her madness that an experienced eye can pick out. She's a minimalist with the thrusters, giving them only what she needs to keep us off the ground, and rather than sticking to a straightforward vector, she curves along the paths she means to take.

In short, she's flying the Beamer right into its weaknesses, and the ship shows it. I flinch as the rear of the craft groans and the rotary thrusters sputter. Gal glances back at me as we arc out over Isla's northern suburbs. He looks mildly nauseated. The way Adela's flying is a negotiation in and of itself, and there's no countering it.

We're losing. By how much depends on how quickly we fold. I give him a short nod.

"Seven K," he says over the scream of the struggling engines.

Mercifully, Adela levels off on a steady vector and flips on the autopilot. "Come again?" she asks, even though it's clear she heard him the first time.

"We'll take the initial offer. Seven K for the Beamer, no questions asked."

Adela grins with her butcher's smile, and I have to tear my gaze away.

We save the minutiae of the deal until we've landed safely back in the vacant lot. I perch on the end of the cargo ramp as Gal and Adela wrangle the details inside, staring bleakly at the life we've stuffed into the pair of backpacks waiting at my feet. *It's done,* I keep telling myself. *Gal and Adela shook on it.*

But I can't shake the sensation that we're throwing away our biggest asset for something so intangible. If that money disappears into the digital void, these bags will be all we have left.

A hand comes down on my shoulder, jolting me from the spiral of my thoughts. A strange, guilty relief washes through me as I realize it's metal. "C'mon, kid," Adela says. "No need to sulk. You cut a good bargain, all things considered." She glances back into the ship's interior, then bends closer. "Your boyfriend's doing a sweep to make sure you haven't forgotten anything."

"He's not my—"

"Shut it. Look, I can't help but notice your circumstances. *Yours,* especially."

With a jolt, I realize her accent is shifting slightly. The broad vowels of Corinth are falling away, leaving a familiar sharpness in the cadence of her voice that sends a chill up my spine. But it's not all the way Umber—there's a painful collision between the clipped syllables of an Umber voice and musical tonality of an Archon accent, one I'm all too familiar with.

"I think I get why you would have deserted an Umber academy," Adela continues. "And if that really represents your feelings, I wanted you to know there's a place for you in this empire. I can introduce you to some people."

Panic wipes out every rational thought in my head. If she's hinting at what I think she's hinting at, I can't afford any part in it—not when my sole mission is to keep the Umber heir safe. But I can't let on that I'm escorting an Umber prince, which means I need a better reason to reject her offer than the fact that Gal would have a full-blown panic attack if I have anything to do with Archon refugees.

If she's hinting at what I think she's hinting at.

"I . . . I can't . . ." I stammer, switching my gaze back to the packs before the smarting in my eyes gives me away. "We're just trying to get home to our families." I'm so used to lying through omission that the flagrancy of the one I'm telling right now burns on my tongue. I have no family to go home to. Gal's mother has made sure of that. By all rights, I belong with people who can sympathize with the pain that's hollowed me out.

Adela lets out a sigh so surprisingly soft that my eyes flick her way to make sure it's hers. I expect her to look angry or betrayed, but there's nothing but tired sadness written over her sharp features. "Fair enough," she says. "But look, you seem like good kids. If you need a place to stay for now, I know a guy with cheap rooms that get cheaper if you use my name. I'll point you in his direction."

"Thanks," I tell her, and at least that sounds earnest.

True to her word, Adela guides us to a run-down building on the northern edge of Isla's downtown, where the owner sees her face and immediately halves the price of a tiny room on the third floor. It's about the same size as our academy bunk, but something about the grimy lightlessness of the place makes it feel far smaller.

And of course, there's only one bed.

Gal flops onto it, throwing down his oversized pack with a heavy thud. We tried to take everything that could possibly be useful, from the tools in the toolbox to the ration packs in the kitchenette. My shoulders ache from my own load, which includes the deflector armor I wore during our escape, all the clothes and towels I could find, and basically anything else that wasn't bolted down.

We have no idea what's ahead, but we're as prepared as we can be for two guys with no ship.

"Remind me," Gal groans against a pillow, "*never* to introduce that woman to my mother. I think they'd burn the galaxy together."

I nearly laugh out loud at his obliviousness, but a sudden crumpling of his expression gives me pause. I sit hesitantly on the edge of the bed as Gal starts to curl in on himself. "What's up?"

He closes his eyes, trying to bury his face into the pillow. "Not important."

"Hey, no. You don't get to lie to me anymore." I reach over and try tugging the pillow away. "You're . . . totally out of lies—*give me that*," I snarl as Gal tries to yank the second pillow over to replace the first.

"Fine," he huffs, relinquishing both. He rolls onto his back, scrubbing his palms over his eyes. "I was thinking about my mother. And about how she came to the throne."

That'd do it. In the end, Iva emp-Umber bore the true blood of the Umber line, but she wasn't the eldest heir. Iva was sixteen years old and still shadowed, running trade empires at the knee of the Bahren System governor, when her older sister Ximena turned eighteen, revealed herself to the galaxy, and began the succession process. Ximena never suspected there might be another Umber heir waiting to step in, and two years into her developing reign, her guard was down.

Iva could have chosen differently. She'd retain her emp-Umber name and its many privileges for the rest of her days. In a different life, maybe that would have been enough for her. Iva could have been content playing backup to Ximena in the tenuous time between the start of the empress's reign and the day her heir came of age and began to share power with her. There were so many other ways she could have served her empire.

But to an Umber mind, the empire wasn't *hers* yet, and that had to be corrected.

When Ximena began to consider marriage alliances, Iva saw her opportunity to prove her right to the throne—to prove her blood ran stronger than her sister's. She disguised herself among the young nobles vying for her sister's hand. Managed to get a moment alone with Ximena. Needed no more than a moment to carve her sister's throat open in the heart of the citadel.

Iva cloistered herself in the Imperial Seat for a week, turned eighteen, and claimed her bloodright. And unlike her sister, she wasted no time finding a match. Yltrast sys-Gordan, a governor's son standing to inherit one of the most critical interior systems, was among Ximena's candidates. Rumors whispered that Iva had confided her identity to him before she slew her sister, and he helped arrange the circumstances. Some even suggested that it might be a love match.

Iva's ascension was ruthless. Calculated. Effective. Decisive. And now I'm starting to understand exactly what's eating at Gal.

Because everything his mother did, she did to establish her bloodright. She did it to secure her rule. And like any good ruler, Iva emp-Umber knows her rule doesn't end with her time on the throne. An empress can hold the empire in her hands for only a few decades.

A dynasty can hold it forever.

In a way, everything Iva did, she did for Gal too. He's part of her unshakable rule, born a scarce two years after his mother killed her sister and began her succession. Iva carved him a legacy.

Now Gal has to live up to it.

When he uncovers his eyes, they latch onto the worrisome stains and cracks that scatter across the ceiling. Gal's expression tightens. "I . . . I know I'm not like them. Not enough. And I know that's going to be a problem soon. When they find out I *ran*—"

"You had to," I say automatically, but he stiffens, and I know it wasn't the right thing to tell him.

Gal heaves in a deep breath, his brow furrowing. "Even with the bloodright, my rule's not . . . It's not . . . I have to be better than this. Better than running and hiding and sneaking back into my empire's bounds. Blood only earns so much." He swallows, his eyes darting back and forth across the patterns that cheapen our new digs. "I'm scared, Ettian. Scared of what it might take."

I want to touch him so badly—to reach over and take his hand. "You've been practicing for this," I murmur instead. "All that time at the academy. You had dismantling and avoiding violence down to an art. Now it's just a matter of putting it into practice and . . ."

I trail off, unsure what to say next. Gal's the one who's got this all figured out, not me. Once he's crowned, he begins a years-long process of sharing his mother's power, and after that the crown will be his and his alone, to pass on to only his blood's true heir. It'll be a hell of a fight to twist the empire's policy away from his mother's course, but he's been preparing for that fight for years.

And I have to trust he's grounded in his principles, trust that he'll hold out against the most fearsome ruler his empire has ever known. I know he's not like his parents—he never could be. I wish I knew how to make him see that for the blessing it is. Being raised as a shadow heir turned Iva into a woman willing to slaughter her sister for power. But Gal was positioned in military leadership, not the cold halls of trade. He's full of heart and camaraderie, not calculation. He wouldn't make her choices. He wouldn't ask me to follow him down her path. That's not the Gal I know.

He reaches over and prods me on the shoulder, jarring my thoughts. "You're systems away, buddy," Gal murmurs, and I let out a long sigh that trails into a wheezy little chuckle. "What's going on?"

I snort. "What *isn't* going on? We're on the run in a foreign empire. We sold our only solid shot at getting home for practically peanuts. I think I hear something dripping in this room. And oh yeah, my best friend's the Umber heir."

Gal grimaces.

"And I'm sharing his bed."

There's a terrifying, frozen moment where I want to reach out into the space between us, grab the stupid joke by its tail, and stuff it back down my throat before he has a chance to press the issue. But then Gal lets out a loud, undignified snort, and within seconds we're both laughing like idiots over this stupid, impossible situation. Here we are in this small, shitty room, all but free from the machinations of galactic politics and the danger that's been locked onto our asses since the moment of his unveiling. Here we could almost believe we're just two guys lying side by side, both wanting each other so bad it hurts. We could almost believe that it's possible to have every-thing we want.

"You know, there's a bright side to this," I mutter, nodding vaguely to the room around us.

Gal's breath hitches. "Oh yeah?"

"Even if you tell them, no one's gonna believe you're a prince now."

I fully deserve the pillow.

CHAPTER 10

I SET OFF on my own early the next morning, slipping into the streets as Isla starts its morning rituals. As a planetary capital in a borderworld system, it plays host to thousands of intersecting cultures that blur together across my senses as I move down the wide roads that sprawl through this part of town. I spot variations on noodles, flatcakes, tea, and even something that looks and smells suspiciously like my region's own flatbreads and sauces. Corinth can't match the richness of the Umber interior's abundance, but from the variety available in the street food, it's clear they're a step above Archon's thin soil. I resist the urge to investigate. We took those ration packs from the *Ruttin' Hell* for a reason—we need every single Corinthian bit in our pockets.

Gal chose to stay behind today. He's waiting in the safety of the room until I've secured a new ship. It's an unnecessary risk to have him wandering the city, but I can't help but think that leaving him alone is just as bad. He tends to fare better when I'm there to look out for him.

But—and I'm a total asshole for thinking this—I need a breather from being around him. We've spent five days locked up in a ship with nothing but each other's company, and after what happened at the river, the tension between us has been reaching unbearable levels. Solitude lifts that burden from my shoulders, but it pinches as it goes.

I travel on foot, even as buses, trolleys, and wiretrams trundle past me, relishing the openness of these wide roads and the sky above and fantasizing about what I could be flying soon. With the 6K and change in our pockets, we won't be able to get much, but we don't need much. We don't even need something with guns. Just a ship that can fly fast and true to the Imperial Seat.

I round a corner and find what must be this system's heaven. Ships stretch along a dirt alley as far as the eye can see, prices written on their windows in colorful soap as dealers lounge in lawn chairs in their shadows, smoking heady cigars and shouting back and forth across the road. The air is filled with the dueling sounds of the haphazard, jazzy riffs Corinthians like to call music blasting valiantly from radios at each dealer's throne. Potential buyers wander in and out of the lots, rubbing their necks from craning up at some of their prospects.

If Gal were here, he'd mutter, *Keep it in your pants, Ettian*. And he'd have a point. My eyes immediately find the slickest ships on the lots, speedsters and sun-sailers with no prices marking their windows. It'd probably cost what's in my pocket just to sit inside those things for five minutes, and the worst part is I'm tempted.

But the fact remains: I'm here to buy a beater.

Those things aren't readily on display. I duck into the first lot, summoning the willpower I need to walk past the fancy models to the back, where they stash the ones that barely fly. I feel the eyes of the owner on me, but I think I've made my agenda clear enough, and when I glance back at his lawn-chair throne, the man goes back to reading his newspaper.

My stomach sinks as I find what I'm looking for. Faringian Toruses with missing heat shielding. An Utar Feldspar that on first glance looks like it might be worth its price until I notice that it's propped up on a rock in place of one of its landing legs. I scowl, knocking the hunk of granite with the toe of my boot. Even though logically I knew I wasn't likely to find what I was looking for in the first lot, I didn't anticipate my prospects being this dismal. If I'm going to get Gal back to safety, I need a ship that can actually get us there in one piece.

So lot number one is a bust. On to lot number two.

They start to blur together. I see the same flaws over and over again, my eyes getting far too used to picking out reasons a ship won't fly. Interspersed here and there are a few likely candidates. Most of them are outside our price range, but I circle them carefully, marking the flaws I could start a negotiation over. Maybe I'll take a page out of Adela Esperza's book and take one of them for a harrowing test drive to knock a few thousand bits off the asking. The thought turns my stomach. All the Umber military training in the worlds couldn't make me brave enough to fly one of these things the way she did.

My mood goes sour as the sun climbs, cooking the lots. I start to sweat through the loose shirt I'm wearing. Gal's counting on me to find *something* by the end of the day, and the prospects are looking grimmer and grimmer as the time pressure mounts. We need to get off Isla, off Delos, into the black, and onto our vector.

And yet, there's a part of me that's imagining staying in Corinth. Somehow convincing Gal first that he doesn't need to run home right away and then that he doesn't need to go home at all. Here, we're both nobody. And if we're both nobody, there's a *chance* . . .

A sly, guilty smile creeps over my lips.

"Like what you see?"

I blink, realizing too late that I've been staring. Not at the girl who asked, but at the ship behind her. It's a skipship—an older model, built in Umber shipyards instead of Umber-controlled Archon belts, but it's still sleek. No price on the windows. Barely any dust on the wings. Maybe it's brand-new on the lot. It's the kind of ship I wanted to fly out of the academy instead of the Beamer, and a twinge of annoyance rattles through me as I realize my job would be a whole lot easier if I'd had a ship like that to sell in the first place.

The girl clears her throat, and my gaze drops to her. She straightens in her folding chair, tipping her rainbow-patterned umbrella back so I can see her face. She wears a wicked smile as plainly as the ragged skin that graces the right half of her features. Burn scars, if I had to guess, and what isn't burned is spotted with acne. Her narrow eyes shine in the afternoon light as she bats her eyelashes at me.

"I . . . uh." Everything about her makes me lose my train of thought. I think back to my pilot training, to lessons on gyro control and how to keep a Viper oriented when you feel like your head's about to spin off. "Sorry, not really . . . interested."

"Of course you are. I've been watching you."

"I zoned out. I wasn't actually looking—"

She waves her hand, cutting me off. "You've been prowling these lots for hours, looking at beaters, and turning your nose up at every single one you find."

"How—" There's no way she's been able to see me the whole time from her seller's perch.

"You've got a good eye. You came here on a mission to stretch your money as far as it'll go. I can make that process easier." She snaps her umbrella shut and swings it backward, rapping its tip against the skipship's hull. "This right here is the best ship in the Corinthian Empire, and I'll give it to you for a price you should be weeping over."

I take a wary step back, holding up my hands. "Now, wait a minute—"

"I'm serious."

"Would you let me finish a sentence?" I snap, and the girl closes her mouth, raising an eyebrow. "I'm not interested."

"Six K."

"You're ruttin' kidding me."

"Hand to the gods, I'll give you this ship today, right this minute, for 6K."

"Does it have an engine?"

She snorts. "Take a look if you'd like." She slings her umbrella back over her shoulder, straightening her spine, and for a moment she looks downright regal—far more regal than a girl in grimy clothes has any right to appear. "Wen Iffan," she says, sticking out a hand. "Looking forward to doing business."

"Ettian," I tell her, keeping my hands to myself. "And I wouldn't count on it just yet."

If her offer's serious, I owe the ship a glance. I can't tell if she's pulling my leg when everything she says sounds like a joke—I have to see for myself. Shaking my head, I mount the ladder up to the sleek, aerodynamic cockpit.

I freeze mid-climb when I realize Wen is scaling the ladder behind me. "Go on," she says, patting a rung. "It's sturdy enough."

I tighten my lips and keep climbing until I haul myself up into the cockpit. The skipship's interior is just as impressive as the outside. While the seats are by no means new and the dashboard has some wear and tear, it's an objectively *nice* setup, and my fingers itch for the controls as I slip into the pilot's seat. It's been a week since I last flew a Viper, and I'm craving the kind of rush that comes from flying a viciously well-equipped machine.

"So, Ettian. Interesting name. Where're you from, Ettian?"

"I don't see how that's relevant." I keep my eyes fixed on the instrumentation as Wen clambers into the cockpit and plunks herself in the copilot's seat.

"Just making conversation. Gotta figure out if the guy with the pretty smile planning on buying my precious ship is trustworthy."

"If *I'm* trustworthy?"

Wen shrugs. "You can make conversation back. Ask me questions, too, you know?"

"Fine," I snap. "What's your deal? Why are you selling this ship?"

Wen shrugs. "All started the day I got this." She beams, prodding gingerly at the uneven, burned-looking skin on the right side of her face. "Wanna know how?"

"No, I want you to answer my ques—"

"Got a bit too close to the tail end of a Solstice-VI." Something dangerously close to pride radiates from her, and I start to wonder if this ship is worth the proximity to this little maniac.

"You're telling me a *thruster* did that to you?"

"Nah, a Cutter lieutenant. The thruster was an accomplice."

"A—" My incredulity knocks me silent. I heard chatter about the Cutters on the local airwaves as we approached the city. Vicious mobsters who've taken root in Isla's north side and become nigh impossible to weed out. Not the sort of people I can afford to be anywhere near.

Wen apparently doesn't do too well with silence. "I was a runner for the Cutters. Guy thought I was skimming—which I wasn't—or deliberately jumbling messages, which I would never dream of doing."

"So he stuck your head in a Solstice's tailpipe?"

"No, he asked nicely. We had a calm, rational discussion. I told him the truth, and he believed it. They're all talk, those Cutter guys."

"Really?"

"No, moron. He didn't even ask me any questions. Just lit the candle and stuck my face in it until it melted. I'm lucky I got to keep the eye." She shrugs, staring out across the lot through the cockpit windows. "Not like I was going to turn out pretty anyway. Now I scare people, and that's more fun."

"When did this happen?"

Another shrug. "Like a month ago."

I struggle to keep my face blank as I stare at her.

"So, want to see the rest of the ship?"

I glance down at the controls under my hands. This isn't worth it. Even if she gives me this ship for free, there's no way I'm getting involved in whatever mess has tangled around this girl. It isn't even the horrific story behind her burns that gets me—it's the flippancy. Her scars are only a month old, and she's already past caring about them. The fact that she's capable of that scares me more than any gang boss ever could, and I don't want to know what other nightmares Wen Iffan hides. "You know, I think I'm going to keep browsing if that's okay."

Wen deflates suddenly, slumping lower in the copilot's chair. "Oh, come on. I'm handing you the perfect ship on an iron platter and you're going to drop it because of my face?"

"I'm not . . . Look, you have a good face. Great eyes, yeah?" Which isn't a lie—there's something downright entrancing about her eyes, but I'm not about to let them suck me back in. "I need more time to think over what I've seen."

"I don't have time, *Ettian*. I gotta make a sale today, and I wasted precious minutes trying to get you to see how great this ship is."

I stand, and Wen ducks her head. A twinge of guilt hits hard in the left side of my chest. She'd better not be—nope, she is. She's crying. "Please don't," I hiss.

"I thought . . . something was going right for a change."

"Don't guilt me into this, Wen."

"No, it's fine. You should go."

"I—"

The sudden crack of boltfire cuts me off. I drop to the floor on instinct, peering out through the open door. A squad of twenty people dressed in black have assembled in the dirt outside the skipship, all of them staring up at the cockpit. Is it obsidian black? My heart hammers against the floor.

Their leader steps forward, lifting a megaphone to her lips. "We know you're in there, you turncoat bastard."

Ruttin' hell.

CHAPTER 11

WEN LUNGES FOR the cockpit door, slamming it shut and throwing down the locks. "Rocks and *rust,*" she mutters under her breath. "They're after me."

"They're after *you*?" I stagger to my feet only to flinch when another bolt slams into the skipship's side, warping the door where it hits.

"I may not have been honest about a few things," Wen says, dropping to her knees, flopping on her back, and tearing open a panel under the ship's controls. She pauses. "You thought they might be after you?"

"No, you go first. Explain."

She reaches into the ship's wiring, sticking her tongue between her teeth as she pulls and twists. Her tears have mysteriously vanished. "So hey, big surprise—this ship isn't mine. And I stole it from . . . Well, I shouldn't have gotten you involved, and I'm sorry in advance. Your turn."

I grab her by the ankle, dragging her out from under the dashboard so she can look me in the eye. "Whose ship is this?"

Wen stares up at me, and *now* there's terror in her eyes. "Dago Korsa," she whispers with holy reverence.

"Who the rut is Dago Korsa?"

She points a shaking finger at her face. "Boss of the guy who did this. Head of the Cutters. The worst man in Isla to cross."

"And you *crossed him*?"

"*He crossed me first!*" she snaps so vehemently that I nearly duck. "Look, it was a risk, it almost paid off, but then *you* didn't buy the ship, so really we're all to blame here." Wen kicks free from my grip, crawling back under the dashboard.

"What are you d—" I break off, pinching the bridge of my nose. I don't want to know what she's doing under there. Probably causing more problems. "Rut this. I'll get us out of here." I cross back to the pilot's seat and drop into it, my fingers gliding over the dash as I bring the ship to life.

"I wouldn't . . ." Wen starts, then goes back to burrowing in the systems as if whatever she wanted to say isn't worth the breath.

"Just hold on to something," I mutter, and throw down the throttle.

But instead of lifting off the ground, the skipship stays resolutely anchored. Instead of filling with the smooth rumble of flight machinery, there's nothing but the buzz of the electricity powering the lights and another dull thud as a bolt slams into the hull.

I frown, leaning over the instrumentation as panic crackles through me. "No. No, no, no. This can't be . . . Why—"

"Because the ship doesn't have any engines, dumbass," Wen snaps.

A faint sputtering noise leaks from my throat. If this ship has no engines, she's locked us inside a death trap, and I'm not even going to *start* on the fact that she tried to sell me a ship with no engines. "I'm handing you over," I announce, rocketing up from the pilot's seat.

"You think passing me off to Dago Korsa is going to stop him from melting your face? Or worse?" Wen continues to dig in the ship's guts, unbothered.

"I'm a goddamn bystander."

"You're an accomplice. You were going to take Korsa's ship off my hands."

"*You* were trying—"

"And that's exactly what I'll tell them if they take me alive, so I'm sorry to say you're in this thing with me."

"I'm not . . . I have my own thing—" But I break off, knowing she's right. I don't know anything about crime in Isla. Wen seems to know too much. There are people outside shooting at us. Maybe it's time to listen to her. "What do you need me to do?" I ask, flinching as the shriek of a saw sounds outside the cockpit door.

"Knew you were smart. Hold these." She thrusts a pair of pliers into my hands. "Almost done."

"With what, exactly?" I can't help but turn and face the door, wishing I had a blaster on my hip or deflector armor or *something* that could stand a chance against twenty angry mobsters. But Wen doesn't offer any answers, only a scarred, grimy hand. I take it and haul her to her feet.

"The hatch," she says, kicking it open to reveal a ladder that drops into the ship's core. She's shaking all over, but there's something giddy about it. Maybe narrow escapes are how she gets her kicks.

I'm fine with that as long as we get out of this alive.

"Follow me." Wen mounts the ladder and slides to the bottom, her palms shrieking against the metal. "Thirty seconds!" she shouts from the bottom.

"Until *what*?" I call after her, but she disappears into the skip-ship's cargo hold. I toss the pliers aside. The saw's buzz grows louder behind me, and I don't need telling twice. I drop down the ladder into the cavernous hold. It's lit only by the soft orange glow of emergency lights. Wen's shadow flickers against them as she beckons me over.

"In here." She grabs me by the collar before I can move and stuffs me into a mercifully cool, terrifyingly enclosed space. "Ten seconds." Before I can ask again, she tucks herself into the darkness with me and pulls a panel shut behind us.

I let out a shaky breath, wrinkling my nose against the scent of two sweaty bodies. "Are we supposed to wait for them to find us?

Because that's a horrible, horrible plan. They know we're in the ship. They—"

My next words are blasted away by a world-shattering *boom*. A wave of heat flash-cooks the compartment. Wen's knocked back against me like a bag of bones, and somehow I already know her well enough to know she's grinning through this. I feel like I'm slipping back into my own body as the ringing in my ears crests a peak and starts to dissipate, leaving me curled into my knees.

Wen grabs my collar again, kicking the panel open, and I blink against the harsh cut of sunlight streaming in. Smoke clots the air, and my lungs burn with every breath. Wen mouths something and hauls me forward. We tumble down the ship's cargo ramp—suddenly open in the wake of the explosion—and out into the dirt of the lot.

It's chaos. Shoppers and dealers scatter. The people in black rush to help their comrades caught in the blast from the cockpit. The skipship's upper deck is a bombed-out husk, belching ugly black smoke into the sky. The ringing in my ears elides into screaming.

Next to me, Wen's already scrambling on hands and knees to her folding chair and the colorful umbrella she was shading herself with barely minutes ago. Her fingers close around the umbrella's hilt, she pops to her feet, and I flinch when she presses down the button, expecting some new horror to burst forth.

Instead Wen snaps the umbrella open, ducks beneath it, and pulls me into its shade. "Arm on my shoulders," she shouts in my ear. "Move fast, but not too fast." Her own arm slips around my waist, and she pulls me into the jumbled mess of people fleeing the scene.

I hazard a glance back at the skipship, trying to clock the mobsters, but Wen dips the umbrella, blocking my view. "Don't let them see your face," she says. "Always assume you've gotten away with it until the second someone says otherwise. Elsewise you're looking suspicious." Belatedly I realize that she's talking at a normal volume again, which must mean my hearing is restoring itself.

"You . . . You . . ."

"Rigged the cargo door to pop when the explosives did, stashed us in the empty engine mounts, and blew up most of Dago Korsa's ship?"

"Yeah, that. Where the hell did you get that kind of ordnance?"

Wen shrugs. "Engine money."

I gape, and she laughs merrily. I don't know whether to be impressed or terrified, but I'm leaning toward the latter. Sure, it *worked*. It created enough chaos to slip away, even if it nearly cooked us and blew out our hearing. But then there's the fact that she had the explosives in place before the Cutters showed up. And the fact that she honestly thought she'd get away with selling me an engineless ship.

And the fact that I was so taken in by the prospect of a cheap skipship that I climbed into the cockpit and got stuck in this situation.

I've got enough problems with one liar in my life. No way am I getting stuck with another. Before Wen can tighten her grip, I knock her arm off my waist and duck out from beneath the umbrella.

"Ettian, *no!*" she yelps, but I'm already out of reach. "You—they're gonna see us. You've gotta—"

I start running. I don't "gotta" anything. I didn't sign up for this—I need to get as far away from it as possible, before it blows up in my face. Or, more accurately, before Wen blows something else up in my face.

Two hundred pounds of black-clad muscle has something to say about that. The man comes out of nowhere, wrapping an arm around my neck and throwing me down into the dirt. The breath explodes from my lungs as my cheek rakes across the ground, and I choke down dust.

Indignation burns through me, fury on its heels. I lash out with one leg, finding purchase in a soft inner thigh, and my attacker reels back. Not today. Not ever. No one throws me back in the dirt I crawled out of. I push to my feet, my teeth bared.

The Cutter draws his gun. A shiver runs up my spine. No deflector armor to protect me now.

Instead I get Wen Iffan, a rainbow umbrella, and a swing so mean the man's head snaps back like an elastic band. She doesn't wait to see if that blow alone does the trick. The umbrella's wickedly sharp tip flashes in the afternoon sun as she spins it around, but before she can slash it over the Cutter's throat, he rolls to the side, reaching for the gun he dropped.

I lunge forward and kick it away, then dive after it. My fingers close around the grip, sliding into the trigger, squeezing so desperately tight that it fires, kicking in my hand. The bolt goes stray, slamming into the hull of one of the sun-sailers, and I hear a distant, indignant shriek—no doubt its dealer. I whirl to find Wen and the Cutter locked together, the man trying to wrestle the umbrella away from her as she clings to it ferociously. He's easily twice her size. Overpowering her. Out of the corner of my eye, I spot more figures in black sprinting toward us.

My heartbeat pounds in my ears. The urge to run bites at my heels. They're after her, not me. But Wen rushed in and saved my ass—the least I can do is this one small thing. I check the setting, lift the blaster, and pull the trigger.

The Cutter goes limp, and Wen jumps back, dropping the umbrella and shaking her hands where the bolt's charge leapt into her. She seems confused. Maybe no one's stepped in for her like this. Maybe never in her life.

Her hesitation breaks. She slips her toes under the umbrella's handle, flips it up, and snatches it out of the air. Then she turns tail and dives into one of the lots.

I sprint after her. There's only one reason someone as reckless and impulsive as her has survived this long. Wen is whip-smart and slippery as all hells. My best shot of getting out of this is on her heels. I keep my grip locked tight around my stolen blaster, my feet skidding on the loose gravel as I track her shadow through the hulking ships. Boltfire chases me, slamming into hulls, kicking up dirt, whistling past my ears.

I miss the certainty of a Viper's controls. My own legs don't feel anywhere near as sure. Somewhere in the distance, sirens howl. The local police are closing in. It doesn't faze the Cutters on our tail.

Wen's slight form dives headfirst under one of the massive ships' bellies, disappearing into a dark hole in the dirt. I pause, but only for a second. Moving keeps you alive. Doubt gets you dead. It's like I never left the back alleys of Trost.

I stick the gun's grip in my teeth and crawl after her. The darkness closes around me, my elbows scraping awkwardly against the tunnel walls. Ahead, I catch a flash of light and Wen's shoes disappearing. I try to wriggle faster, cursing the length of my limbs and praying that the heavily armored Cutters behind us will be even slower.

By the time I squirm out of the tunnel's other end, Wen's ducking around the corner of a building. I haul myself to my feet and glance back. We've burrowed out of the dealers' alley entirely, coming out on the other side of the chain-link fence that binds the lots. The ship the tunnel undercuts blocks us from sight, and relief stirs in me as I pluck the gun from my mouth and whip around the corner after Wen.

A hook catches my ankle, and I go sprawling. I twist to find Wen flipping her umbrella's handle back into her hand, looking nonchalant as ever. "Now's the part when we lay low," she says, beckoning me into a narrow alley. "They expect us to go for distance, so we wait for them to spread out."

I stagger to my feet and lurch after her, tucking the blaster in my waistband and wiping halfheartedly at my shirt. It's a lost cause at this point—I've been knocked into the dirt too many times.

Wen hauls open a hatch in the alley's wall and beckons me forward. "After you, flyboy," she says, clapping me on the back as I duck into the darkness.

Too late the smell hits me. Too late I realize this is a garbage bin.

Wen slams the hatch shut. A moment later, she clicks on a penlight. The tiny glow casts her burns in sharp relief. Even worse, she's grinning. "You saved my life back there," she says, falling back on her haunches and leaning against the bin's wall. "I think that means I owe you some sort of debt."

"No, no—I don't want anything like that."

"I'm serious, Ettian. I can help you. You need help."

"Not the sort you give." I hug my arms against my chest, terrified of what I might brush up against in here. I'm no stranger to spaces like this, but that doesn't mean I'm going to accept returning to them so easily. "Look, I just wanted to buy a ship. I didn't ask to get caught up in this mob nonsense."

"And then you shot a Cutter. I've spent a whole month dodging them, but I'm good—they only caught on today."

It takes all my willpower to keep my voice at a whisper. "Because you were trying to pawn off their boss's ship!" I hiss through my teeth.

"Among other things."

"*Among*—" I clamp a hand over my mouth as my outburst echoes in the tiny space.

"You should be thanking me. I saved our asses by blowing the ship."

"So the debt is paid."

Wen's brow furrows. She looks like she's crunching numbers. Weaving checks and balances into a net. A sinking feeling overtakes me. From what I've seen so far, Wen's a chaotic opportunist. This debt thing isn't a matter of honor. She has none. It's her chance to squeeze something out of me. Sure, she says she owes me, but she also knows I was in the market for a ship. The 6K offer was enough to get me to take a look at one, which means there's at least that much in my pockets.

I have to get out of her grip before she takes me for everything I have.

"You saved my life, even though you didn't have to. You could have turned and ran, but you didn't." Wen's voice is soft, her narrow eyes half-open, focused on the tiny light in her hand. "That matters. That's not something people do, usually. It means something, doesn't it?"

She's so relaxed here. So comfortable, even though we're hunkered down in the smell of stale garbage. This is *normal* for her, and what I did wasn't. I sigh, slumping slightly, trying to inhabit this space the way she does, to imagine being used to this.

It isn't that far a stretch. Less imagination, more remembering. I was here—I was *her* seven years ago. When I had no one to fight for me. It didn't last, but I didn't know that at the time. A flashback takes hold of me like a hook in the gut, the feeling of my throat collapsing under a hand far too large for me to pry away. It was the first time I'd been caught stealing and the first time I truly understood how alone I was. There was no one who could have saved me from whatever revenge that woman had wanted to take. After that incident—after she let me go with a kick in the ribs that felt like it nearly snapped me in half—I knew I had to trick someone into watching my back.

It took years to figure out the logistics, but I was able to attach myself to the Umber reconstruction, to the Umber military when they opened the academy, and eventually to the Umber heir himself. I saw opportunities, grabbed them, and didn't let go. I know exactly how the game goes.

But that doesn't mean I agree to be a piece in Wen's.

"Sorry, junker. I've got to get moving."

"Wait—"

With one quick kick, I pop the hatch open, squinting as light spills in. I choke down a breath of fresh air and glance both ways. Nothing. No one.

I've been gone too long. No doubt the newsfeeds will be covering the incident at the dealers' alley—Gal might already be mid-panic. I need to get back to him before anything else goes wrong.

"Ettian," Wen hisses from behind me. Her fingers curl around the edge of the hatch as she peeks out. "It's not safe."

I take off at a brisk stroll, shoving my hands deep in my pockets. Only a few Cutters saw my face, and it was in the midst of Wen's hurricane of chaos. Even with my darker-than-average skin, I'm not distinct enough to draw their attention. They're looking for a half-burned girl.

I don't look back as I round the corner.

The closer I get to our building, the more the tension leaves my shoulders. I'm hopelessly dirty and smell faintly of garbage, but I'm in the clear. Still without a ship, but the important thing right now is getting back to Gal.

I duck under the shade of the building's awning, pull open the iron-handled door, and step into the cool, stuffy darkness of the lobby. Above my head, a bell rings.

The owner, a portly man named Jusun, gives me a nod from the desk, and I freeze in my tracks. Bent next to him is a woman clad in black, peering at something laid out on the table. Her eyes flick to me, then back to the paper. They don't return. I give her two extra seconds to draw her gun on me, and when she doesn't, I make for the stairs.

Fast, but not too fast. Eyes focused on where I'm going, but not too focused. One hand in my pocket, the other on the rail as I creak up the steps. My stolen blaster burns a hole in my back where it's hidden under my shirt.

The bell rings again. I glance back. My stomach lifts like I'm at apogee. The woman at the desk straightens, blinks, and takes three seconds too long to register that Wen Iffan and her rainbow umbrella have slipped into the lobby.

I launch into a sprint, thundering up the stairs three at a time as the room behind me erupts into chaos. Shouts, muffled thuds, and the shriek of boltfire chase me as I climb. I spill out onto the third-floor landing as someone mounts the stairs behind me. I don't look back to see which of the three.

My fingers fumble on the key in my pocket as I reach the door. "Gal?" I call, my hand shaking too badly to get the sliver of metal into the lock.

The door flies open, and I lunge into the room, blowing clear past Gal to the corner where we've tossed our unpacked bags. "Ettian?" he asks. His eyes are wide, his hair messy, but at least he's not in pajamas again. "What's going on?"

"We gotta get out of here." I throw anything I can reach into the bags, stuffing unfolded clothes down in messy heaps. My velvet bag is somewhere at the bottom of my pack—I feel for it to be sure.

Gal's hand comes down on my shoulder, and I startle under his touch.

I glance up. First at him. Then at the door. Unlocked. Unbolted. Before I can leap across the room, the handle turns.

Wen slips inside, then locks herself in with us.

CHAPTER 12

"OH. YOU BROUGHT home a girl," Gal says flatly.

I storm across the room, catching her by the throat and pinning her against the door. "Ettian, I can explain," Wen chokes. Her skin is rough under my thumb, smooth under my fingers. She doesn't try to pry my hand away—just lets me pin her, waiting for me to clench down.

"You followed me. You brought the Cutters here. You're endangering—" I break off, glancing back at Gal. "I don't need an explanation. I need you to get out."

"I might need an explanation," Gal interjects.

"Well—"

A sharp jab in my stomach cuts me off. I look down. Wen's got her umbrella angled up, its bladed point digging into the soft spot beneath my sternum. She braces against the door as my fingers tighten on her neck. "Cutters were already on your tail. I was trying to warn you—they're closing in. We don't have time for this. If you throw me out now, they'll catch all of us. You're a little bit stuck with me." The burned side of her mouth goes taut, somewhere between a terse look and a cruel smirk.

I scowl. "Down in the lobby. What happened to that woman?"

Wen reaches around behind herself and pulls a blaster out of her waistband. She keeps her wrist limp, the weapon pointed at the floor. Her umbrella sports a few fresh red patches.

"Gods of all systems," I mutter, letting her go and taking a step back. She keeps the umbrella pointed at me. "What about Jusun?"

She gives me a blank look.

"The owner? The guy—"

"Oh, he locked himself in his office. But the Cutter got a call off to her fellows before I took care of her, and they're probably tracing her location. We've got a minute, maybe more."

"Does anyone feel like telling me what's going on?" Gal asks, his voice dangerously low. I turn to find him backed into the corner, his eyes fixed on the gun in Wen's hand. My heart drops. In all of this chaos, I nearly forgot what we're doing here. What's at stake. How *stupid* it is to let someone like Wen anywhere near him.

"Who's he?" Wen asks.

"You don't want to know," I say, and Gal smirks despite himself. The sight of it grounds me from my panic. I have two and a half years of academy training under my belt. I have a minute to work with. I can get us out of here. "Wen," I bark, and she snaps to attention. "Put the gun away. Gal?" He straightens, relaxing slightly as Wen slips the blaster back into her waistband. "Get that deflector armor on. I wish there were time to explain, but we need to get moving."

Gal crouches by the packs, pulling out the armor I wore during our escape. I dig into our gear and find my grappling gun. Wen creeps closer, hovering over my shoulder as I check the device's charge. "Where the rut'd you get gear like this?" she asks, clutching her umbrella tighter.

"Unimportant. More important—you know the city. You know where we go to lose them, right?"

Wen bares her teeth, and something tells me I'm going to like this place even less than her last hidey-hole. But it's all the confirmation I need.

Gal finishes strapping on the armor and pauses, glancing between us. "Which one of you smells like garbage?"

I shrug. Wen says, "Both."

Gal sighs.

I cross to the window, glancing down into the street below. Our room is around the corner from the main entrance, so if there are Cutters on their way, we're none the wiser. Foot traffic's light—we're in the midafternoon lull between when most people take their lunches and when they start heading home for the day. Still, people will see us. We have to make this fast.

"Wen, you any good at climbing ropes?" I ask, popping the window's latches and hauling it open.

"Up or down?"

"Down."

"Not a problem."

"Great." I kick out the screen, lean into the open air, and fire a grappling line into the wall adjacent. Two quick yanks to check that it's rooted. One nod to Gal, who hands me my pack without a word. I lean out the window, loop the line around my foot, and set the gun to unspool.

Voices sound outside our door. "Go," Gal whispers, slinging his own bag onto his back. Wen turns to face the noise in the hall, bringing her umbrella up like a knight's vibrosword. I grab the line with my free hand, shift my weight onto my foot, and drop, wincing as the woven fibers strip skin from my palm. I hit the street, kick free from the line, and immediately press back against the building, switching my grip from the grappling line to the blaster tucked against my back. Five seconds later, Gal hits the pavement. His hand finds my shoulder, and I let him brace against me as he slips his foot out of his loop.

The line shudders and sways, and I glance up to find Wen leaning awkwardly out of the window, the hook of her umbrella's handle clenched in her teeth as she tries to replicate the way we used a loop around one foot to slow our descent. People in the street stare up at her, and I hiss. "Wen? You sure you've got this?"

Gal grabs the line to steady it, but it doesn't do much for her. She slips out the window and thuds gracelessly against the building's side as she swings. The blaster topples out of her waistband, and both Gal and I duck to dodge it. "I'm fine," she calls, the words muffled by the umbrella in her mouth.

I really have to stop falling for everything she tells me. "Try to twist it around your leg," I offer, and Gal swings the rope to help.

But before Wen can get the line positioned, her attention snaps up to the window. I don't catch the words she says, but I can taste the venom behind them. Wen plummets down the line, her fall barely controlled. Gal and I dive out of her way. She hits the street so hard that she crumples. A nearby woman shrieks, and I glance up to find people clad in black sticking their heads out of our abandoned window. Gal's grip on my shoulder tightens.

Wen staggers to her feet with the help of her umbrella, looking winded. Her palms are crossed with furious red lines. "Gotta run," she mutters, blowing a stray strand of hair out of her eyes.

Her gaze flicks to the gun she dropped, but I shake her by the shoulder, bringing her attention back to me. "Which way?"

She squints, the circuits of her brain firing in rapid blinks of her eyes. "Wiretram. Next block over." Before we can get anything else out of her, Wen bolts down the sidewalk without a backward glance. Gal and I launch after her, both of us looking up in time to catch the shadows overhead disappearing back into the room.

"You've certainly had a busy day," Gal says as we chase Wen's slight form.

"If we get out of this, I'll tell you all about it," I reply, wishing we hadn't stuffed so many extra tools into the packs we're carrying. Why the rut did I think we'd need every size of wrench on the *Ruttin' Hell*?

Wen pauses at a corner up ahead, waiting for us to catch up. "Right down this way," she says, pressing against a wall and pointing to a squat-looking station where the wires that cross the city skyline dip and converge. A tram is approaching, trundling along at a good clip. "One minute until they dock. Two until they launch. We get on board, and we should be in the clear. You got fare?"

I nod, my gaze sweeping the open ground between here and

there. I don't like it. It's too exposed. We'll be spotted the second we break across it. And then there's the matter of the tram—I've never used public transit, and I'm fairly certain Gal hasn't either. In post-reconstruction Trost, I'd heard its reputation for being slow and un-wieldy, and I don't see why a Corinthian borderworld would be any different. How the hell are we supposed to escape the mob with a bunch of commuters on a known route?

I glance back, expecting to see black suits sprinting toward us, but we're only getting weird looks from passersby. Gal presses into my shoulder, the deflector armor humming to life against my arm.

The tram glides into the station. *"Now,"* Wen commands.

We run like every system's hell has unleashed its horrors on our heels. Shouts chase us, and a distant buzz sharpens in my ears. I glance back over my shoulder.

Three motorbikes come howling up the street, dodging between pedestrians. Two Cutters apiece. I will my legs to go faster, my gear to get lighter. My pack traps the blaster I stole against my back, and the one in my hand fires only grappling lines.

Wen dodges around one of the massive poles that support the wiretram lines, and something clicks in my head. I plant my feet and skid, whirling as I lift the grappling gun and fire a line clear across the open street, the bolt at the end taking root in a building's façade. I run the line twice around the support pole, and it snaps taut as the motorbikes close. The drivers try to divert, skidding and swerving to burn their momentum, but one of them takes the wire full-on, clotheslining the gunner off the bike as the driver ducks.

I abandon the grappling gun and take off after Gal and Wen. They've reached the station, and Gal's fumbling with his datapad at the till. Wen beckons me over frantically, her eyes on whatever's going on behind me.

The wiretram driver starts yelling something at Gal in a thick Corinthian accent, his vowels so broad that they threaten to bowl him over, shaking his head vehemently and pointing at the Cutters in the street. I blow past them, grabbing Wen by the collar and hauling her on board. The commuters shrink toward the back end, the front bobbing up as the weight redistributes. I glance back. Three Cutters are on their feet and running for us.

"Launch the tram," Gal commands, and his imperial voice shoulders through the tram driver's last scraps of resistance. Or maybe it's fear of the Cutters closing. No matter the reason, the man moves to the controls, throws up the gates, and releases the brakes as the motors spin up. The wiretram sways forward.

Not fast enough. As it gains speed, the Cutters run alongside. They leap, catching the rear handholds as the tram lifts clear from the station, and my stomach drops as three black-clad mobsters haul themselves into the tram with us. A glance down confirms even worse—the other three have gotten their bikes under them. They come screaming after us as the tram gets up to speed, running along the parallel streets beneath.

"This doesn't have to get messy, Iffan," one of the Cutters says, stepping through the commuters. Her eyes are shielded by her helmet's visor, giving us nothing but beetle-black plastics to read her through. "The boss wants you alive. Not a scratch on you, he said, or we'll be the ones hung out to dry."

Wen shrinks behind me, her lips thinning. "Doesn't fill me with confidence. Dago Korsa just likes to know which work is his."

A lazy smile cracks across the lower half of the woman's face. "Didn't say anything about these two, though," she says, nodding to me and Gal.

"Now—" Gal starts, the word heavy with his negotiator inflection, but before he can say anything else, I've launched clear across the wiretram. The woman fumbles for the gun on her hip, but I knock it out of her hand, sending the weapon flying. She swings, her knuckles grazing my cheek as I yank my head back.

Her two companions reach for their guns. They draw fast, but I'm faster, slamming a stunner bolt into the one on the right before he has a chance to fire. He goes limp, his helmeted head cracking against the wiretram's floor, and one of the commuters shrieks. The woman grabs my wrist, yanking my aim astray before I can target the other Cutter.

The fight sings through me. Pounds in my blood like drums. I drop low and jam my elbow up under her chin, striking soft flesh. She chokes, but her grip remains, her other arm coming around as she tries to plant her weight and wrestle me into submission. She's lighter than me, but I'm several years removed from the last time I had to scrap for my life. I try to break her grip on my wrist, but she twists viciously, and the gun pops free, clattering to the floor.

Out of the corner of my eye, I see her companion shift his aim to Gal.

The rational part of my brain knows Gal's wearing the deflector armor. Knows any bolt shot at him will go astray. Knows I need to focus on not letting this woman crack my head open on the wiretram's plastic seats. But the rational part is no match for what takes over. I plant my feet and heave, using my weight to twist the Cutter woman in front of her companion before he can get a shot off. She kicks off one of the seats, redirecting her momentum straight into me, and I stagger back, collapsing as she drives a knee into my chest.

But before she can pull back her fist and do some major damage, the wiretram lurches, the brakes squealing, and the woman goes flying down the aisle. I tilt my head back to find Wen at the controls, throwing a manic grin my way as Gal holds off the driver. I struggle to my feet and shrug the pack off my back as the tram reaccelerates, bouncing slightly along its line as we climb above Isla's skyline. We're going fast—far too fast for normal travel speeds, fast enough that the noise of the motorbikes beneath us is fading.

The Cutter woman lunges for the fore of the tram, and Gal steps forward to meet her, his fists up. I try to rush after her, but a hand comes down on the back of my shirt, and I whirl to face the other Cutter. I don't know where his gun has gone—maybe he lost it in the braking—but in any case, his fists do just fine. He snaps a right hook across my face, and my vision goes starry.

The tram lurches again, and I dodge to the side as the Cutter stumbles past, grabbing a bar to keep myself upright. The commuters in the back scream, pressing against the walls, clinging to their handholds, some of them holding up their datapads to capture the moment. I scoff. Guess we put on a good show.

As my opponent regains his bearings, I glance to the fore of the tram in time to catch Wen tossing her umbrella at Gal as he dodges the Cutter woman's swing. He grabs it by the hilt and spins it around, catching her upside the head. With the helmet she wears, it only disorients her, but Gal follows through with another spin that slashes the bladed tip over her arm.

And like the blood blooming in the wake of his slice, a smile the likes of which I've never seen spreads over Gal's lips.

Bile rises in my throat at the sight, but I can't afford the distraction. I leap sideways as the male Cutter charges me. But instead of taking a swing, he dives past me for one of the blasters. Too late, I dive after him. He rolls on his back to meet me, firing a shot that rattles my teeth as it cracks past my ear, and I land hard on his chest, elbows driving into his sternum. The Cutter chokes, and I use the distraction to pin his wrist before he can take aim.

But before I can pull my fist back and drive it under his chin, a kick catches me across the side of the head, knocking me onto the grimy tram floor. I roll on my back to find the other Cutter—the one I dropped with a stunner bolt—is on his feet again. He's woozy from the aftereffects of the hit that took him down, and maybe it's that wooziness that mercifully drives his next kick into my shoulder instead of my head.

"Ettian!" Wen hollers from the front of the tram. "Our stop's coming up."

Here's the trick behind fighting to the top. The way forward when it looks like you've lost everything. You have to make it convincing. Disappear, sink to the bottom, let any threat you pose evaporate.

Go limp.

I let my arms sprawl out as I close my eyes, heaving a defeated sigh. I feel the pause—one Cutter crawling to his feet, the other bringing his foot back down from the kick he was aiming.

And then I feel the hilt of the blaster underneath the tram seat. Out of their sight, but not out of my reach.

One second to get it in my hand. One second to crack my eyes open. Two quick pumps of my trigger finger as I snap the weapon out and aim it, first to the right, then to the left.

The Cutters collapse. I push to my feet, gritting my teeth against the throbbing in my head. With a few nudges of my toe, I check to make sure they're properly stunned, then stuff the gun in my waistband. The tram sways into a wide turn, and I glance to the fore.

Gal and the Cutter woman dance around each other. She's flagging fast, drained by dozens of tiny slices that arc across her body. Her flesh flashes white and red beneath the black suit in the places where Gal opened it.

He remains untouched, keeping her at the end of the umbrella as he weaves from side to side. His hooded eyes are dark and vicious, and another wave of nausea hits me as I realize he seems to be enjoying this. Gal doesn't fight like the sloppy cadet I thought I knew. He's not scrapping for his survival, scrabbling for that upper hand like I was two seconds ago. He fights like an imperial, dismantling her piece by piece, and even though I'm on his side, I feel the impulse to step between them for the Cutter woman's sake.

I look at Gal emp-Umber and see something that I don't recognize. And it scares the shit out of me.

"Thirty seconds to our stop," Wen hollers.

I glance out the tram's open windows. We're a hundred feet up, well above the buildings, and the wiretram shows no signs of slowing. I don't want to know what she means. I stagger toward the fore.

Wen skips back from the controls, waving the driver back in. He hauls himself out of the corner he backed into and dives for his post. A moment later, the brakes howl overhead as the tram burns off its speed.

The Cutter woman staggers back, collapsing against a row of plastic seats. Gal brings the umbrella down gently, resting the bladed point against the softness of her neck. A slight sneer lifts the edge of his lips, cruelty that I've never thought him capable of flashing in his eyes. She shakes her head, holding up her hands without another word. She's done.

"Fifteen seconds," Wen says. She snatches the umbrella out of Gal's hands, and a look of confusion flickers over his face like he's surfacing from a trance. He blinks once, taking in the bleeding Cutter woman, then glances up at me, lips parting as if to make room for an explanation, a curse, a plea for forgiveness.

Wen's the only one of us not frozen. She flips the umbrella handle-up as she pulls a release on the tram's wall and forces the gate over the door open. "Ettian, get over here."

My eyes flick to my pack, wedged halfway under one of the seats in the scuffle.

"*Leave it,*" she snaps.

But that's not happening. The velvet bag—my only memento of my family—is in my pack, and goddammit, I've let go of enough in the past two days. I dive for my gear, wrestling it onto my shoulder, and turn to find Wen reaching out the door with the umbrella's hooked handle. Gal has one hand clenched around the umbrella's stem, the other locked around Wen's waist. She's beckoning frantically for me.

I throw myself at them, my arms outstretched. Catching. Clinging.

My momentum topples us out of the tram, and for a terrible second, we fall.

CHAPTER 13

WHEN THE UMBRELLA'S hook catches on a line, we're all reduced to the same instinct. The three of us hold on with everything we have. Grips slide, muscles ache with tension, and my teeth clench so tightly that for a moment I fear they might shatter.

We fly along the wire, wind whistling past as the city rises to meet us. Our speed flags as the rooftops get closer and our weight drags the cable parallel to the ground. "Let go," Wen shrieks between her teeth.

Gal and I fall away, tucking into ungainly rolls as we spill onto the roof of an eight-story building. I settle on my side, every bone aching. But that doesn't matter. I pull my head up, ditch my pack, and drag myself over to Gal as fast as my body will let me.

"Ettian, I'm fine," he says, coughing as he pushes off his stomach and onto his knees. "I'm . . . honestly surprised, but I'm fine."

There's a part of me that can't possibly believe that. A part that won't believe anything it can't feel for itself. And before I can stop it, that part of me is reaching for him, cupping his face gently, turning his head side to side to make sure he isn't lying.

Gal leans into my palm, his wide brown eyes meeting mine

steadily. "I'm fine," he repeats. "Breathe, Ettian." He grins. "Or don't—I like you breathless."

I jerk my hand back and cuff him on the shoulder. Gal winces, sucking in a breath through his teeth, and I smirk. "Ruttin' *liar*."

"Didn't say I was completely unscathed. Just said I was fine."

My gaze drops to the hole that's been torn in the knee of my pants. "So I found trouble," I mutter with a sideways glance. Trouble's on her way.

"This rooftop's secure," Wen calls, slinging her umbrella over her shoulder. She barely looks winded. "We don't have to run any-time soon."

I sit back on my haunches, groaning. "There's no *we*, Wen. Go home."

"Technically don't have one. Whole city's fair game." She drops onto her knees beside us, tossing her umbrella down next to her. As she leans back on her rear, she runs a hand through the stringy, wind-tangled mess of chest-length hair on the unburned side of her head. The burned side grows out short and spiky, a testament to the freshness of her scars. Wen's attention shifts to Gal as she starts to pick out the knots and braid it. "So you're, uh . . . Ettian's boy-friend?"

"Yep," Gal says, sticking out a hand.

Oh come on, I groan internally, but I don't need Wen questioning why Gal would lie about that.

She pauses her braiding, reaches out, and shakes Gal's hand. "Wen Iffan."

"Gal Veres. And how do you know our dear Ettian, since he doesn't seem to plan on telling me anytime soon?"

"Now, hold on—" I start, but it's too late. Wen's eyes light up as she launches into her side of the story. She spins it for maximum sympathy, of course, casting herself as a poor orphan out on the streets. Only sixteen, trying to escape the mob, trying to earn enough money to get off-world and out of the Cutters' clutches forever. All she needed was a fast sale, but Ettian—a cruel, nightmarish knave—

came along and insisted on inspecting the ship, unwittingly trapping her inside when the Cutters came calling.

I know it's pointless to interrupt as she moves to the explosion—the backup plan she'd rigged in case the worst happened. Only, she had to change it around to work so she could survive it in the safety of the ship's engine mounts, because she never anticipated being *inside* the skipship when it blew. But Ettian—unthinking, dim-witted Ettian—forced her to improvise. Even worse, he tried to run and drew the Cutters' attention, pulling Wen into an all-out brawl in the middle of the dealers' alley.

"It was *one* guy," I mutter under my breath, but Wen ignores me.

She skips the part where I saved her life and moves right along into graciously sharing her hiding place—"A trash bin," I insist—with ungrateful, careless Ettian, who ignored her advice and ran off. She saw the Cutters on his tail and knew she had to warn him, so she followed—and good thing, too, because there was a lieutenant in the lobby of his building.

"That woman didn't know me," I snap. "There would have been no trouble if you and your recognizable face hadn't followed me in."

"You know that for sure?" Wen asks, smirking. "I'd bet everything in my pockets that she was waiting for you to settle in and drop your guard."

"How much is in your pockets?"

Wen reaches into them, roots around, and pulls out a few pieces of gravel and a hairpin. "Good point." She coils her finished braid at the base of her neck and fixes it there.

"Unbelievable."

"You guys wouldn't have made it out if it weren't for me. You owe me."

"Gal, don't nod—don't encourage her." I pinch the bridge of my nose. My head is woozy from the blows I took, and I don't even want to think about how high up we are or how we're supposed to get off this roof. Or, even worse, how we're supposed to get a ship and get off-world with the local mob on our tail. At this point, getting Wen off our case would rank as a minor miracle.

"Hypothetically," Gal says, his voice dropping low and smooth and charming, "what would we owe you for your trouble?"

"All three of us seem to have a mutual interest in getting off this rock," Wen says, leaning in. "Take me on."

"Take you on?"

"As your pilot."

Gal snorts. And because he snorts, I scoff, and because I scoff, he breaks completely, collapsing into laughter that echoes across the rooftops. I jam my fist against my lips as if that will keep the giggle trapped inside me.

For maybe the first time in the hours I've known her, Wen looks thrown. She frowns, waiting for Gal's mirth to die down, her eyes flicking back and forth between us.

"You're so far off the mark that it's almost adorable," Gal says at last and chuckles.

"You guys wanted to buy a ship for 6K. I'm the best junker pilot in Isla. I'm not *that* off the mark."

I run a hand over my scalp. I think I might be close to crying. "Wen, *we're* pilots. Both of us could probably fly any junker better than you—you should have seen the thing we came here in."

"And where did you come from?" she asks. If she was thrown before, she's back on track now, all demands and fire, with a voice just as exacting as Gal's.

We glance at each other, neither one of us sure exactly how much we're supposed to give her. But I'm not the one with the most at risk, so I tilt my palm up at Gal and let him tell the story.

"We're deserters," he starts. All the best lies are grounded in an easy truth. "We fled the military academy on Rana and crossed out of the Umber Empire's borders to escape the people on our tail. We sold the ship we came here in, and we're looking for a way to get back to—" His voice breaks, and I pray Wen doesn't pick up on the uncertainty that nearly unmoors him. "Back to our families," he concludes.

A knife twists in my stomach, and I notice the way Wen's lips twitch taut. A family to go back to is a luxury only one kid on this roof possesses. But then that tautness turns into a slow smile, and suddenly Wen Iffan looks like we've delivered her the best news she's heard all day. A cold shard of fear replaces the twist of the knife. She can't be planning on turning us in to the authorities—Wen's probably as disenfranchised as we are in the eyes of the Corinthian Empire. Even if she tried, who'd believe that?

No, she has something else. Something that makes her wicked and devious, far more terrifying than any tiny sixteen-year-old should be. "You guys are Umber ex-military? Trained on Rana?"

I don't like where this is going one bit, but Gal is already nodding.

Wen's smile gets wider, her lovely eyes sparkling. I'm going to have nightmares about the victory in her expression. "Like I said, we want the same thing here. Or close enough to the same thing. You guys want to get back to the Umber Empire, and I want to get off this planet—doesn't matter where I end up, as long as it's out of Dago Korsa's reach."

"I'm listening," Gal says.

"So we join the Archon resistance."

The hunger and hope in Gal's expression evaporates in an instant. My hands start to tremble. I try not to let it show, but Wen's clued into something. Her confidence slips, and she blinks. "You're going to have to explain exactly what that is," Gal says, and I swear there's an edge of menace in his voice.

"When the Archon Empire fell, people ran here. You know that, right?"

We nod. I remember the night after the surrender, when blockade-runners tried to escape Rana's atmosphere and the guns of the dreadnoughts long enough to go superluminal. Few slipped past the cityships. The darkness shone with the rain of broken ships reentering, shredding as they fell, and the skies echoed with the distant thunderclap of heavy boltfire slamming into the atmosphere. There was no chance I'd go on one of them. I was stuck on Rana, doomed to the occupation along with most of the population. But that night, I looked up at the sky and wished that I could take the risk.

I glance at Gal. To him, those were his rightful subjects, mandated by the power of his blood, fleeing his eventual rule. I wonder if I'll ever be able to tell him how much I wanted to be one of them.

It wouldn't—shouldn't—matter. I'm here now.

"The refugees organized with assistance from the Corinthian Empire. Our imperials have a vested interest in keeping Umber from overreaching again, after all, but an even more vested interest in appearing uninterested in conflict with the Umber Empire. They built camps for the Archon folks at first, spreading them across the borderworlds where we had the space and the resources. But after a few years, there was a shift in their priorities. Those who wanted to integrate peacefully into Corinthian society did just that. But those who wanted revenge—they have our emprex's support. So much so that for the past five years, they've been operating a resistance movement out of a base right here on Delos. I don't know exactly what they do over there, but if you're deserters from a former Archon territory, they might welcome you. And me along with you. And maybe they could get all three of us where we need to go."

Gal looks ashen. He grips his knees, staring at his knuckles, and his breaths are so measured that I know he must be counting. One, two, three, in. One, two, three, out.

A different sort of counting echoes in my heart, a steady rhythm I've known all my life. The beat Tatsun Seely tapped into my shoulder finds resonance in my bones. I push myself to my feet, trying not to look off-balance even as my mind reels. "Wen, could you give me and my, uh, *boyfriend* a second?"

I reach down and help Gal up. He shrugs out of his pack, and I loop an arm around his shoulders, shepherding him toward the edge of the roof. When I glance back at Wen, she's sprawled on her back, her hands folded behind her head as she stares up at the late afternoon sky.

Gal's tense under my touch, his eyes downcast. I glance at the city street beneath us, half expecting to see Cutters racing up on bikes, but instead I see the reason Wen knew for sure we'd be safe on top of this particular building.

"A police precinct," Gal mutters. "Rut me sideways."

"She's . . ." I don't know how that sentence ends. Part of me wants to call it cleverness. Part of me wants to call it luck. Most of me wants to get as far away from her as we can. And all of me knows that's impossible now.

"She's something," Gal agrees.

I heave in a deep breath, staring out at Isla's distant downtown. It shimmers and glitters in the haze, the sky above woven with the vectors of ship traffic. My old wounds ache, my old loyalties prickling at the back of my neck. The ghosts of drums thunder in my ears.

I feel like I'm being torn in half, like the person I've been pretending to be for the past seven years is being ripped away, leaving that fragile, bitter, vengeful ten-year-old in his place. I fight the sensation. I trained at the academy. I'm a loyal soldier of Umber, trying to get its prince home. I have no loyalty to the shattered remains of the Archon Empire, the empire that abandoned me to the rubble of Trost.

It's dead. It's gone. I can't carry it with me.

But apparently it's not dead. Not gone all the way. And I've carried enough through the years that the idea of a resistance movement out there, still fighting after all this time, is lighting a small fire in my heart.

I don't want to join them. But I have to know what made it through those blockades.

Gal's arm snakes around my waist, and I stiffen. The simple fact—the inescapable fact—is that going to the Archon resistance would be handing ourselves over to the enemy. If they find out who Gal is, we could be giving them all they need to take back their empire. They might already know. They could have been in contact with the academy officer who organized the attack that outed Gal as the Umber heir—the assassination attempt that would have succeeded if it hadn't been for me.

"She might not be telling the truth," Gal mutters, sneaking a glance back over our shoulders to make sure Wen's a safe distance away. "What's your read on her?"

"I don't know," I tell him honestly. "She kicked things off by trying to sell me a ship with no engines. But she helped me escape the Cutters. Helped *us* escape the Cutters, even though she was the one who brought them down on us in the first place."

"She's trouble."

"Undoubtedly."

"A junker girl."

"A waypoint."

"A distraction."

"Chaos incarnate, more like." I pause. "But she's smart. Terrifyingly, brilliantly smart one second, and then the next she's blowing up a ship. And somehow that was smart too."

"So you think what she's suggesting is smart?"

My breath hitches, and I know he can feel it. I duck my chin against a sudden swell of confusing emotions. "No," I try to say with confidence. I fail utterly. "Yeah," I admit, but that doesn't sound wholly true either. "Look, if there's an Archon resistance out there, sponsored by the Corinthians, we can't sit by and do nothing. *You* can't sit by—not after you ran."

The dig at the insecurity he confessed last night is a cheap tactic, but I feel it work—Gal's spine goes a notch stiffer under my arm. "There could be an . . . *opportunity,* I guess," he suggests carefully.

There's a note in his tone that reminds me of the way he dismantled the Cutter woman—imperial, sharp-edged, and utterly ruthless. An ache blooms in my chest. I don't know the boy I have my arm around. Not the way I thought I did. Today I saw what Gal is capable of. What his mother's blood makes him capable of. Does it matter that he spent his entire academy career theorizing about dismantling the violence of his legacy if in the moment he defaults to the vicious impulses that define his line?

At least it seems to be eating him up inside. There's a cosmic storm in Gal's expression as he stares out over this unfamiliar city. The summer wind tugs at his unruly hair, the late-afternoon sun deepening the shadows carved by the purse of his lips. He looks severe and regal, and my heart aches, urging me to pull him closer.

I wish I'd tried to keep him here, to enact that whim I had before this all went sideways. Keep him from his blood's potential and the way he cut that woman until the fight drained out of her. Keep him harmless. I wish I'd realized he was never harmless to start.

What I saw today could be just the beginning, but the more he flexes that merciless edge, the easier it'll be for him to use it. I know what it's like to walk down that path, feeling as if you have no other route. I know how hard it is to pull yourself back from it once that instinct is ingrained. And I know how easy it is to give in to it when you tell yourself it's the only way to survive. I suppress a flinch at the thought of how viciously *I* fought today—how much I want to forget where that came from. I wasn't raised to feel the give of a skull under my fists, but I have, knowing all the while how disappointed my parents would have been to see me reduced to such violence.

Gal's parents probably would have applauded.

If we go to the Archon resistance, he'll run right up against the ledge of that opportunity. I want to believe in the way it seems to tear him up inside. But his duty to his blood is everything.

My stomach twists. "We can try it. We'll strike out and see what's there for us. And if it goes sideways, I've carried you out of worse."

Gal's gaze drops to the streets, his eyes tracking a few pedestrians far below. "Someday there's going to be a time when you can't," he says, swallowing like the words are caught in his throat. "You keep making all these sacrifices for me. I can't possibly live up to them."

"It's not an *exchange,* dumbass."

"I know," Gal says sharply. "I just don't . . . I don't want to be the terms that decide your life's path, Ettian."

It's a little late for that, but I don't dare say it. "Let's focus on our path out of this mess," I tell him. "And speaking of messes . . ." I tighten my grip on his shoulder, crushing him against my side. "The *rut* were you thinking, telling Wen that you're my boyfriend?" I snarl in his ear.

"Sorry."

"No ap—"

"Shut up. Look, I was hoping it'd get her off our case. No one wants to be a third wheel, right?"

The comment stings, but not for the reasons he might assume. If Gal understood anything about what it's like to be out on the streets, he'd know that being a third wheel is the difference between a groggy, paranoid stupor and a solid night of sleep, between a mewling, weak stomach and enough stolen food for everyone. I sigh. "Well, it looks like we're stuck with our third wheel for the time being. Which means we're stuck in this charade, unless you want to explain to her why we've suddenly decided to call it quits."

Gal grimaces. "She's too smart. She's going to figure out something's up."

"Hey, you're a good liar." I jostle his shoulder, and his arm tightens around my waist.

"I suppose. And if we're going to march right up to an Archon resistance base and try to dismantle it from the inside," he says, leaning so close that his breath ghosts over my cheek, "I'm going to need an excuse to whisper in your ear."

Stop that, I groan internally. One way or another, this adventure is doing its damnedest to kill me.

When we make our way back across the roof, we find Wen lounging in the shade of her umbrella with her head propped up on my pack. She cracks her unburned eye open as our footsteps approach. "Decision made?" she asks, sitting up.

Gal bends to scoop up his own pack. "If you think the resistance can help, lead the way."

Wen scrambles to her feet, swinging the umbrella up onto her shoulder. She kicks my pack at me, and I flinch, thinking of the precious cargo buried in it. "Better get a move on, then. Daylight's wasting, and it's a long way by rooftop." She turns on her heel and strolls off toward the edge.

Gal leans close and hisses, "Is she serious? I can't tell if she's serious."

Wen snaps her umbrella shut, tucks it under her arm, and takes a running leap, landing crouched on the next building over.

I sigh. "She's serious. Let's go."

CHAPTER 14

TRAVERSING THE ROOFTOPS of Isla's north side isn't the worst way to travel, but it wears me down in ways not even the academy's drills could have prepared me for. My shoulders ache from my pack, and after a certain point, I feel like there's no way I'll be able to make the jumps from building to building. Gal flags beside me. Wen, as always, skips on ahead.

"There's a monorail that goes straight to the base," she explains while we're bent over, catching our breaths. "But with the Cutters on alert, we're better off waiting until tomorrow morning to catch it." I glare, and she shrugs. "They're ruthless, but they sure aren't morning people."

So as the sun settles on the city's horizon, Wen leads us to a cache. Tucked under a loose metal plate on the roof of an apartment building is a ratty spare blanket, a can of some variety of beans, and a few spare clothes—though I'm not sure some of the shredded scraps qualify.

Gal and I exchange a glance, but Wen's already wrapping herself securely in the tattered blanket, leaning back under the overhang that protects her makeshift hidey-hole.

Don't feel sorry for her, I tell myself over and over again. *Once you feel sorry for her, you start getting attached, and once you start getting attached you start letting your guard down. And once you start letting your guard down, she slits your throat and Gal's with that goddamn umbrella and takes everything you carry.*

Gal crouches next to her, rooting in his bag. He pulls out a ration pack and hands it to her so carelessly that it hits me all at once how unfamiliar he is with hunger. Wen holds the pack loosely, glancing between it and Gal like she's not sure if he actually meant to give it to her. He doesn't notice her hesitation, already digging back in for another meal.

Wen's gaze flicks to me. I don't know what to do with it. As I crouch and settle under the overhang with her, I give her a nod that tries to be encouraging and probably ends up condescending. She purses her lips.

"So," Gal says as he rips his own ration pack open. "We rest here for the night?"

Wen nods. She sets aside the can of beans and pinches the plastic in her hands carefully, tugging it open with unexpected daintiness, like she means to save it for later.

My heart sinks at the sight. I pull my own dinner out, my stomach rumbling. I haven't eaten since the meager breakfast I stuffed down my throat this morning before I set off to buy a ship. The ration pack doesn't offer much in the way of flavor. The meat-based mush inside is meant to be reheated, and the crackers that accompany it are dry and tasteless—probably manufactured somewhere in the Archon territories. Still, it's difficult to resist the urge to inhale it all at once.

Wen doesn't. She eats like the food's about to disappear and licks the plastic tray when she's done, draining the last bits of juice into her mouth. When she catches Gal staring, she makes a face at him, and he laughs like he's charmed.

"Tell me about yourself," he says in between careful, moderated bites of his own rations. "How'd you get into this mess in the first place?"

Wen hesitates, turning the tray over and over in her hands. "Destiny," she says at last, leaning back and tossing the container aside. "Born for it. You know how it is."

"You're going to have to be a lot more specific than that."

Wen bares her teeth. "Nothing on any world for free, prettyboy."

"I'd say you're getting one hell of a favor if you're using us as a ticket into the resistance."

She considers it. "If you ask around these streets, you'll get the story easily. But no one tells it right, so I guess that's up to me."

Gal's self-satisfied smirk is barely a flicker on his lips, but I pay a little too much attention to them to miss it. I let my own lazy smile spread, settling against the wall behind us. Wen closes her eyes, drawing a deep breath like she's gathering herself in. When she opens them, we both lean in.

"It all starts with my mother." Some of her braid has fallen out, and she tucks it back behind her ear. Her voice is low and filled with snarled edges, like she's used it far more than she's used to. "Sixteen years ago, Mom was at the top of her game. She ran a crew called the Burners, she'd carved her place in these streets, and she felt secure enough in her territory and her place at the top to have me."

Wen's smile goes soft. "She raised me for my bloodright like a proper heir. Kept me at her knee whenever she held court, even though I was so young that most of it went over my head. She wanted me to take her place someday—wanted to give me the whole city. She'd tuck me into bed each night with that promise. And for eight years, she kept me safe, ran her little empire, and pushed her borders. She wanted the whole north side. She should have gotten it."

My gaze flicks to Gal. Already my palms are sweating. Already I want him to stop her from saying what comes next. She shouldn't have to relive it for his entertainment. But Gal doesn't know what she's about to go through. Gal's parents are still alive.

"When I was eight years old, the north side cracked open. It was summer, and everything . . . boiled. I was locked in a dark, cool room for most of the day, waiting for Mom to come off the streets. She'd always sweep in with her hair plastered to her face, her body armor stinking from whatever she'd sweated and whomever she'd gutted."

Wen breaks off, frowning. The distant noise of traffic fills the missing space her voice leaves, and it takes her a while to find her next words.

"I never thought I'd miss that smell."

Gal looks like he's on the edge of asking a question, but I roll my foot, nudging his hip and giving him the slightest shake of my head. She doesn't need to say any more.

"When a boss falls, whoever struck them down snaps up their people. Their lieutenants, their foot soldiers, even the kids who do the running. So when Mom went, I went to Dago Korsa. There wasn't anywhere else for me to go anyway—I had no papers, couldn't make any other kinds of arrangements. It's a rusted thing that I'm actually *grateful* he's not worse. Not the sort that puts kids to work doing . . . well, what you hear about kids being forced to do sometimes. Dago Korsa uses the littlest morsels as an information network. Had us sweeping the streets with open ears, begging for our meals while trying to wheedle information out of anyone we could. And I can look back at that and think it wasn't that bad, but . . ."

But it was the end of the world. It was the lowest thing, bending to serve the man who'd stolen her bloodright, stolen her entire reason for *being*. Who'd slaughtered her mother. Who ran the streets she'd been born to inherit. I close my eyes.

"Korsa knew he had to watch out for me. I learned fast not to scramble any information I ran—the punishment was always far worse than anything they gave the other kids."

Her fingers tap a series of scars that run along the back of her shoulder.

"I guess all of that was to make it seem generous when an apprentice mechanic position opened up in one of his chop shops and he *graciously* suggested I should be the one to fill it. And it worked, for a time. I was content there. I felt like I was carving my own place. Stopped thinking I was owed stuff because of my mother's blood. I got good at tricking out Cutter junkers, and nobody beat me if I screwed up. Korsa's play for my loyalty worked. Until it didn't."

She stares at her feet. Her shoes are nearly worn through, covered in scuff marks, her laces tattered at the ends.

"A ship I worked on crashed during an important run. Boss was on board and everything. I didn't make the mistake that brought it down, but that didn't matter. Korsa knew exactly how it read, and he leaned hard into what he could do to me because of it. He tossed me out of the chop shop and reassigned me to a Cutter lieutenant with a known temper. And, well. Ettian knows this part. The lieutenant snapped on me one day and stuck my face in a Solstice's tailpipe. That was a month ago. And honestly, it was exactly what I needed."

Gal makes a strangled noise. He hasn't had a chance to get used to her flippancy. The burned corner of Wen's lips lifts.

"I spent half my life owned by the guy who killed my mom and took what should have been mine. I wasn't going to let him take a second more from me. I ran. Healed. Built a few caches like this throughout the city. Kept out of the Cutters' reaches for as long as I could. Tried to muster every drop of my mother's blood, to make something of myself without playing into the hands of her killers. And then I jacked one of Korsa's skipships. I knew it would get shot down if I tried to leave the city in it, but I figured if I could slice it up, make it unrecognizable enough to sneak into the dealers' alley, and milk every last bit of cash I could get out of it, maybe I'd pull together a way to get out of here. And hey, it's on its way to working, right?"

My brow furrows. "I thought you wanted to get back at Korsa. Why leave?"

Wen laughs. "I've seen so many people go up against him. It always ends with them in pieces. There's no winning when Korsa controls the game board. I need to get clear of his turf. Take my time, use my blood, see what I can do without him constantly breathing down my neck. And then I'll come back and annihilate him."

Gal and I blink.

"It's a loose plan. Needs workshopping. But hey, if this thing with the resistance pays off, I've got time." She notes our blank looks and claps her hands. "Next question?"

Gal nods. "Was your mother as mad as you?"

Wen gives him a feral grin. "If the stories are true, Mom made what I do look like child's play."

I'm having a few second thoughts about dragging the Umber heir to this lawless borderworld city. From a distance, I thought that the Corinthian rim's loose frontier infrastructure would make it easy to slip in unnoticed. Up close, I see the way that same looseness has allowed crime to run this city unchecked. In a way, Isla reminds me of what Trost could have become after the bombardment if Umber hadn't stepped in to pick up the pieces and flush out the riffraff. There were plenty of people back then who saw the broken city as nothing but the pieces of their future kingdom—people I avoided at all costs. I knew bloodright rule would come back to the city, and I wasn't about to get caught in the trash when it got taken out.

But bloodright rule has never touched the Corinthian Empire. Their emprex is appointed by a democratically elected council, and a similar system trickles down to the lower echelons of planetary and city government. It all sounds very egalitarian—and it seems to have done wonders for Isla's transit infrastructure—but its weakness is made readily apparent in how fiercely the mob has taken root in this city.

Better for us to get clear soon.

Gal crumples up his ration pack and tosses it behind him. With a wary look toward Wen, he clambers around to my other side, dragging his pack with him. Isla's glow cuts through his rumpled hair as he settles next to me. The open night sky is leaching away the summer heat fast, but not fast enough to calm the nervous sweat that prickles across my skin as he scoots closer.

"So that's it, then?" Wen asks, peering around me.

"That'll do." Gal reaches into his pack and pulls out a jacket, tugging it over himself. "Wake me if they find us," he mutters into my arm as he slumps against me.

I roll my eyes, resisting the urge to shove him away. Wen gives me a look, but I don't know her well enough to read it. "He's had a long day," I say. A weak excuse, but it's enough for now. Wen slumps back against the wall, folding her blanket tighter around herself as she stares out toward the downtown. The lights glimmer in her eyes. From this angle, I can't see her burned side at all, just her pitted, uneven skin smoothed out by the darkness. "Sorry," I offer.

She keeps staring, but her lips tighten. I think she's done talking for tonight.

Which stings, because I've finally figured out the only question I want to ask her. *How?* I want to whisper, low enough that Gal can't hear. How did she do it? How did she keep a thirst for revenge alive for eight years? How did she keep her fire when her enemies literally tried to scorch it out of her? Listening to her story made me realize how inadequate all of my excuses are. How did I end up broken, empty, and twisted into an Umber soldier when she's still fighting, even though she's the only one left who carries her cause in her heart?

I need to figure it out. And that means that we're sticking with her for as long as that takes.

So I sit between them. Gal on my left, pretending to sleep— I know he hasn't dropped off yet, because he always twitches when he does. And Wen at my right, her eyes fixed on distant heights. I wish I could dip into both of their heads. Know exactly what's causing Gal's brow to wrinkle as he tries to slow his breathing. Feel the same things Wen does as she looks out over the rooftops she was born to own. I don't know what forces conspired to bring me here to this moment, perched between the two of them, but I think the god of this system must be playing a cruel joke on me.

On my left, power without fathom in the fragile body of a boy. On my right, a nightmare of a girl who should be ruling these streets. And in the middle, there's me.

And I know a little of what it is to be both of them. To leave your life behind. To watch helplessly as the world turns over. To fight from the bottom to carve a place in the new order. My mind circles and circles around the places we intersect, the way everything we've ever done has brought us to this quiet rooftop and the three of us drifting off under an open summer night.

All the while, I push away the inescapable fact that one of us is destined to rule the galaxy.

I sleep, but not really. My consciousness comes and goes in flickers. More than once, a loud, distant crack or the rumble of a nearby engine jolts me fully awake, sending my heart hammering back to my early days on the streets, to the muffled thunder of buildings the bombardment hadn't quite finished with collapsing in the night. Gal slumbers on, undisturbed, but when I look to my right, Wen's watching like she already knows why that instinct is locked so deeply inside me. When our eyes meet, there's a flicker of understanding between us. A moment where we recognize some deep, ingrained *sameness*.

Then we both close our eyes and drop off again.

As the sky starts to gray with the oncoming morning, Wen slips off, muttering something about finding a convenience store with a bathroom. My anxiety spikes the second she drops out of sight down the closest fire escape. If she ducks out on us now, we're basically humped.

Rather than sit here and worry alone, I nudge Gal awake. He's shifted during the night, tucking himself under the warmth of my arm, and he startles at my touch, rolling back to reclaim the distance between us once he sees that Wen is gone. "Already?" he groans, even though he's the one who managed to sleep the longest.

"Wen's scouting a bathroom."

"Oh, good. My mouth tastes like rotten meat," Gal says as he rolls onto his back.

"Tragic." I chuckle, tilting my head up. The ship traffic above the city is sparse, the travel lines barely drawn as speeders trace their vectors several thousand feet above our heads. "What does she want from us?" I ask.

Gal shrugs. "A fast pass off-world seems straightforward enough, doesn't it?"

"Not when that fast pass means marching right up to an Archon resistance base."

"Honestly, I've warmed to it. I'll take it over another night on a rooftop, that's for sure." Gal stretches, twisting until his spine pops. "And you still think it's our best option, right?"

There's a layer to his question that I wish I couldn't notice. He's wondering if I'm still with him.

When I don't answer immediately, his face falls. "I know I'm asking a lot. I never thought it'd go this far. And look, if you want to drop the fake relationship—if that's too hard—"

I shake my head. "You're right. We need an excuse for privacy."

"I . . ." He groans, pinching his brow. "I feel like I'm driving you away. And nothing is worth that—if I lose you, I have nothing left."

But you will, I think. "But you won't," I tell him.

His weary, sleep-glazed eyes turn up to find mine. And even though his breath reportedly tastes like rotten meat, for a dizzying instant, a tug in my chest reminds me how easy it would be to lean over and close the distance between us.

"Should get moving," I mutter, and the cold truth of that statement is enough to dislodge the dangerous moment.

CHAPTER 15

THE MONORAIL STATION is nearly empty before dawn. A few people wander the platforms, and even fewer wait out on the farthest one, where our train is due to arrive. We blend in well among them—most people outbound from the city at this hour are coming off night shifts.

I stretch out on a bench with Wen curled up beside me while Gal orders tickets at a kiosk. She wears a hoodie Gal loaned her, keeping the burned side of her face tucked safely in its shadow. "You watch him like he's going to disappear," she notes, then pulls a face when I scowl at her. "Just saying. I know from experience. Sometimes when you come up from nothing, it makes you hold on too tight."

I purse my lips. With Gal at a distance, it's tempting—*too* tempting—to let Wen know how much I understand her. How much we've lived along similar lines.

And she must sense it right away, because she averts her eyes and asks, "How long?"

My breath catches, and my eyes fix on the rail. Better there than on Gal, which will make the gulf between us feel wider, or on Wen, who's already too close for comfort. "Two years. The war rolled through when I was ten and took my parents with it. Finally got taken in and cleaned up by a charity program at twelve."

Wen lets out a low whistle. "What took them so long?"

"Reconstruction. Regime changes don't happen overnight, especially not in bombarded cities. Social work was out the window until they wrung out Trost and let the war dry off it. The Umber Empire's efficient about conquest, but they're not *that* efficient. They couldn't pull me out of that hell any sooner." I break off, frowning. For five solid years, I thought I didn't have the words to talk about this stuff. But the words came flooding out like I had them locked and loaded this entire time.

For Wen.

She reaches out, patting my arm like she's not quite sure how to make it comforting. I close my eyes, haul in a deep breath, and release it with a deeper sigh. I don't want her pity, but we don't always want the things we need, and I can't deny that something about letting even that little bit of information out has made my chest feel a thousand times lighter. It's a scarcer luxury than any imperial metal or stone, feeling understood.

It hits me like boltfire—I'm glad she's here. I went to that shipyard for a way off this planet, and instead I found a mirror with a half-burned face. Someone who knows what it's like to have your life pulled out from underneath you, to scrape yourself together from what's left and keep surviving. "Understood" is only part of it— I was *alone* before and never realized how much that hurt.

We hold the same burden between us, and I can't believe how freeing it is to share the load.

"Train should be here in a few minutes," Gal says, and my eyes snap open. He perches himself on the bench between us, handing us each a scrap of paper. My stomach twists as I see the name of our destination, something heavy and low thudding inside me like a mallet on a drum.

Henrietta Base.

They named it after our fallen empress.

I choke back my emotion before either of them can pick up on it.

———

I don't relax until the monorail's cleared the suburbs and broken out into the open far beyond Isla's city limits. I lean my forehead against the window, watching as the greenery blurs past me and trying to soothe the unsettling feeling of traveling so fast so smoothly on a rail. Gal naps against my shoulder, and Wen's folded in on herself in the seat across from us, pulling the strings of the hoodie so tight that nothing but her half-burned nose is visible through the opening.

I doze, but don't sleep. Even though I'm bruised and battered, even though the only people in this car are a little old man and a mother with a baby strapped to her chest, even though I probably need it far more than either Gal or Wen. My brain keeps on churning, and the smooth hum of the monorail isn't soothing it.

Two and a half years. Two and a half years we've known each other, and he's never known the part of me that Wen was able to extract with one day and two words.

And I thought I knew Gal too. I mean, Gal loves rainy days more than sunny ones, because the noise drowns out the world around him, and it helps him clear his head. And also because he doesn't have to fly on rainy days—the academy never wants to risk Vipers in uncertain weather. I used to be so proud, knowing that about him. That I could look to the sky when I woke up and know what he was thinking.

I thought knowing him in that way would be enough.

Now I know that the heir to the largest galactic empire history has ever seen brushed his teeth in a convenience store bathroom's scum-ridden sink this morning. I know the storm that brews in his eyes as he dismantles his enemies. And I know that he's never going to understand what it's like to live on the streets. He might claim to after last night, but it's not the same thing in the slightest. Gal's always had a safety net. We had a plan, gear, food, clean clothes, weapons—even if one of those weapons is a suspiciously sturdy umbrella. We're well-off, and it kills me a little knowing this is probably the most destitute Gal emp-Umber will ever be.

The more I turn it over, the more I realize that I cracked open in an instant for Wen because one look at her tells me she's been through the same kind of hell. When I tell her that I spent two years sifting through the ashes of Trost, she doesn't have to *imagine* what that might entail. She knows about the cold nights, the hard choices, the moments you have to cover your ears or close your eyes or tighten your fist around that rock and swing harder. I don't have to worry about her judgment. I'm terrified of Gal's.

Is it enough to make me want to push him away?

No, I decide before the thought has a chance to settle. No, I have to fight through this. Gal and I only have so much time left, and if there's anything the streets of Trost taught me, it's that the worlds are cruel and friends are fleeting and you've got to hold on to the good things as tight as you can. Maybe if I keep talking to Wen, keep working on it, I'll figure out how to stop hiding this part of myself from Gal before we're out of time.

Our paths were always destined to diverge, and diverge they will. Sooner rather than later.

The monorail hits a wide turn that pushes my forehead into the window and Gal into my shoulder. I shift my arm around him without looking, my gaze fixed on the line of the tracks as they carve through the landscape, speeding us closer to the moment when I lose him for good.

When the automated voice announces our arrival at the base station, Wen snaps awake all at once, clawing the hood off her face as she rolls off the seat and onto the train's floor. Gal jerks up at the thump, blinking. "Already?"

He casts a curious glance at the arm I've draped around his shoulders, and I withdraw it sheepishly, bolting to my feet in time for the train to brake and nearly send me hurtling into Wen's seat before I can grab a handhold.

We're *here,* and I have no idea what we're supposed to say to the resistance to bring them over to our side. This movement is born of the same resentment that sparked the Archon loyalists within our academy into an assassination attempt that we barely escaped. These are patriots devoted to the resurrection of an empire seven years dead.

These are my people. They made it out safe, abandoning me to a hungry ruin. They've had the luxury of sticking to their convictions. But the fact remains—they kept their cause alive. I let mine wither and die.

I don't know how I can face them.

"Don't go all wild-eyed on me, flyboy," Wen says, popping to her feet with the assistance of her umbrella. "Gonna need you to appear calm, cool, and collected. You, too, prettyboy." She cuffs Gal on the shoulder, and his eyes narrow at her.

I bite back a snort.

As the monorail's speed fades, we make our way to the sliding doors, swinging from handhold to handhold until the train comes to rest. I peer out the narrow window by the door, fidgeting with the straps on my bag. We've arrived at the base's support town, a strip of small businesses flanked by suburbs that house the personnel not cleared for lodging on base proper. In the gaps between buildings, I spy the fence that marks Henrietta Base's perimeter.

The sight of the town ratchets my anxiety up another tick. It's so developed, so *large*. Wen knows nothing about the resistance's actual numbers, but from the size of its support, it's already far more established than I anticipated. I thought there would be a ragtag army, pop-up tents, stolen shuttles.

Gal peers over my shoulder and says exactly what I'm thinking. "It looks like the academy."

Wen leads the way off the train, through the station, and onto streets that are prickling with familiarity, lined with supply shops, groceries, and even a little cantina with its shutters down. She keeps her hood drawn, which isn't helping my nerves. Why would she still hide her face? There's no way Dago Korsa's presence extends to a small town a hundred miles from Isla. But something has her on edge. Or she's planning something.

Either way, I don't like it. We're drawing attention with all our attempts at not drawing attention. Gal and I are haggard and stubbly, dressed in day-old clothes, and Wen's ragged pants and hooded face aren't doing us any favors. None of us look like we fit in here, and as a passing man dressed in fatigues tracks me with a suspicious eye, my spine gets stiffer. "Wen?" I growl through my teeth.

She drops back, slotting herself between me and Gal. "Problem?"

"Several. How exactly do you plan to get us on the base?"

"The same way everyone gets on the base," she mutters, leaning up so I can catch the words. "We go in a shuttle."

Wen tips one finger toward our destination, a distant lot where rows of simple transporters are parked end-to-end—Corinthian in manufacture, judging by their iron trimmings. The ships are dusty and roughened from use, but they're well made. Intimidatingly so. The resistance has resources. The support of the Corinthian emprex themselves. And if this is what they use for jaunts into town, I'm not sure I'm ready to face what they keep on the base.

Gal catches my eye over the top of Wen's head. His eyebrows lift, his eyes bugging out as if to say, *Seriously?*

I agree. "Wen, are you saying they'll let us hitch a ride on one of the shuttles when it goes back to the base?"

In the shadow of her hood, I catch the flash of teeth. I know exactly what it means.

"You're kidding."

"Give me a better plan, flyboy. The soldiers in town can't transport anyone without ID. Base policy."

"Hold on, are you saying you've tried to join up with the resistance already?"

Wen shrugs.

"And I'm guessing this was after the whole . . ." I motion vaguely at the left side of her face.

"Who better to shelter me from Dago Korsa than an army, right? Except, turns out this army needs a goddamn ID card just like any other potentially useful thing in this empire. *But* with you two in hand, if we can get onto the base . . ."

"Tell me we're doing something else," Gal groans.

Wen's face lights up when I shake my head. "Sorry, Gal," I say, eyes fixed on a shuttle that looks like it will handle like a god-given dream. I let my hunger devour my nervousness. Let myself dip into the mentality that makes Wen a living nightmare. "We're jacking a ship."

Five minutes later, Gal and I are in a full-blown argument on the edge of the shipyard. "It's reckless," he says. "Irresponsible. We're *better than this,* Ettian."

I cast a nervous glance at the sole pilot on the lot. He sits on the folded-out steps of his shuttle, a joint dangling from his fingers, and his eyes are fixed intently on us. "Keep it down," I warn. "We're drawing attention."

"I could punch you in the face right now—how's that for drawing attention?" he spits through his teeth.

"You like my face too much to do that."

Gal lets out a bark of laughter, still pacing back and forth. "You asshole. I thought you were on my side."

"First of all, I can't be on your side for everything. Just because we're best friends doesn't mean we're the same person. I think this is our best option. You disagree."

"And you should *listen to me,*" Gal snarls, turning on me with so much fervor that I take a step back. He collapses the distance between us, going up on his toes to get right in my face.

"Why should I listen to you?" I give him my smuggest smile.

"Because I'm the—"

"Careful," I warn. Gal's eyes flick to the smoking pilot, who's watching with even more intensity now.

"Because I'm the brains of this outfit, how about that?"

"The brains, really?"

"Someone has to be!" he shouts.

The shriek of boltfire from across the lot cuts off my retort, punctuated by a soft thud. We both glance over to where the shuttle pilot slumps in the dirt with Wen standing over him, my stolen blaster smoking in her hands. "All clear," she says, waving us over and holstering her gun.

"How'd we do?" I ask as we jog up.

Wen grapples with the pilot's unconscious body, dragging him up the steps by the shoulders of his fatigues. "Gal, you overact. Try to tone it down next time—you push it past the realm of the believable. Ettian, your dialogue is so generic—you're just throwing out questions that egg him on. Not super engaging."

I grab the pilot's legs and help her hoist him up into the cockpit. "But we gave you the time you needed?"

"That and more. I wanted to see how far you guys would take it."

"Can we focus?" Gal hisses, clambering up after us as he glances back across the lot. "All clear, but the noise is going to draw attention. We gotta move."

I turn to find Wen perched in the pilot's seat, throwing switches. The unconscious pilot's joint is pinched in the corner of her smile, and the look in her eyes is verging on that dangerously manic glint she wore when I first met her. She glances up at me, letting out a smoky breath that clogs the air. Gods of all systems, Corinthian weed is not messing around.

"Absolutely not," I tell her, and grab her by the shoulders, dragging her out of the seat as she kicks and twists and fights.

"Come on," Wen yelps. "I told you—I'm a pilot."

"I'm not taking any chances." I shrug off my pack and dive into the pilot's seat before she can scramble back in.

"Drove the tram fine yesterday."

"*It was on a wire*. Gal, how're we looking?"

"One second," he says, jamming his fingers against the door controls. "We've got incoming—soldiers who heard the shot. All on foot. We good to go?"

I glance up at Wen, who blows another puff of noxious-smelling smoke in my face. "Rewired permissions on the landing gear, and I think I did what I needed with the engines."

"You *think*?"

She gestures to the controls as if to say, *Try me*.

I spur the engines. A powerful rumble overtakes the ship as they spin up, and my own manic grin breaks loose. The transporter is no Viper, but it runs with smooth confidence, a far cry from the *Ruttin' Hell*. I punch the thrusters, and my stomach swoops as the shuttle takes off.

Gal slips into the copilot's seat, and a second later the navigation flickers to life. "We're two miles away from base proper," he says, tapping the location with a finger. "Want to see how fast we can burn them?"

I wheel our nose onto our vector. "Hey, Wen? Make sure our guest doesn't bump his head. And put that damn thing out before you hotbox the cockpit."

There's shuffling behind me, followed by a vaguely affirmative grunt. I glance back to find that Wen has one hand wound in the webbing overhead meant to be used as a handhold and the other fisted in the pilot's jacket. She lets the joint drop from her lips and drives her heel into it, giving me a nod. "Punch it," she says.

I oblige her. The transporter leaps forward, sinking me deep into my seat as we streak over the town and toward the towering fence crowned in barbed wire that marks the border of the base's territory. Just for fun, I let us dip down until we clear it with mere feet to spare. It's been two days since I last flew and over a week since I last flew something *good*. I'm not letting this go to waste.

We're barely forty feet past the fence when an incoming communication chimes. "Shuttle Thirty-Seven, this is Henrietta Base. Your report time was noon. Please state the reason for your unscheduled approach."

I nod to Gal, and he picks up the line. "Base, this is Shuttle Thirty-Seven. One of our guys passed out. We're bringing him back so medical can have a look at him."

There's a brief pause, the static crackle of an open line. All three of us stare intently at the dash.

"Base to Shuttle Thirty-Seven, who is this?"

"Heavens and hells," I mutter.

"Shuttle Thirty-Seven to Base, I'm gonna be honest with you," Gal says. "We're out for an audience with the leadership of the Archon resistance, and I realize this isn't the best way to start a relationship—"

"Where is the authorized pilot, Lieutenant Briggs?"

Gal glances back at the pilot, squinting at the nametag pinned to the front of his uniform. "Lieutenant Briggs is aboard, but . . . indisposed. Please don't shoot anything at us. He doesn't deserve this."

Wen giggles, swaying. I hitch the shuttle up with a burst of the attitude thrusters, and she nearly topples over. We streak across an open plain, running parallel to a well-worn dirt road. I keep us close to the ground, but not too close.

On the horizon, I catch the distant forms of low, flat buildings. Hangars. Dormitories. The silhouette is different, but the sensation is the same. It feels like the academy.

It feels like coming home.

But the feeling doesn't stick. Dread builds in me as we get closer and closer. This place is *big*. Bigger than I ever could have fathomed. This is what the Archon-loyal have been doing while I gave myself over to our conquerors and became a soldier in their hands. Seven years of work went into this establishment, and I don't know if I'm ready to face what that means about me and my loyalty, not only to the Umber Empire but to its heir himself.

My hands fidget on the controls, my fingers tapping out a soft beat where neither Gal nor Wen can see.

"Base to Shuttle Thirty-Seven, we're authorizing a landing pad for you. If you surrender there, we'll take you in peacefully."

"Understood," Gal says, and closes the line. A moment later, the navigation flickers with a beacon laid over the resistance compound. He slumps back in the copilot's chair, running his hands over his eyes.

Wordlessly I reach over and lay a hand on his shoulder. His fingers find mine, and my heartbeat stutters at how natural it is, how natural it shouldn't be. With Wen in the cockpit, there's nothing I can say to comfort Gal directly, but maybe this is enough—the quiet, unwavering reassurance that I'm here, I'm watching out for him, and no matter where he goes, I'll be there to defend him.

Even if it's wrapped in layers upon layers of deception.

Even if it can never last.

CHAPTER 16

I'M THE FIRST one out the door. With the unfortunate Lieutenant Briggs propped up against me, I stagger down the steps and onto the tarmac, which is already boiling in the summer sun. Eleven soldiers wait for us, and a flicker of relief lights in me when I see that none of them have their guns drawn. Two approach, and I hand Briggs off to them.

"It was a simple stunner bolt," I say. "Should be up in a matter of minutes."

They nod, but neither of them look particularly grateful. I take a step back, lifting my hands with my palms turned out. Gal descends, tugging Wen after him. She's doing her best not to look stoned, her brow furrowed in concentration as she wrestles with the smile threatening to break free from her lips.

Stumbling out of a stolen shuttle, flanked by the haggard and the high. This is how I come back to my people.

I scan our surroundings, checking the roofs of the buildings around us for sniper barrels, but all I see is how many buildings there are. How well made everything is. The compound may be hewn from Corinthian granite, but the soldiers' uniforms are decorated with patches woven in green and silver. Emerald and platinum. The Archon Crown's metal and stone.

Gal's mouth opens. And in the suspended seconds between him drawing the breath he needs to steel himself and the moment he starts to speak, something crumbles inside me. I feel the rumble and drop, the wall giving way, and the next thing I know, I'm stepping in front of him.

"We're deserters from the Umber Imperial Academy on the planet Rana," I announce. I have to yell to be heard across the tarmac. "We have useful intelligence about the academy and its defense of the former Archon interior, which we're willing to exchange for assistance with returning to our families."

"Ettian, what are you doing?" Gal hisses in my ear.

"Starting things off on the right foot," I reply, but suddenly I'm not so sure about that. Gal's the negotiator. I just fly the ships. It's not my place, and yet I all but shoved him out of the way to take point.

"Hold up—that girl isn't a deserter," one of the soldiers says as she steps out in front of the group. "That's the thieving urchin we threw out three weeks ago. She's been warned to stay away from this base."

Wen shrinks behind us. She grabs the hem of my shirt and holds tight, her gaze flicking anxiously back and forth, absorbing every potential threat and every potential hiding place.

"She's with us," I say. "And if you want the information we carry, you'll treat her as one of us."

Gal's shoulders stiffen.

The woman looks skeptical, and Wen's obvious state isn't helping. I don't blame the soldier. She's sworn to an uprising based on seven years of hurt, and she doesn't have time for kids playing games.

I remember one of my earliest lessons. The last-ditch way to save a crumbling ruse. I kick out another wall inside me—one of the old, stalwart things that stands between me and my younger self. I let the desperation show in my eyes. "Please," I say, my voice a tad hoarser than it needs to be. I drum my fingers against my palms, tapping out the triumph rhythm I've kept buried under my skin for seven years. "Rana was my homeworld. If there's even the slightest chance we can restore it, I want to do everything I can."

The soldiers soften. Sympathetic smiles creep onto the corners of a few mouths. The woman at the fore keeps herself in check, but there's something dangerously close to pride in her eyes. "We'll escort you to a holding cell," she says. "Once we get clearance from the higher-ups, we'll see what we can do."

I nod. The relief I show is genuine. But as the soldiers flank us and lead us off the tarmac and toward one of the squat granite buildings, Gal catches my eye. His face is set with an unfamiliar look—or at least, one I've never seen directed at me.

He looks furious. But worse than that, he looks suspicious.

In the cell, I lose track of time. We wait in silence, unsure whether the room is bugged. Gal simmers with pursed lips, Wen leans against the wall for support, and I pace until finally the door opens. Four soldiers beckon us out and escort us down the hall to a narrow interrogation room. Three chairs wait on one side of the table, and a bare bulb illuminates the space, casting everything in sharp relief. Wen's eyes are still blown out, and Gal helps her into a chair, making sure she's steady before he sits.

I stay standing, thinking. Three chairs—none bolted down. The door has the sort of handle that could be jammed by one of them. The glass on the two-way mirror is probably reinforced, but the ceiling tiles are accessible if we stack a chair on the table. A slight smile twists my lips as I remember the day Hanji realized she could disappear from the restrooms via the dropped ceiling and reappear a few rooms over to the terror of everyone inside. Looks like the same trick might apply here.

Only once I'm confident I know the way to escape this room do I sink into the chair on Gal's other side. I don't miss that he's taken the middle seat, placing himself at the center of this negotiation. He's not giving me a chance to take the lead again.

He's an imperial, and he's born for control. In the face of his enemy, he can't forget it.

But when the door opens to admit a walking ghost, control goes out the window. I jolt backward, Gal nearly stands, and Wen outs herself as a Corinthian by simply blinking.

He's tall and broad, the kind of man you imagine when history mentions a great general. His olive skin is weathered but unscarred, and he wears his hair long—longer than I remember—and bound back in braids. His uniform is trim and fitted, betraying his heavily muscled frame with every movement.

And he's supposed to be dead.

"General Iral," I whisper.

Maxo Iral gives us an enigmatic smile as he closes the door behind him. "In the flesh, against all odds," he says, approaching the table. Even in this cramped room, his voice resonates like the thunder of an imperial skin drum. "Don't believe everything you see on the news."

Five years ago, Iral's execution was broadcast across the entire galaxy. It was the most spectacle surrounding an execution since the Archon imperials ascended the Umber citadel, and for the people of Archon, it matched the devastation of Knightfall. Once again—inevitably, it seemed—we lost our heroes. I was two weeks into my placement in a foster home, and I'd been cutting vegetables in the sink when every screen in the house went live to show the captured general hung on an electrified crucifix before the Imperial Seat.

I brush my thumb over a thin line on the edge of my index finger. The slaughter of the suited knights was the beginning of Archon's downfall, and even though the beheading of the Archon imperials was supposed to have marked the end of the empire, the execution of their most critical general was its immolation. With that final blow, Iva emp-Umber had all but guaranteed the totality of her victory.

But here Iral is, the leader of the resistance. The one we came all this way to see. And everything I was supposed to say falls aside. "How?" I ask. It's the only word my brain feels capable of releasing.

Under the table, Gal's fingernails dig into his palms. His face has frozen as he tries to figure out which reaction to present. Is he a hopeful deserter who's found salvation? An Umber kid suddenly doubting his empire's might? Or a wayward prince coming face-to-face with the greatest threat he's ever known?

I hook my foot around his, trying to divert his attention before he thinks his way into a heart attack.

Iral sighs, folding his arms as he stares down at us. "It's a long and complicated story, but the unfortunate fact is that I had a twin brother. Omat preferred to work from the shadows—few people beyond the imperials themselves knew of his existence. Safer for him, easier for me since he wanted no part of the glory I'd been cultivating. But when the empire fell, neither of us ran. Maybe that was our first mistake."

Gal stares up at Iral unblinkingly. He's shaking—subtly, but the tremors are on the rise. I nudge his foot, and he stills for a moment. *That's it,* I think. *Calm down, asshole, before you blow our cover.*

Iral continues, unaware. "We waged those guerilla wars in the borderworlds for two years, trying to reclaim even the smallest foothold in the name of Archon. But Umber's grasp on the interior was too strong, and we could never muster the resources to match them, especially not once they started stripping the belts for their ships. We'd lost before we began. And as enemies of the Umber Crown, there would be no quiet escape for me or my brother. There was only one gambit that would distract the imperials enough that the rest of our forces could escape to Corinth."

General Iral's eyes glimmer faintly against the bare bulb. Gal's, too, but I can tell that gears are shifting in his head, fear giving way to something closer to wrath. The wrath I've been afraid of ever since I saw what he did to that Cutter woman. I press my toes over his, trying to bring him back.

"It was Omat's plan," Iral says. His tone goes hollow. "He was always braver and smarter. He gave himself and a significant portion of our forces over, let them think they'd caught the great General Iral, and the rest of us slipped into the black. Thanks to his sacrifice, I stand before you today, with a proud army rising from those who took shelter here. So now that I've told you my story, how about you go ahead and tell me yours?"

The question catches Gal off-guard, cracking his composure. His lips curl and his brows lower—I can all but see the mind-numbing anger he grapples. "We're . . . uh."

I blink. Gal never uses filler words.

"Deserters," he blurts. "Umber deserters—well, I'm Umber, but he's not. He was born in Archon, and he got swept into service but he found it unconscionable, and we ran away together. And this is Wen, and she's helping us, and—"

I grab him by the shoulder, digging my fingers into his bones before he has a chance to float us even worse. Gal clamps his jaw shut and slumps back in his chair.

"What he means to say," I start, and Gal tenses under my hand, "is that we're former cadets of the Umber Imperial Academy on Rana, which provides the heart of the Archon territories' defense. And yes, I was pressed into service as an orphan of the Umber conquest, but my true loyalty lies with the Archon Empire."

I shake Gal, and if there were a way for resentment to melt human bones, I think I'd be feeling it now.

"I couldn't have made it out if it wasn't for Gal here." It's not exactly false. "And he never would have let me leave alone. But escaping drew more attention than we anticipated, and now we're wanted across the systems. We're afraid that we won't be able to make it home safely on our own."

Iral lifts an eyebrow. "Why return at all?"

"My family," Gal mutters, his act restored. "My family's in the Umber interior. I just want to get back to them." He bares his heart in those words, splits himself open raw for the general to see.

And the general's been primed for the sight. He's recounted the death of his brother, and if that wound has scarred over, it's torn anew now. His steely gaze drops to the ground, and he heaves a deep breath. I tighten my fingers on Gal's shoulder, and he allows a faint smile while Iral isn't looking.

"My heart goes out to you boys," Iral says. "And I'm grateful beyond measure that you've found your way to us."

I brace for the turn.

"But we can't send you to the Umber interior. Our fight isn't there—it's with our people in the former empire. It's not within our means to allocate resources like that."

I nearly blurt something rash, but Gal's eyes cut to me, and I catch the words before they leave my mouth. My hand slides off his shoulder, and I do my best to look disappointed rather than furious. All of this effort—we came all this way, we ditched the mob, we tried to save Wen—and for what?

"You told the soldiers outside that you wanted to help us," Iral says, his eyes narrowing in a way that worries me. I don't want to disappoint this man. After Iva emp-Umber crushed my fantasies of knighthood, I decided it was *him* I wanted to be like when I grew up—not a lone warrior, but a great leader, a common man who rose to fight for the empire when it needed him most. I forgot that ambition. It hung on a crucifix when I thought he did. But it's difficult not to get swept up in it now.

"We can," I blurt, though internally I'm reeling for something, *anything* to back up that statement. We didn't come all this way for this to be a dead end. We just need time—time and a decent bargaining chip.

"I was an aide to the academy head," Gal announces shakily, covering up my floundering. "I don't know how what I know can fit in with the intelligence you already have, but that's worth something, right?"

Iral's head tilts as the thought takes hold. My brain should be scrambling for our next escape route, trying to figure out what we do if the resistance throws us back out on the streets, but my focus hitches on the tautness in his lips and stays fixed there. For a moment, I'm not in front of my childhood hero—instead, I'm yanked back to the long moments I spent sitting stiffly before frowning authority figures choosing my future, from settling and resettling me in foster homes to admitting me to the Umber Academy itself. I've been on this knife's edge before, and as ever, it feels like eternity.

"I can put together a meeting with some of my staff tomorrow," he says at last. "I'll give you the night to draw up the intelligence you think would be helpful. In the meantime, we'll set up a dorm room to accommodate you and figure out your clearances." General Iral pulls himself up to his full height, his chest swelling with a momentous breath. "Hope rides on the shoulders of contributions like this. With enough of it, victory might be within our grasp."

"Victory?" Gal asks. My heart hammers in my chest.

"Victory. The chance that someday we might retake Rana and build the Archon Empire anew."

There are no constants in flight. Your mind has to be athletic, your spatial awareness unrelenting. Lose your landmarks and you lose any hope of staying oriented. The only thing that'll save you is bringing your ship to stillness, giving your head time to catch up with the way the galaxy spins around you.

But there's no stillness in Henrietta Base's intake office. Soldiers and secretaries rush back and forth, sticking out datapads for me to print, then wrenching them away before I can read half of the information. I'm at the eye of a bureaucratic maelstrom, and nothing about it gives me room to process what's happened.

Iral, alive.

The resistance, thriving.

Victory.

Victory. The word hasn't been associated with Archon for half a decade. And yet, when I heard it from Maxo Iral's lips, I couldn't doubt it. This base was supposed to be our ticket off this planet, not something that could resurrect a rutting *empire*.

My choices are no longer hypothetical, no longer inevitable. My apathy's been shredded. And one wrong step could get Gal killed.

As a secretary orients me in front of a camera, I realize I've lost track of him in the confusion. My nerves snap taut with panic, and I turn my head as the flash goes off. The secretary groans—I give him my best apologetic smile, but I don't turn back to the camera until I've spotted Gal.

He's in the far corner of the room, talking to two officers. He looks relaxed, at ease—he's *smiling*—and I scold myself. Gal's safe. They think they need him, and now that he's recovered from the initial shock, he's back on his game, lying like he's been doing it all his life.

And in case the worst happens, I've already identified three ways of escaping this room.

When the secretary hands me the freshly printed badge, I take a moment to check the photo. My gaze is serious, my mouth unsmiling, but I swear I see the relief of that moment—the relief of seeing Gal safe—forever captured on this little piece of plastic.

I look up, and the secretary catches my eye. "I know you guys probably want to settle in, but if you need to unwind after that, the cantina's in the building directly across the quad from this one. People usually start trickling in after sunset, and I think there was talk of getting a game of Float or Sink going tonight. You're both welcome to join."

"I'll . . . uh. I'll keep it in mind," I stammer, trying to force down the panic sparking through me. It's not just that I barely remember how to play Float or Sink. I shouldn't get friendly with anyone here—and yet I yearn for it. I want to know how every single one of these soldiers got to this base. I want to understand how they could keep their fire going in the seven long years since the war ended while mine guttered and died.

But the mention of a cantina plunges an uncanny ache through my chest. I left so many friends behind when I grabbed Gal and booked it out of the academy. Hanji, Ollins, Rin, Rhodes—it's *them* I want to be drinking with after a long, hard day.

And if this dream of retaking Rana and restoring Archon anew goes into motion, they'll be caught in the crossfire.

My head is starting to hurt. A pair of soldiers ushers me out of the intake office, across a field, and into a dormitory. A swipe of my new card gets me into a narrow dorm room that, like most things here, looks uncannily similar to the ones at the academy. I barely have time to flip on the lights before Gal joins me, accompanied by his own escort. Our wide-eyed, unsteady gazes meet, and I see the way this day is tearing him in half.

Behind us, the soldiers close the door.

Gal's eyes drop to the bottom bunk. "Looks like they brought our stuff from the ship." Our packs are stacked together, Wen's rainbow umbrella propped up against them. The sight of it puts me at ease. No need for an escape plan when that battered, bloodstained, outrageously colorful thing is in here with us.

I grab it by the handle and heft it, testing the weight, then turn it over in my hands. Part of me expects to find secret triggers for even more nonstandard modifications, but another part is barely surprised when I don't. "She'll probably want this back," I muse, pricking my finger on the bladed tip. "Did you see where she ended up?"

When I look up, Gal's giving me a look I can't parse. Somehow my knuckles are already tightening around the umbrella's handle before he speaks. "I told them they could send her back to Isla."

CHAPTER 17

I'M OUT THE door before Gal has a chance to explain. The soldiers who escorted us here are only a couple paces down the hall, and none of them seem ready for the sight of a manic Umber deserter streaking past them with a rainbow umbrella tucked under his arm. I'm around the corner before they remember they have blasters on their belts.

I was stupid, so stupid. So fixated on Gal, on Archon, that I forgot we're not the most vulnerable ones here. We had something to offer the resistance, but Wen had no bargaining power whatsoever. And she was still coming down from those hits she took, and she was so quiet during the negotiation, and I got so distracted by Iral. I should have noticed sooner.

I clutch the umbrella tighter as I plunge down the stairwell. I hear voices, footsteps, people in pursuit, and there's a wild part of my brain that thinks I can take them because I have Wen's umbrella in my hand. They can't dump her back on the streets for Dago Korsa to find. I don't know how she fits into this resistance gambit, but no one deserves to go back to that.

"Hey, kid!" someone shouts behind me.

It only spurs me on.

I spill out of the stairwell and into the ground-floor corridor to find three soldiers squared up with their guns drawn on me. They give me two merciful seconds to react, enough time to throw my hands up in surrender. The umbrella clatters at my feet. "Please," I choke through a ragged breath. "I have to speak to Iral—someone— the girl has to stay."

"The girl?" one of them asks.

"Wen. Wen Iffan. They can't send her back to Isla. She's with us—she's part of our bargain."

"The junker? The Corinthian?"

I bare my teeth, shaking my head. I've always felt doomed to let down anybody who dares to rely on me. I can't let that happen to Wen—not when I know exactly what she's been through. "She stays, or there's no deal."

I'm not sure what their guns are set on. They could have me in the sights of a killing bolt. My arms start to shake, my lungs shuddering as I try to bring my breath under control.

The soldier at the head of the group cocks his head, listening to something in his earpiece. He lets out a deep sigh and says, "Stand down." One by one, the soldiers lower their guns. "She's in the main shuttle hangar. We'll take you there."

I don't trust their word until I see her. Wen sits on a crate at the edge of the hangar, flanked by two guards, running her hands over her wrists like she's been freed from cuffs. Her face lights up when she spots me—not with joy, but with surprise that she quickly smothers with a look of cool regard. "Ettian," she says.

"Wen."

"They tried to, uh—"

I take a knee next to her, glancing at the soldiers. "Wen, I'm so sorry," I murmur. "I should have been paying attention."

She nods. Her hair is loose, and she keeps her head bent forward so that it curtains her burns. "Wouldn't be the first time," Wen says. Her smile has a cruel edge to it. "My face isn't so easy to forget, but it feels like the rest of me kinda makes up for it."

"It's the last time," I tell her firmly. "You're with us, okay? We're getting you off-world. No one's forgetting you."

"You can't make good on that."

"Is that a challenge?"

She lets out a short laugh.

"I swear, Wen. You know what? Every person in every system is going to know your name someday. I'll make it my personal mission. No one's going to forget Wen Iffan again."

"Now you're making fun of me."

"Someone's gotta." I hold out her umbrella, and she plucks it delicately out of my hands, turning it end over end. Her eyes catch on the bloodstains and darken. "C'mon," I say, standing. "Let's get you set up here. ID, room, everything."

Wen rises and grabs my elbow before I have a chance to offer it. The evening outside is melting into night, and in the cool blue light of the darkened hangar, I barely catch her softer smile. "You're never getting rid of me. You know that, right?"

"I know." When I first met her, that sentiment would have been terrifying. But I need more constants in my life, and even if this one comes with mob trouble, wields a rainbow umbrella, and nearly blew me up yesterday, something in my gut tells me she's worth it.

Wen pops the umbrella open, slings it onto her shoulder, and pulls us along the edge of the hangar as the guards trail in our wake. When we duck out a side door, we nearly run headlong into an emissary from General Iral, who offers the general's most profuse apologies for the misunderstanding. I glance down at Wen, wary. I don't know if she knows Gal was the one who allowed them to send her away, and I'm not sure if I should tell her. For the sake of Gal's safety, it's probably better that I don't.

"She's staying," I assure the woman after an awkward pause. "She goes where we go. And she won't be stealing anything. Right?"

Wen smiles, pulls a knife, three wallets, and a printed photo of a toddler out of her pockets, and presses them into the emissary's hands one by one. I give the woman my falsest, most apologetic smile, then march Wen out of her sight before she has a chance to create any more chaos.

I know what's waiting for me in that dorm.

The time it takes to get Wen her own badge and room gives me plenty of chances to envision the way this is about to go down. I stand on the edge of the intake office with my arms folded as she flashes the camera a toothy smile, trying my best to get a handle on the simmering fury inside me.

Gal needs me to be calm. He needs me to be rational.

But then Wen gets her card—a legit ID, maybe the first one she's ever carried. I escort her to her first comfortable bed in months and watch over my shoulder as one of the soldiers points her toward her first hot shower in years.

And then I blow into our room like dreadnought boltfire.

"How the *rut* can you justify telling them to send her away?" I roar.

Gal startles—his datapad topples out of his hands, and he scoots back against the head of the bottom bunk. "Ettian—"

"Don't . . . Don't try to . . ." I rub my hands over my face, feeling the furious heat that's built up in my cheeks. "She was lucky to get away half-burned. She has an entire army of mobsters out for her blood in that city, and you tried to send her right back to them *alone*."

"Wen can handle herself," Gal says, straightening up. His hands are balled into fists at his side. He's holding something back.

I'm not. "That doesn't mean she should *have to*! What the rut is wrong with you?"

Gal moves so fast that not even my Viper-honed instincts have time to react. In the blink of an eye, he's on his feet, his hands catching me across the chest as he shoves me back against the wall. My head throbs where it hits. Gal's forearm digs into my collar, making my breath go shallow.

He leans up slowly, carefully, his lips curving around to my ear. "I've checked every inch of this room for bugs and cameras, but I'm not taking any chances," he snarls, the words barely audible over the rush of my blood in my ears. "If you *insist* on an explanation, I'll explain."

Logically I know I'm bigger than him. A better fighter than him. I could overpower him easily. But I'm so goddamn afraid of him in this moment—of that vicious rage, the blood of his mother—and it freezes me. A terrible question roars in my heart, one that started on the wiretram and has only gotten louder since we made it to the base.

Are we strangers? Are we strangers? Are we strangers?

I stammer, and Gal shakes my shoulders. "There's only one goal in all of this that matters. If I lose sight of it, I'm dead. We have to get home to the Umber interior. And I can't afford a liability like that junker girl."

"She got us to the resistance," I hiss. And because I can't think of any other way to fight back, I slip my hands up around his hips. If anyone *is* watching, they'll get a very different idea about what's going on in here.

Gal barely blinks at the contact, but a line in his neck goes taut. "Yeah, she walked us into an active military operation that would *string me up* if they knew what I am."

A slow, sinking feeling is dragging down my stomach. A familiar fear, one that's been eating at me ever since we left Jana behind at the academy. "She doesn't have to have *utility* to be worth saving, Gal," I snap. "Is that all we are to you? Tools to get you to your throne?"

His grip on me loosens. My grip on him tightens, and I lean back to look him in the eye as he grapples with the question. "I'm not . . . *You're* not . . ."

"What? I'm not like her?" A cruel smile edges out of the corner of my lips. I let it sit there like armor.

"You're my best friend, and she's a girl we met yesterday. You're *nothing* like her."

My smile vanishes, and I catch the flash of fear in Gal's eyes as he realizes how deep his words cut. "Not true," I say, low and dangerous. "And if you had any idea what that's like, it wouldn't even cross your mind to put Wen back on the streets."

"*You* don't know what it's like!" he shouts, then claps a hand over his mouth as our tiny room throws the sound back at him. After a moment of stunned silence, he bends his head forward, reeling me in with a tug until his forehead brushes my shoulder. He's shaking even harder than he was in the interrogation room—no reason for him to hide it now. "When I agreed to come here, I thought it would be spies, instigators, a few stolen shuttles. Not a base this huge. Not General Iral. I . . . I couldn't even leave the *citadel* when he was still living, and now I've looked him in the eye. And you think I can keep track of a junker girl with a death wish while that's on my plate? She's permanently scorched from the last bridge she burned, and I have an empire's future—"

He pauses, and when his voice is strong enough to come back, it's suddenly drenched in despair. "I could feel the blood inside me boiling back there. I understood my mother. How she could . . . How she keeps . . ."

My hands go soft at his hips, and I slip them around until I'm pulling him into the embrace he so desperately needs. The last notes of my anger rattle through my skull, but the broken fear in Gal's voice is more important than anything I could yell at him.

"You don't know what it's like," he repeats, the words pulsing against my neck. "No one knows what it's like. To be alone like this and know it's never going to change. To be raised for shaping the galaxy, to know that nothing else matters beyond surviving to eighteen. So many people out there are hell-bent on making sure that doesn't happen. And now—"

His voice catches, and against my better judgment, I hold him tighter.

"The general got right under my skin," Gal admits. "When I was a kid, I had nightmares about what he'd do to me if I ever fell into his hands. Even after Archon fell, he was unstoppable. The biggest threat the Umber Empire ever faced was Maxo Iral's revenge. And then we crucified him in front of the citadel, and I thought it was over. I never dreamed . . ."

I close my eyes and nod, mostly to keep him from stammering through an explanation that's only going to shake him more. Gal never dreamed that the threat General Iral posed wasn't over. He never dreamed that the Shield of Archon had escaped the Umber Empire's reach. He never dreamed that man could amass a new army among the refugees with sponsorship from the Corinthian Crown itself. And now we're stuck on this base, bound by the promise to give Maxo Iral critical information—information he could use to launch a whole new offensive.

"It's my responsibility," Gal whispers. "Billions of people live in the former Archon territories—people who depend on what we've built for them, people who were starving under Archon rule." An urge to correct him lodges in my throat. He's too freaked out to react well to any attempt to untangle the propaganda he was raised on from the facts. "I have to stop this somehow. I have to protect them from what's brewing here, from *him*. I can't bring them another war. It's only been seven years."

I stiffen, trying to press down the wild mess of thoughts threatening to overtake my head. Gal's breath hitches, and he draws back slightly. My eyes open and find his, dark and searching, as if he can extract all of my secrets from a look alone.

"Ettian," he whispers. "I know . . . I know you were born on Rana. I know you don't have anyone left. But I need to know . . ."

I should tell him. It was so easy this morning—when Wen asked, the truth slid out clean. I thought that step meant more would follow. I thought I might be able to talk about those two years after the collapse of the old empire without feeling like the scars were being hacked open. But being here, surrounded by a small army dreaming of reclaiming the Archon territories, is like having the blade still buried in my flesh. There's no hope of closure. It only gets deeper. It only gets worse.

"You know enough," I say, the words laced with bile. "You know I shattered with the empire. You know I built myself back from what was left."

I catch the flicker of disappointment in his eyes. Something twists in me, equal parts guilt and anger. I don't owe him my history, but I feel like I should, especially now that Wen knows more than him. He's shared his own story with me, after all. Twelve years in the citadel, three on Naberrie, and two and a half as my roommate on Rana. But for him, my story starts on the day he took the top bunk. Everything before that moment is lost in a fog.

I can't stand to be touching him anymore. I pull away and cross to the bottom bunk, where I drop on my haunches as the weight of the day comes crashing down on me. My mind is caught in the tumult of a zero-G spinout. I pull over my pack and dig through it until I reach deep into an interior pocket and find my velvet bag with its drawstring still knotted. I squeeze it in my palm, letting its familiar weight ground me.

Gal sets himself down on the edge of the bed, and suddenly the bag is scalding in my hand. I stuff it back into its pocket, clamping down hard on the shame and nausea roiling through me. He leans close, and for a moment I'm seized by the irrational fear that he's going to try to kiss me again. "I'm sorry," Gal whispers against my ear. "I shouldn't have . . . I'm sorry."

"No apologies," I mutter.

The silence hollows around us, inside us.

"Please don't blow up at me again, but . . ." Gal says quietly. "You're with me, right?"

I close my eyes. "Of course."

"You're sure?"

I hate that he has to keep checking. When I overrode him on the tarmac earlier, it was like something came over me, ripping out the lacing that's been keeping me together for the past seven years. And if that wasn't enough, I had to look General Iral in the face as the man I've idolized since childhood laid his hope on our shoulders. I may hate that Gal has to keep checking, but there's no question *why* he feels the need to do so for the second time today.

But through all of this, through every part of this mess, the only thing that's ever mattered is Gal. There's only one side that has my allegiance. It's not Archon, which fell and fled, or Umber, which conquered and reshaped. It's not the past. It's that possibility of a better future. It's only ever been Gal.

Gal emp-Umber, but that isn't exactly helpful at the moment.

"I'm sure," I tell him. I'll tell him as many times as it takes. "No matter what, I'm with you." The pure relief of that simple truth cuts through the confusion. I was caught in the swell of an ocean wave before. Now I've found my footing in the sand. "But we need to decide what we're going to do."

He takes his time before answering, his fingers tangling in his lap. "There's no way out but through. If we withhold information from the resistance, they'll get suspicious. They'll investigate. And if they find out who I am, we've handed them the greatest weapon they could possibly have. With the right negotiation, they could probably ransom their ruttin' empire in exchange for me."

The urgency in his voice has brought him right up against my ear, and I slip my arm around his shoulders to steady him. He doesn't tense up at the contact—instead, he relaxes right into it, melting against my side in a way that has *me* tensing at how easily we could topple into something out of control. "So we have to feed them information," I whisper, trying to get my thoughts back on track. "The kind that forces them to keep us. Maybe even . . . the kind that gets them moving where they're headed."

Gal stiffens. It's no innocent comment coming from my lips, not when he's seen firsthand what this place seems to awaken in me. I can't *want* the resistance to launch an assault. I *don't* want the resistance to launch an assault. Not when our friends would be caught in the crossfire. Not when it's only been seven years since the last war.

I take a deep breath, trying to sort through the facts. First, we have to give the resistance information. Second, we need the resistance to make it back to the Archon territories.

But a third fact slips into my mind, one with ramifications that go far beyond the crisis we're facing. Third, and maybe most important, Gal needs to return to his empire with a show of strength. Something massive, something bloody. Something that will leave a mark.

And this plan doesn't need the resistance to win.

"So we give them information," I say slowly. "But not all of it. And not always the right information. We know the interior defenses inside-out."

Gal straightens, inhaling deeply. I turn my head to find his face taut, his hooded eyes pinched shut. I know he doesn't want me to go on. I also know he doesn't want to finish the thought out loud himself.

So I lean forward, my lips skimming his ear. "We could convince them it's possible to win Archon back. And then we walk them into a trap. Iral only escaped the first time because he had a trick up his sleeve that can't be repeated. Imagine telling your mother that you didn't flee—that you came here to pursue the Archon uprising that tried to out you as heir and obliterate you. You could take the throne with the defeat of Maxo Iral and his final rebellion on your hands."

He stares at the crooked nest of his clenched fingers, and hangs his head. "The galaxy would bow to me. If . . . If I . . ."

If he brings her Iral's head. If he stoops to the violence it took for Iva emp-Umber to claim her legacy and outdoes her a thousandfold. If he finishes what she started, crushing the Archon Empire before it has a chance to rise again.

"It's necessary," he says, but the words are more question than statement. "We have to stop all of this. If we start a war, the death toll would easily outnumber the people on this base. But then that makes me an asshole if I choose to see it all in sums, using the math to decide who lives and who dies. And I don't want . . . I know what my mother's blood makes me capable of. I could come at Iral with every ounce of hate in my heart for the way he dragged out the destruction of the last war for another two years. If he had laid down arms when his imperials did, so many lives would have been spared. And I can stop him from doing it again, but then what does that make *me*? And . . . why are you looking at me like that?"

I'm looking at him like that because *this* is the Gal I know. Iva emp-Umber's brutal reign will cede to a boy whose heart is torn in half at the thought of destroying the man he's feared since he was small. Gal and his uncertain heart will steer Umber away from a legacy of conquest and bloodshed, away from the ruins of his parents' war.

And I've also realized something else. Something I can never tell him, because it's only going to shatter us completely. It sits on the edge of my tongue like a lit fuse. And Gal is looking at me expectantly, waiting for *something*. "I . . . can't process all of this," I tell him, because adjacent truths are more manageable. I keel backward, pulling away from him and stuffing the pillow over my head.

"Yeah, okay." The mattress bounces slightly as Gal pushes himself to his feet. "We need some real sleep. And then we'll figure this out."

I listen to him puttering around, getting ready for bed. I know I should change and shower, but I can't even bring myself to sit up again. I feel like the weight of this day is pinning me to the bunk. Everything I've done, everything I've learned, everything I've chosen. And yet, I don't know if I'll be able to sleep—not with all of that tumbling through my thoughts nonstop.

On the other side of my eyelids, the room goes dark.

And then there's a slight dip in the mattress again, the pressure of a single knee sinking in like a testing of the waters. "I know it's weird, but . . ." Gal murmurs.

Wordlessly, I roll to the side.

Now I *really* can't sleep.

Gal dropped off in a matter of seconds, his back turned to me and his breathing deep and steady. The gulf between us feels charged, and even though I have so many things to keep my mind off it, I can't help but fixate on the bare inches separating us in this narrow, narrow bed.

I lie on my back, staring at the underside of the mattress above me. The thin light that comes through the crack beneath the door barely illuminates the geometric patterns of the stitching that holds it together. I try to count the stitches, but I keep losing track.

Tomorrow morning, we'll be expected to give the resistance information. Tomorrow we'll start the slow, deadly process of poisoning them from the inside. I'll let Gal do the talking, but he'll be guiding them into a trap that's ultimately *my* design. My idea. My fault.

But I don't believe in the empire that pulled me out of the rubble and glued me back together. And I don't trust the empire that crumbled to dust and left me to die. My only allegiance is to an empire that doesn't exist yet, to the possibility of Gal's future rule. Maybe that makes me a traitor. Maybe it forfeits my soul. But for him—for this disastrous boy sleeping next to me—I would, I will.

CHAPTER 18

I WAKE TO a hand clutching my chest. Disoriented, I snatch it by the wrist and turn my head to find Gal half-awake and doing his damnedest to fight his way free from the blankets that pin him to the bunk.

"Hey, whoa," I murmur, but my voice is nowhere near enough to snap him out of the raw animal panic that has him in its talons.

Whatever's got him so worked up, we can't afford it. No one can ask questions about why he's so high-strung. He tries to rip free from my grasp, and I fight back, wrenching his arm against my chest as I loop my other arm around him and pin him.

He kicks and flails for a few seconds before his brain seems to register why he's being held down. I roll on top of him for good measure, and he lets out a hoarse, helpless croak.

"Hey. You're okay. You're fine. Deep breaths."

As he takes them, I key into three rhythms all at once. The first is my own heart, rattled from the sudden shock of waking. The second is Gal's, fluttering underneath me like a trapped bird.

The third is the low, sonorous rudiments of skin drums outside. It wasn't a bad dream that sent Gal into a panic. It was the nightmare of his reality. "They're just the wake-up call," I mutter into his ear.

His nose hitches against my collarbone, and his breathing starts to steady against our chests. "Sounded like Seely."

My heart aches, and the terror of that moment comes rushing back to me. Of course—the last time he heard an Archon rhythm, it was the one our classmates were pounding into their Viper dashboards as he fled from their fire. To wake to that—and to have no context to distinguish between a rallying beat and a simple wake-up call—must have been the worst possible way to greet a new day on Henrietta Base.

Gal makes a low noise beneath me that shudders through my entire body. Only then do I grasp that I've wrapped myself around him, he can feel almost every part of me, and *yep*, it's the morning.

How bad would it be? a terrible part of me croons. Because for two people who've resolved not to do this, we're *really bad* at not doing this.

Then I remember that I didn't shower or change last night, and I hate myself for letting *that* be the reason I peel off him, shuffle over to the edge of the bed, and let the chill of my feet on the floor shock some sense into my system. "You good?" I ask, and nearly double over laughing at how falsely casual those two words can sound.

"Ettian."

"I'm gonna take a shower."

He doesn't press the issue.

When I get back, we slip into our old academy routine, staggering around each other and getting dressed, communicating mostly in grunts and shrugs as the gray dawn outside fades into a clear, bright morning. Gal's datapad chimes with an alert as the base system delivers our itineraries. "Breakfast in ten, meeting in an hour," he says, tilting the pad so I can see.

I tap Wen's name on the schedule, seamlessly inserted alongside our own, and Gal grimaces. "I didn't tell her it was you."

His eyes dart away guiltily. Maybe he thought he'd dodged this topic after the turn our conversation took last night.

"She deserves an apology."

"And a reason to gut me with that freaky umbrella?" Gal massages his temples with both hands, then tugs nervously at the jacket he's shrugged on. "No. I know she *deserves* an apology, but—"

I shake my head, crossing to the door. "Even if you don't tell her you were the one who sent her back, I think it's fair to say you're sorry for letting it happen." I pause with my hand on the handle. "It only gets worse if you let it fester. Sooner you talk to her, sooner she puts it out of mind. Tell her now."

You're one to talk. I bite down hard on a grimace.

Gal rolls his eyes, stalking past me as I open the door for him. "Fine, *Gold One,*" he scoffs.

I step out into the hall and find myself greeted by a disconcertingly happy-looking face. "Morning!" the soldier chirps, pushing himself off the wall across from the door as he fumbles with his earpiece. He's warm-skinned and slight-framed in a way that tells me he did most of his growing on Archon rations. I'd call him handsome if he didn't look way too chipper for the hour of the morning. "Name's Sims," he continues. "I've been assigned to escort you for the first few days to get you acclimated to the base. I'm also your security, so uh . . . don't try anything funny, I guess?"

He gets the pair of blank looks and blinks he deserves.

"Right then," he says, unfazed. "Breakfast. Onward!"

Sims leads the way, guiding us down the stairwell and out of the dorms. Gal keeps his gaze turned pointedly away from me the whole time. Calming him this morning feels like a distant dream, and all it took was the mention of Wen's name. I know he's scared. I know he's stressed. And I know he's not convinced we need to keep Wen around. But even though I promised I'm with him, I can't abandon her a second time. Gal needs me, but Wen needs somebody— *anybody*—on her side.

We rendezvous with her and her guard in the cafeteria, which is already packed with soldiers and choked with a smell I don't clock as familiar until I see Gal wrinkle his nose at it and realize he's never encountered genuine Archon food before. Wen gives me a smile that matches the buttery sunlight streaming through the windows. She's dressed in her tattered clothes from yesterday, and I make a mental note to see if the resistance can outfit her with something better.

"Sleep well?" Wen asks, nudging a bony elbow into my ribs as we hop into the mess line.

My self-pitying chuckle gets stuck in my throat when I catch the conflicted pinch of Gal's brows. He squares his shoulders, and for a terrifying moment I'm seized by the impulse to step between them before the inevitable brawl breaks out. But then Gal's soft, apologetic smile splits his face, and he says, "Wen, I'm sorry. I heard about what happened last night, and I'm glad Ettian caught you before it was too late."

Wen pauses, her hand outstretched over a pile of toast. "Thanks," she says, then claws a handful of slices together, to the horror of the cafeteria staff.

Gal shrugs as if to say, *Good enough*. He looks relieved, and it lightens the tension between us marginally. But then his gaze shifts to the long tables of the mess hall, and his jaw clenches.

If we had any remaining illusions about this being a scrappy group of freedom fighters, they're shattered by the number of people in this room. The facilities could be explained by the Corinthian sponsorship. All those impressive buildings could be empty. But here's the future of the empire's revival, chowing down and making rowdy noise as they jostle their way through their mornings. General Iral doesn't just have a fancy compound.

He has an army.

An army we'll have to destroy.

As we move toward an empty table, one of the soldiers catches my eye and gestures invitingly to the empty space next to her and her companions. I try to adjust my course, but a tug on my jacket's hem brings me up short. "We can't interact with them," Gal whispers urgently against my ear.

"We need intel. We need to actually talk to these people."

He gives an almost imperceptible shake of his head. "We can't afford to get close. *You* especially."

The notion rankles me. "What do you mean by that?" I let a dangerous edge into my tone. If he doesn't trust me to talk to these people because he thinks I'll abandon him, he has another think coming.

"Ettian, I'm not worried about your loyalty. I'm worried about your heart."

I stiffen, caught between the delight of being known so well and the shame of it. Of course Gal would notice how this situation tears me in half. Of course he would care about what it's doing to me, to be here in the midst of a rebellion for an empire I thought was long dead. I don't know why it's become so surprising to realize that Gal is as invested in my well-being as I am in his.

Maybe because I don't deserve it.

I shove that intrusive thought away and follow him to an empty table instead. As we settle on a bench, Gal's attention goes distant. His eyes are unfocused, his mind awhirl with plots and schemes, waging war against the constant fear he feels when he's surrounded by Archon soldiers. I wish there were something I could do to free him from it, but a part of me knows it's better like this. Not better for him, but better for our chances of making it out alive. He needs to be sharp and afraid.

Just as we're about to dig in—me with enthusiasm and a little too much emotion for the early hour, Gal with trepidation verging on distaste—Sims tosses a tray down next to me. Wen's guard plops down on the other side of the table. I hesitate, torn between taking my first bite of properly seasoned food in *years* and acknowledging their presence.

"Don't mind me," Sims says, toggling his earpiece. "Audiobooks," he explains when he catches my brow furrowing. "Ever read anything by Huron Vayner?"

I shake my head, struggling to settle my expression somewhere closer to consternation than pain. "Weren't a lot of Archon authors on my syllabi."

"I'll put a chip together for you if you want," he offers.

I catch a worried glint in Gal's eye across the table. "That's . . .

very nice of you," I stammer, trying to sound noncommittal. Not sure I'm going to have much reading time around here anyway.

At my right, Wen's already licking her plate clean. There's something deeply satisfying about the wonder in her eyes as she stares down at her gut. I remember it well—that unshakable sense of security that came with a full belly, dispelled only by the knowledge that it could all go away tomorrow.

She glances back at the mess line, no doubt wondering if she can get away with a second helping. Instead, I push one of my pieces of toast onto her plate.

Wen smirks. "You know you owe me more than that," she says.

I think she's right.

Once Wen's finished stuffing herself to her heart's content, our guards lead us to a conference room on the top floor of the base's administrative building. As Sims beckons us through the door, we're greeted by the sight of General Iral standing at the head of a long table packed with people. When he said he was putting a room together, he really wasn't messing around. There are three seats left open for us, which we take. Gal positions himself carefully between me and Wen—whether to separate us or protect himself I'm not entirely sure. I shrink closer against him as I take in the rest of the room. Even though they're dressed down, I pick out signs of rank here and there, from mission patches on sleeves to platinum stars on collars to rings of emerald-green embroidery on cuffs. The upper crust of this resistance base has turned out to grill us.

We're collaborators, not prisoners, I remind myself. We're sitting at a table, not chained to one. But when General Iral's heavy gaze locks onto my eyes, I feel my secrets teetering on the edge of my lips anyway.

"I realize it's a daunting task, trying to parse your years of experience down to their most useful bits," the general starts. "To help, we've put together a packet of the information we find it appropriate to declassify."

At my right, Gal's fists are already tight. I wonder how long it will take for this resistance gambit to play out, weighing it carefully against how long it will take for him to snap under the stress. The sums aren't favorable. We have to work fast.

With a flick of his fingers across the conference table's surface, Iral brings up a projection of Tosa System and its known defenses. I lean back in my seat, my eyes fixed on the tiny holographic version of my homeworld that slowly circles its sun. I've never been so far from Rana. Never been so uncertain about my chances of returning to it. Never even realized I could feel something like homesickness for a planet where I lived through hell.

I glance across the table and find General Iral's eyes fixed on the same spot, shimmering in the light of the projection. My heart swells before I can stop it.

Gods of all systems, I think. *I'm in over my head.*

Iral gestures to Rana. "Our best hope of restoring the former empire is to hold the center."

He collapses the projection until we're looking at the entirety of the former Archon territory. Tosa System is nothing but a pinhead at its core. Long vectors meander in the vast dark between worlds, and it takes me a moment to recognize them for what they are.

"Our scouting so far has isolated these pathways as the routine patrols for dreadnoughts throughout the former empire," Iral says, tracing his finger along one of the glowing threads. "But these are essentially public record. There are more 'notties in the black than these, and it's those ones that have the most potential to sink us before we start. If we had a way through that mess, we might stand a chance of reclaiming the capital and then expanding outward. We have the resources to launch that kind of campaign."

He wipes aside the map and starts pulling up data. First the ships—hundreds of carrier craft stationed in orbit around the planet, thousands of fighters, a veritable armada with platinum trim curling across their hulls. Then the personnel—thousands and thousands of displaced Archon citizens who have answered their general's call and trained for the single purpose of retaking the empire.

For a dangerous moment, I imagine a life lived among them. A life where I got out on those refugee ships, where I never felt the abandonment that tore out my love of the Archon Empire. A life where my purpose was always clear.

But it would have been a life without Gal, and that makes it incomprehensible.

He sits at my left, his fingers fidgeting as he nods along. When the general falls expectantly silent, Gal tries his best to draw a deep breath without looking like he's steeling himself. "So you're saying you could mount an assault right away if you had intel that could get you past Umber dreadnoughts?" he asks, sounding out each word like he's stringing them along a tightrope.

"'Right away' is optimistic, but . . . soon, yes," Iral confirms.

"I'm not sure if anything I know could help," Gal says, "but I can give you everything I can think of and let you be the judge of that."

I take a steeling breath of my own. No matter what, Gal *can't* give Iral information on dreadnoughts' weaknesses. Those ships form the core of Umber's defense—not just in the Archon territories, but throughout the empire. Handing them over to Maxo Iral might give the general the power to punch a hole clear to the Umber interior.

I may be in over my head, but the Umber heir has it light-years worse.

The meeting ends, mercifully, after nearly an hour of Gal tiptoeing around information the resistance likely already knows. It's enough to establish good faith, but not enough to get Archon birds in the sky.

Yet.

When we leave the conference room, we're greeted by Sims fumbling with his earpiece and trying not to look caught off-guard by our sudden reappearance. "Your schedule's clear for the rest of the day," he tells us. "I switch off to my other shift in a few hours, but I can show you around in the meantime. You guys are pilots, right?"

Gal grimaces, I nod, and Wen nods even more enthusiastically.

Sims grins. "I'll take you down to the hangars. Personally I couldn't fly if you put a gun to my head—my nerves can't take the pressure—but I think we've got a few things you might get a kick out of."

"What *is* your specialization?" Gal asks as we're escorted into the elevators.

"Demolitions," Sims replies with a shrug.

We emerge from the administrative building to find the summer heat and the base operations in full swing. The air is thick with humidity, and the familiar noise of firing engines rumbles toward us from a distant runway.

We follow Sims on a long, meandering path, nodding along as he points out landmarks, until we reach the hangars at the outer edge of the base's cluster of buildings. The tarmac boils under my boots, and the trickle of sweat down my spine only fuels my anxiety as a line of Cygnets—sleek fighter craft twice the size of a Viper—taxis past. I wish for a cockpit. In the cockpit, I'm always sure of myself, of where I stand, of what I'm doing. Or maybe it's that in a cockpit, I just follow orders.

Out here, I have to choose my own path, and it's growing more and more difficult by the day.

I'm so caught up in the sight of the Cygnets maneuvering into their launch positions that I miss the moment Gal's hand slips around my waist. Suddenly he's tugging me into the shade beneath a stack of cargo containers, his back colliding with one of them as he loops his arm up around my neck. Language drops out from under my feet, leaving to meet him with nothing but a soft, confused warble as his lips stop inches from mine.

He tips his head, peering over my shoulder. A sly grin cracks across his face, and my racing heart stills. I turn to follow the line of his gaze and find Wen and Sims sauntering purposefully away, glancing back at us with equally mischievous smiles.

I try to step back, but Gal keeps his grip tight. "We're in the clear," he says. "We ditched the extra eyes, and there's no way there are any bugs out here. We can talk."

I let out a shaky breath. "Don't do that."

"Do what?"

I lift my eyebrows, nodding at the lack of space between us.

"Hey, it *worked*."

His hold on me loosens, but I can't bring myself to pull out of it. "I know it worked, just . . . Y'know, if you're gonna try to kiss me, I want you to mean it."

Gal's face falls, and he slumps back against the container. "Look, I don't know when our next chance to strategize will be, or when we'll need a plan in place. And we need a plan fast."

"The dreadnoughts," I mumble, closing my eyes.

"The dreadnoughts," he agrees. "There's no way into that system that doesn't involve going up against cityships. But we can't . . . I can't . . . If Maxo Iral knows how to beat the Imperial Fleet, the galaxy is doomed."

A sudden roar from the runway startles us so badly that we both jolt, clutching each other tighter. I crane my neck back in time to catch the Cygnets streaking overhead. A vicious thread of envy seeps into my bloodstream—not at the sight of them, but at the speed with which they disappear. My feet have been on the ground for an entire day, and it's already too long.

"It would be easier if we could let the dreadnoughts take care of all those ships they just flashed in front of us," Gal says, bringing me out of the sky. "But they're never going to buy a plan that would walk them into their path. They don't trust us enough."

"So how do we get their trust?"

Gal shrugs, glancing overhead. The darker smudges beneath his eyes have grown. "We have to figure out how to beat a dreadnought without actually beating a dreadnought. We give them a way through, they trust us, and then we walk them into the system defenses."

I nod. "And how the rut are we supposed to figure out how to take down a 'nottie?"

Gal's nose wrinkles. "Gods, you're talking like them already."

I bristle, pulling back out of his grip. General Iral used the old Archon slang for dreadnoughts in the meeting, and the word got under my skin. Or maybe it was under my skin to begin with, and hearing Iral pulled it to the surface. I don't know how to justify using it without sounding overly defensive, and I don't know how to defend how *right* it felt to use it.

Gal reaches out like he's going to reel me back in, then thinks better of it. "Hey, I didn't mean . . . I know it's weird for you."

Weird doesn't even begin to cover it, but I want to get us back on track. "Dreadnoughts. Only way to beat dreadnoughts is *with* dreadnoughts, and there's no way any of the ships in the Archon fleet can cut it." I take a step forward and turn, slumping shoulder to shoulder with Gal against the cargo container.

"Even if we did have dreadnoughts of our own, our generous Corinthian hosts would have strong objections to using them in an assault launching from Corinth. That starts a whole new war." His eyes focus on something in the distance. "Speaking of Corinthians . . ."

Farther down the runway, Wen's chattering animatedly with Sims—about blowing things up, if I had to guess. I sigh.

"She needs something to do," Gal mutters, and I throw him a sharp glare. "Don't start with that utility stuff—I just mean that she spent the whole meeting this morning sitting on her hands. She doesn't have anything to contribute—Ettian, I'm trying to be nice about this, but it's *true*," he says, crossing his arms as I throw up my hands. "If we don't find something to occupy her, she's going to start making trouble. She probably already has."

"When you say *we*—"

"I mean you."

I roll my eyes. "I'll figure something out."

"You always do."

Silence settles over us, punctuated only by the noises of the base in motion—soldiers drilling, machinery humming, and a gentle wind blowing in from the south. I can't shake the unsteadiness that keeps on threatening to knock me over. Ever since we got to the base, there's been an inescapable sour note in every conversation between me and Gal. I don't know what to blame—this place, where we come from, or worst of all, some sort of fundamental disconnect between us that's only surfacing now. I can't lose him. We've come too far for this.

"Why do I trust you?" Gal asks.

My blood runs cold.

But Gal's tone isn't cruel or calculating. It's hopeful. Warming. He's on to something. "Maybe you don't trust me—I wouldn't blame you if you didn't, after everything—but I trust you with my life. I know I can trust you because you throw your life on the line to save me. Time and time again, no matter how little I deserve it. You've sacrificed everything for me."

He shifts his gaze skyward. I don't know if he's looking for the Cygnets, a merciful cloud to break the heat, or this system god's absolution.

"So that's what we have to do for them."

CHAPTER 19

I GOT USED to feeling helpless a long time ago.

During the final days of the war, when Trost was under bombardment, I found myself wrapped in an uncanny calmness. I knew there was nothing I could do—that the bombs would fall, the buildings would collapse, and only chance would save me. As the days wore on and the bone-shaking rumbles grew closer, it got easier and easier to accept.

At the academy, that detachment served me well. I could disconnect from my body during grueling drills. Disconnect from my fear in a Viper cockpit. I was a perfect soldier—one who could follow orders without hesitation or limitation. I stopped caring about what happened to me, and it made everything easier. I could sit back and watch things take their course, knowing there wasn't anything I could have done to change it.

Now I watch Gal set out on the course I plotted, leading Maxo Iral toward his ruination, and for the first time in years I feel like I *should* do something.

"Tracking the movement of dreadnoughts can only get you so far," Gal says. He stands at the head of the conference room, combing his fingers through the vectors on the projected map. General

Iral watches him from the side, his dark eyes fixed on the lines Gal traces. "As you said, there are ships ghosting in the black whose vectors aren't a part of the public record."

I'm seated farther down the table, sandwiched between members of the base's senior staff. It's been two days since our first briefing. Two days of getting acclimated to the base's layout, to the base's schedule, and to the rhythm of Delos's slightly longer rotation. The dark smudges under Gal's eyes have faded, but they aren't gone completely. In those two days, we've found plenty of time to put our heads together and strategize, but the kind of thing we're trying to pull off usually takes months of planning preceded by decades of military training.

All we have on our side is bloodright and nerve.

And speaking of nerve, Wen's been scarce. On the one hand, I'm thankful. It gives us time to plot, and she hasn't started to suspect us yet. On the other, I'm worried. The less we see of her, the worse trouble she could be getting into. She's stopped coming to the strategy meetings, instead asking for recaps that I dole out while she stuffs her face in the mess.

Gal collapses the projection, plunging the room into darkness. The lights slowly readjust, but he waits until they're at full to speak. "There's an easier way to the interior. An easier way to engage the dreadnoughts that guard it, with a lessened risk to your own assets. We've talked it over," he says, nodding to me, "and we're willing if you are."

General Iral folds his arms, waiting.

Gal takes a deep breath. I know part of it is the act—playing the moment up for effect, making it look like bravery to say the words. But part of that breath is steeling himself. Once he speaks, we're committed.

"Use us as bait," Gal announces.

Murmurs roll across the conference table as the senior staff processes the idea. "To what end?" Iral asks. My throat goes dry at the note of suspicion in his voice. Gal was able to sway him once. Now we'll see if the negotiator can do it again.

"The Umber military doesn't rut around with deserters," Gal says, his eyes downcast. He looks just the right amount of scared. "The empress doesn't tolerate disloyalty at any rank. It's a policy I learned . . . too much about while working for the academy head. If we're caught, we'll be strung up and fried in front of the rest of the academy. And if a dreadnought gets word that we're in the system, their orders are to divert and come after us. But they won't fire—not if there's a chance we can be taken alive and made into an example. I mean you saw . . . You've seen . . ."

A pained look flinches across General Iral's face. He's seen plenty. The emperor and empress he served faithfully. His own twin brother.

"To take us alive, they have to deploy their own fighters and physically herd us in," Gal continues. "And when they open up those launch tubes . . ."

He doesn't have to say much more than that. The tension drops from the face of every officer in the room as they realize exactly what they could do with those openings. I lean back in my chair as the chatter rises around us, each colonel already jockeying for the mission lead. *We've done it.* Gal's eyes flick my way, and I catch a tiny smile on the edge of his lips, half-relieved and half-smug.

And it rattles me where it shouldn't. In that momentary tilt of his lips, he seems to enjoy what he's doing. Gal's a good actor, but there's no need for him to act pleased with himself over the trap he's laying for Iral.

Unless the rest was the real act. A tremor of uneasiness rattles up my spine as I remember the look in his eyes on the wiretram and every time he's checked in to see that I'm still with him since then. What if Gal's hesitancy to commit violence is a front to keep his war-orphan getaway driver on his side?

Whatever smile might have been there vanishes in an instant when General Iral sets a hand on Gal's shoulder. Gal startles, then catches himself on the edge of the conference table. His knuckles stay pale even after he gets his balance.

"You're sure you would do this for us?" Iral asks, his voice low and barely audible over the senior staff's talk.

I jolt to my feet, ready to step in and cover for him, but Gal only wavers for a second. "I've spent my whole life being raised to serve an empire that can never quite justify the way it'll use me," he says, staring not at Iral's eyes but at the platinum-and-emerald weave on the shoulder of his uniform. "But this—*this* is . . . I don't know how else to say it. It's right."

He's going to make a hell of an emperor someday. His words are exactly what General Iral wants to hear. Exactly what he *needs* to hear. A child of the Umber interior is telling Iral that his war is just and he's noble to wage it. His cause is so righteous that a kid who should be Umber-loyal wants to stake his life on its success.

I'm three feet away and utterly powerless when Gal emp-Umber becomes a hero in my hero's eyes.

A half hour later, I'm sitting in front of the door to Iral's office with the sensation of a Viper nose-dive tugging at my stomach. When the meeting was adjourned, Gal got caught up in a tide of praise from the senior staff, and I ducked out of his periphery. With all of them focused on shaking his hand, it was easy to slip away unnoticed.

The guilt struck not long after. I should have told Gal I was coming here. Should have made sure he was okay with me leaving him alone in a room full of seasoned Archon leadership. But in the moment, it seemed too important to flag Iral down, and the general disappeared before I could get to him. So I headed to his office and slumped against the wall, trying to tamp down the frantic pounding of my heartbeat that hasn't stopped since the moment I spotted Gal's little smirk.

A door opens down the hall, and I'm on my feet in a blink.

"Ettian?" Iral asks.

"Sir," I say, the word coming out cracked and sudden. "I wanted to talk."

He nods. There might be a smile in the edges of his lips, but he's carved of stone and nigh impossible to read. "And I've been meaning to speak with you."

My heart lurches against my ribs. *He's your con's mark,* I remind myself. *He's not the Shield of Archon. He's not the man you idolized back when you still had hope for the empire. He's the man who will kill Gal if you slip up, so don't you dare slip.*

"I was wondering if—" I start. But before I can get the rest of my question out, General Iral swipes his badge and opens his office door, and the words collapse in my mouth.

Iral crosses the room and settles behind his massive, stately desk. He pulls up its interface and begins tugging information from his datapad onto the display. The desk's surface is clear, but the walls behind it make up for the neatness tenfold. I take a hesitant step forward as my eyes sweep back and forth over the chaos, recognizing things here and there. Platinum medals and pins, some framed, others hanging on hooks. Ceremonial chains and garb, the formal uniform Iral would have worn at public functions. Printed photos. A battered pilot helmet with mission stickers papering it that pre-date the Umber War of Expansion. A twenty-year-old flight suit, the emerald on its patches faded and the left sleeve torn and burned.

Iral catches me staring at it and wordlessly pulls up his uniform cuff to bare matching scars on his forearm. "I was fresh out of flight school, flying supply carriers on a borderworld campaign. Got shot down by rebel raiders, had to land the ship while half of the cockpit was on fire."

"Oh, I know," I blurt, drawing up the courage to step all the way into the room. Only then I see it. Standing straight-backed in the corner, polished to perfection. I freeze, nearly choking on my next breath. "That's . . . But that's . . ."

"A knight's powersuit," Iral confirms, and for the first time I hear his bold voice waver.

I move toward it with heavy limbs, feeling like I'm in a trance. It stands a good head higher than me, human-shaped—but promising so much more than that. It's crafted from the most advanced alloys the Archon Empire ever produced at its peak and wired with tech Umber could only dream of, all put together in a sleek carapace that shows both the nicks and dents of something worn and the proud shine of something loved. "I thought they were all destroyed at Knightfall."

"So does the empress." Iral lets out a low chuckle.

"This wasn't supposed to survive," I croak, turning my burning eyes toward Iral. "None of this was supposed to survive." *You weren't supposed to survive. We weren't supposed to survive.* Too many things are coming dangerously close to the surface. My resolve is crumbling out from beneath my feet. I reach for the suit cautiously, half-expecting my fingers to go through it.

But instead I lay my palm against sturdy, hard-packed tactical weave. Strong enough to catch a bolt with no damage. Light enough that it wouldn't keep a knight pinned to the ground when they fired their boot and palm thrusters and took to the skies. A beautiful, twisting design, the knight's personal sigil, is etched at the sternum.

I think I recognize it. "This was Torrance con-Rafe's, right?" I don't remember many details about her—only that she was a second child of a continental governor from one of the Archon border-worlds. Rather than challenge her sibling for the right to serve as heir, she chose to train as a knight and eventually earned both her powersuit and the right to protect not just the continent that her bloodright could claim but the Archon Empire as a whole. "Wasn't she the knight who held up that building?"

"That she was. It was structurally unsound, it started to collapse as Tor—as Rafe was patrolling nearby, and she planted herself like a cornerstone and kept the damn thing upright until everyone inside made it out."

"Did you see it?" A bitter wash of shame flushes through me as I realize how *boyish* I sound—like some kid at his parents' knees, begging for one more knight story before bed.

Iral doesn't reply right away. I glance back over my shoulder to find his face stricken, his eyes dark and damp, his lips pressed around a grief I'm only just now comprehending the shape of. "I wasn't on that world at the time. Seemed like I . . . was never there for her when I needed to be. But I saw the footage from that day."

"I'm so sorry—" I start, but Iral clears his throat, cutting me off.

"Tor was remarkable not just in her strength and skill with a powersuit, but in her selflessness. Acting for the good of others was so instinctual to her that she never hesitated to jump in where she was needed."

No wonder Iva emp-Umber decided she had to go. I run my fingers carefully along the support struts and motorized joints that would have turned her into a living weapon. On the battlefield, a suited knight was a devil unleashed. The tech to make these suits was all but destroyed at Knightfall. Nowadays, with Umber dreadnoughts to wage wars, there's not much point in consolidating this kind of power in a single person.

"I *was* there at Knightfall," Iral says, before I can beg him not to. He squares his shoulders and pinches his eyes. "I heard the bombers. The blast. I ran into the wreckage of her headquarters, even as the buildings around us were still crumbling. We only ever found . . . parts of her. Not enough to bury. But she'd shown me where her vault was, and I was able to recover her powersuit."

He takes a deep breath, and in the space of it I see him rebuild himself from a shattered lover back into the leader the Archon people needed.

"When I found it, I knew I had a choice to make. To declare the find would paint a fresh target on anyone in proximity. The Umber empress didn't want to kill just the suited knights—she wanted to kill the *idea* of them. So instead, I swore my troops to secrecy and put a call up the chain of command. Days later, the Archon imperials themselves reached out."

Iral turns in his chair, his gaze locking onto the photos that paper his back wall. I drift away from the powersuit, closer to his line of sight. Some of the pictures are informal—soldiers with their arms slung around one another, a laughing woman lit from underneath like she's sitting next to a fire, a sleeping baby curled around a stuffed animal. One shows Iral smiling alongside a carbon copy of himself who can only be his twin brother, Omat. Next to it, where the general's dark-eyed stare has fixed, there's a picture of three people standing on the raised dais of an imperial court—Iral in the middle, with Henrietta emp-Archon and Marc emp-Archon flanking him on either side.

I haven't seen pictures of the emperor and empress in years. I take another step forward, nearly tripping over one of the chairs on the other side of the desk. Iral startles at the clatter. The tautness in his eyes softens. "They took a vested interest in my career after I made that choice. Everything I am today, I am by their grace."

"What were they like?" That question sounds even more childish than my ones about the knights. Iral was a tool in the imperials' hands. Seeing him stand next to them is like seeing a man walk among the gods, and expecting him to speak to their true nature is just as unlikely.

But the general only nods. "No ruler is perfect. A good leader will always have faults and failings, and the things that may endear them to one person might be the same reasons another can't abide them. The most you can do is try to do right by everyone who depends on you. That was the principle that governed our empire while it stood. A leader was a servant to their people, not the focal point of their power the way our conquerors see it." He pauses, then bows his head. "And the most important thing I could tell you about the Archon imperials was that they were *always* trying. They listened to their people, they served with dignity through that hellish war, and the galaxy is worse without them."

The room feels far too small for everything in it.

After a long moment, I decide I might as well ask one last stupid question. "Do you think someone could ever wear that suit again?" I glance back at it, my eyes raking over its deadly edges even as the persistent fact of its emptiness drives a stake into my heart.

Iral shakes his head. "I think Iva emp-Umber did exactly what she meant to at Knightfall. No one believes in the heroes of old—not after she showed us how cruel this galaxy truly is. Even if someone wanted to take up the mantle, they'd only be daring her to take aim again. And then there's the matter of finding someone brave enough to strap four starship engines to their extremities and hurtle into battle. It's not the most common quality."

For a moment, I imagine myself in that suit. Imagine what it would be like to rocket through air and space at starship-level speeds without thousands of pounds of metal around me. Imagine the ability to hold up a crumbling building, to steer a foundering ship to safe landing, to do the kind of mythic deeds only a suited knight would be capable of. But then I remember what I'm doing here, what I *am*. I don't deserve to wear this suit. If I had any commonality with the suited knights, it died with the Archon Empire.

Iral leans back in his chair, turning to face the wall. The corners of his eyes tighten like he's staring into a bright light. "I keep the past behind me when I work. But it's always here waiting for me when I walk into this room. All the things I've done. Everything I couldn't do." He spins slowly back around to face me. "The past is always here to drive us, but when I work at this desk, I'm looking forward. And from where I sit, the future of our empire looks bright."

His gaze is searing, and I lower myself into a chair to avoid meeting it. It feels twisted and wrong to build up Maxo Iral's hope. He's devoted the past seven years to resurrecting the empire. He works with the shadow of his failure always looming over him and the hollowness of Torrance con-Rafe's empty suit staring him in the face. And Gal and I plan to turn on him. The assault we've just convinced him to launch will *ruin* him. And Gal will use the general's head to secure his throne.

I don't know how much longer I can stand to be in the same room as Iral, thinking of a future that's not distant enough. "Sir, I came by to talk about Wen Iffan," I blurt.

Iral's brow creases. "Ah yes, the Corinthian. I've been meaning to ask you what she's doing here."

I grimace. "I understand, and I want to give her an opportunity to contribute more meaningfully. She's a pilot too, you know."

"Is that so?"

"So she tells me." I steel myself as the plummeting sensation in my stomach sharpens. "But if she's going to be a part of our future, I need a favor."

CHAPTER 20

ON THE MORNING that marks our first full week at Henrietta Base, Gal and I awaken not to drums—which he's grown used to—but to a sharp knock that sends him scrambling back against the wall of the bunk. I prop myself up on my elbows and meet his frenzied gaze, torn over whether I should reach out and reassure him.

"If they knew," I hazard softly, "they wouldn't be knocking."

Still, I'm the one who answers the door. I'm the one who greets the tired-looking soldier who's come to tell us Wen Iffan has been detained for trespassing and attempted sabotage.

"I thought you said you were going to keep her occupied," Gal hisses the moment the door is closed again.

"I did—I was . . . I'm working on it," I mutter, rubbing the heels of my hands over my eyes. "Iral was supposed to . . ." Well, it barely matters what Iral was supposed to do now. According to the soldier, they caught Wen in one of the hangars, elbows-deep in a ship's guts. There might be a rational explanation for what she was doing, but probably not one that the resistance will see as justified.

I pull on fresh clothes and stagger into my boots, avoiding Gal's glare. He's not leaving the bunk. This is clearly my problem to deal with. And the look he's giving me is saying everything he wishes he could scream—that Wen causing trouble is going to bring scrutiny on us, going to get us caught, going to get us killed.

I'm halfway across the base when I realize how thankful I am to leave him behind in the dorm. The sky overhead is rosy with dawn and tinted blue by one of the moons, and the grass on the drill fields glimmers with undisturbed dew. Ever since we put this scheme in motion, I've found myself second-guessing every minute I'm around Gal, waiting for his mask to slip again. But for a moment, I can lose myself in the steady rhythm of my strides. I can let things be simple.

Then I reach the detention block, and simplicity goes out the window. For nearly an hour, I'm batted back and forth between the supervisors as each of them tunes out my attempts to negotiate and deflects me to their counterpart on the other end of the building. By the time they give up and let me have her, the sun is high and the dew's been trampled by the morning drills.

Wen has the conscience to look guilty when she sees me, though only half of her face can pull off contrition. Her wrists are furiously red from where she was zip-tied, and she shoots a foul sneer at the back of the officer who escorted her out of the cellblock.

"I was trying to help," she mutters as I grab her by the elbow and pull her down the hall. "That Needle was on the verge of collapse when they stuffed it in the hangar last night. The pilot didn't notice. I thought I could put it right—then at least I'd be doing *something* useful around here."

As we burst out into the heat of the early afternoon, I realize I'm too angry to put things into words. Instead, I drop her arm and storm along the path to the hangars. After a moment's hesitation, Wen follows in silence.

I track the familiar scream of engines until I reach the edge of an open drill field. A runway sprawls on the far side of it, where a unit of light fighter craft are doing touch-and-go landings. The summer heat makes the distant pavement of the runway shimmer, and the ground beneath my boots is parched.

Wen barely bats an eye when I turn on her. "I thought I told you I was working on something," I snap. "I told you to be patient."

She shrugs, and the rage inside me flares hot. "I'm not gonna sit around and wait to be told where to go and what to do." Though she speaks with an easy cadence, her tone is measured like she's toeing a line.

I'm crossing one. "You don't understand what's at stake here, Wen!" I shout, throwing up my hands. "This is a military operation. You can't just—"

"You're right!" she yells so suddenly that I nearly stagger a step backward. "I don't know what's going on here. I'm trapped in this place on a promise that I can get off-world, and I barely know what the Archon Empire *was,* much less what it means to you. I . . ." Her voice goes soft, and the fierceness in her eyes drops abruptly, leaving only the hollowed-out look of a girl with no roots. "I thought it was my best option. I thought *you* were my best option."

It hits me all at once—this isn't the fight I'm spoiling for. I sink down on my haunches, the grass crackling beneath me as I sit with my boots pointed toward the distant runway.

Wen joins me a second later. She wraps her arms around her knees and tucks her chin between them. "I'm sorry. I know I jeopardized your position. Gal was probably right to try and send me back."

It takes me a moment to process what she's said.

Wen catches my wide-eyed look and gives me a bitter grin. "Thanks for fighting to keep me here, even if it wasn't worth it."

"Gal wanted . . . I mean . . ."

"It's okay, Ettian." She stares up at the distant tail of a fighter craft as it screams along a nearly vertical vector. "I wouldn't have kept myself around either. Like I said, not much for me to do around here, and I have no idea what's going on."

I grimace. "I could give you a recap, but I can't promise an unbiased one."

Wen's eyebrows rise. *Go on,* she gestures.

So I do. Starting at the very beginning, when the ancient genera-tion fleets were roving down the galactic arm. On Lucia, settlers found a rich world with vast swaths of arable land, and the Umber Empire grew from that abundance. On Rana, they found hard ground and thin air—and the Archon Empire rose to that challenge. It took centuries for terraforming to spread through systems, for powers to condense into the empires we know, and for an actual border to form between the two entities. And, while they had their differences, they managed to coexist peacefully despite them.

And then Iva emp-Umber came to power drenched in her sister's blood. In the decade after her ascension, the system governors be-neath her jockeyed to prove to her that they were just as vicious. To keep them in line, Iva needed more dreadnoughts than the Umber Empire's mined-out belts could provide and an excuse to unite them against a common enemy.

She looked to her Archon neighbors and saw the solution to both problems.

When I pull back and explain it like this—a game of resources and power, an inevitable consequence of ruling philosophies—it makes the war logical. Inevitable, even, the way history tends to be. I'm halfway to spitting the old propaganda about freeing Archon's starving people from their imperials' mismanagement and justifying it completely. But then I remember Umber warbirds razing the sky-line of Trost during the final month of fighting. The way the walls of the bunker would shudder around us. The helpless noises it wrenched from my throat.

"You know about the suited knights, right?" I ask, wincing at how sudden the change of vector feels.

Wen shrugs. "Bits and pieces. They were like . . . vigilantes?"

"What? No!" I laugh. "They were at the service of the Archon imperials themselves. They were heroes. Sure, they had barely any jurisdiction, but they operated under a strict code of honor passed down for centuries."

"I think the technical term for that is *vigilante*. Vigilante with fancy sponsorship."

"Okay, well, these 'vigilantes' were total badasses. Arceley Vitto once took a C-27 cannon burst to the chest, got up, and kept fighting. Lamar plan-Rana tore the engines off a skipship and rode it through an atmospheric burn. I even heard a rumor that one time Ala Rutger split a fighter clear down the middle with her vibrosword."

Wen lets out a sharp giggle. "There's no way that's true."

I grin. "That was the point of the suited knights. Yeah, they were ordinary people. Some of them had bloodrights, others didn't—but they were all united by the drive to serve their empire and the wild bravery it'd take to wear one of those suits. They could do anything." And then I picture Rafe's empty powersuit, and the grin falters as I remember where this line of conversation is supposed to go. "So Iva emp-Umber coordinated thirty simultaneous strikes across the Archon Empire to kill them all and launch her war."

There isn't much more left to say after that. With the story wrung out of my head, I stare at the runway, watching another featherlight fighter dip down, skim it with its landing gear, and then go howling back into the summer sky.

"Gal doesn't understand it, does he?" Wen asks after the jet's faded to a shimmering speck.

"Understand what?" I don't try to hide the wary edge in my tone. Increasingly, I'm finding it difficult to hide anything from this girl.

"What it took out of you. He doesn't see you with a before and after. He just sees what's left."

I think about her own before and after. Before, when she was destined for glory. After, a place filled with dirt and burns and uncertainty. I flop back, folding my hands behind my head, and a second later, Wen joins me.

"There's not . . . much left," I admit to the broadness of the sky. "I don't understand how there's so much of *you* left."

I expect her to fire off some sort of snappy quip, and I'm surprised when she doesn't. Wen stares up contemplatively at the distant contrails left by transports far above us. "I lost my mother," she says at last. "You lost an entire empire."

"I lost my mother too," I whisper, and my heart seizes in my chest. It's a truth that's always been wrapped up in the larger tragedy. A truth so obvious that I've never said it out loud like this.

If I said it to Gal, he'd follow with a question, or with sympathy that would only double the sensation of a weight crushing my ribs. But Wen just nods and says, "I had to fight for what I kept. I had to keep thinking about it, keep the hurt fresh. And . . . I don't think I like what it's done to me. Part of me wants to know what I'd be without this revenge quest eating up my spare time."

And I want to know what I'd be if I kept my fire the way she has.

"I don't know," she says and sighs, twisting her heels against the dirt. "It's so much to live up to. But for you, it's good to be here, right? To find out that you lost less than you thought? To know so many are fighting to restore it?"

I can't bring myself to lie to Wen directly, and so it startles me when I admit, "Yeah, a little. More than a little." After a moment, I add, "But we're just trying to get back home."

"To *Gal's* home."

I nod, my jaw tightening. "I go where Gal goes."

"Even if the resistance retakes Rana?"

"I go where Gal goes," I repeat.

"Fair enough," Wen says, but nothing in her sounds convinced. Which is fair, because what I said wasn't exactly convincing. I haven't allowed myself to consider what I'd do if our plan falls through and Archon actually regains territory. My thoughts flick to my velvet bag, to what I owe my parents' memories, to what I owe myself after what I've endured in the seven years since the empire fell.

My lips go taut around a question I'm afraid to ask. Finally I spit it out. "When you take down Korsa, would you take his place?"

Wen sighs. Somewhere on the runway, another jet comes down, engines roaring, then rears back into the sky. "Mob rule is mob rule, Ettian," she says. "The people under Korsa's thumb wouldn't be much different from the people under mine. I have to repay him for what he took from me, but I don't have to take it back."

"But if you burn him, what fills the hole he leaves?"

"In me or the city?" she asks, and it's far too insightful for my liking.

"The latter," I decide after a pause.

Wen groans. "I don't want to be responsible for that. Someone worse could take his place, or someone better."

"You could be someone better. Your mother's blood must be strong in you."

"You sound like an imperial," she snorts. "Half the time, I don't believe in this bloodright stuff. In this empire, a council of planetary representatives elects the emprex, but the idea's impossible to root out of the criminal sector—they *love* the notion that the amount of power they hold in their bloodlines justifies their reign. I mean, my own mother . . ." She catches herself, her expression darkening suddenly. "Anyway, it always seems to be the choices that make a person, not the people who rutted to make 'em."

"That's one way of putting it." I roll my head to the side, my eyes meeting hers.

"Whose side are you on, Ettian?" Wen asks, and I know I'm humped before the words have left her lips. I can't look away without shattering her trust in the next thing that comes out of my mouth. Can't take too long to say it, or else the lie is obvious. Can't lie to her anyway.

"I'm still deciding," I tell her, because it's the closest thing to the truth that I can articulate. But the fact that my answer to that question used to be "Gal's" without hesitation—*used* to be—is twisting something horrible in me.

I almost tell her, right then and there. Who Gal is and what it means. The full extent of the war that's been waging inside me since the moment I realized he might not be everything I thought he was. Everything we've been through on the journey here, and how it feels to have the fate of two empires tethered to your every choice.

But that truth would lead to other truths, ones I'm not ready to put into words, and so instead I glance toward the hangars at the far end of the runway. "I asked Iral for permission to take you out on a test flight. He's working on the clearances, and it might take longer after what you pulled this morning, but I swear I'm going to get us in the sky."

Wen's smile could give the brutal summer sun a run for its money, and something tells me it has everything to do with the word "us."

CHAPTER 21

IT TAKES AN extra week to get clearance but only twenty minutes for Wen to drag me by my collar into the cockpit of the waiting Cygnet as soon as the verification comes through.

She's somehow procured a flight suit. I'm not sure if it was a gift from the resistance or if she simply nicked it from the laundry. Wherever she got it, it's a little too big for her, and she rolls the sleeves up as she settles amiably in the copilot's seat. That alone curdles my suspicion—I'd have thought she'd be adamant about being the one to take us out.

Wen notices my hesitation and grins, something leering in the corner of her smile. "Let's be honest, Ettian—you need this more than I do."

I roll my eyes and climb past her, swatting her on the side of the head as I drop into the pilot's seat. Wen cackles, wedging her helmet over the messy braid she's snarled her hair into. The visor drops over her eyes, replacing them with a silvery mirror.

I settle into the gel-seat, hands gliding over the dashboard as I spin up the ship's preflight checks. The set of the controls is familiar, but this ship—Corinthian-made, with a little more emphasis on form than function—still feels a little alien to the touch. Outside, the hangar bustles with activity. I track a group of soldiers as they wheel crates of artillery toward one of the larger cargo ships for transport to orbit. Slowly but surely, the assault is coming together. With every passing second, my heart creeps higher and higher up my throat.

And it's not helping that ever since the mission was green-lit, Gal's been pulling away from me. With the constant threat of discovery hanging over his head, he's been getting more and more withdrawn, and even the tiniest of irregularities causes him to lock up in panic. It's been days since the last conversation I had with him that didn't involve our subterfuge, and even longer since the last time we managed to speak without fighting.

The deeper we get into this scheme, the less I see of the real Gal—or the Gal I want to be real. All I see is the way he squares his shoulders and marches into meetings that I can't even stomach attending, his unflinching willingness to pave our path to the Archon interior with bloodshed. When we're in sight of the resistance, he acts like a model cadet. When we're alone, it feels like there's barely anything left of him. All he wants is to be on the other side of this, and I worry about how hungry that makes him for our plan's brutal end.

I don't know what to do. All I *can* do is quietly ache.

But today I have a distraction. Gal wants me to prove that Wen can be useful, and Iral needs to see that she's as committed to his cause as we are. So today I'll get her in a pilot's seat and see what she can do. But that's not all we're trying to accomplish—Wen's implication is also dead-on.

I really, *really* need to blow off some steam.

The Cygnet hums under my hands, its engines hot and eager. As I spur it out of the hangar and onto the open tarmac, my heartbeat syncs to the vibrations of the ship beneath me and I feel myself lock more firmly into the controls' layout. The Cygnet is a two-man fighter, built lean and athletic, twice the size of a Viper and twice as armed. And unlike a Viper, this bird doesn't need a running start to get into the air.

I pull the safety harness down over my shoulders, snap my helmet's strap beneath my chin, and stare pointedly at Wen until she does the same. "Henrietta Base, this is Green Twelve," I announce. "Preflight checks are clear, awaiting confirmation of launch permissions, over."

A moment later, the base tower chimes back. "Green Twelve, this is Base. Sky's clear, you have permission to launch, over."

Wen bares her teeth. I don't miss the way her fingers itch toward the weapons panel. The ship's been unloaded, but the temptation is all too real. I double-check that the firing mechanisms are disabled. She sticks her tongue out at me.

In reply, I throw the engines hot and blast the forward thrusters, rearing our nose back as the Cygnet leaps into the sky. The force crushes us into our gel-seats, my vision fringing with black, and I cut back our burn before the acceleration wrings the consciousness out of me. Wen tries to howl, but it comes out as a scream through gritted teeth, and belatedly I remember that she's probably never been in a ship this fast.

So I pop on one of the attitude thrusters and throw us into a corkscrew for the hell of it.

When we level off, her smile is savage. I laugh as I set our vector, pulling our trajectory southward. Isla's spires glitter in the distance beneath us, and Wen leans forward, pressing her helmeted head against the cockpit window. A slight burst of wind buffets us, but the Cygnet's sleek aerodynamics slice through it like a well-honed blade. "Had enough?" I ask Wen.

She braces herself in her gel-seat, her lower lip pressing against her upper teeth, every part of her daring me to do my worst.

So I let loose. My instructors at the academy tried to steer us away from aerial acrobatics, but every cadet did their part to steer back. I have a whole arsenal of maneuvers, all of them stomach-twisting, hair-raising, vision-stealing. I cut our main engines, let us glide, let us fall, push the attitude thrusters to flip us end over end as we tumble toward the ground. Then level off into an even glide, reeling from the effects of the g-forces that make my heart feel like it's in a hydraulic press. Then gun the engines as hot as they'll go, pushing the fighter until we've surpassed the sound barrier four times over.

When I pull us back into a cruise, Wen lolls her head toward me, her mirrored visor pointed right at my eyes. "Shown off enough yet?" she asks. There's a slight weariness in her voice, like maybe I've shaken her up too much.

I flip on the autopilot and sink back in my seat. "Give me a minute."

Wen's already clawing out of her harness. There's no floor space in this cockpit, so she braces against the bulkhead behind us, her feet sinking into the gel of her seat as I unstrap and worm over to the copilot's side. My legs and arms shudder, my body betraying the aftereffects of my stunts. Wen climbs over me and drops into the pilot's seat with a *whump*. "Ten seconds to strap in, flyboy," she says, slipping into the harness.

My knuckles tighten around my own belts as I buckle them. Something tells me a measly safety harness isn't going to do much against whatever I'm in for.

Wen hisses her countdown through her teeth as she knocks her hands around the dashboard. It seems like she's memorizing the feel of it—where each control is, how to bully each thruster into doing exactly what she wants.

My worries run wild. She's only ever flown junkers. She has no instinct for this kind of craft. Heavens and hells. We're humped.

"One," Wen whispers.

And burns.

My vision goes dark instantly as the engines crush me into my gel-seat. But that doesn't stop Wen. Not even divine intervention could do that. Blacking out doesn't matter anyway—she's memorized the shape of the controls. The ship steadies under her hands, carving through the turbulence. Somehow, impossibly, it keeps accelerating, and I fear worse than blackouts as the Cygnet hitches against another bad spot of wind. But finally we hit our limit, my vision comes back, and I lift my head from the gel to find Wen hunched forward over the controls, her teeth bared like she's intimidated the ship into submission.

The miles fly beneath us in swaths of forest woven with rivers, cities, and highways and air traffic far below and far behind. "How the rut . . ." I choke. The speed on our dashboard doesn't seem feasible. My hands shake as I bring up the ship's status.

"Spun down unnecessary systems—air circulation, mostly. Gonna get stuffy in here if we want to keep going this fast," Wen croaks. Her chest heaves up and down, and it takes a moment to realize mine's matching. Both of our bodies are floundering to recover what the acceleration crushed out of us.

"But I mean . . . How . . ."

Wen grins. "Just 'cause I fly junkers doesn't mean I don't know what to do with a good ship on a good day." She pulls the Cygnet's fins, lifting our nose to the sky as the engines rattle behind us. "You know, you should think about learning some mechanics. I could teach you a few tricks, if you're not busy."

As our altitude climbs, I glance at our navigation, making sure the path ahead is clear of other ships' vectors. "Wen?" I ask as she ups our angle, sinking us against the backs of our gel-seats.

"Yeah?"

"You do know you're going to space, right?"

She nudges the engines in response.

"Just checking." I'd assumed we'd stick to atmo today, but clearly she has other ideas.

"Wen?" I ask again, after a few minutes have passed. The gravity is bleeding away beneath us, and Delos's landscape blurs together at the edge of the cockpit windows.

"Yeah?"

"You ever flown in zero-g before?"

There's a too-long pause. Her lack of an answer is all the answer I need. I scan the dashboard on the copilot's side for something—*anything*—that will save our skins the second this goes sideways, but all I have is guns filled with blanks.

I let out a long, resigned sigh. Even though anxiety hums at the base of my skull, I know there's little I can do to stop her. "Well, no time to learn like the present."

"That's the spirit," Wen mutters, and spurs the Cygnet until we see stars. The rush of air fades away, first to a whisper and finally to the silence of the void. Wen spins down the main engines—they're no longer needed with no drag to tear us back. As our acceleration fades, we drift out of our seats against the harnesses. I sneak a side-long glance at Wen. An unfettered grin has overtaken her lips, one I know all too well. You never forget your first time in orbit. For a moment I'm back above Rana, the lone still point in a shuttle packed with cadets quite literally bouncing off the walls, unsure how to handle the fact that for the first time in my life, my birth planet's gravity is no longer dragging me back down.

"Okay," I say, once I've given her mind enough time to process the emotion and her body enough time to get its bearings. My eyes stay fixed on the navigation in case any other traffic starts to brush up against our flight path. We're out over an open area, clear of any cities and too close to the planet to be a bother to any of the orbiting satellites. "Now, adjust our vector fifteen degrees to the right."

Wen punches the attitude thrusters on the left side of the ship. Our nose tilts against the black, but our vector stays the same, sailing us crooked along it. Wen frowns.

"Engines," I remind her, forcing my voice to remain steady. With no gravity to tug us in one direction, the ship only goes where pushed. The attitude thrusters have the force needed to rotate a craft, but to change its vector, we need a contribution from the Cygnet's actual firing power.

Wen gives the main engines a boost, and our course skids sideways. I watch our vector on the readout, but I don't dare urge her to go any faster. Caution trumps speed when a new pilot's testing the vacuum for the first time.

"How was that?" Wen asks the moment we've locked onto the target vector.

"Could be better. Use the gyros to point us, not the attitude thrusters. It's more precise."

Her lips purse, and she falters on the controls, probing the gyro stick like she's not sure what to do with it.

"Gently—" I warn, but it's too late.

Wen spins the Cygnet like a top, the forces jamming me back in my seat before I have a chance to rip her hand off the stick. The last thing I see is her fingers flailing, scrabbling, trying to claw their way back across the dashboard as the force of our spin throws her into the side of her harness. Then my vision goes dark.

My head smashes sideways, my helmet digging into my cheek as my jaw does its best to make contact with my gel-seat. I fight with everything I have, arms straining, fingers reaching, fumbling over the unfamiliar controls on my side of the craft.

You've endured worse in your academy training, my mind screams. *Remember the centrifuge? Remember the stress tests?* My body screams back that all of my blood is pooling in all the wrong places.

I find the weapons panel. The ship's loaded with blanks, no actual firing power in any of our guns, but maybe blanks are enough. Blanks will have to be enough, because I'm starting to feel like I could take a nap. I root through what's left of my brain until I get the calculation right. Spinning one way. Fire the other. Slow the ship.

I run my hand over the ridges that distinguish each knob. The bones of my fingers feel like they're about to shatter. I find the button— I hope it's the right one. Either it makes our situation better, or it makes it a whole lot worse.

Only one way to find out.

I jam down. If we had bolts enabled, I'd be depleting our entire arsenal, firing a whirling barrage of death into the void. I hear the guns behind, beneath, chugging their emptiness into the black. Each blank sends a shudder through the ship, and each shudder skims away some of our speed like a hand brushing against a spinning wheel. I choke out a breath as my lungs finally find the strength to expand, then lean forward against my harness until my fingers brush the gyro controls on Wen's side of the ship. I spin them counter to our rotation with a twitch of my hand, breathing a long sigh of relief as the spots fade from my vision. With a few long burns of the attitude thrusters, I scale the Cygnet's vector back to a point.

Wen's slumped in the pilot's seat, unmoving. Her arms drift in front of her in a dead man's float. Panic snaps through me, and I jam my fingers under her chin, digging for a pulse in the soft flesh next to her trachea. Her head rolls, but a weak, slow beat rises through her skin.

I sag back in my own gel-seat, closing my eyes.

At the academy, our introduction to flight in a vacuum was gradual. We worked in simulators aboard a training station—nasty, finicky, slow-moving things, but they had safety measures imposed that kept us from centrifuging ourselves into cadet-sized puddles. Even when we graduated to an actual cockpit, we spent days watching a skilled pilot fly before we were allowed to touch the controls.

I neglected that, caught up in the thrill of seeing Wen fly, and it almost got both of us killed.

Gal and I have spent the past two weeks consumed by the fear that we'll be caught and executed, and somehow an untested pilot in zero-g nearly took me out instead. I realize with a jolt that I never actually said anything to Gal this morning. Never said goodbye—I'm not even sure if he knew we were going on our flight today. He's been waking up each morning already consumed by thoughts of war and treachery, and he collapses into bed—my bed, still—each night thoroughly worn out by them.

If Wen had killed us with her spinout, Gal would have been left all alone in the midst of his enemies. I would have abandoned him to face Maxo Iral, the man he's feared since childhood, for a chance to blow off some steam in the cockpit of a fast ship. I've never vomited in zero-g before, but a tickle of nausea climbs up my throat at the thought of Gal alone on the base.

I think I owe him an apology. Maybe a thousand apologies.

I remember Wen's question. *Whose side are you on?* I remember how the answer wasn't him, and my nausea doubles fiercely. Gal told me on that rooftop back in Isla that he didn't want to be the terms I lived my life on. Now I think that fear's farthest from his mind—not just because he's preoccupied with our gambit but because I've been letting him slip away so easily. My eyes burn, and heat flushes my cheeks. With no gravity to pull it, the water floats in my vision, blurring the controls in front of me.

I could have died without him knowing anything. Not what was going on in my head when I took off this morning. Not the past I've buried for so long. And not the realization I had that night we came up with the plan that's supposed to restore and redeem him in the eyes of his vicious empire. I owe him more than an apology. I owe him the truth I keep running from, the one that drives me to fling myself into the sights of would-be rebels and mobsters and Maxo Iral himself.

The burn behind my eyes gets stronger.

Next to me, Wen stirs. She rolls her head for a moment, then lunges forward against her restraints, clawing at them like a trapped animal. It takes a good fifteen seconds for her to wrap her head around her circumstances, and only after she's wrenched her helmet off and pitched it into the cockpit window. It bounces back at her, she catches it, and then she glances sidelong at me.

"That . . . was a hell of a thing," Wen says. In null gravity, loose strands of hair sway around her face, and she blows them away with a huff. Her eyes drop to the controls, fixing on the gyro stick. She looks rattled, but not entirely discouraged.

"It's sensitive," I tell her flatly, two minutes too late.

Her gaze snaps to me. "You okay, Ettian?"

Something in my voice must have betrayed me. I give her a terse nod, glad for my own helmet's mirrored visor. Beneath it, I blink rapidly, trying to clear my vision. It doesn't do much. "Vacuum flying—nothing stops you from spinning once you start. If you lose control, sometimes there's no coming back." I'm talking way too fast, my words as out of control as the Cygnet was.

Wen leans forward over the dashboard, but she stops when she sees me tense up. "Oh, come on," she groans, setting her helmet back on her head. "It's not the kind of mistake you make twice."

"Like hanging around with the likes of you?"

She sticks her tongue out at me.

"Just . . . Just go slow."

"You sure you're okay, Ettian?" she says. Her hands pull back from the controls, and her impenetrable mirrored gaze feels locked on me.

I pause, my breath catching. I've spent so long avoiding this kind of talk—seven years, if I'm being honest.

I haven't been okay for seven years.

And once that thought is in my head, it can't be taken back. Gods of all systems, what a horrible time for this to sink in. I laugh, because it's the only thing that feels right.

Wen's not laughing. She pulls off her helmet again and leans over, patting my sleeve with one tentative, scarred hand. "You want to fly?" she asks, her other hand working on her harness. "C'mon, give me something. Stop giggling. It's weird."

I run one hand over my mouth, trying to get my emotions under control. Water beads catch on the inside of my visor, skirting along the rim.

"Look, I'll close my eyes if you want. Do what you need to do," Wen says, then presses her nose into the crook of her elbow, folding around the helmet in her lap. I wave one hand in front of her face, just in case, then duck my head and pull my chinstrap loose. My head feels so much better without the helmet compressing it, and as I rub down my eyes, some of the weight lifts off my shoulders.

The radio crackles. "Henrietta Base to Green Twelve, we noticed anomalies in your flight plan," the tower announces. "Do you need assistance?"

"Green Twelve to Henrietta Base, all good up here," Wen answers, because she knows I can't. After I settle the helmet back on my head, she lifts hers. I feel the edges of a question in the air between us, but she doesn't ask, and I nod, and she jams the helmet back over her head, her hands dropping to the controls. With a burst of the main thrusters, she sends us sailing. I brace myself, my fingers already on the weapons panel.

Wen's survived this long by learning hard lessons fast, and her first encounter with the gyros has taught her well. She probes the stick cautiously, tensing when it tilts us into a lazy spin, then locks us onto a steady new vector.

My eyes drop from the weapons panel to navigation, watching our flight path's curves bleed into lines. She flies with steady hands, cool under pressure, learning the ship more and more with every burst of the thrusters, with every spin of the gyros, with every second that passes.

I wait for the moment I have to open my mouth again. Wait for the need to correct her, the certainty that I have to step in. It doesn't come. Wen melts into the Cygnet's controls, into the cradle of the void, into perfect, natural flight. She escalates slowly, pushing boundaries, testing edges, experimenting with all the ways she can hurtle the ship through the dark. The Cygnet in her hands is eager and athletic, and soon she's flying it the way she did in atmo, using its mechanical quirks to push it to its full potential.

When she scales the Cygnet's vector down to a point, she lets out a long, enthralled breath. Our nose is pointed away from Delos, out into the black, and this far over on the night side, the darkness ahead shimmers with a thousand stars she's never seen under the city lights of Isla. "So?" Wen asks.

"You're not flying in space."

"But I'm flying?"

I pretend to mull it over, just to work her up. She nudges me with her elbow—softly at first, then over and over until I give in, laughing and shoving her away. "I'll have to talk to Iral, but I think we need a pilot with your kind of tricks."

"I want a 'nottie," Wen says plainly.

"Someday."

"Promise?"

I don't lie to her. I don't think I *can*.

"Promise."

CHAPTER 22

WHEN WE SPILL out of the Cygnet, smiling deliriously and unsteady on our feet, Gal is waiting in the hangar. A laugh drops back down my throat as I meet his sunken, tired-looking eyes. Wen glances between us, then tugs my helmet out of my hands and sets off across the hangar to the equipment lockers without a backward glance.

"Have a good flight?" Gal asks. His voice is flat, but I can't tell if it's from exhaustion or something more.

I stuff my hands in my pockets and approach him with a caution I used to reserve for stray dogs. After my breakdown in the cockpit, I know I need to talk to him. I also know this scares me more than any system's hell.

I can't lose him, but somehow it feels like I already have.

"Wasn't all bad. Cygnet handles like a dream, but it's no Viper." I try to keep my tone light, but I know it's a lost cause. Gal can read me better than anyone else, and I'm too nervous to keep my thoughts off my face.

"How'd Wen do?" he asks. His hand finds my elbow, pulling me ever so slightly closer toward him, and the touch should put me at ease.

Should, but doesn't.

"She's one hell of a pilot. Took to zero-g like a fish to water after a . . . slight hiccup."

"She spun out?"

"She spun out so hard. We were basically humped—" I break off, noticing a slight twitch in his jaw. Something about it makes his whole face shut down. "Gal?"

He blinks. "Sorry, it's just . . . Can I show you something?"

Before I can respond, his grip tightens on my elbow, pulling me behind him as he sets off across the hangar.

We move along the highlighted paths that wind between rows of Cygnets, dodging the pilots running back and forth to their exercises. A distant rumble shakes the hangar doors as a ship takes off somewhere beyond them.

The whole place is abuzz, and so am I. There's an electricity crackling down my arm to the point where Gal's fingers lock around it, charged by the thought of what I'm going to tell him. I resist the urge to pull free, instead leaning into his grip as he pulls me out a crew door on the far side of the hangar.

I almost ask for an explanation, but then I see the way his lips are pressed together, the way his dark eyes narrow. Gal's not telling me anything until he's ready, and he won't be ready until we get where we're going.

Under the blazing afternoon sun, we cross the tarmac, the soles of my boots softening in the summer heat. We duck into the shadow of a large hangar, and I nearly open my mouth again. We've tried to stick our heads in here during our exploration of the base, but our keycards wouldn't get us through the door. Gal lets go of my elbow, pulls his out, and swipes it through the reader next to the crew door, which unlatches with a cheerful beep. He hauls it open for me, gesturing, and I step into merciful, ventilated coolness with all of the questions inside me unanswered.

But the inside only holds more questions. Rows and rows of ships greet us, but unlike the hangar we came from, there's no order to their layout. Some are massive transports, fit to carry a hundred people in comfort or three hundred if pressed. Others are skipships, built for speed and athleticism. Still others—

My breath catches. Fighters. Not just any fighters. Vipers, their hulls striped with obsidian and brass.

Every ship in this hangar is of Umber make.

Gal takes in my surprise with a wry smile, nudging my shoulder with his. "You haven't even seen the best part."

He grabs my hand this time, his fingers slipping easily between my own, and I let him drag me across the hangar floor, under a canopy of ships' wings. Their hulls glimmer with the official markings of the Umber Empire, and every ship looks like it's fresh from the factory. I resist the urge to reach out and trail my fingers along the thin brass lines drawn in perfect parallels on a skipship's hull. We dodge around it, and I'm met with two familiar faces.

The first is Adela Esperza consulting with a small cluster of mechanics and detailers, her grubby dealer getup traded for a crisp uniform with platinum-and-emerald trimmings.

The second is the *Ruttin' Hell*.

She's been repainted, the marks we scraped off her restored to their original glory, but I'd know this Beamer anywhere. I let out a short laugh, and Gal's hand tightens on mine.

Adela's head whips up, and a sharkish grin spreads over her features. "There's the other one," she says, tipping her cybernetic hand in a rakish salute. "I told you there was a place for you in this empire. Would have been a whole lot simpler—and cheaper for the both of us—if you'd taken me up on the offer."

Gal beams, letting me go so he can step forward and shake her hand. "Colonel Esperza, you'll have to forgive his gawking," he says. "Ettian never dreamed he'd see his long lost love again."

Adela—no, *Esperza* cackles. "As you might have noticed, we're stockpiling anything Umber that comes through the borderworlds. It's been a pet project of mine—hard to convince the general there's any use for junkers like this one. I mean, Umber ship design is . . . inelegant, shall we say, but it turns out they're going to be the crown jewel of our attack strategy. And thanks to you two, yours truly snagged the mission command."

Something dark flashes in Gal's eyes, and it dims my smile. I can't get caught up in the joy of seeing the *Ruttin' Hell* again when there are deeper machinations turning. If Esperza will be leading the strike, and the strike is meant to fall through . . .

"C'mon, let me introduce you to the ship," she says with a wink, dismissing the mechanics with a wave. Farther down the hangar, I spot another ship coated in scaffolding, a hive of detailers drawing careful lines of paint across its exterior. The markings match academy specifications exactly, and as I look around, I realize most of the paint in here is fresh.

My eyes slip to Gal, who's already following Esperza up the Beamer's cargo ramp. He's always had a talent for memory. It's one of the things that makes him so good at holding grudges.

As I step onto the *Ruttin' Hell*'s ramp, a shiver of nostalgia runs up my spine. The smell of the cargo hold hits me, and I nearly freeze in my tracks. I didn't realize the scent of the ship was something I'd memorized. It's been barely half a month since we sold the *Ruttin' Hell,* but it feels like a lifetime has passed, and it makes me yearn for the days that were, if not uncomplicated, at least a thousand times less so.

"C'mon, Ettian," Gal calls from up the ladder. He seems downright giddy, and I have to admit that it's a relief to see him break from the serious, tormented look that's been shrouding his face since we arrived on the base. But no matter what's in his head, a smile's only part of the act.

Still, it's a damn good act.

I clamber up the ladder, down the hall, and into the cockpit, where Esperza is already installed at the controls. I brace myself for her to do something reckless, even though it's difficult to reconcile the messy, grungy Adela we met in the undercity with the woman decked out in a colonel's uniform. Her casual slouch in the pilot's seat helps with that.

"The mechanics have been going wild on this thing," Esperza

says, running her flesh hand affectionately over the dashboard. "The little rutter's been souped up to every hell and back. No more handling like a doped-up puppy. Want to see?" She reaches for the ignition, but Gal holds up a hand.

And she freezes. Grins. Sits back in her seat.

My eyes narrow, flicking between them. Two weeks on the base, and already Gal has enough clout that a *colonel* is taking cues from him?

"Suit yourself." Esperza rises from the pilot's seat, ducking the instruments and crossing the cockpit. "It'll fly better than anyone expects, which makes it a profoundly valuable addition to the arsenal. So thanks for that."

"I feel like we should be thanking you," I reply.

She smirks. "Given what the general has planned for it, I wouldn't thank me yet. But that's a topic for another dull meeting, and I've got other shit to do."

"We'll leave you to it," Gal says with a nod. "My associate and I need to talk anyway."

My stomach bottoms out. *Here we go.*

"He's all yours," Esperza says. "Let me know if you change your mind about that test drive. This thing's got some surprises in it that might be worth your while."

Gal waits until the sound of her boots has faded down the ramp before he lets out his breath. In that instant, he transforms from hungry rebel upstart to exhausted young prince. "So with these ships, the assault plan is getting a lot more concrete," he says, dropping into the copilot's seat. I try to reconcile his cold, factual tone with the Gal who curled up in that chair over two weeks ago, wild-eyed with raw panic. I come up empty.

I stay standing, leaning against the back of the pilot's seat. The cracks in the cushioning are familiar. It isn't another Beamer, cleverly painted to look like our ship. This is the vessel that carried us out of Umber, the one that I dodged missiles and ran a blockade in.

The one he pressed me against when he tried to kiss me.

Has he changed so much since then? Or was this the truth of him all along?

"Enjoying yourself?" I blurt. The words come out so sharp that I want to swallow them immediately to spare him from their edges.

Gal's head snaps up, eyes narrowing. "Do I *look* like I'm enjoying myself? How the rut could you think—"

"I don't know what to think," I snap. "One minute you're chumming with a woman who scammed us out of a ship—"

"We stole the ship."

"*Hush.*" I bury my face in my hands, groaning. "Every day, I see less and less of you. Or of the person I thought you were. I thought you *were* starting to like this—that maybe you . . ."

Oh gods, this is *not* what I was supposed to be telling him.

When I peek out between my fingers, Gal has slumped low in the copilot's seat. The look he fixes me with is cool and guarded, and it makes me doubt myself even more. "Finish that sentence," he says, a slight tremor in his voice.

"That maybe you . . . you've been putting on the act for me. That you really are the Umber heir through and through, every inch your parents' blood."

Gal lets out a low, humorless snort, turning to face the windshield and the sprawling salvaged fleet outside. I brace for the inevitable confirmation of every sneaking suspicion that's wormed into me over the past weeks.

"Ten thousand troops will fit in the ships we've gathered," he starts. "They'll be packed tight for four days, but the soldiers are willing and the mechanics have made adjustments to the life-support systems to handle it. We'll be taking the fight to the dreadnoughts, catching them off-guard. Cutting the head off their leadership, commandeering their troops. Swarming as many as we can. And then we take the assault to Rana."

I nod. All of it fits together with the snatches I've caught from the briefings I've been able to stomach.

"And when we reach Rana, every single one of those ten thousand people falls into the jaws of this nightmare I created. Every last one of them dies, and the best, the brightest among them will probably do so painfully and publicly on the steps of the citadel."

Bile rises in my throat, but I can't look away. Gal's brows drop, his lips tightening around the words stuck in his throat. He breathes deeply through his nose, clenching and unclenching his hands.

"I chose it all. I drove them into this. All of this is my *fault*. And you expect me to live on this base, to watch it happening around me, and be the *same*?" His voice is getting quieter and quieter, hissing through his teeth, forcing me to lean forward to hear what he's saying. "I said it before—you don't know what it's like, spending every day surrounded by people you're going to kill and knowing what they'd do to *you* if they knew what you were. If they catch us, there's a chance for you. You're one of them. They'll make all sorts of excuses. But me?" He breaks off with a low laugh, leaning forward to jam the heels of his palms against his eyes. "I just want to stop a war, and it's probably going to kill me."

"Gal," I murmur, taking a step toward him, but he shrugs away from my outstretched hand. "I had no idea—"

"Don't start now," he groans, fixing me with a vicious glare. "You . . . Gods, this whole gambit was your idea in the first place, and you've left me alone to see it through. Left me to go off gallivanting with *Wen*."

"Don't you dare drag her—" I start, but Gal breaks my gaze, sinking his knuckle against his lips as he stares petulantly out at the hangar.

"I've never seen you like this with anyone," he says bitterly. "It took you months to even have a real conversation with me when we first met. And yet you stumble across this stupid girl who almost blows you up and all of a sudden you're ride or die for her?"

Nothing he's saying is false, and yet I want to protest it with every fiber of my being. "I'm not . . . It's different. It's not what you think."

"Is there something I should be thinking?"

The cockpit stills. My lungs have frozen, my breath trapped as I fight down the words that feel like they *should* be coming out now. *Not like this. Not like this. Not like this.*

Finally Gal breathes out a long sigh, tangling his hands in his hair. "I've been trying so hard to keep it together, and you keep . . . slipping away. I can't stop it. I probably shouldn't stop it. I thought . . ."

I step around the pilot's chair and round the copilot's. I fight back the building dread, even though everything in me wants to flee. I've spent my whole life running from anything that mattered, anything that felt too huge to confront. But nothing is going to matter more than this.

"It's not working," I start, but have to cut off around a thick swallow. Gal's eyes widen in obvious panic, and I hastily correct, "It's not working because we're doing this all wrong."

It's so clear now, looking at him. I should've trusted my instincts from the start—they always point me back in the same direction. Him, him, always him. *Save him. Kiss him. Tell him.*

I go through my days working off the base assumption that I can't have what I want. That maybe I never should. So even when it seems like I might, I push my chances away.

Now I reach out and cup my chance gently on the jaw, bracing for him to pull back. "Ettian." Gal whispers. He doesn't move.

There's more I should say. A better explanation for why I've finally come around. I know he probably needs it.

But I think we both need this more.

He's going to stop me. He should stop me.

He doesn't stop me.

And the weight of all my fears leaves me as my lips seal over his. I prop one knee up on the copilot's seat to keep from toppling over as he pulls me down against him, his arms winding around me so enthusiastically that for a moment I forget why I was ever afraid in the first place. This isn't an everyday sort of kiss. It's deep. Hungry. Terrifying. Momentous. I'm kissing the Umber heir, and he's kissing me back.

And I was right. I was so right. We're slipping into alignment, clicking into place, solid and sure. Resisting this has been destroying us. Allowing it is putting us back together again. We should have been honest—we should have been doing this from the start.

The urge to make up for lost time is a little terrifying. "Gal," I mumble against his lips, trying to break away. He lets out a soft, protesting hum, and the corners of his mouth tighten. I slide my hand down to his chest and push, pinning him against the seat so I can look him in the eye. "I'm sorry. And don't you dare say it—don't you dare tell me 'no apologies.'"

He blinks up at me, looking dazed and giddy and so gorgeous that it takes a significant amount of willpower to keep from kissing him again.

"I've been holding myself at a distance because I thought I saw what I was afraid of. I saw how much you want this plan to succeed— I knew you *need* it to, but I kept expecting the worst, reading into everything the worst way."

Those were the instincts that used to keep me alive, and only now am I seeing how much they twisted my perceptions. They let me turn Gal into the monster I feared he might become, giving him no chance to prove himself otherwise.

"And I'm sorry I went off with Wen today," I blurt, the words cascading out of me in a rush. "I didn't think. She nearly killed us when she spun out, and all I could think about afterward was how I could have left you here all alone, never having . . . Not knowing . . ."

The thought is too terrible to complete. Gal's hand trails along my hairline, across my jaw. I lean into it, closing my eyes. "Ettian," he murmurs again. His hand slips lower, his thumb moving to circle the jut of my throat. I make a surprised noise, but Gal doesn't clench. Doesn't threaten, or if there is a threat in this motion, it's the softest one I've ever received. A notion flickers in the back of my mind— Gal's the only person in seven years to touch me with this much tenderness.

Or maybe he's the only one I've ever allowed. Maybe the only one I ever *will* allow. It doesn't seem possible that in a galaxy where empires rule entire systems, where cityships wage war, where annihilation is a threat that can be made good on, there's room for something as small and tender as a boy's gentle hand on my throat.

Slowly Gal lets it slide, moving around my neck until he cups the back of my head. His thumb brushes over my wiry, buzzed-short hair. When he speaks, he breathes his words against my collarbone. "I'm sorry too. I didn't want to make this harder on you, and I thought you wanted . . . Every day I wake up terrified that I won't be able to come back from this. It seemed so much easier to shut down, to not feel anything at all, and I forgot what that would look like to you. I can't . . . I need . . . I'm so glad . . ." He breaks off, inhaling deeply. "No empire is worth it if I don't have you too."

This time I tilt my chin down and let him come to me. In the darkness of my closed eyes and the hush of the cockpit, my world reduces to the slight hitch of his breath as he leans up and presses his lips to mine.

There's no hurry. No resistance outside, no brink of war on the horizon, not even the thundering urgency inside me for *more, more, more*. Just the slow tilt of his chin. The warmth of his mouth. The way my shaking hands move up his sides. I feel him grin—nearly catch myself on his teeth.

And a deep certainty washes over me as his hands find my hips, skim under my shirt, run up my back. He's never going to leave me behind. He never could. I pull back, trailing my fingers over a brow meant to wear a crown of brass and obsidian.

It feels ridiculous to say it now. For gods' sake, we just caved into this. But two and a half years is more than enough to know, even if you've only been kissing for a microscopic portion of them, so it doesn't feel shameful in the slightest to whisper, "I love you," into the inches between us.

And it feels a thousand times more ridiculous when Gal whispers, "I love you too," back.

He leans in for another brisk kiss, his nose smashing awkwardly into my cheek. "Tell me what you need," I mumble against his mouth. "Where to be. When to be there. I'm never going to let you down again."

Gal laughs, nuzzling my neck. "I need you here. With me. For as long as we can stay in this ship. I need them not to question that I want to sleep here. But most importantly, I'm gonna need you to kiss me again and tell me not to do something *really* stupid."

"Really stupid?" I ask before obliging him.

When I break away, his eyes are downright wicked. "Do you want to steal the paint, or should I?"

Gal swipes the can from one of the scaffolds while the workers are looking the other way, covered by the thumping beats of the Archon music the detailing team is blasting from a haphazardly but lovingly rigged stereo system. He sprints back across the hangar with the paint in one hand and the detailing brushes clenched tightly in his other and dodges around the *Ruttin' Hell*'s rotary thrusters, nearly running headlong into me. A glob of thick, brassy paint slips over the edge of the can, dripping onto the hangar floor, and Gal tries to wipe it away with the toe of his boot.

Instead he smears a streak of gold across the concrete. He laughs, bracing against my shoulder, but only makes it worse as he scuffs his boot along the floor. "Ruttin' hell," he mutters. The paint's already starting to dry. "Whatever. Did you pick a spot?"

I point to a panel in the juncture between the ship's body and the branches that hold the rotary thrusters. It's clear of the heat shielding so the paint won't get scorched off by the reentry burn, and it's low enough that we don't need a ladder to reach it.

Gal holds out a paintbrush, but I raise my hands in protest. "Your handwriting's way better. You should do it."

"It's for the both of us—we should both have a hand in it."

"You write one word, I'll write the other?"

"You first."

I roll my eyes and take the brush, moving past him to run my hand over the chosen panel. "If I rut this up, I'm blaming you. And don't you dare make me rut this up."

Gal holds out the can of paint, but the mischief in his eyes makes no promises. I dip the detailing brush's fine tip in, swirling it once before pulling it out and raising it to the hull. "How big should I make it?" I ask Gal, poised to strike.

"One foot per letter," he says, and I snort. The point of this exercise is moot if our addition gets noticed and scraped off the hull. I trace my *R* carefully, then trace over it again, trying my best to lend some elegance to my strokes. It doesn't work. No childhood penmanship lessons survived the fall of Archon, and my hand is shaky even at its slowest.

"Don't laugh," I mutter as Gal starts doing exactly that. I dip the brush back in and finish my work with haste, leaving the *R* overly dense and the "uttin'" traced in brisk, inch-high strokes. I step out of the way in time to dodge Gal's brush.

He writes his "Hell" with perfect balance, the letters so measured that it looks like he drew them with guidelines. Against my rough font, his hand is ridiculously smooth, each character carving a graceful, shimmering arc. I jab him in the ribs with my brush as he's finishing the last *l,* and he jumps sideways, accidentally streaking paint from the base of his work all the way down to the heat shield.

"Heavens and hells, Ettian," he groans, flicking his brush at me. Brass spatters across my nose, and I flinch, grinning. "Give me your hand."

I hesitate, but he sets the paint can down and grabs my wrist, flipping it palm-up before I can get a word of protest out. Gal runs his brush over the pad of my index finger, then pulls me down so he can get more paint.

"This stuff had better be washable," I grumble.

"Agreed," he says, glancing at the damage I did to his shirt.

"And nontoxic."

He hesitates, his eyes flicking to the paint can's label.

I shake my head, chuckling. "Whatever. They have a medical ward here. Do your worst."

Gal finishes painting my finger, then taps a spot on the hull beneath our unofficial christening. I catch his drift, raising my hand

and pressing my fingerprint into the *Ruttin' Hell*'s metal. My finger comes away still dripping paint, and I reach out and wipe it on Gal's brow before he can stop me. "Seriously, Ettian?" he yelps, trying to rub it off. The brass is only a few shades shy of his natural skin tone, falling short of blending into his golden visage.

"My turn," I say, dip my brush, and paint the finger he offers. Gal marks the hull to the left of me, his own print a bit smaller than mine. And then, because he can't resist revenge, he smears the leftover paint on my cheek. "Oh come on," I groan. "It stands out way more on my skin than on yours."

"I know."

"We're going to have a hell of a time explaining why we look like this," I say, shaking my head.

Gal beams. He lifts his hand and draws a defiant line across the rest of his forehead, crowning himself in the metal of his blood. "I've talked these people into hijacking dreadnoughts. A little paint is nothing."

CHAPTER 23

THE NIGHT BEFORE Archon's reckoning departs, Henrietta Base lets out a long, needed breath.

The first bonfire lights at sundown, and by the time night has settled over the base, hundreds of towering flames are scattered across the drill fields. Whatever air isn't choked with smoke is washed with the sharp scent of raw polish. Palpable relief hangs over the thousands of soldiers, technicians, and other personnel swarming the fields, celebrating their last night on this planet. The fires are fueled by possessions accumulated over five years on Corinthian soil—everything that these people won't be taking with them when the fleet launches tomorrow.

I slip through the thick of it, blunted and unsteady. I'd rather be back in the dark corner I just stumbled out of, tangled in a rumpled, desperate mess with Gal, but the combination of bonfires, polish, and an unsupervised Wen Iffan has enough potential for disaster that I've extracted myself and waded out into the fray.

And there's a part of me that knows it's time to come clean. Before the assault launches, before she gets snared in the trap we've laid. Tonight, with the remnants of the life we've built on Delos in flames, there's no better time to do it.

It takes me nearly an hour to track her down. I find Wen seated at the edge of one of the largest fires, part of a captivated crowd watching as Colonel Esperza narrates a story with a bottle of polish tucked under one arm and nothing attached to the other.

"So there I was," Esperza says, gesturing expressively with her stump. "Back to back with Lietta Omoe—her in her powersuit with a fully charged vibrosword snarling in her hands, me with no ruttin' armor and one ruttin' pistol. The most honorable Nova Knight and a ratty Umber-born pirate who didn't realize what she was getting into when she targeted this particular freighter."

I hate to tear her away—especially with the way Wen's eyes keep flicking back to the unmistakable burn scars that wreath Esperza's missing wrist—but I don't trust myself to hear whatever knight story the colonel is spinning and maintain my emotions. Not on a night like this. I tap Wen on the shoulder and hitch my thumb toward the darkness and quiet that fringes the fires.

She pulls a face, but comes willingly. I offer my arm, seeing the way she sways when she stands, and even though she scowls at the implication, she takes it. The feeling of her hand slipping around my elbow sinks a heavy stone through my conscience, sobering me almost instantly.

Wen trusts me to hold her up.

And I'm only going to let her down in the end.

"What's up?" Wen asks, staring out at the distant shadows of ships staged along the runways. All preflight checks have been done, all practice runs have been flown, and all that remains is to strap in tomorrow morning and blast off for real.

I brace myself, trying to summon the truths she needs to hear. "I wanted to talk to you before there's no going back. I want to be sure you're . . . *sure*."

That earns me a reproachful look. "I've been committed since we got here."

"I'm just saying, there are easier ways to get off Delos. If that's all you want to do, there's no need to throw yourself into a fight you have no stake in."

"If you don't think I have a stake in this fight, you haven't been paying attention," she replies with a wry smile and a nudge of her shoulder.

Under any other circumstances, I'd be moved. But now I just feel sick. "It's a war, Wen. It's going to be a war."

"I was born war-ready. I've been at war my entire life. You, though," she says, her voice going soft with concern. "You seem like you're worried you might not be able to handle another war."

She doesn't know the half of it. How terrifying it is to see this war looming on the horizon. How far I'll go to keep it from happening. She's getting swept away in stories of heroism and missing the brutal reality of the lies I've woven around her. If I were noble, if I were anything near *good,* I'd tell her the truth right now.

But the thought of an oncoming war has reminded me of a fact I can't escape. After all of the grief I got about finding Wen a role in our scheme, I've made sure no one can contest that she's needed.

Which means I *can't* give her a chance to walk away.

Wen trusts me absolutely, and on the other side of this assault is the moment she sees me for what I really am. The moment I lose her for good—because I have no illusions that it could go any other way. It's going to break my goddamn heart, and I'll deserve every ounce of the pain.

So instead, I let her lean on me for a moment longer, breathing in the smoke, soaking in the electric night around us. "I'll be fine. I've done it before," I mutter, and Wen squeezes my arm.

"I believe you," she says, then ducks back toward the fires before she can notice how deeply those words cut.

The *Ruttin' Hell* departs the next morning, her cargo hold packed with ten hungover Archon soldiers and all of their tactical gear. I fly, with Gal sitting rigidly in the copilot's seat and Wen lurking behind us, belted to an attendant bench that folds out of the rear of the cockpit.

It'll take four days for the assault fleet to make it to Tosa System, and that's including one full day at subluminal speed as we move to the outer edge of this system's speed-limited zone. Our timekeeping switches from Delos's long days to the shorter galactic standard, but the hours drag long in spite of it. I stay camped in the pilot's seat, all too aware of the soldiers starting to stir in the hold. One of them is Sims, our persistently friendly former guard, who seems all but ecstatic to curl up with his audiobooks for the duration of the journey. Despite sitting in briefings together, I don't really *know* any of the others, which seems like a prerequisite for people you're flying into battle with—doubly so when you're sharing a cramped Beamer with a single lavatory for four days.

But knowing what we have planned for these people, it's better not to know them well. Gal's warning from our first morning at Henrietta Base sticks in my brain. I have to guard my heart.

So I let the first day pass in silence. And when the fleet gathers at the edge of the system, pointing our noses along a uniform vector, I break that silence only to announce, "Brace for superluminal."

I hit the booster, the black goes gray around us, and just like that, we're on our way to war.

On the second day, the stories start.

Gal and I sleep in the crew bunk with Wen overhead, and when I shrug off his arm late in the morning, I hear them drifting under the door. I slip out into the corridor as quietly as I can, trying to pick out the shapes of words in the faint noises coming from the hold. My bladder pulls me to the lavatory, but my curiosity's got it beat, and I drop into the shadows of the hall as I creep closer and closer to the ladder into the bay.

". . . telling you, Meridian has Chorta beat by a long shot," a sharp voice declares.

"*Parts* of Meridian, sure," Sims's voice shoots back.

"Come on, Chorta's like ninety percent ocean. It's underdeveloped."

"Yeah, well maybe I just like beaches."

"They've got beaches on Meridian too," the first voice scoffs. I sink against the wall, trying to peer out and see which soldier Sims is talking to without losing my place in the darkness.

"Anyway, what I was *saying* was that Mom and Mama would take us out in the skiff before dawn, and I stand by my statement that there isn't a prettier sight in all the worlds than a sunrise on Chorta. All three of us were small enough that we'd sit on one bench, and Mom was big enough to take up the other one entirely. Mama always manned the motor, and she gave us these little nets to scoop up the . . . Did you guys have them on your worlds? They might have been a regional species—we called them glowers, but they probably have a scientific name too."

I know Chorta was an Archon world, but my knowledge of the former empire's been buried over the years. My brow furrows as I try to place its system. It must have been a borderworld or a system's minor planet. A sour taste builds in the back of my throat. I should *know* this. And the fact that I don't has me clinging to the wall, greedy for the next words that float my way.

"They were these tiny bioluminescent jellyfish—we'd put them in jars and keep them by our beds. There'd be fields of them out there below the waves, waiting for the sunrise to tell them it was time to return to the deep. Someday I'm gonna make it back. I have to know if my moms are still there."

Before Sims can continue, his companion's sharp voice cuts in. "The empire's glory wasn't in its beaches, Sims. It was in its cities—the shit we *built*. You wouldn't know it from any of the settlements on Chorta, I'm sure. But Golgorath was the emperor's favorite jewel for a good reason."

"Henrietta was the emperor's favorite jewel," Sims counters, and the hold fills with quiet chuckles of agreement.

"Right, but of the *cities*," the interjector continues, undeterred. "Of the cities, Golgorath was the greatest. Those spires were miracles of engineering."

"*Were,*" someone else interjects pointedly, and a sober silence sweeps over the hold like an Umber warbird's passed overhead.

They're dancing around a question without asking it. What's left for them if they take back their homeworlds? The empire will never be the same again. Governments have been ousted, power redistributed, cities burned and built. I close my eyes, picturing Trost as it once was and Trost as it is now. The imperial palace and the system governor's estate that replaced it after the warbirds bombed it into a husk. The massive crater of the Warning Shot, visible from the city's downtown. The landscape of the old empire simply doesn't exist anymore. These soldiers are wandering in memories that have no match in the Umber Empire's reconstruction.

"What are you doing?" a voice whispers in my ear, and I reel back, nearly toppling into the hold.

"Wen," I snarl, but it's too late. All of the soldiers are looking up at us. Some of them look guilty, like they shouldn't be talking about Archon-as-it-was. Others soften when they meet my nervous gaze. Sims offers us an encouraging smile. "You're from Rana itself, aren't you?" one of the snipers, a willowy woman named Tarsi, calls out.

"She isn't," Arso, the squad leader, says, nodding to Wen. I recognize her voice as the sharp-edged one from before. "You're Corinthian, ain'tcha?"

Wen shrugs. "Guilty."

Arso lets out an ungrateful scoff, and Sims checks her on the shoulder. "Wen was just curious," he says. "Come on down, you two. Plenty of stories to go around."

"I actually gotta—" I start, but Wen's already scrambling down the ladder into the hold. The soldiers have laid out their cots with five packed against one wall and five against the other, and most of them are sitting propped up on them, hands folded on their laps. The conversationalists sit cross-legged on the floor, with dice and cards scattered around them. Wen drops to her knees at Sims's side. She glances back up at me, grinning slyly, and waves me down.

With one last forlorn glance toward the lavatory, I descend after her.

———

By the third day, my silence is getting suspicious. The soldiers talk their way around it, always bringing up Rana, the war, and the aftermath and waiting for me to fill in the gaps. Sometimes I'll nod along, acting like I'm expecting someone else to fill the hole in the conversation. Other times, I'll excuse myself to check on the autopilot. We've passed into Umber territory, and all of our proximity sensors are dialed up. So far, the only thing on our scanners is a few members of the assault fleet, traveling in staggered formation along slightly crooked vectors that will eventually coalesce at the rendezvous.

Gal's joined us in the hold. Like me, he's been listening in on the conversations, his own silence noticeable but justified. The soldiers don't care too much for him—even Sims's easy smile tenses whenever the two of them make eye contact. No matter how instrumental he's been in arranging the assault and how heroic the senior staff paint his role as dreadnought bait, they can't ignore that he's not an Archon citizen, a fact they like to jokingly throw in his face over and over again.

He shrugs off their barbs with strained, diplomatic smiles that mask his guilt. After his apology for walling himself off, he's trying to make up for the way he shut down on the base. But his eyes get more and more hollow with every story. If all goes according to plan, these soldiers are eulogizing themselves, and we'll be the only ones left to carry their memories.

"So Ettian," Arso starts, steepling her fingers. "You might know—in the Feda System, same one that hosts Meridian, there's a planet called Vilt. Kinda backwater, low population, mostly mining colonies. I had uncles out that way, and . . ."

I rack my brain, frowning. In between the storytelling, it's been a constant barrage of questions like this from the soldiers, each of them worried about relatives on worlds I barely remember. The war separated them and the secrecy of their exile silenced them, but they still hold out hope that there's something left to go home to.

I try not to let my envy show.

"We went to Vilt," Gal says, and Arso's eyes snap to him, stunned. "There was . . . Ettian, you remember?"

Horrified, I nod. Better for me to complete the thought than him. "The planet was one of the first to be mined out completely for dreadnought metal. We went there on leave once. There's a base in the southern hemisphere with an adjacent resort town. There was, uh, recreational climbing. In the quarries, or . . . well, what was left of them."

Arso's pride keeps her disappointment off her face, but a spark of hope in her eyes winks out. My stomach twists. I can't pretend to know what it's like to have your family's world transformed from a home to a plaything for Umber officers.

And I feel the resentment for the three of us reaching a peak. We've each had our own hardships, but in their eyes, we've never been touched by the horrors of the War of Expansion. Gal and Wen certainly haven't.

But I can't stand the guilt anymore. "I was ten," I start, and every eye in the hold snaps to me—even those of the soldiers who've been drowsing on their cots. I stare at my feet.

Can't look at Gal. Can't look at Wen. Can't look at any of them.

"My parents were a part of Noam plan-Rana's advisory board, and we lived adjacent to the planetary governor's household in the heart of Trost. I think my mother worked on the planet's defenses. I didn't see her much in the last days. There was an airstrike, and—"

Smoke in my lungs. The world shattering around me. The woman who was supposed to be looking after me gone, a twisted red mess in her place. Shouldn't have panicked. Should have stayed put for the rescue crews. But I was ten and terrified, and the world around me had descended into a twisted hellscape, and the only thing I had any presence of mind to do was run until I reached a part of the city that was still intact.

"In the aftermath, there was no one left for me. No one would help—in those days, everyone had their own battles to fight."

But that's not quite right. I went to no one. Did nothing. Hid in an underground garage for three days, until the hunger was unbearable. Started stealing. Started fighting. Started telling myself it was all necessary. Went feral—for how long, I'll never be entirely sure.

"I had no identification, no friends, nothing. I did what I had to do to stay alive, one day to the next, for two years. By then, Umber had installed social welfare programs, trying to wring the war out of the city. They cleaned me up, put me in a foster household, even arranged for me to attend a school. A propaganda-heavy school, where Archon children were raised into proper Umber citizens. And I guess it worked, because I went straight into the academy when I was fifteen."

I break off, feeling like I've already said too much. It's like my outburst at the train station with Wen all over again. The parts of me that I thought were blasted away like that big stupid crater outside Trost have come squirming back to the surface again. And this time makes the information I told Wen look like a trickle in comparison.

I'm bracing for the soldiers to scoff, to call me on the places where my voice rang false. But instead Arso softens. She reaches over and pats me gently on the knee, and when she speaks, her rough-edged voice is low and soothing. "You don't have to say any more," she reassures me.

"I . . . uh. I need to go check on the autopilot," I say, standing before anyone can protest. Across the hold, Gal's dark eyes find mine. *Now?* he seems to ask, an ember of fury in his watery stare. *For ten soon-to-be-dead strangers? That's when I get to know you?*

But I think it's more than simple jealousy that I withheld my history from him when everyone else on this ship brings it out effortlessly. By throwing my story in with the rest, I've made it abundantly clear that I'm just as much a victim of Gal's rise as everyone else on this ship—and *that,* more than anything else, cuts him deep.

I break his gaze and head up the ladder before he has a chance to say anything that might stop me.

The autopilot is fine. On course. One more day of travel. The twisting sensation in my gut misses Delos's longer cycle. On the galactic standard, it feels like we're hurtling even faster toward Tosa System.

And once we're there, it all goes into motion. The dreadnoughts will drop onto our tail, and we'll see if Colonel Esperza can pull off the miracle it will take to commandeer them. If we manage it, we'll lead the fleet into the jaws of Tosa System's defenses. And then we betray every person in our hold and every quiet hope they've shared.

I drop into the pilot's seat, trying to ground myself and stop the tremor that's leaching into my hands. It's been so long since I've brushed up against that part of my past, and I'm helpless against even the quickest glance into the memories I've kept buried. I let my eyes unfocus as I stare out into the gray. A silent moment passes.

"What do you want, Wen?" I sigh.

"It was a good story," she says from the shadows of the hall, low enough that her voice won't carry back into the hold. "But someday you're gonna have to tell me why half of it isn't true."

CHAPTER 24

WE'VE BARELY SCRAPED the outer fringes of Tosa System when a dreadnought locks onto the *Ruttin' Hell*'s tail. Assurances of certain annihilation flare on the instruments as the cityship adjusts its vector and burns onto our rear. Gal's face reflects the ashen gray outside our cockpit windows. He bends over the navigation, his fingers tracing long, unsteady arcs between us and the rest of the assault fleet, between us and Rana, between us and the distant promise of the Umber interior.

I fly, trying to ignore the fact that I've already sweated through my shirt. My brain struggles to process the pieces at play—even the concept of the dreadnought on our rear is difficult to comprehend. It's two thousand times our size, and yet, if all goes right, we walk away from this confrontation as victors. Nothing about that math adds up.

Behind us, Wen sits in eager silence. When this is over, she takes the helm. She wants this over *fast*.

"Drop superluminal at my mark," Gal mutters next to me, holding up one hand as his other swipes through communications channels that will put us in contact with the rest of the assault fleet. "Three. Two. One. Mark."

I flip the booster. The gray snaps back to black as stars sprinkle across the cosmic night. A long, ragged breath bursts from my lungs, and somehow my next one feels fresher. After four days cooped up inside this tiny ship, I don't understand how that's possible.

"We're sure this is going to work?" Wen asks, not for the first time.

"Dreadnought's popped out, matching speed," Gal mutters, eyes unblinking, ears unhearing. "They're hailing." With a careless flick of his fingers, he dismisses the call.

"They could fire on us. I know you said they want to take deserters alive, but one burst from those guns and we're ash in the void."

I suck in my lips. Gal's brows lower.

"Someone start talking," Wen hisses, kicking the back of my chair.

"The 'nottie won't fire on us," I tell her, trying to sound confident.

"You're *sure*?" she says, and I glance back to find her straining for a glimpse of Gal's readouts.

"Of course we're not sure, but where's the fun in that?" Gal says, smug and princely. With the *Ruttin' Hell* flying brazenly into Tosa System, we're begging to be caught, and the only threat we pose is if Gal tries to run again. The dreadnought won't fire. Not when they've identified this Beamer as the one that hauled ass out of the system a month ago. Not when there's a chance the Umber heir's on board.

It doesn't do much to combat the sweat trickling down the column of my neck.

Gal pulls up the intercom line, and the distant speaker in the hold crackles with his voice as he reminds the soldiers to strap in good and tight. No matter what happens next, things are about to get shaky. I double-check my own harness, and behind me there's a slight jingle as Wen does the same.

"Another hail," Gal says, dismissing it in the same breath. "Dreadnought's closing the gap. Time to about-face." He gives me a nod.

I burn the rotary thrusters. The stars swerve outside our cockpit, and briefly my eyes lock on the distant glimmer of the star Tosa. Somewhere in its orbit, Rana waits. Sometime today, we'll be back on my homeworld's soil.

But not yet.

I bring us all the way around, lining up our nose along our former vector's inverse, and find a distant shard of light bearing down on us. According to our instruments, they've started their deceleration, easing out of the burn that ensured they'd catch up to us. And with our rear pointed squarely away from them, they know we're not running.

The question is how quickly they'll figure out why we're letting them come to us.

The next hail flickers across the dash, but Gal doesn't dismiss it immediately. Instead he pulls up the ship's information embedded in the signal, peering intently at the data. "Not Umber imperial. This fellow is the *Torrent,* under the command of Governor Berr sys-Tosa." He gives me a savage smile. "Not by presence. By proxy."

So Tosa's not on board. We've hooked a member of his fleet, eager to prove their worth by reeling in the governor's secret prize. Part of me is a little disappointed. It would have been so *clean* to humiliate Berr sys-Tosa in the course of engineering Gal's return to the interior. But no governor means the ship isn't traveling under delusions of power. It might make it easier to capture.

Or it might make it more openly desperate to bring us in.

The *Torrent* noses closer, its form becoming distinct. The ship is bulbous, sickening in shape. It has no need for aerodynamics when it's far too large to survive an encounter with an atmosphere. Most of it is built for brute acceleration. The parts left over are crafted for war. My eyes are drawn unwillingly to the main batteries, the cannons that could vaporize us at a whim. They lie inert, but a single order could change that in an instant.

An order that could easily be encouraged by our reluctance to answer their calls. Not for the first time, I wish Wen weren't hovering behind us. If she weren't here, we could open that line, let them know for sure that the prince they're after is aboard, and guarantee that those guns stay inert. My fingers itch for the weapons panel, but we can't risk their interpretation if we start to look aggressive. If the *Torrent*'s guns go hot, our only defense is my flying, and no modification in the galaxy can keep the *Ruttin' Hell* out of a dreadnought's sights forever.

Another hail. Another dismissal. Another minute passes as the distance closes.

I pray that Gal's right about what's coming next.

"Wait for it," he mutters under his breath, spinning up the Beamer's scanners to watch the *Torrent*'s hull. With his other hand, he's got lines open to the rest of the assault fleet, feeding them information from the extra sensors Esperza's techs packed into our ship. No doubt the *Torrent* is performing a similar examination, trying to make sense of all the unconventional aspects of this seemingly unworthy little transport. Within the cityship, orders are snapping along the synapses of command, knee-jerk reactions transformed into strategies in a matter of seconds. Our instructors at the academy used to say that with a seasoned captain in charge, a dreadnought can react like a single, massive organism.

Now we find out if Gal successfully anticipated that response. I lean toward him, my eyes drawn to the readouts underneath his hands. I know my focus should be on the *Ruttin' Hell*'s flight controls. I should wait for orders. Gal's in command. But ever since we left the academy, it's been my duty to keep both of us alive, and with twenty miles of dreadnought bearing down on us, that directive is the most urgent it's ever been.

Impossibly, my eyes move to Gal himself. His mop of unruly hair curling over his forehead. His hooded eyes—his mother's eyes. The way his throat bobs as he swallows. The way fear bends him low, even though he'll never let it consume him fully. And a razor's edge saws through my worry. With him at my side, we'll always fly true.

"C'mon you ruttin' bastards," he whispers. "Do it."

The readouts beneath his hands flicker. The *Torrent*'s hull buzzes with activity. Launch-tube doors peeling open. The silent glimmer of air venting into the black. Gal's fingers twitch, counting the apertures, calculating the chances.

His thumbs yank up the comm line. "We have our opening. All teams *move*."

Forty Vipers breach from the *Torrent*'s flanks, wheeling in the void as their gyros point them squarely at us. Their engines are hot, but their guns are cold as ice. They burn for us, curving out in arcs that weave their vectors together in a net. They're here to herd.

Just as Gal predicted.

Space doesn't react when a vessel drops from superluminal. There's no flash of light, no noise—in a vacuum, there's nothing to react *against*. So when a hundred members of the assault fleet come screaming out of the void between stars, it happens in a blink. One moment there's nothing.

Blink.

Ships.

Their calculations are precise. Their pilots are far more skilled than I'll ever be. They match the *Torrent*'s forward vector and arrive with just enough distance to avoid pancaking themselves on the city-ship's hull. From our distance, they're barely visible, motes of dust next to the dreadnought's might.

But our instruments and the flurry of information coming in through the comm lines paint a different story.

The carrier-ship crews haul open their launch doors, puffing a blast of air into the void along with the resistance Vipers lined up inside their bays. The fighters are locked and loaded, ready for launch, their pilots howling through the lines as they dive headfirst down the dreadnought's exposed tubes.

"First teams are *in*," Adela Esperza announces through the comm from her spot at the flagship's helm. War drums echo in the background of her line, Archon's thunder rising again. "Let's clear a path for the gentleman, shall we?"

In the rear of our ship, the soldiers pick up the rhythm. The *Ruttin' Hell* shudders with the stomping of their feet, the slapping of hands on bulkheads, the pounding of fists on chests.

"Ettian," Gal reminds me, "time to split."

I rip my eyes away from the battle unfolding on the instruments and tune out the drumming, my hands jerking on the *Ruttin' Hell*'s controls. With a hard burn of the rotary thrusters, I bring our nose spinning around, gunning the main engines at the same time. We catapult across the black as I lock our vector onto the distant speck of Rana. "Vipers?" I ask through gritted teeth.

"Recalculating," Gal replies.

I glance down at the instruments, watching our gambit play out in points of light. The *Torrent*'s acting captain has to make a split-second decision. The Archon forces have pinned down the *Torrent*'s flanks, their guns poised to blast away any Vipers that launch from the hull. The *Torrent*'s scrambled fighters could bully us in, securing her grasp on the Umber heir and the favor of a ruthless system governor. But if she has any hope of saving her ship from the commandeering Archon forces, she needs to target the assault fleet, not one measly Beamer.

Only, if the prince gets caught in the crossfire, she'll have to answer to both Berr sys-Tosa and the Umber imperials.

And the prince has every intention of jamming himself squarely into the crossfire.

Right on cue, the Vipers split, their formation blooming like a flower as half of them peel off, wheeling back toward the *Torrent* and the flickering battle around it. "Ruttin' hell," Gal mutters. "That's what I would have done."

Behind us, the *Torrent* is accelerating again, bearing down on our rear as the Archon forces struggle to match speed. The twenty Vipers still on our tail spread out, burning their engines as hot as they'll go.

Casting the net. Waiting to cinch it closed.

Wen's fingers creak in my headrest as she hauls herself forward to look at the instruments. "Not good," she seethes. "Not good—they're going to fire on us."

"They won't," I tell her firmly, spinning the Beamer around once more with an athletic twist of the thrusters that wouldn't have been possible a month ago.

"They're in attack formation—"

"They're herding us."

"There are twenty Vipers on our rear! Why are neither of you acting like it? Why are we turning the ship around? Why are we playing *chicken* with a cityship?" Gone is the calm, cool, collected Wen, the one who walked casually away from the remains of the bombed-out skipship, who didn't hesitate before jumping off the wiretram, the one who flew the Cygnet like a dog chasing its tail.

She must have finally realized that she stands at the center of a web of lies. Finally realized that something is *off* in a way she can't pin down. Trapped in deception and uncertainty, all that's left for her to do is panic.

Well, that *and* switch her grip from my headrest to my neck. Her uneven fingernails bite hard into my skin, and I swear vehemently as the ship's vector wavers under my hands.

"Wen!" Gal yelps, twisting in his seat and lunging. Her nails bury deeper as he tries to pry her off me. From a distance, belted to his chair, he's less effective than I'd like.

Even with my jugular twitching under her grip, I can't blame her. The trouble we're giving the *Torrent* doesn't match their neglect to fire *anything* at us. And as the Vipers circle closer and closer, trying to steer us onto the vector they want, their guns are as cold as ever.

"Get—c'mon, get off him, Wen," Gal grunts, twisting one of her wrists. "For the love of . . . *We're* in the ship with him. He's not going to fly us into something that gets us killed."

Her grip loosens, and I choke down an unsteady breath. *Us. We.* Words that mean worlds to Wen. Gal knows exactly how to win her.

"You know Ettian would never throw our lives away. So let's let him do his thing, okay? Wen?"

The negotiator's worked his magic. Her hold goes slack, and he yanks her hands back before she has a chance to rethink. I feel a slight wetness and a chill in the indents left by her nails. Pushing the stinging pain aside, I throw the *Ruttin' Hell* into a spiraling dive, feinting one way, then the other, teasing the Vipers' herding formation wide open.

I spare an odd, grateful thought for Tatsun Seely—thanks to his assassination attempt, I've had practice with this kind of flying. With an extra burst of speed from the main engines, I thread the ship clean through the hole I've opened and streak for the *Torrent*'s flanks, where the second half of the scrambled fighters tangle with the Archon forces.

"*Ettian,*" Wen warns.

"What did I just say?" Gal grinds out between gritted teeth, still twisted around in his seat. "*Trust him,* you little asshole. We've put our lives in your hands, like, eight times before. Try it the other way 'round."

The void around us starts to flicker with stray boltfire as we close in on the fight. The drumming in the cargo hold grows louder, like the soldiers can sense it through the silence. The Archon artillery outmatches the Vipers, but their agility can't be beat, and they keep the resistance forces pinned against the *Torrent*'s hull like a firing squad. There's no outmaneuvering them—not without risking the wrath of the dreadnought's main batteries.

That is, until the *Ruttin' Hell* comes screaming between them. The Vipers' guns flicker out like snuffed candles. They swing their noses away from us, trying to get clear for a shot at the Archon ships, but we run right through their formation, dragging the other half of their force behind us to add insult to injury. The two Viper groups tangle together, veering wildly to keep distance between themselves and the unruly Beamer in their midst.

I sneak a glance over my shoulder for the joy of catching Wen's slack-jawed confusion. Then a glance to my side, for the breathless, wild grin I knew Gal would be wearing.

Chuckling, I spur us farther along our reckless path. The *Ruttin'*

Hell hums cheerfully beneath my hands, and I throw a loop into our vector to taunt the *Torrent*'s command. No matter how much they doubt Gal might be aboard, they can't run the risk of firing until they know for sure. I almost feel sorry for them. The *Torrent* is a mighty annihilator, and a surprisingly slippery Beamer has reduced it to a carnival sideshow.

And the humiliation on the outside is nothing compared to what's going on beneath the dreadnought's skin. The initial force, led by the Vipers we stuffed down the open launch tubes, has cleared a path for the true invasion, forcing open hangar doors to bring in ships brimming with Archon soldiers. In turn, they cut through the *Torrent*'s internal security officers with a combination of boltfire and strategic venting of the ship's air supplies, facilitated by techies jacked into its systems. They're wrestling their way down through the architecture to the heart of the *Torrent*, where the armored bridge sits.

It's laughably early when another hail flickers across our dash, the broadcast code confirming its origin as Archon. Gal picks it up, grinning wide as Adela Esperza's sweaty, grimy face glows in front of us. She tucks a strand of inky hair back behind her ear, pulls her ponytail taut, and tips a salute with her mechanical hand.

"Attention, all local vessels," she announces in an even voice that barely betrays her delight. A faint triumph rhythm pounds beneath her words. "The acting captain of the *Torrent*, Nita con-Silon, has ceded command to me, Colonel Adela Esperza. I claim this ship and all its assets in the name of the Archon Empire. Those who have any sort of quarrel with my command will face the *Torrent*'s fire. Those who wish to surrender . . ." She pauses, her eyes glimmering with pride and rage and a thousand other emotions I know I shouldn't be feeling. "Get in line."

With no superluminal drives, the scrambled Vipers have no choice. Their launch tubes open welcomingly, the shimmer of vented air inviting them in. The Archon forces abandon the *Torrent*'s hull, leaving the path to the Vipers' surrender clear and unquestionable. One by one, they wheel toward their berths. One by one, their guns go cool.

Another ship appears on the radar, winking into existence ahead of the *Torrent*'s fore. It's the size of a city block, but it seems insignificant against the scale of the dreadnought. It faces down the conquered *Torrent*, proud and unyielding.

Maxo Iral has arrived to claim his victory.

My heart thunders in time with the triumph drums as the soldiers in the hold pick up the beat. For a moment, I forget that I'm not supposed to want this. For a moment, everything feels *right*.

Gal finally twists back in his seat—finally relinquishes Wen's hands, I notice with a smirk. There's a slight tremor in his fingers as he drags them across the navigation, his eyes fixed on the newly arrived flagship, and suddenly I'm sunk in the reality of what's happened. The victory we're celebrating is nothing but the first stage of a plan that ends in Archon's final defeat. "No going back now," Gal mutters under his breath.

Behind us, Wen inhales sharply. I turn around to look her in the eye, and she scowls at me. On the unburned half of her face, the expression is already uncompromising, but the burn triples her fury. "One of you, start talking," she demands.

"Start talking about what?" Gal asks, still focused on the communications bouncing around the assault fleet as they solidify their victory.

"What that was? How we did this? How any of this is possible? They were well within their rights to vaporize us, and they didn't. You said they wanted to take you alive, but they deployed *forty Vipers* to try to bring you in and then didn't fire a single shot at you."

I keep my face blank. Impassive. She can't see through me now.

"They should have shot us down. They should have let us fly into their fire. Why—"

"Wen," I say, my voice low and deathly serious. "Has it occurred to you that if we could explain, we would have already?"

She slumps back against the bench, her hands tightening into fists. "I'd take Korsa any day over this shit," she growls, and my heart seizes, knowing I'm already losing her.

"We've got a second dreadnought inbound," Gal says, tapping

my side of the dashboard. "Due to hit in seven minutes. Time to do this all over again."

I turn to face the stars outside, and instinctively my nose points straight at the distant speck of Rana.

But the fight isn't over. The drums are switching over from triumph to a call to arms, that familiar rhythm Seely tapped into my shoulder on the morning this whole mess started. And though my blood is pounding for home, I pull the *Ruttin' Hell* back into the fray.

CHAPTER 25

RANA LOOMS IN our windshield. From a distance, the planet looks peaceful, but my heart rate is escalating with every mile that collapses between the *Ruttin' Hell* and its goal. When we reach the planet, one way or another, this all goes to hell.

My hands itch for the Beamer's controls, but I've been replaced at the helm by Wen Iffan. She wears a deathly serious look, her lip stubbornly set as she holds the ship steady on its vector. In the co-pilot's seat, Gal flicks away incoming hails. He still hasn't allowed any communications between us and the Umber defenses, leaving them uncertain about whether he's aboard and unable to shoot the *Ruttin' Hell* down. The closer we get to the planet, the more frequently the hails come.

"Only a matter of time before we get an escort," Gal mutters, glancing back at me. "You should get to the cargo bay."

I shake my head. I'll leave his side when I have to, and not a moment sooner. "Gotta make sure Wen knows how to treat the lady," I joke, knocking my knuckles against the bulkhead above me.

Gal blows an exasperated sigh out of his nostrils, but he doesn't argue the point. I reach forward and set my hand carefully on his shoulder as he turns back to the instrumentation. He relaxes a little.

We left the dreadnoughts far behind. At our last point of contact, Maxo Iral had managed to bring three of the monstrous ships under his command, and a fourth was on the way. Soon they'll be turning tail and going superluminal to meet up with the remainder of the assault fleet in the deep black between star systems and escort them into Umber territory. The rest of the assault ships stuck to their skirts, waiting for the next commandeering.

And the *Ruttin' Hell* streaks for Rana completely alone.

"Inbound," Gal says, dragging up the sensors as he homes in on two ships. "Skipships. Weapons cold, but they're moving fast."

"Want me to tease 'em?" Wen asks, nudging the stick. Our path veers away from the approaching escort, and a boost of the engines sinks us all back in our seats.

"Fly casual," Gal replies.

"I can tease casually," Wen shoots back, and it gets a little grin from him. I should have flown these two through a battlefield ages ago.

"Fine," Gal says, and sighs. "Put some heat on their tails."

I have about a half a second to find something to hold on to before she obliges him with a hard burn of the rotary thrusters. The Beamer plunges, breaking for Rana's atmosphere, and Wen lets out a wild whoop, leaning to check the pursuit on Gal's side of the dash. "Watch it," I warn as the first gasps of air start to rush over us, flickering with a hint of fire. "Don't hit atmo with our heat shield belly-up."

"Unclench, Ettian. We've got time," she says, then cackles, tilting the ship into another vicious course adjustment. Somewhere behind us, I hear a heavy thump, followed by a groan from one of the soldiers in the cargo bay. We should have warned them before turning Wen loose, but Arso hasn't started yelling at us, so I think they caught on fast enough.

"Wen," I choke as she swerves again.

"Twenty seconds till we hit the hard part," Gal agrees.

"*Fine,*" she seethes, hauling on the *Ruttin' Hell*'s throttle. She cuts the main engines and throws the rotary thrusters into a lazy spin that curves the planet through our windshield before bringing it to rest squarely beneath us. "Happy?" Wen asks, holding her hands up.

"Don't—" I start.

Gal lunges across the controls, firing the thrusters as the atmosphere blazes around us. The *Ruttin' Hell* lists before aerodynamics take hold, and Gal fights to keep the Beamer level as the deceleration bends him over the dash.

I release my handholds and crumple, trying to save myself from the uncompromising force. The armor around my chest and the helmet on my head keep my vital bits from cracking, but my legs and arms are about to melt into the bench. The straps over my shoulders feel like forty-pound weights.

Gods of all systems, I think, and it's halfway to a genuine prayer.

The first thing I hear when the roaring dies down is Wen cackling. She throws her head back and howls, leveling the ship off, and Gal glances back over his shoulder with a look that says, *You're leaving me alone with* this?

I give him a slow, tight-lipped nod.

"They're catching up," Wen notes, bringing our attention back to the Beamer's instruments. "Looks like they're trying to get on either side of us."

"And they're hailing. Again." Gal dismisses the communication with a well-practiced swipe. "Five minutes until we're in academy airspace. Best to look complacent until then. Let them think they wore us down. Do whatever they bully you into."

"Yes, sir," Wen says with a roll of her eyes and a jab that engages the autopilot. She can't commit fully to the sarcasm—not when she knows that it's almost her time to shine.

Gal glances back at me. "You should be in the hold."

"Should," I agree, but don't move. Terror is creeping up my throat as the distance to our goal closes. Not because I've got a helmet on, gear strapped to my back, and a wingsuit webbing my arms and legs, begging to catch the prairie air over the academy.

No, I'm terrified because all of a sudden I'm not so sure about what we're doing. No matter how hard I've tried to flush it, I can't rid myself of the giddy joy that swept over me when I saw Archon take its first victory in years. I tried to tell myself it was an illusion. It's all going to come crashing down.

I'm going to bring it all crashing down.

I feel the weight of my little velvet bag pinned against my chest by my armor. There's no telling what will happen next, so I slipped it in my front pocket when nobody was watching. Now it scorches me like the reentry burn has seared it. What would my parents say if they could see me now? Would they even bother saying anything?

Or would they just see how forsaken I am?

"Ettian," Gal warns. The Beamer shudders around us, and one of the skipships noses into the windshield's periphery.

I unstrap, standing on shaking legs. I want to pretend it's the aftereffects of reentry or fear of the jump, but I'm so ruttin' sick of lying to myself. "Wen?" I croak.

She tips a gentle salute up at me.

I salute back. "Look out for him, will you?"

"You got it," she says, then turns her gaze pointedly to the dash so I can bend down and pull Gal into a rough kiss.

His fingers find my collar, tugging at the wingsuit. "Be careful," he murmurs against my mouth, and I hate how final all of it feels. I want to tell myself that there will be other chances, but everything beyond this moment is mired in the uncertainty of battle. So I sink hard into this kiss, my hand tangling in his hair, my head filling with just him, just this moment, just lips and tongue and teeth.

And when we break apart, my terror triples. Because it's not enough—all of him, the promise of his future, everything I've thrown my soul away for. It's not worth what we're about to do.

I can't let it show on my face. Gal cuffs me gently on the side of my helmet, then knocks his knuckles against my chest. The deflector armor beneath my wingsuit hums, ready for action. His eyes catch on its shape, and his lips twist bitterly. We've always flown into battle side by side. He's always had my back. And now this carapace is all I have to protect me when I need him the most.

"Keep flying," I whisper hoarsely, the roar of the air around us stifling the words as they leave my mouth. "No matter what, keep flying."

He gives me a grim nod, and with that, I leave him.

When I drop into the cargo hold, I find it transformed. The narrow cots have been packed up and pressed against the walls, and everything's been tied down. The ten Archon soldiers are dressed in the same garb as me, their weapons strapped to their chests, their gear carefully distributed across their bodies. As I scramble down the ladder, Sims lifts his hand in greeting. The demo guy looks ten times more threatening with heavy ordnance strapped around his ankles, but the effect is somewhat offset by the silky wings bridging his limbs and body. "Ready?" he asks, nodding to the cargo door.

"No," I reply honestly, pulling my goggles up from around my neck. I can't look him in the eye. I might have been able to before I heard about his moms and the jellyfish, back when he was just a smiling face leading me around Henrietta Base, but now, knowing him, knowing what I'm about to do to him . . .

"Don't look so grim, you two," Arso says and chuckles, clapping her hands. "It's gonna be good to stretch our legs and get some solid ground under them."

"You're leaving out the concerning distance between here and that solid ground," Tarsi mutters from the back wall. The rail-thin sniper is pressed as far from the bay doors as she can get, and I don't blame her. With her proportions, she's going to be a leaf on the wind.

"How many drops have you got on you?" Arso asks her, shouting to be heard over the burn of the rotary thrusters as Wen adjusts our vector.

"Two hundred and eighty-five in total, hundred or so on missions, and I hated every single one of them," Tarsi snaps back.

Arso lets out a booming laugh. "What about you, kiddo?" she asks, looking me up and down.

I crack a nervous grin. "Forty-seven. All in training. And one ejection seat, but I don't think that counts."

"You'll be fine. And if you aren't, well . . . It'll be fast."

Tarsi blanches.

"Coming up on the target," Gal announces through the intercom. "Dropping the ramp in thirty seconds. Hold on to something."

We line up along the walls of the cargo bay, our fingers finding purchase on canvas handholds stitched along the wall. I check my watch. Our altitude is closing on a thousand yards fast, the skip-ships forcing us lower and lower. The academy must be in sight by now, and I switch the line of my gaze to the seam where the cargo ramp meets the edge of its frame.

Against all odds, I'm almost home.

"Hold tight, people," Wen announces. "Slight course adjust-ment."

My fingers clench as she throws the ship into a disorienting swerve. My feet fly out from underneath me, and I add a second hand to the canvas. Confused muttering rises from the soldiers, and I know they must be checking our position on their maps.

We're supposed to be targeting the academy's communications tower—the relay point for an entire system of command. It's all but guaranteed that no missiles will target this ship a second time, giving the *Ruttin' Hell* all the clearance it needs to drop a team in, blow it to hell, and then get out.

At least, that's what the Archon soldiers think is about to happen.

"Ruttin' junker girl," Arso mutters, craning her neck toward the cockpit as our feet settle under us. "Hey, kid!" she barks, pounding a frustrated beat on the bulkhead. "We're off course! Fix it!"

The Beamer flies level, unhurried, unbothered.

Arso's eyes narrow beneath her goggles. "Ettian, tell your pet project to get this ship on track," she snarls.

I don't meet her gaze. "Trust her. Focus on the jump."

The intercom crackles overhead. "Communications check go," Gal shouts. A burst of static rings in my ear, and the voices of the other soldiers drop from shouts to normal levels as our comms start filtering the noise.

"Testing, Red One," Arso says. "Sound off. Make it snappy."

Call signs ring out one after another, moving around the cargo bay in a circle until I announce, "Red Eleven," with as much conviction as I can manage.

"Communications clear," Arso declares, though I don't miss the look she sneaks at her watch. We're still off course, and it's eating at her.

"Communications clear," Gal echoes. "Opening the cargo door."

The low rumble of the engines gives way to the howling wind as the ramp thunders down. The *Ruttin' Hell* sways in the air, our nose listing dangerously upward, and I grip the handhold tighter to keep from sliding out the rear. Someone's jacket whips past my head, and laughter snaps through the comm as the soldiers scold whoever failed to pack their gear right.

The ground is close. Horrifically close. We're well under a thousand yards, and even though part of my brain knows that jumps have been made from as low as two hundred feet, there's nothing I can do about the survival instinct screaming at me to never let go.

"Ten seconds to drop. Wait—" Wen's voice cuts off abruptly as the Beamer swerves.

Spins.

And then, even worse, flips.

Pain shrieks through my wrists as my hands twist in the canvas. The comm fills with confused shouts as every soldier in the bay goes ass over head. I find myself staring down at the ceiling of the cargo hold, trying to decide whether to let go and try for a better grip or let the canvas straps slowly wring the life out of my fingers.

"Get this ship—" Arso starts, but another vicious twist of the Beamer's controls chokes her silent.

"Ettian," I hear Gal whisper.

It's time. Gal's scrambled the navigation, tricking Wen into flying a mile off from the communications tower we're targeting, positioning us squarely over a patrol that the Archon soldiers won't see coming until it's too late. My gaze fixes on the bay door, the open ramp, the welcoming sight of the prairie below.

"On me!" I shout, and let go.

Gravity steals me, pulling me hard into the floor as Wen rights the ship. I tuck into an awkward roll, spreading my wings, and tumble clean off the ramp. The world spins wildly, and I struggle against the buffeting winds. My suit catches me, yanking my arms back as I level my chest against the horizon. The comm in my ear buzzes with the confusion of the soldiers behind me, but when I twist my head, I catch ten shadows in my periphery as the *Ruttin' Hell*'s engines scream into a rapid ascent.

I let go. All animal. All instinct. In a Viper, you retain a little of your humanity. In free fall, you're a missile. But there's an uncanny moment when the air pushes hard against my wings—a moment where I'm not clad in silk but in the lightweight, impenetrable armor of a knight's powersuit.

A moment when I'm invincible. A moment I feel *right*.

"Ettian," Arso's razor-edged voice warns in my ear. She's spotted the communications tower—so far from our current position that there's no chance we'll make it.

"Trust me," I shout over the wind.

And for once, my words ring true. I shift our course with an abrupt dip of one arm, veering us away from the tower, away from the patrol, away from anywhere anyone expected us to end up. I wait for the objection, but none comes. Another glance over my shoulder finds the soldiers nosing into formation behind me. The plan has fallen apart, and they know I'm their best hope of making it safely to ground.

Which is happening in a matter of seconds. We're close enough that I can pick out the individual tufts of prairie grass. I hazard a look over my shoulder, catching both the distant spires of Trost gleaming in the late-afternoon sun and the far-too-close plume of dust kicked up by a patrol truck veering toward us.

"*PULL*," I bellow, and grapple for the cord on my chest. A flap, a flutter as the pilot chute unfurls and yanks the main chute out, and then my chest feels like it's about to snap in half as the straps go taut. I glance up, making sure the chute's unfurled completely, then down in time to swing my legs up and catch the ground.

I go down hard, stumbling, staggering, finally managing to throw my weight backward, dig my heels in, and plant my ass firmly on the prairie. Dust clots the air around me, and I desperately try to quiet my gasping lungs enough so I can hear how close the patrol truck is. The rest of the soldiers swoop past overhead, steering their chutes expertly enough to land on their feet.

With a tug of the releases, I shed my chute, then rip my helmet and goggles off. The whine of the patrol truck's engine sharpens in the distance. I stagger upright, tamping down the urge to jog after the rest of the squad.

Arso whirls on me. Her eyes narrow when she sees how I've planted myself apart from them. "C'mon, kid," she snaps. "Everyone form up on me. Guns up."

I hold steady.

"Get your ass over here," Arso snaps.

I flick a switch on my chest, and the comms go dead. Her voice drops from my ear to several feet ahead of me, flanked by the confused mutters of the soldiers.

"There's a way out," I call, grateful for the way my volume disguises the otherwise-obvious tremor in my voice. "Dead ahead is the least-staffed gate on the perimeter. Ten soldiers can take it easily, and there'll be a truck you can use to get a head start. To get somewhere safe before this all goes to hell."

"What do you mean *all goes t*—oh, you son of a *bitch*," Arso hisses. In an instant, her gun snaps up, and her boltfire slams hard into my chest.

Into the deflector armor she doesn't know I'm wearing beneath my wingsuit.

I go down hard, my back slamming into the dirt. There's no question it's where I belong now. Arso rushes toward me with the soldiers at her back, ready to beat me senseless or shoot me in the head while I'm down. "There isn't *time*," I plead, rolling onto my knees. "A patrol's coming. You have to go now. I can head them off for you."

She stops short, her teeth bared in a snarl vicious enough to knock a dreadnought out of orbit, but I see the calculation in her eyes. The immediate satisfaction of revenge versus living to fight another day. With so much at stake, there's only one right choice. The one she's made before.

"You have to go," I repeat. "I can't save the Archon fleet, but I can do this much. I'm so sorry."

Arso shakes her head, spitting into the dirt. "Traitorous whelp," she growls, but her gun goes down all the same. Over her shoulder, I catch Sims's despondent eyes, and my gut twists. I knew this would happen when I got to know them, and still I let it happen. Sims, the kindly, well-read soldier dreaming of finding his moms and their oceans again. He's done nothing but make me feel welcome, and in return I've welcomed him to my homeworld with a knife in the back. I deserve every inch of how much it crushes me to face my betrayal head-on.

With one last snarl, Arso turns tail and jogs off, the rest of the squad closing in formation around her as they head for the gate ahead.

I crawl to my feet, watching them go with my heart in my stomach. Somewhere in the free fall, I'd convinced myself that this would feel *good*. Heroic, even. That I was finally going to do the right thing.

I feel nothing but sheer, mind-numbing terror as I turn toward the distant plume of the patrol truck's dust, lift my hands over my head, and start walking.

CHAPTER 26

WHEN THE TRUCK rumbles to a halt, six armored Umber soldiers pour out. Their faces are shielded by helmets and goggles, but one of them nearly takes off at a run when he recognizes me. "Ettian?" Ollins shouts, like he can't believe what he's seeing.

Despite everything, I have to hold back a grin. "Been a minute, hasn't it?" I call back. The tension in my stomach lessens as I register that not a single gun is pointed at me.

"We counted eleven chutes," the squad leader says, narrowing his eyes.

"Those were Archon loyalists who thought they'd be taking out the big fellow over there," I say, nodding to the communications tower in the distance. "When they realized we'd dropped them off the mark and I intended to meet up with you fine folks, they cut and run for the nearest gate. You might be able to catch up to them, but I think it's more pressing to get me in a room with the academy head. I've got intel for him from the Umber heir himself."

The Umber squad blinks at me.

I hold out my wrists.

Ten minutes later, I'm crouched against the mounts of the chain gun in the bed of the truck, sitting shoulder to shoulder with Ollins and worrying away at the zip ties binding my hands together. The relief of still being alive is tempered only by the fact that I have absolutely no idea where Wen and Gal ended up. They must have made it to our rendezvous point. I have to believe that, because the alternative is too crushing to think about.

The fact that I've betrayed Gal is less crushing, but it's dragging my thoughts to a dark place as we rattle along the dirt road leading back to the academy compound. I try to convince myself that it doesn't matter. From our point of view, the plan is still on track. We didn't need those Archon soldiers captured—we just needed to make sure they didn't take out the main relay and destroy the nexus of Umber's military communications network in Tosa System. With their comms fried and the base alerted to their presence, the Archon squad won't have time to relay my treachery to the main fleet until well after Gal and Wen have made it to safety.

All that's left for me to do is meet with the academy head and tell him every detail of the Archon invasion strategy.

The thought of it, combined with the swaying of the truck, is bringing a swell of nausea slowly but surely up my throat. I duck my chin, trying to brace more firmly against the chain-gun mounts.

Ollins leans over. "Just tell me, was he with you?" he mutters in my ear, low and urgent. "He's alive, right?"

My orders are to save the details for the academy head, but I oblige Ollins with a tiny nod.

His shoulders go slack with relief, even though his grip on the rifle slung around his chest stays tight. "Knew it. Knew there had to be more. They tried to tell us you were some kind of seditionist after you took off, you know? But everyone thought that was bullshit. Anyone who knew you and Gal *knew*. Heavens and hells, I gotta tell Rin and Hanji. And I think Rhodes owes me money."

The mention of our friends sends another guilty pang through me. They never gave up on us. On me. And with the invasion force closing on Rana, there's no telling what they'll be roped into if Iral's advance isn't stopped in time.

If I don't tell the academy head exactly how to stop it.

The next part in our grand plan to destroy Iral's onslaught happens in a tiny interrogation room on the third floor of the academy's detention center. The squad leader gives Ollins permission to cut my zip ties, and I strip out of my wingsuit, shrug off my deflector armor, and hand it over. The six of them leave me alone, facing a mirror that pretends it's only a mirror.

I sit down at the table to wait, eyeing the ring in the middle meant to be threaded with a pair of handcuffs. The fact that they haven't seen fit to chain me to it bodes well. It means that they don't suspect that I let the Archon soldiers go.

Or it means that they have bigger fish to fry. The muffled rumble of scrambled ships is near constant, and thundering footsteps fill the hall outside. War is coming to Rana again. Archon has risen, and they're inbound with dreadnoughts of their own. No one believes there will be the mercy of another Warning Shot. The base is in chaos.

When silence falls outside, I know I have only seconds to compose myself. I sink back into the chair and try to relax my shoulders. Try to look like the loyal Umber soldier they need to see, not the shattered kid. Not the truth.

The academy head sweeps into the room. He's dressed out and ready for battle, deflector armor on, a coat trimmed in brass over it. "Where's the prince?" he asks, setting his datapad on the table. With quick movements of his fingers, he flickers through communications, tracing his replies instantaneously. He doesn't look at me, but I can feel the usual contempt radiating off him like the heat that clings to a bombing site.

"The prince is safe. He has orders for you."

The head scoffs. "The only reason you're still alive is because we need to find the Umber heir. There's only one order that will be passed in this room. It's simple, and it's already been stated. Tell me where the prince is."

"The only reason *you're* still alive is because Gal emp-Umber thinks you can be useful," I shoot back, and that earns me his eyes. The head's pointed brows lower. "He's confident that you want to earn his forgiveness after the way you tried to hold him here a month ago. And no one wants the empress to find out about that little accident with the automated defense system, do they? The Archon fleet approaching is the least of your worries. You aligned yourself with Berr sys-Tosa, and the system governor has made himself the worst of enemies. There's no need for Tosa to drag you down with him."

His lips twist sourly, and he locks his datapad. "I'm listening," he says. It might be the most grudging way I've ever heard a man save his own skin.

I steel myself. This saves Gal. It saves Hanji, Ollins, Rin, and Rhodes. It spares the former empire from being torn asunder by a new war. It's worth the cost of my soul.

"The Archon attack is Gal emp-Umber's doing," I start, and can't help but savor the look of confusion that flickers across the head's face. "He discovered Maxo Iral alive and mustering an army in Corinth, and he ingratiated himself with the Shield of Archon. Convinced him to use our knowledge of Rana's defenses in an assault against the planet. Iral is inbound with his fleet of commandeered dreadnoughts and every ship the resistance has collected over the years. And Gal emp-Umber is making ready to impale them on the planetary defense. How would you like to win a war in a day, sir?"

He doesn't answer. He doesn't have to. I see it in his eyes—the heady mix of fear and hunger that drives people to fight wars in the first place. And it didn't hurt to address him as a superior. The head leans forward, holds out his datapad, and fixes me with an expectant stare as he unlocks it.

So I lean forward in turn and tell him everything. Exactly how Maxo Iral plans to attack. Every way in which Gal's deceived the Archon general. The codes and call signs necessary to trick the fleet into thinking they've managed to destroy the communications relay, to bait them inward, thinking the planet is theirs for the taking. I spill my guts, and somewhere in the middle of the process, I learn to love the freeing lightness that comes from hurling yourself past a point of no return.

The head's eyes gain a savage glint the moment Gal's strategy clicks for him, and it triples the churn in my stomach. Does it even matter how much it tore Gal up to think of this? Divorced from his moral crisis, the plan is nothing but annihilation. The planetary defenses will cleave the Archon attack in half. Every single one of Iral's expectations will lead to his bloody ruin. The brutal mechanics of Gal's mind are laid bare, separate from his heart.

His mother will be proud.

It takes nearly an hour. The time stretches even longer as frantic aides burst into the room with updates on the approaching Archon fleet. The head waves them off, intent on hearing the entirety of Gal's plan. My throat goes raw from explaining, and my eyes start to ache from squinting at the datapad.

But then a new aide bursts into the room, and no matter how many dismissive waves the academy head flaps in her direction, she won't be turned away. "Sir," the girl insists. There's something in her voice that steals mine, and when I go silent, the head finally turns to her.

"What is it?" he snaps, exasperated.

"New orders, sir. From the system governor."

"Tell Berr sys-Tosa that I'm in the middle of saving his miserable capital."

"That's the thing," the aide stammers. "Berr sys-Tosa's retreating to the inner worlds. He's ceded Rana to the Archon forces."

The world's dropped away beneath me. Blank, nihilistic fear washes out my thoughts. Everything we worked for—every plan, every sleepless night, every stress that's been eating Gal alive, every hope we had of stopping this war in its tracks—all for nothing.

The governor's surrendered.

CHAPTER 27

THE ACADEMY HEAD stands up abruptly, snatching his datapad.

"The plan," I stammer. "It'll still work. There's still time."

But the head's back is already turned. He sweeps toward the door, eyes lost in his datapad. I try to follow, but he holds up a hand. "You stay in this room," he says, eyes narrowed.

The brunt of his suspicion hit like a Viper at full speed. His least favorite student appeared out of nowhere, tied up his time with a useless battle plan, baited him with vague promises of saving him from the imperials' wrath, and claimed to have come directly from the fleet invading us. I wouldn't trust it either.

"Wait until you're called on." With that, he slams the door and clicks the lock in place, leaving me staring at my panicked reflection in the mirror that's not just a mirror.

I lunge across the room and try to jam down the door's handle. "Please," I shout, the metal throwing my voice back at me, ringing in my ears. "I can get in contact with Gal—I can find him. We have to protect the heir."

Gal's trapped in that Beamer with Wen at the helm, stuck squarely between a planet that's forsaken him and an army that will tear him to shreds if they discover what he is. I don't know if Wen ditched the skipships on her tail. I don't know if she continued to follow orders after I leaped out the back of the *Ruttin' Hell*.

I never should have left him alone.

A few more rattles of the door handle confirm that no one's listening. No one's on the other side, or if they are, they aren't doing a damn thing to help me, no matter how much I shake the door and shout promises through it.

I catch myself in the mirror, wild and white-eyed. *Be calm. Be rational*. I lash out, kicking the table. Pain snaps through my toes, and I realize too late that it's bolted down. As the agony settles into a dull ache, I let it focus me.

Think. Think. You've crawled through worse. The Cutters. The dreadnoughts. Twenty Vipers on our tail. The fall of Trost, when my world was reduced to rubble and ash, and still I made it out alive.

Breathe in. Breathe out.

The drum of my heart goes steady.

One table. Two chairs. A door with a lever-type handle. I glance up at the ceiling. My lips twist at the sight of familiar tiles. If there's someone on the other side of the mirror, they'd better move fast, because I've already thought this through once before. I hook my aching toes around the leg of the closest chair and sling it around, jamming it under the door's handle with a satisfying crash. An extra kick wedges it in there good and tight.

I round the table, grab the other chair, and hoist it up. Under the clatter it makes as I set it down on the table, I hear muffled voices on the other side of the door. The handle rattles. My blockade won't hold for long. I hop on the table, then clamber onto the chair, throwing out my arms as it wobbles beneath me.

No time for second thoughts. No time for hesitation. It only takes a quick strike with the heel of my palm to pop the ceiling tile up, releasing a puff of stale dust that claws into my eyes before I can close them. I cough, swaying. The rattling behind me grows more insistent.

I feel for the metal struts that form the ceiling's support. The ridges dig into my palms as I test my weight against them. The whole structure creaks, and I wince, reaching deeper into the crawl space. My fingers brush against a support beam. Relief washes through me.

I loop one arm around it and jump, my chest colliding awkwardly with the ceiling's lip. I try to remember which way I was facing before the dust got in my eyes. Pause. Focus. Home in on the noise.

The rattling behind me has been replaced by rhythmic thuds. Someone's trying to kick their way through the door.

I haul myself up by the support, wrestling my legs into the crawl space and looping them around the beam. Dust clots my nose, my lungs—my whole world is fouled by the neglect inside the ceiling. I hazard a peek through my burning eyes, but it doesn't do much for me. I catch the glow of the fluorescents in the interrogation room streaming through the punched-out panel, and the rest is darkness.

So I do it blind. Hand over hand, I yank myself forward along the support, wincing away from the blazing heat of the lighting units as I squirm past them. They're my markers—two lights over and I know for sure I'm in the next room. A turn at a juncture along the beam to throw off anyone on my tail. Another two lights. I nearly burn my shoulder on one of them.

I pause, finally wiping the dust out of my eyes. Coughing before was an inconvenience. Now it could get me killed. I pull the collar of my shirt over my nose and mire myself in the scent of my own sweat instead.

Inventory. I've lost my armor, and they took both my comm unit and the pistol I was carrying when they loaded me up in the truck back on the prairie. I'm left with shirt, jacket, pants, boots, and a little velvet bag pressed against my chest that won't do me any good if I can't get off the academy base.

That starts with getting out of this ceiling. I try to visualize the layout of the detention center—how many rooms there were and where the interrogation room was relative to the rest of the block. If I come down in another room with a locked door, I'm humped, especially if there's no way for me to get back up. Time is working against me, but chaos is working for me. I have to keep moving.

I have to think like Wen.

It's terrifyingly easy to slip into her mind-set. To imagine where her head was when we blew the skipship and jacked the wiretram and scrambled across the rooftops of Isla. It's the animal instinct of flying a Viper and jumping from the *Ruttin' Hell* and clawing through postwar Trost. It's everywhere I've been before.

There's a trade-off between silence and speed. I choose the latter. The crawl space fills with muffled thuds as I scramble along the support as fast as I can, my boots slipping in the dust. Go until I hit a wall. Go until I hit a corner. Ignore any other noise but my desperate breathing and the hammer of my heart. If I thought about this right, I should be exactly where I intended to end up. I brace against the support, stick my leg out, and bring the heel of my boot down hard.

The ceiling tile beneath it cracks neatly in half, and this time I remember to close my eyes against the cloud of dust and particle-board chunks that rises in its wake. I fight back my hesitation, swat once to clear the air, and roll sideways, trying not to take the rest of the ceiling with me as I drop through the rectangular hole.

I land hard on my feet right in front of the door to the stairwell. Checking over my shoulder would only slow me down—I grab the handle of the door and dive through. My legs pump furiously as I thunder down the stairs. I think I'm bleeding in a few places where I must have cut myself in the crawl space. My toes still throb from kicking the table.

All things I can deal with later. I spill out onto the first floor and kick through the emergency door, bursting into the open air.

The base is in an uproar. Cadets and officers scramble every which way, and the hangars are abuzz with ships jockeying for precious runway space. I flatten against the wall as a Beamer—not the *Ruttin' Hell,* not *our* Beamer—swoops overhead, rotary thrusters screaming to lift the stubborn transport into the sky with every bit of urgency it possesses. Berr sys-Tosa's sounded the retreat, and everyone's rushing to get the hell off this forsaken planet.

Think like Wen. Think like Wen. I keep myself braced against the wall, trying to pick out the noise inside the detention center over the evacuation's bedlam. There's no way I don't have pursuit on my tail. Footsteps sound in the stairwell. I tense, watching the door's seams.

When it swings outward, I duck out from behind it and loop my arm around the soldier's neck. He flails for his gun. I beat him to it, snatching the blaster off his belt. No time to check the settings—I flick the safety off, fire a shot into his hamstring, and hope for the best. He immediately slumps, and I leap back from him, pulling a face as the bolt's charge tries to bridge into my body.

The door slams shut. I switch the gun's settings and shoot the latch, melting it into place.

The soldier's blaster goes in my belt. His hat on my head. His badge and identification in one of my jacket's inner pockets. I slip out of Wen's mentality long enough to mutter a quick apology and prop him up against the detention center's wall. He'll come around in a few minutes. He won't be stranded.

At least, that's what I'm telling myself as I take off running across the quad.

The loudspeakers on every building blast orders, but my flight-mode brain takes an extra second to translate them. I hear familiar locations, familiar designations, things that should be ingrained after two and a half years of training here, but my mind is sluggish, my thoughts scattered. I pause in the shadow of one of the main hangars, giving my head time to catch up to the rapid pounding of my heart.

If everything went right with the academy head, I was supposed to rendezvous with Gal and Wen on the south side of Trost once Wen had ditched the Umber pursuit. We said "once." We probably should have accounted for "if."

Now I have no idea where Gal and Wen have ended up. I fried the comm that could have contacted them, and even if I hadn't, the patrol took it on the prairie. We never anticipated the governor's surrender. Not when we were so certain we had gift-wrapped the Archon forces. Gal thought he could outmaneuver Berr sys-Tosa.

Now our plan is ashes at the system governor's cowardly feet.

Now Gal's caught in the middle of a war I was supposed to end before it started. Now I don't know how to reach him.

Get to Trost. Get to the rendezvous. Go where you're expected and let the rest fall into place. Pretend like everything is going your way and don't stop until the second someone tells you otherwise.

I pull my stolen cap low on my head, gritting my teeth. It's easy to blend into the chaos of the base evacuation, but easier still to get lost in it. Somehow I need to pull a ticket off the base out of this mess. As a group of soldiers runs past me, I catch a familiar silhouette. It's Rhodes—I'm sure of it, but he disappears around the corner before I can catch his eye.

My panic fizzles. Maybe there's nothing that can help me in my pockets, but I'm back on my home turf. My resources are all around me. I have a gun on my belt and strength in my legs. I'm going to make it to the city. I'm going to find Gal. And gods of all systems, I'll fly him out of this mess like I always do.

I straighten my spine and plunge headfirst into the academy's turmoil.

Hanji cackles when she sees me lurking in the shadow of a skipship's wing. "Nassun, you slippery son of a bitch," she hisses, ducking under the ship's hull as she drops the munitions crate she was supposed to be loading. "What the rut're you doing back here? You picked a hell of a time. Haven't you heard?"

"World's ending," I agree. "Listen, I need a favor."

"And I need a hot bath and an explanation, but neither of us is getting what we want today, are we?"

I grimace, then jump when a hand slaps me squarely between the shoulder blades. "Ettian Nassun, you slippery—"

"Already said that, Rin," Hanji snaps, cocking an eyebrow at the smaller cadet.

Rin glares up at me like I owe her an apology. I probably do. "Officers are going to notice we've skipped off," she mutters, glancing around the skipship's hull. "Kinda an all-hands-on-deck moment here. No thanks to you, I'm assuming?"

I shrug. "Been a busy couple of weeks. Look, about that favor—"

"Favor?" Rin asks, eyes narrowing. "What makes you think you get to waltz back in here and ask for favors?"

Unwittingly, my hand slips around the hilt of my stolen blaster. "I'm on a mission, okay? Things have gone sideways faster than Ollins on two shots of polish, and I need all the help I can get."

Hanji smirks. "You float, Ettian. What's your leverage?"

"*Gal* is my leverage," I snap. "Me, I'm worthless. Nobody. Nothing. But the Umber heir needs our help, and that means I need a way to Trost. Please, Hanji . . . You work the tower. You know the schedule. What's leaving?"

Rin and Hanji glance at each other. The calculation plays out on their faces. The amount of their loyalty that's based on survival factored against their true loyalty to the Umber Crown. The years we've trained together divided by the way I disappeared in the middle of the night. And all of it pressured by the way time ticks steadily onward, waiting for one of the other soldiers to notice us.

"Lot B, down by the east gates," Hanji says, just as I'm about to get desperate. She pushes up her glasses and slips her datapad out of her pocket. "There's a convoy of buses scheduled to leave for the city in twenty minutes, out to collect officials with no off-world transport of their own and bring them back here for evac. If you can get on board, that's your ticket."

I nod, picturing the layout of the lot and the buildings around it. "Gonna need a distraction to make sure that happens."

"Oh no, no, no—I don't have the time—"

"Ollins owes you money."

That shuts her up fast. Ollins has the luck of a devil where wagers are concerned, and Hanji's cantina debts are the stuff of legend.

"That bet you made on Trisu—the one about me and Gal."

Her jaw drops. "You did *not*."

"It happened. About two weeks ago."

"Holy ruttin' shit. He's the *prince*. Ettian Nassun, you *maniac*. Who made the first—no, never mind. Details later. Rin?"

The smaller girl snaps to attention, grinning. "Yeah?"

"There must be something we can do for our dear friend Ettian, right? After all, he's given us so much."

Rin pretends to think, her brow furrowing comically. "But what could possibly be loud and distracting enough to turn every head on the tarmac?"

"If not Ollins, what about something of yours stashed under his bunk?"

"Thought you'd never ask."

CHAPTER 28

FIFTEEN M NUTES LATER, I've wedged myself into the undercarriage of a bus. My hearing's coming back in parts, and I'm still frantically trying to beat out the embers of Rin's homemade fireworks where they've singed my shirt and pants. The engine rattles my teeth, and I tuck my legs close against my chest, praying that the driver sees no need to check the luggage compartments before she takes off for the city.

Gal and Wen were counting on me. Now it's my turn to count on them. They made it. They *must* have made it.

The rumble grows into a roar. The bus sways forward. I close my eyes and wait.

When the driver cuts the engines, I don't hesitate. No time to listen to voices, to guess if I have an opening. I pull the release that pops the luggage hatch. Light streams into the narrow compartment as I tuck and roll out of it.

And Trost welcomes back its native son with open arms. I'm five years off these streets, and yet my bearings lock into place so quickly that I nearly trip over my feet, as if I'm unused to the length my legs have grown in the time since then. Confused shouts rise around me, but I don't have room to process any of the words they're yelling. The only thing I can hold concretely in my head is the layout of the city and my place in it, the grid that had two years to etch itself into my bones.

There. I lunge forward, all but diving headfirst into an alley ahead. Stone and brick snatch at my clothes—I wasn't nearly this big the last time I slipped between these walls. Behind me, the shouts fade. The soldiers think I'm a deserter, and with an evacuation to manage, they don't have time to deal with it. I throw myself around the next corner, slam back against the wall, and heave a deep sigh of relief.

The shriek of starship engines takes that relief by the throat and pins it, sending my fingers scrabbling into the brick for a handhold as a shadow passes over me. My memories tangle with my present as all around me I sense the utter *wrongness* of a city trying to flee. *It's not the same,* I tell myself, swallowing back the bitter wash of nausea creeping up my throat. The armada approaching Trost is a sympathetic one. Archon is committed to serving its citizens, not dominating them like Umber. There will be no bombs falling upon the fleet's arrival—or, at least that's what I'm telling myself, knowing all too well how the past seven years have changed *my* priorities.

After all, I once crawled out of a dark tunnel not far from this block with my innocence intact as the world began to end around me. It didn't take long for me to cave to what was necessary to keep myself alive. My fists clench, remembering the shapes of a hundred different pieces of rubble in my hand, the sensation of blood slicking off them, the twinning triumph and despair at the fact that I had lived. I wasn't made for violence, but I learned it fast and well under Umber-ruled skies. I don't want to go back to the city I knew years ago and what it will take to survive it.

But this time is different. This time it *has* to be. This time, there are people waiting for me at the other side of this nightmare. And it's that thought—the thought of the relieved look that'll break over

Gal's face and the wry smirk that'll tug at Wen's lips when I make it to the rendezvous—that has me pushing off the wall and diving headfirst into the tumult of the evacuation.

I steel myself against the sights and sounds of people fleeing the planet in droves. The bawling children being dragged by their wrists through the crowds, unable to comprehend leaving their home behind. The shouts and sudden clusters of people that ring where a fight has broken out. The omnipresent voices of newscasters echoing against the buildings as they do their best to keep the population calm. The near-constant rumble and scream of starship engines as yet another shuttle launches, sometimes with people banging on the doors, begging them to let just one more passenger aboard.

I've seen it all before, but it doesn't get any easier—not even with the knowledge that this is a homecoming, not an invasion. My heart's in my throat. My eyes keep flicking to the sky as if the ships will be in sight any minute. There's no thrill to Archon's victory this time. War is marching toward us, and the people of Trost are doing everything they can to get out of the way.

As I cut through a square choked with advertising billboards, their screens flash red with an update. My stomach twists as loudspeakers hum to life across the downtown. A shaken-looking newscaster appears, clutching a datapad against her chest as she stares into the camera. "Citizens of Rana," she reads from an unseen teleprompter. "The latest in the unfolding of events surrounding the secession of the planet. This is a broadcast from General Maxo Iral, thought to be executed five years ago, now appearing to be in command of the approaching invasion."

The image cuts to Iral standing before the Archon crest. In the last broadcast I saw, he was disheveled, his voice urgent as he issued commands from his stateroom. Now his hair is swept back, carefully combed and rebraided. He wears the former empire's uniform, and his eyes are filled with cool confidence.

"My fellow citizens," he says, and my heart wavers, my loyalties dragging themselves back to my childhood empire, my childhood hero. Everyone else on the street has frozen in their tracks. Distant murmurs reach my ears—surprise, wonder, and fear mixing together.

"Today we celebrate the first stage in the restoration of the Archon Empire. The false governor installed by the Umber establishment has ceded, and my administration is prepared to step into the absence he left. The Umber occupation of our territory will cease. We will retake what is ours by right. And already we've taken a momentous step toward the restoration of Archon's glory. Citizens, allow me to present the Umber heir."

The camera moves to Gal.

I feel as if all the blood has drained from my veins. He looks unharmed but scared to pieces. His wrists are bound in ceremonial chains—brass, the metal of his empire. Maybe to mock him, but more likely because the chains came from one of the captured dreadnoughts. I sag back against a wall, my eyes burning.

I can't blink. Can't miss a second.

Gal was supposed to make a triumphant return. His unveiling on the galactic stage was supposed to be a moment of victory. He was supposed to deliver Iral's head to his parents and proudly claim his place as heir.

Now he stands as still as a statue while Maxo Iral lays a massive hand on his shoulder. "Sources within the former governor's administration confirmed this boy's identity. He is blood of the blood that stole our lands and razed our cities. Now he bends to us." The rage in Iral's voice is palpable. It thickens the air around me. I watch, helpless, as the general leans his weight onto Gal.

The prince doesn't go easily. He fights, tries to slip the load, tries not to stoop. His worst nightmare has come to life, his greatest fear now forces him down, and still he resists. But in the end, Gal drops to his knees, his head bowed.

Somewhere farther down the street, people start cheering, and my mind goes blank with rage.

CHAPTER 29

I COME BACK to myself in a familiar parking garage. For a moment, it's like nothing's changed in the past seven years. I'm down in the dark, trapped in instinct, overcome by fear and failure. I stare down at my hands, at boots that would have swamped my ten-year-old feet, and a hot pit of shame starts to grow in my stomach.

All of that strife and struggle, all of that effort, and I've ended up back at the bottom of the hole I crawled out of.

I think it smells the same down here, even after all these years. Something about it reminds me of the dust in the crawl space. Or maybe it's closer to dust after rain, flattened down into nothing. It's sterile and old. A mausoleum. A few vehicles are still parked down here, but no one's coming for them.

It's quiet, and it has no right to be. Overhead, everyone with the means is fleeing the planet. My memory flickers, images of broken ships raining from the sky overtaking my senses. The Archon fleet wouldn't shoot down the refugees. They couldn't. But on the edge of my hearing, I swear I catch the deep rumble of bombardment.

My heart rate spikes before I have time to realize it's a car pulling out.

Deep breath in. Deep breath out. I try to reduce my world to nothing but the steady rise and fall of my chest. Only I can't keep it steady. My lungs shudder, and I squeeze my eyes shut as if it will stop the inevitable.

Isn't this what you wanted all along? the voice in the back of my head croons. *It's okay. You can admit it. You wanted the invasion to succeed. You wanted vengeance for the fall of Archon, and now you'll have it. The restoration of the former empire is at hand.*

But no empire is worth it if I don't have him too.

I give in, opening my eyes as the tears come fast. They spill down my cheeks, around the flare of my nose, over lips, chin, throat, collarbone. I feel them melt into the fabric of my shirt and choke back the sob trying to rise from my throat. Everything gets magnified down here, and I don't want the concrete shell around me to throw the noise back in my face like it did seven years ago.

All of this is my fault. I put the idea in Gal's head that he could break Maxo Iral's onslaught and take his throne in triumph. We could have made an opening in our plan for us to bolt for the interior if Gal hadn't been convinced he needed to claim his victory firsthand. If I hadn't convinced him of it.

I gave up everything I had to keep Gal safe, and it wasn't enough. *I* wasn't enough. It's only fair that I'm back in this garage.

My stomach turns over, and I taste bile. It's been nearly a full day since I last ate, but I know that if I tried, I'd see it all again too soon. I rub my eyes, massaging my swollen cheeks, and some of the nausea starts to abate as I realize the tears have stopped. Now I feel so wrung-out that I could keel over and drop into a deep sleep here on the freezing concrete.

"Got it all out of your system?" a familiar voice calls, and I snap upright, yanking my stolen gun off my belt.

I sight down the barrel, searching the gloom for movement. "You've got a lot of ruttin' nerve, Wen Iffan," I try to snarl. It comes out blunted by snot and strangled by the lump in my throat, and the last bit of my dignity withers.

She eases out of the darkness with her hands over her head. Even though I'm furious, I can't help the relief that warms through me when I realize she's unhurt.

"How?" I ask, even though I know the answer's going to piss me off. How is she here when Gal is gone and the world above us is turning inside out?

"Little hard to keep me in a place I don't want to be kept," she says with a shrug. She looks like the day has worn her hollow, and it reflects in the flatness of her voice. "Though I think once they realized I'd slipped the zip ties, gotten into the vents, and wormed out of their perimeter, they decided I wasn't worth the trouble. They had the prince—that was all they wanted. And speaking of the *prince*—"

"I never could have told—"

"That part I get, yeah. But you didn't have to drag me into the middle of it."

"I didn't," I concede, lowering my gun. "But I thought I couldn't do it without you."

Something in her expression twitches from pissed to pleased before she can stop it. She saunters closer, lowering her hands. "So," Wen says, dropping into a crouch next to me.

"So," I repeat. The fury's fading, and I don't want it to leave. I can already feel the emptiness growing in its absence. "How did you find me?"

I stop myself from adding, *Why did you bother?*

Wen shrugs. "I thought like you and took a guess."

I gape.

"Also Gal made me sneak a tracker onto your belt." Wen chuckles at my expression, leaning back and settling herself against the wall. She pulls a pilfered datapad out of her pocket and drops it in my lap as the "distance to target" on its display winds all the way down to zero.

"And how . . . how did you get caught in the first place?"

Wen looks stricken. "I ditched the skipships nice and easy, like you said. Piece of cake once I didn't have to worry about bouncing the soldiers in the hold around like rubber balls. I thought we were supposed to meet up with the fleet after that, but Gal told me we were changing the plan. I asked if you knew, and he said you did, but . . ."

I squeeze my eyes shut. More things I should have anticipated. More reasons the blame for Gal's capture lies heavy on my shoulders. After what Gal tried to pull when we arrived at the base, it's no wonder she'd balk at trusting him without me there to reassure her.

"We were arguing when we got the notification that the system governor had surrendered, and by then I was sure something was wrong. Nothing about today added up, and . . . if I had *listened,* if I hadn't hesitated—"

"You couldn't have known," I say softly, and she shakes her head.

"They were on us so fast. Too many of them," Wen says, her eyes dull, like admitting that is stealing something horrible from her.

I swallow back the lump in my throat as the tumblers line up in my brain. Berr sys-Tosa's surrender makes perfect sense. The *Ruttin' Hell* was sighted. He knew the Umber heir was collaborating with the Archon forces to enact his revenge. And the governor must have decided two could play at that game. He saw his opportunity to eliminate the Umber heir before Gal could ever become a problem. Berr sys-Tosa ceded. He turned Rana into a warren, then told General Iral exactly what he was hunting.

I pick up the datapad and turn it over in my hands, running my fingers along its smooth, glossy surface. A dark urge rises to snap it in half, to throw it across the garage, to take some part of my rage and frustration out on this useless slab of electronics. Instead I pull out my own datapad, stolen from the soldier I took down, and stack it on top of Wen's. Set both of them on the ground between us. Put the blaster on top, followed by the soldier's ID.

Wen lifts her unburned eyebrow at me.

"Our assets. You got anything else?"

She pulls a switchblade out of her boot and tosses it on top of my pile.

"That's it?" I ask, scoffing. It's more than I had last time, but now

I've got Wen with me, and we should probably have more figured out between us.

"Well, I know where they took Gal."

I swat her on the shoulder. "Heavens and hells, Wen—*lead with that.*"

"I didn't want to rev you up—you're gonna say it's impossible. I might not agree, but—"

I shake my head. "Wen, where is he?"

"The general's setting up shop in the governor's palace. Your dear prince is being kept in the court there."

My hand clamps over my heart before I know what I'm doing. Something truly ridiculous has planted itself firmly deep inside me, something I didn't have the last time I was down here.

Wen recognizes it right away. Her eyes flick suspiciously from my clenched hand to my swollen face. There's something mischievous dawning in her gaze. "You know a way in?"

"I know a way in." I give her a moment to ask *how* I know a way in, and when she doesn't, I know for sure I don't deserve her. "Wen, look. I did this all wrong the first time. I need your help—you're all I have left. But if I'm going to drag you into this mess again, this time I'm going to tell you exactly what you're getting into. Sound good?"

She shrugs. "Those Archon bastards took my umbrella. I do kinda want it back." Her wry eyes meet mine, and she cracks a smile that banishes the last of my worries with its sheer devilry. "I told you you're never getting rid of me."

I breathe in. Breathe out. Slide my hand inside my jacket and find the inner pocket. "I'm going to show you something. I'm going to tell you what it means. And then I'm going to double-check that you're really with me."

Wen nods. I take one more deep breath to steady myself.

And with shaking fingers, I pull out the velvet bag.

CHAPTER 30

THE TUNNELS ARE pitch-black, but I know them by feel. I slip through the dark with purposeful steps, one hand trailing along the rough stone wall, the other clenched on my blaster's grip. Wen follows with one finger tucked into the collar of my shirt, never stumbling as she places her feet carefully in my wake.

I gave her the abbreviated history—it was all we had time for—but it was the truth all the same, the truth I've tried to bury for seven years. She *knows,* and she's still with me. It seems mathematically impossible, but Wen Iffan has always been improbable herself, and now more than ever I appreciate that.

The whole notion makes me light. Even though the tunnels smell like rot and ruin, even though it's been far too long since I last saw sunshine. All this time it's been such a heavy load to bear, but now we split the weight between us with no imbalance, no leveraging it against each other—none of what I feared.

I trust her. It's a miraculous thing.

"Two more notches," I whisper into the dark as my fingers pass a precisely carved indent. These passages pre-date the estate above us by nearly four hundred years, built when Trost was only a mining town. My bones hum with restless energy, and the darkness is making the enormity of the task ahead seem larger, like something out of a knight story.

I guess it *is* the kind of absurd attempt at heroics one would expect from a suited knight.

One step at a time. One more notch in the wall. Another. And then I feel the familiar edges of the panel. If there were light in the tunnel, the rusty slice of metal would be a clear incongruity in the hewn rock. It's been roughly six years since the estate's construction, and still this security flaw has gone unnoticed. I shift my fingers to the panel's upper edges and gently pull, tipping it back until I've laid it on the ground. Behind it is nothing but more darkness, but it's welcoming us in with a slight breeze that carries a faint savory smell.

My breathing goes shallow, and Wen mimics it. We've already talked this through. No need to speak. Soundlessly, we slip into the governor's pantry.

I ate well the first time I figured out this way in. Probably too well—the hole I left in the pantry's stock wasn't subtle. Fortunately the trick panel, tucked behind a boiler and shadowed even when the lights are on, was more difficult to notice. I'd squirm in and squirm out whenever I thought I could get away with it. The stakes were higher, but the day-to-day risk was far more preferable to swiping what I could from convenience stores or digging through trash. This used to be my secret.

Now it's one more little truth I've shared with Wen. She presses close against my back as I feel my way past the boiler machinery and into the dusty shelves. This part of the palace wasn't destroyed in the bombing of Trost—it's been hewn out of the rock the building was founded on. The stone walls reflect the sound of our careful footsteps, our rustling clothes, our breaths. But no other sounds join the mix. The estate's new occupants haven't made their way down here yet.

Even so, we make our way in silence. First through the building's dimly lit sublevels, the paths I dared to explore six years ago when I was sure no one else was down here. Then into a narrow servant's stair that winds into the palace's main floor. The bedrock falls away, replaced with new concrete and steel. My knowledge of our position ends.

We switch places. Wen was in the palace briefly, and she got a good look at the layout during her mad dash for the exit. She leads the way through the narrow service corridors that run parallel to the ostentatious halls.

I catch glimpses of soldiers through the spyholes, clearly Archon by the platinum-and-emerald uniforms they wear proudly. They stand guard in the main halls, still new enough to their surroundings that their eyes keep getting caught on the decorations. Berr sys-Tosa dressed his palace to Umber tastes, and I can see the brass-and-obsidian trappings gnawing away at the soldiers forced to look at them for hours on end.

We peer around a corner into the hall that leads to the court's doors. Wen catches my eye with a quick hand motion, pointing to an immense urn tucked into an antechamber across the hall. *There,* she signals, then, *I'll cover you.*

I squeeze her shoulder once to let her know I understood and pass her the blaster. Steeling myself, I pull my datapad out of my pocket, bring up the contacts, and dial.

From a nearby cranny within the hall, her datapad chimes in answer. At full volume, it blasts a bombastic choral rendition of the Archon Anthem, backed by a battery of imperial skin drums, and my heart swells. In the main hall, confused voices murmur back and forth. From our hiding place, we have eyes on the pair of soldiers guarding the gates to the court.

They glance at each other, unsure. One of their comrades playing a practical joke? An obvious distraction? As the song moves from the first verse to the chorus, one of them takes a hesitant step forward. Then another. His hands are tense on his gun.

Cautiously, he moves past our hiding place. We listen to his footsteps, and then the steps of his comrade as she follows him. When they've both passed us, I give Wen a nod.

Time for some real knight shit.

She whips around the corner and fires two quick bolts into their backs. The noise is deafening. The chorus roars. The drums rumble in a triumph rhythm. As she sprints for the cover of the urn, I take off running for the gate, skidding to a halt in front of the brass handles. With a monumental heave, I pull the doors open and step into the court, the music blasting at my back. I resist the urge to turn around and check on Wen. The boltfire she lays down as cover tells me enough.

Head held high, I march into the court like it's my right.

This is how I come back to my people.

The room is massive, the vaulted ceiling decorated with inlaid obsidian that glitters in the evening light streaming through the great windows. Hundreds of eyes turn toward me as the noise in the room fades to whispers, and I find myself facing down Archon officials, resistance officers, and soldiers who point their guns and wait for an order. I hold up my empty hands as an offering to the dais at the head of the room, where Maxo Iral looks up from his datapad and shoves through the knot of officers gathered around him.

My eyes glance off him and find Gal farther along the dais, still wearing the brass cuffs, with two soldiers standing guard over him. I can't bear the look in his eyes, the equal measures of hope and fear and love. I look away.

The beady lenses of six cameras swing around, and their presence, along with all of the officials in the room, emboldens me. With all eyes watching, they can't gun me down. I straighten my spine and stride forward, lifting my chin.

"Ettian Nassun," General Iral says coolly. "I was wondering when we'd see you next."

I turn my right hand around, flashing the sparkle of emeralds, the pale glint of platinum, the signet ring in all its glory, freed from its velvet prison. The anthem's last notes fade.

"Not Nassun. Ettian emp-Archon. And you will address me by my bloodright, or not at all."

CHAPTER 31

NO ONE KNOWS what to make of me. *I* don't know what to make of me. The silence grows deafening. The fire in the hall outside goes quiet, and a moment later I hear Wen's familiar footsteps stop short a few feet behind my back.

So I just stand there and let the truth sink in. It isn't difficult to see. I have my father's large brow and my mother's full lips. If you're looking for one, you'd miss it. If you're looking for both, you could never. But no one's ever scrutinized me, not since the fall of Archon. I'm a street kid, raised from nothing, one of a thousand scrappy young things who shook off the rubble of Trost.

Only, that's not quite how it happened.

What I said on the *Ruttin' Hell* was a partial truth. There was an airstrike. It had been too risky to sneak me off-world this far into the war, and so I stayed deep in the palace's recesses, in the stone-hewn rooms that raised and sheltered me. But we weren't deep enough when the bombs hit. My world came raining down around me. My caretaker crushed. Every exit blocked by rubble. And somehow I still lived.

I still lived, but I couldn't survive for long down there. Not until a world-shattering rumble sent tremors through the ground that freed an opening in the wreckage I had spent days scrabbling at, trying to dig a way out. Not until I found the panel behind the boiler and walked a mile in the dark of the mine-cut tunnel, my feet bleeding, my fingers scraped raw, my royal garb tattered beyond repair and recognition.

By that time, the war was over—the Warning Shot fired, my parents captured, our armies crushed, and Iral's crusade of revenge only beginning. My useless bloodright hung on a platinum chain around my neck, the signet ring too large to fit on my ten-year-old fingers. In the parking garage, I wrapped it in one of my torn sleeves. I didn't get the velvet bag until much, much later.

Now I hold the ring high for the whole court to see. Every camera and every pair of eyes fixes on the metal and stone, the pale platinum stark against my darker skin. They all know what it is. They all know what it means.

I wait for the doubt to find its voice. I may look the part, but maybe that's luck. The ring could be forged. The imperial inflection I gave my voice when I announced my true name could be the product of careful practice.

I can't look at Gal. Can't bring myself to face his reaction. I only have eyes for Iral, the font of power that flows into the rest of this room. His gaze is steely, but I catch a glimmer of something that looks suspiciously like hope. He's the first to speak. "Why now?" he asks, the first question I would have asked too.

The one I'm ready for. The one that will hurt the most to answer. "Because of him," I say, still not looking at Gal, even though everything in my voice points in that direction. "Because I needed the Umber heir's trust more than I needed an army that might lose. I needed to keep him close. He was the most valuable bargaining chip I had. He's enough to win our empire back, and until the moment you took Rana, I wasn't sure it was possible without him."

The flattery eases the suspicion in the general's eyes. The explanation wipes some of the disbelief from his uncertain smile. But there's something too proud in the way he stands. He won't back down easily—not for some punk kid trying to snatch his victory, no matter how well he knew my parents. "Grateful as we are that you've survived, the empire's not won yet," Iral says, and some of the officers around him stiffen.

"And when you win the empire, who do you win it for?" I ask, stalking closer. I lower my hands to my sides, slipping one of them into my pocket. "You're the Shield of Archon, Maxo Iral, but you don't have the blood to rule it."

In one quick motion, I draw Wen's switchblade, flick it open, and trace a thin line over the palm of my left hand. The pain sinks in like a burn, and I clench my fist around it. The general takes a step backward as I uncurl my fingers and offer him the red mess of the imperial blood in my veins.

There will be genetic tests later, I'm sure. They'll all confirm the truth I'm shouting into this room. But I don't have time for the science with Gal mere feet away from Maxo Iral. Right now I have to *be* the heir they're expecting. I have to be imperial, and that always comes back to bloodshed.

"Your oaths to Archon are meaningless without this," I tell him, my voice swelling to fill the vaulted ceiling overhead. I will not ask for my throne. I will not beg for it. I am the son of Marc and Henrietta emp-Archon, and I will stand here bleeding until I am recognized.

Iral knows what I want. I wait for his pride to allow it. Even with my ring, my features, and my blood, I'm still a bone-tired kid dressed in dirty fatigues, and I've spent years relying on how hard it is to see past that.

Iral's spent five years preparing for a revolution he thought he'd be leading. Maybe he expected to lead the people of the Archon Empire too. If he was in it for power, he's showing his true colors with every second of hesitation. If he's in it for the sake of our people and everything we've lost, he knows exactly what he needs to do.

I'm gracious. I give him time. The court's silence holds.

General Iral comes down like a skyscraper, and I swear the ground shakes when his knee hits it. He bows his head like he's meant to, like he used to when he presented himself in my parents' court.

And slowly but surely, every Archon soldier in the room follows his example. I'm the epicenter of a shockwave, the focal point of a hundred kneeling citizens who never dared to hope for this day. I glance back behind me to find Wen bent at the waist, my gun tucked behind her back, peering up at me with her half-burned, crooked smile. I smile back, my fingers tightening on her knife.

We've done it. My heart is racing, my back is damp with sweat, my muscles shake with fatigue, my toes *still* hurt from kicking that table, and blood is leeching steadily out of the cut on my hand, but here I stand. Recognized by my bloodright. In command of the Archon resistance. With Rara under my feet, completely *mine* for as long as this army can hold it. With a rightful imperial to guide it, Archon will rise again.

But most important, Gal's fate is now entirely in my hands. Now I can keep him safe from Berr sys-Tosa, safe from Iral, safe from the wrath of Archon's vengeance. No one can stand against my authority.

I turn to face the dais again, and the grin fades from my lips.

Because there's one person in this room who isn't bowing. One person who doesn't have to, the only one who stands as a true equal—even if he's an equal in chains. Gal emp-Umber looks at the truth of me, and his gaze is scorching. Fury twists his lips into a sneer, narrows his eyes, makes his hands shake so much that I can hear the cuffs rattling.

My throat remembers the gentle feeling of his fingers around it. That quiet moment on the *Ruttin' Hell* when we thought we'd finally gotten it right. I look in his eyes now, and as always, I know what he's thinking. The hesitation is gone. No more second-guessing. No more fear of his own violence.

He's every inch his mother's son now, and if his hands were around my neck, he'd squeeze.

EPILOGUE

IT TAKES TWO weeks to fashion the crown. The original diadems my father and mother wore were taken along with them when the empire fell. They sit at the heart of the Umber citadel, balanced carefully on top of my parents' skulls. A display for the system governors, planetary governors, and any other members of the imperial court who might need reminding of what the Umber Empire does to those who stand in its way.

But they're just metal and stone, and that's nothing against the authority of my blood. The resurgence of the Archon Empire demands a fresh start anyway. I issue the order, and the crafters get to work.

It's strange to see Trost and think of it as home instead of hell. From the academy head's former office, the spires glitter in the late-afternoon sun brightly enough that I have to squint. The expanse of the prairie around us is dotted with pale green, new growth breaking through as winter's hold loosens and spring shrugs off its grip. I take an extra moment to relish the sight and the swell in my chest that accompanies it, then turn back to the desk.

General Iral sits on the other side, his mouth set in a firm line as he scrolls through today's reports. It's overwhelming work, coalescing Rana's resources and strengthening its defenses. Iral has learned well from his failures to establish supply lines, and with the Umber infrastructure that's been installed over the past seven years, we have advantages we never could have mustered last time. But we also have to gain the trust of our people again, trust that's been whittled away by years of Umber propaganda telling them they're better off under their new empire's thumb. This whole fight is for nothing if our people start starving the second the Umber yoke lifts.

And the war isn't waiting. Already our instruments are detecting imperial dreadnoughts skimming the outer edges of our system. Colonel Esperza works fast to capture and turn them. Our fleet is growing steadily, but not quickly enough.

"We can't afford to stagnate in our first victory," Iral warns as I settle onto the edge of the head's cushy chair. I don't dare sink back into it. I can't afford to look soft. Can't be seen enjoying any of the luxuries I'm technically entitled to. I still dress as a soldier, though I'm not sure how much longer that'll fly once I'm crowned.

"I'm aware," I reply. "How's the scouting around Imre?"

Wordlessly he hands me the datapad. Dread bleeds into my bloodstream as I read. Berr sys-Tosa has reined in his resources and made the inner world his fortress. He knows that this revolution won't be considered a success until we hold the entire system, and he's determined to make it as difficult as possible. A little cut on my palm is nowhere near what it'll take to establish my bloodright after years of Umber domination.

We need to crush him, and we need to do it fast.

When I look up from the reports, Iral steeples his fingers. "The Corinthians are wary. The emprex expected to collaborate with us to establish a more democratic power structure, and they're concerned about the ideas of leadership seven years of Umber rule have impressed on you. And with fears of Umber retaliation also in play, they aren't supporting us further until we have Tosa System completely secured. The emprex has made it clear we're on our own until we prove that we can restore the interior."

"That could take months."

"Not necessarily." The general watches me closely as I straighten a fraction. Iral plays the noble warrior, trying to atone for his faults and failures, but I haven't forgotten the breathless seconds it took for him to kneel. He's looking for an opportunity to establish himself as the real power here.

So I'm watching him closely in return. "Draw up your strategy," I tell Iral. "Run it by me when it's ready."

"Understood." Iral pauses, a muscle in his jaw twitching. "Speaking of Corinthians—"

I snap my fingers, and he immediately falls silent. "Wen's doing her job."

Truthfully, Wen slid into her role as my operative like she was born to play the part. Nobody knows what to make of a half-burned Corinthian girl acting as the hand of the young Archon Empire, but few dare say anything about it.

Iral is one of those few. "The fires from her stunt in the undercity took three days to put out," he growls, squaring his shoulders.

"And it'll probably be months before another Umber resistance pocket tries to organize while Trost is under her watch."

"Whispers around court are already calling her the Flame Knight."

I have to fight to keep the pleased smile off my face, even though I know how dangerous those whispers are. If Wen gains a reputation that puts her in the same caliber as the suited knights, it will paint a target on her back that Iva emp-Umber won't be able to resist. But to be a suited knight, she'd need a suit anyway, and General Iral is keen on protecting Torrance con-Rafe's legacy from anyone he deems unworthy.

"She needs oversight," Iral continues.

"No, General. *You* need oversight. All Wen Iffan needs is a target." I've vowed on the blood inside me that this girl is never going to feel useless again, and this time around, I'm a man of my word.

"Then there's the matter of the coronation."

If I'm forcing him to drop one subject, of course he'll bring up the other one I've been avoiding. I push up out of the chair and turn back to the sweeping window.

"Your Majesty, it would be the perfect message," Iral continues. In the glass, I catch the reflection of him rising to his feet. "It reinforces the legitimacy of your ascension, it represents the restoration of power to its rightful blood, it's an unforgettable way to make your debut to the public—"

"And it's cruel," I say quietly. My gaze drops from the distant spires of Trost to the emptiness of the academy base. The Umber military and all of their assets fled on Berr sys-Tosa's tail. The Archon command is still moving in, and most of our forces are out on the fronts, leaving the base a desolate husk. Nothing is left of the place I once called home.

"It's effective," the general counters. "You can't appear to be lenient with the Umber heir. The relationship between you two was unambiguous, and if you're to rule—if you're to *win*—you need to bury that history decisively. The rest of your advisory is in agreement."

The skies above the academy are the same as ever. Brisk winds push feathery clouds across the upper atmosphere, and contrails net the air. I know there's no going back to the way things were. But it hurts to see the vastness and know I'll probably never be at the controls again.

Gal hasn't spoken since the moment I stepped into the court. He goes where ordered and doesn't put up a fight. I freed him from the brass chains and gave them no replacement. I keep him in comfort and watch over him carefully. His rage has gone down to a simmer, barely detectable if you don't know him.

But I *do* know him. I can't un-know him, and the truth's a heavy burden. If that's the cost of keeping him safe, I'll bear it.

I close my eyes, trapping myself in darkness. "Fine," I say. "Make the arrangements."

———

The morning of the coronation dawns bright and passes quickly. Outside the governor's estate, the noise of the gathered crowd grows from a low murmur to a steady roar, the windows rattling every time a news transport passes over. A platform has been erected in the center of the lawn, and as we make our way out to it, the roar triples in intensity, encouraged by the thundering victory rhythm played on the newly constructed imperial skin drums that line the walk.

I let it sink in. The beat resonating through my chest. These thousands of people cheering for me, for our victory, for the reclamation of the Archon Empire. For everything I've done for them and everything I might do.

Gods of all systems, I hope I'm enough.

As I ascend the platform, my legs start trembling. Claiming my legacy to save Gal was one thing. Claiming it to take the reins of a war is something else entirely. The platinum trim on the sleek suit I wear feels far too heavy for my shoulders.

But heavier still is the crown awaiting me. It looks so delicate, with curved metal loops weaving together around emeralds the size of my eyeballs. Gal holds it like it scalds him. His ornamentation is slight—a trim black suit, a brass circlet around his brow, his hair doused in oil and slicked back. Two massive platinum cuffs are locked around his wrists, symbolic reminders of his status within my court, in case the guards behind him didn't make it clear.

He stares impassively out at the crowd that roars for me, not him. His lips are thin, his eyes sunken. The broadcast where Gal knelt to Iral was widespread, but this is historic. Every empire, every system, every planet, every *person* will see what he does here today, and it will forever be remembered as the first public act of the Umber heir.

As the drums fade and General Iral's sonorous voice begins the ceremony, Gal glances over at me, and for a moment I swear he's about to speak. I lean forward to catch his words over the crowd's drone.

But he says nothing and wrenches his gaze away.

When Iral's speech is finished, I turn to face Gal again. He turns to face me.

I could kneel—*should* kneel, to spare him the humiliation. But on this day, there's a message to be sent. Archon will never bow to Umber again. So I keep my back straight and my head held high, forcing Gal to reach up. Forcing him to look me in the eye as he does it.

The crowd screams my name—*Ettian emp-Archon, long may he reign.*

And he crowns me.

ACKNOWLEDGMENTS

Here they come: the thank yous. The people I couldn't have done this without. It's been over three years since I first set out to tell this story, and so many people have helped me along the way that I'm almost certain I'll leave someone important out. So if you get to the end of these and don't see your name and feel left out, here is your PREEMPTIVE THANKS.

Now on to the real stars of the show.

To Thao Le, who told me I couldn't write space vampires, so I wrote this instead. Thank you for never giving up on this book through nearly a year of submission. I'd promise I'll write an easy sale eventually, but c'mon—we've been working together for half a decade at this point. You know me. Thank you as well to everyone at the Sandra Dijkstra Literary Agency, especially Andrea Cavallaro and Haneen Oriqat, for all you do for my work.

To Sarah Peed, editor extraordinaire, for hopping fearlessly onto this galactic romp with me. Thank you for your boundless, infectious enthusiasm for my space kids. Thanks to everyone at Del Rey who had a hand in bringing this book to life: Cindy Berman, David Moench, Mary Moates, Julie Leung, Ashleigh Heaton, Scott Shannon, Keith Clayton, and Tricia Narwani. Special thanks to David G. Stevenson for the *gorgeous* cover design.

Tara Sim, you monstrous delight—I couldn't have written this book in the first place if I hadn't wanted to impress you. Thank you for being my go-to throughout this entire process. To Traci Chee, who is too smart for my own good, and Jessica Cluess, without whom I'd have to do all of my complaining in a mirror. Here's to our little Avengers squad outlasting the original Avengers.

This would be a much lonelier journey without the scores of writer friends, both in LA and in the digital sphere, who've supported me along the way. Special thanks to the ladies of Cobbler Club—Gretchen Schreiber, Alyssa Colman, and Alexa Donne—all the badasses on #TeamThao, and the Sweet Sixteens who've been in the trenches with me since the start.

No writing could get done without a life outside the craft, which is why I can never be thankful enough for the friends I have who have nothing to do with this job. Thanks to Marisa and the rest of the Wop House gang for getting me to go on vacation once a year, to Ali and the rest of my day job cadre for making me enjoy earning my health insurance, and especially to Mariano: *no u*.

This is another book I wrote during the year I lived at home after college, so I can't thank my parents enough for tolerating my un- and under-employment and continuing to feed me while I figured things out—both in this sprawling galactic empire and in the direction of my life. Sarah, I hope you've been paying attention. Ivy, you weren't just good—you were the best.

Thank you to every bookseller, blogger, tweeter, bookstagrammer, and reviewer—no matter how large or small your platform, the fact that you're spreading the word about my work means that I can never fully repay you for what you've done for me. I can't wait to share even more of it with you.

And to you, the reader, whoever you are. Thank you for joining me on what is shaping up to be the most ambitious creative venture I've ever embarked on. Stick around for this one—it's gonna be a wild ride.

ABOUT THE AUTHOR

EMILY SKRUTSKIE was born in Massachusetts, raised in Virginia, and forged in the mountains above Boulder, Colorado. She attended Cornell University and now lives and works in Los Angeles. Skrutskie is the author of *Hullmetal Girls, The Abyss Surrounds Us,* and *The Edge of the Abyss.*

skrutskie.com
Facebook.com/emilyskrutskie
Twitter: @skrutskie

ABOUT THE TYPE

This book was set in Sabon, a typeface designed by the well-known German typographer Jan Tschichold (1902–74). Sabon's design is based upon the original letterforms of sixteenth-century French type designer Claude Garamond and was created specifically to be used for three sources: foundry type for hand composition, Linotype, and Monotype. Tschichold named his typeface for the famous Frankfurt typefounder Jacques Sabon (c. 1520–80).